HARPY OF THE TON

Misfits of the Ton
Book Five

by
Emily Royal

© Copyright 2024 by Emily Royal
Text by Emily Royal
Cover by Dar Albert

Dragonblade Publishing, Inc. is an imprint of Kathryn Le Veque Novels, Inc.
P.O. Box 23
Moreno Valley, CA 92556
ceo@dragonbladepublishing.com

Produced in the United States of America

First Edition October 2024
Print Edition

Reproduction of any kind except where it pertains to short quotes in relation to advertising or promotion is strictly prohibited.

All Rights Reserved.

The characters and events portrayed in this book are fictitious. Any similarity to real persons, living or dead, is purely coincidental and not intended by the author.

ARE YOU SIGNED UP FOR DRAGONBLADE'S BLOG?

You'll get the latest news and information on exclusive giveaways, exclusive excerpts, coming releases, sales, free books, cover reveals and more.

Check out our complete list of authors, too!

No spam, no junk. That's a promise!

Sign Up Here

www.dragonbladepublishing.com

Dearest Reader;

Thank you for your support of a small press. At Dragonblade Publishing, we strive to bring you the highest quality Historical Romance from some of the best authors in the business. Without your support, there is no 'us', so we sincerely hope you adore these stories and find some new favorite authors along the way.

Happy Reading!

CEO, Dragonblade Publishing

Additional Dragonblade books by Author Emily Royal

Misfits of the Ton
Tomboy of the Ton (Book 1)
Ruined by the Ton (Book 2)
Thief of the Ton (Book 3)
Oddity of the Ton (Book 4)
Harpy of the Ton (Book 5)
The Taming of the Duke (Novella)

Headstrong Harts
What the Hart Wants (Book 1)
Queen of my Hart (Book 2)
Hidden Hart (Book 3)
The Prizefighter's Hart (Book 4)
All I Want for Christmas is My Hart (Novella)
Haunted Hart (Novella)

London Libertines
Henry's Bride (Book 1)
Hawthorne's Wife (Book 2)
Roderick's Widow (Book 3)
A Libertine's Christmas Miracle (Novella)

The Lyon's Den Series
A Lyon's Pride
Lyon of the Highlands
Lyon of the Ton

CHAPTER ONE

"THERE'S A MAN in the garden, miss—and he's *naked!*"

Arabella glanced up. Her maid stood at the window, her face flushed pink.

"Come away from the window, Connie," she said. "You shouldn't ogle men like a common harlot."

The maid's blush deepened. "Sorry, miss."

"I don't want you to be *sorry*—I want you to behave as a lady's maid ought. And not just any maid—*my* maid. How you behave is a reflection of me. Did you find my parasol?"

"Yes, miss."

"Then bring it, and go."

Apprehension flickered in the maid's eyes.

Good. Servants should fear their betters, to ensure proper behavior.

Or so Aunt Kathleen said. And she should know—she'd replaced her maid six times due to inappropriate behavior such as *talking back, disrespecting her betters*—and, worst of all, *expressing an opinion.* According to Aunt, opinions were not for the lower classes.

The maid held out the parasol, and Arabella took it, dismissing her with a curt nod.

She watched Connie's retreating back and sighed.

What might life be like if she ignored her aunt's instructions to set herself apart from others and, instead, sought out friendships?

Arabella pushed the notion aside. Nobody in Society wanted to be *friends* with anyone. She was an object of envy. No, not envy—*resentment*. Envy implied that her rivals wanted to be in her position. But they didn't. Instead, they wanted to see her position stripped from her, as punishment for having been born into beauty, wealth, and a title.

She rose and exited her chamber.

A duchess. She was to be a *duchess*—the ultimate prize for a woman.

So Aunt Kathleen said.

Arabella descended the staircase, each stair creaking beneath her feet, gripping the banister with her free hand.

If she slipped and fell, would anybody care?

She drew in a sharp breath and stopped at the foot of the stairs to concentrate on maintaining her balance.

"Lady Arabella—are you well?"

A footman approached, his boots clicking on the floor. He reached for her arm, and she jerked free.

"Don't touch me!" she snapped.

"Very good, miss." He bowed, his expression impassive, and withdrew.

She didn't know what was worse—the dislike she'd expected, or his indifference to her incivility. But, to the footman, she was merely a means to earn a living. She had no control over his life. In time, he would secure employment in another household and effect his escape.

But for her, there was no escape.

Arabella made her way through the hallway along the east wing, overlooking the garden. She'd made such a fuss about its redesign, but it was one of the few aspects of her life over which she'd been given a speck of control.

She glanced through the window, and her heart fluttered as she caught sight of the gardener. His back to her, he brandished a shovel, his body half concealed behind a stack of shrubs lying on their side.

Connie had been right—he *was* naked.

She approached the window, her pulse thickening.

Not completely naked—merely shirtless. His broad male torso, bronzed by the sun, was in sharp contrast to her own pale skin, protected by layers of lace, her parasol, and Aunt Kathleen's instructions that tanned skin was a sign of savagery.

And he exuded savagery—with a body toned through a lifetime of toil and rough, broad hands. The muscles of his torso rippled as he drove the shovel into the ground in a smooth, repetitive motion. Then he stopped and picked up a shrub with one hand, as if it weighed no more than her parasol, and placed it in position. Then he began piling earth around the base of the shrub, securing it in place.

He stepped back to admire his handiwork, then turned toward the window. His face was strong featured—a nose bearing a slight kink, full, sensual lips, and clear, slate-gray eyes. His chest could have been sculpted by Michelangelo himself. Thick muscles nestled in pairs, covered with a dusting of dirty blond hair that grew denser lower down, leading toward his waist, where his breeches fit his form like a second skin, clinging to his thigh muscles. And below his belt…

Oh my…

The material of his breeches stretched over a thick bulge below his waist.

Slickness formed on her palms, and she tightened her grip on her parasol, drawing in a sharp breath to dissipate the fog in her mind. But she couldn't temper the lick of desire in her belly—the sensation she couldn't fathom, other than to recognize its wickedness.

It was a sensation she'd experienced only once, when she'd come across a stallion rutting a mare in a stable yard. The beast had needed little effort to subdue the female before mounting her, thrusting forward with deep, primal grunts, the sheen of its pelt rippling with each movement while it drove into the mare, impelled by the purest of needs.

The need to mate.

She'd hidden then, as she hid now, unable to avert her gaze, her senses overpowered by the scent of beast and straw—and the thick, sharp scent of mating that had intensified when the animal reached completion.

She placed her hand at her throat, where her skin burned.

How hot it was! And not just inside. Sweat glistened on the man's skin as he moved and beaded at the ends of his hair, the occasional droplet splashing onto this chest.

The man plucked a cloth from his breeches pocket, wiped it on his brow, then tied it around his neck. He stooped to pick something up—a bottle, which he held to his lips, his throat pulsing as he drank greedily and savagely. Then he tipped his head back and poured the rest of the contents over his head. Liquid ran over his face and down his chest, forming rivulets, trailing a path across each pair of muscles until it disappeared beneath his waistband.

He shook his head from side to side, and droplets flew from his hair, forming an arc in the air, glinting in the sunlight before dispersing. Her lips grew dry, and she flicked her tongue out to moisten them.

He reached for his belt and gave it a tug. Arabella let out a small cry as the material of his breeches shifted over the bulge at the center.

Then he glanced toward the window, and she shrank back.

Surely he'd not heard her?

Footsteps approached, and her gut twisted with apprehension. Heavens—he *had* heard!

But the footsteps came from inside, their rhythm ungainly and overly familiar.

The passion that had been coursing through her veins moments earlier shriveled and died as she turned to face—*him*.

Her betrothed.

"*There* you are, my dear. I've been looking all over for you."

Even his voice was thick and fleshy, its nasal whine reminiscent of a nasty schoolboy who tortured his subordinates for nothing more than puerile satisfaction.

But he was a duke. *The Duke of Dunton*—and, by virtue of his title, one of Society's most desirable catches. Arabella had reigned triumphant over her rivals in securing her place as his future duchess.

Something he never failed to remind her of.

She suppressed a shudder as he drew near and thrust his fleshy face close to hers. His pale brown eyes gleamed with fervor—a sheen she'd come to associate with the stench of harlots. But if smothering himself in doxies kept him from foisting his attentions on her, so much the better. Her gain was their loss.

He moved to kiss her, lips parting in expectation. She held her breath to avoid the assault of his breath on her senses, and stepped back.

"I see the work on the garden has begun," she said, gesturing toward the window. "It's most generous of you to indulge me."

He glanced at the window, his brow furrowing in confusion. Then he nodded.

"The garden, yes. Exactly so—nothing's too much for my future duchess." He gestured around the hallway, sweeping his arm in a large, imperious arc. "Now I have the means, I'll soon restore the honor attached to my name."

"The means?" she couldn't help asking. "As in…my fortune?"

The weak expression in his eyes hardened, then he stroked her hand, as if petting a dog. "That's not a subject a lady should bother herself with, my dear," he said, his voice carrying an edge that sent a cold fingertip running along her spine. "You shouldn't fill your pretty head with such vulgar notions. Crawford can deal with that on our behalf."

"Who's Crawford?"

"My lawyer."

"I thought Mr. Stockton dealt with my fortune. He—"

She drew in a sharp breath as he gripped her wrist.

"You must desist, my dear," he said, his chin wobbling. "Your aunt will think you've grown quite uncouth if she hears you speaking of anything related to…*commerce*."

He spat out the last word, as if it left a nasty taste in his mouth.

"But…"

"I trust you're not going to prove to be as troublesome a wife as you are a fiancée." The laughter in his voice belied the cold expression in his eyes. He took her face in his hands, and she stiffened in anticipation, clamping her lips together. But rather than kiss her, he stroked either side of her face. His fingers caressed her chin before settling for a brief moment on her neck and curling around her throat.

He lowered his mouth to hers, but she turned aside, and his lips brushed her cheek. A brief flare of anger shone in his eyes.

"All in good time, my dear," he said. "All in good time. When you're my duchess, you'll belong to me, utterly and completely—will you not?"

"Yes," she whispered.

"Yes, what?" His fingers twitched, tightening against her throat as if by accident. "Yes, what?" he repeated.

"Yes, Your Grace."

He smiled, then patted her cheek.

"Sweet young thing—what am I to do with you? *Your Grace*, indeed! I'd prefer *my lord*, or *sir*. But nothing will be as delectable as to hear the word *husband* fall from your lips. And fall it shall."

Arabella lifted her chin in the manner of the haughty debutante Aunt Kathleen had schooled her to be.

"Yes, my lord," she said coldly.

"That's better." He patted her cheek. "And now, my dear, I must abandon you once more. Important business that cannot be avoided."

"I'll bear your absence with fortitude, my lord."

Before she could withdraw, he lifted her hand to his mouth and kissed it, sliding his lips across her skin.

Then he bowed and retreated.

Arabella glanced at the back of her hand, which glistened in the afternoon sun, reminiscent of the sticky trail a slug left in its wake. Gritting her teeth to temper the bile rising in her throat, she wiped the back of her hand against her sleeve.

How would she stomach the bridal kiss at the altar—let alone the wedding night?

She reached for her necklace—a thin gold chain with a tiny pearl pendant. A gift from her parents, the mother and father she'd never known, always just out of reach in her memories, beyond the wall of fire she couldn't penetrate. Not even in her dreams.

Had they lived, would they have insisted she accept Dunton's hand? Or, had they had a son, would she have remained at the home of her birth, rather than be evicted?

What if...

That was a question she'd asked almost daily since her come-out.

She let out a sigh, glanced out of the window, and froze.

The man outside was staring directly at her.

Eyes the color of sharp steel met her gaze, their expression rendering her helpless, as if she were the prey mesmerized by her predator, understanding the futility of any attempt to flee. But rather than the lust she saw in most men—lust for her fortune, or her looks—his gaze was searching, probing, threatening to expose the weak, vulnerable soul hidden beneath her façade. He had only to reach out…

No—stop it!

She stumbled back, retreating from the window until he was out of sight.

She wasn't some coy, lovesick maiden ready to make a fool of herself over a gardener.

She was Lady Arabella Ponsford—soon to be the Duchess of

Dunton. She had status.

And for a woman in her position, status—not freedom—was the best she could hope for.

CHAPTER TWO

SWEET SWIVING HEAVEN—SHE was the loveliest thing he'd ever seen. She must be Dunton's fiancée—Lady Arabella Ponsford.

Bella…

The name suited her, for she *was* beautiful. With her pale face and expressive blue eyes, she reminded him of a princess trapped in an ogre's lair—her porcelain features bred into her through generations of aristocrats. Doubtless she could trace her ancestral line to William of Normandy's conquest.

How amusing that those Society layabouts considered themselves better than others by virtue of knowing who their ancestors were—as if it mattered! More important was who, and *what*, a man was. Here and now.

And the woman in the window—here and now—was exquisite.

Doubtless, like all fine ladies, she'd disintegrate at the slightest touch.

Which didn't bode well for her wedding night with that lecher Dunton and his bulbous belly and multiple chins. Not to mention his voracious appetite for bedsport that was enough to turn the stomach of even the most hardened whore.

Lawrence's mind drifted to last night, and Millie's ministrations. Millie—with her ripe, round curves, plush lips, and ready thighs that had parted so eagerly for him, and the anticipation of his coin.

He'd not begrudged Millie her shilling. She'd earned it well, riding his cock until he exploded with pleasure—then, for an extra sixpence, she remained in his bed until dawn, when she woke him in a very delectable fashion, pleasuring him with that luscious mouth more before she slipped out of his chamber to resume her duties at the inn.

The best harlot at the King's Head, the innkeeper said—and he wasn't wrong. Worth every penny, Millie was. She sold her body well.

The woman in the window—Lady Arabella—had sold herself for a title. But she'd take little pleasure from it. She had surrendered herself to a man she hardly knew—her chaperone would have made sure of *that*. She would surrender her freedom at the altar, whereas Millie enjoyed the freedom to select her partners at will, taking her own pleasure from each one while she earned an honest living.

No doubt the lady in the window considered herself the more fortunate of the two. Like an exotic bird bred in captivity, she knew no other life. She'd never know the sheer joy that Millie—or any woman who relished her sexuality—expressed when she cried out with pleasure at a man's touch.

His manhood twitched as he allowed himself a wicked thought…

What might it be like to take Lady Arabella—to have that brittle body bloom at his touch as he taught her pleasure? Or to hear her sighs of ecstasy as he entered her for the first time, having prepared her for his cock?

Or scream his name while he fucked the ladylike demeanor out of her?

He drew in a sharp breath to temper the urge to bury his fingers in her hair, to tear out those hairpins keeping those pristine little curls in place…and to rip that prim little gown off her and pull her into the dirt—to his level, where men and women drew every last droplet of pleasure out of rutting.

She's not for the likes of you.

His conscience—the rational, practical part of him—shattered the dream and returned him to reality. He was a widower, with three children to feed, and, as such, should keep such fanciful thoughts to himself.

He drove the shovel into the ground, focusing on the motion as he dug a hole for the next shrub. A symmetrical pattern—that was what Dunton had instructed. Bloody symmetrical patterns, forcing nature to conform to straight lines. Didn't those soulless aristocrats realize that working *with* nature, enhancing her natural form, would create a far superior garden?

But he had to take work where he could find it—even if it was for a foul-tempered duke known for treating his subordinates with cruelty, who stank of unwashed flesh and a gaseous constitution.

Lawrence grinned to himself. At least he wouldn't have to endure the fat duke puffing and wheezing over him in bed while he availed himself of his marital rights.

Or, more likely, *forced* himself…

His mirth faded. What if Lady Arabella was unwilling, and her awakening to the marital bed was filled with pain and terror? Lovemaking should be a mutual sharing of pleasures, not a violation where the woman submitted to the brute who'd purchased her.

Bloody hell—one glimpse of a sad, pretty face, and I'm goin' soft.

He glanced toward the window again. A man—the duke himself—had joined the woman, and he seemed to have his hands about her throat. She withdrew from his grip, and he bowed and disappeared, then she approached the window and looked out.

She stiffened as she met Lawrence's gaze. For a moment, they stared at each other, then she frowned and retreated.

Lawrence resumed work. Moments later, footsteps approached.

"You there—gardener!"

It was Dunton.

"Yes, sir?"

"It's *Your Grace*," the duke snapped, before muttering under his breath, "Disrespectful *peasant*."

"Forgive me, Your Grace," Lawrence said, gritting his teeth and bowing.

"How long will this all take?" Dunton gestured toward the garden.

"About a fortnight."

"A fortnight! I hope you're not expecting to be paid by the day, or you'll be here forever, won't you? I know your sort."

"My fee is fixed, regardless of how long the work takes," Lawrence said.

The duke narrowed his eyes. "So, if you finish sooner than expected, you'll have earned yourself a tidy penny for less work."

Hardly. Lawrence was barely making a profit as it was—what with the cost of the plants and his board at the King's Head.

The duke pointed to the shrub Lawrence had just planted. "Why isn't it flowering?"

"It flowers later in the year," Lawrence said. "But it may not flower *this* year—it often takes a year or two after planting for the flowers to come."

"That's damned inconvenient. What's the point of a plant that doesn't flower? Lady Arabella won't like *that*, and she's insisting on this damned garden."

"I've chosen the shrubs to ensure there's flowers throughout the year," Lawrence said. "You'll find—"

"Don't answer me back!" Dunton stepped toward Lawrence, his eyes gleaming spitefully. How many schoolfellows had he bullied at Eton or Harrow—or whatever fancy school he'd languished in while honest men worked for a living?

But rather than cower, Lawrence stretched to his full height and crossed his arms—the only way to deal with bullies.

A sharp scent assaulted his nostrils—soiled clothes and cheap perfume. Perhaps Dunton was on his way to bestow his attentions on another harlot. If he could find one who could stomach his touching her. Millie said that the girls at the King's Head refused to service him, but there was a brothel at the other end of the village where the women were of a more robust constitution and charged Dunton an extra two shillings to satisfy his tastes.

"Forgive me, Your Grace," Lawrence said. "Perhaps I should discuss the matter with Lady Arabella. Or I could attend both of you—unless you have a more pressing errand? Or we could discuss it at the King's Head. I'm lodging there and have often seen you patronize it and other...*establishments* in the village."

The duke shook his head. "There's no need to disturb her. I'm afraid she suffers from nerves." He gestured toward the shrub. "I'm sure you know what you're doing, but I'll be watching you, *boy*."

Boy?

At thirty, Lawrence hadn't been called a *boy* since he'd left the schoolroom.

"Get on with it, then!" the duke said. "I want this done, and you gone, as soon as possible."

Before Lawrence could respond, Dunton turned his back and disappeared down the path, roaring for a groom to saddle his horse.

Poor horse.

And poor woman.

At least Lawrence's ordeal with Dunton would be over once the garden was complete. He only need endure the man for a fortnight. Whereas Lady Arabella would be bound to him for a lifetime.

Chapter Three

As Arabella entered the breakfast room, the footmen stood to attention—two flanking the door, another beside the buffet, and a fourth attending Aunt Kathleen.

Of her fiancé, there was no sign.

She approached the table, and a footman rushed to pull out her chair.

"Where's the duke?" she asked.

"I don't know, Lady Arabella," he replied.

"You *should* know. He wasn't at dinner last night, either."

"Arabella, that's enough," her aunt said.

"I'm his fiancée. I have every right to know where he is."

Aunt Kathleen inclined her head toward the footmen. "*Pas devant les domestiques.*"

"Surely *they* must know where their master is," Arabella said.

"Child, must you be so petulant?" her aunt cried. "It's not your place to demand where the duke is—not as his fiancée, and certainly not as his wife."

"I won't be his wife, Aunt—I'll be his *duchess.*"

"Must you be so troublesome? Do you want your fiancé to witness such unladylike behavior? He's already going to considerable trouble to accommodate your whims, with that garden of yours."

"With *my* money," Arabella said. "I—Ouch!" She broke off as her aunt gripped her wrist.

"Child, it's *not* your place to ask how the duke spends his money."

But it's not his yet.

"Charles, fetch Lady Arabella some breakfast," Aunt Kathleen said, releasing her grip. "A little scrambled egg, but only one slice of bacon." She turned her pale-blue gaze on Arabella. "We don't want you ruining your figure before your marriage, do we?"

"And afterward?"

"You must maintain your appearance to keep your husband interested, until you've given him an heir. Then it matters not."

Because, at that point, she'd have served her purpose.

"If you behave," Aunt Kathleen continued, "I might be disposed to permit a second slice of bacon every other day. When we next see the modiste for your fitting, I'll decide then whether it would be appropriate."

She cocked her head to one side, expectation in her gaze.

Arabella rubbed her wrist. "Yes, Aunt, thank you."

"Well?" Aunt Kathleen barked at the footman. "Get on with it!"

The footman scuttled over to the buffet, where he deposited a spoonful of eggs and a slice of bacon on a plate before placing it in front of Arabella.

Arabella wrinkled her nose at the odor rising from the food.

The eggs were off.

And…was that a green hue on the edge of the bacon?

She pushed her plate aside.

"Aren't you going to eat it, child, after I took such pains to have it brought over?"

"I'm not hungry, Aunt," Arabella said. "And if the modiste is visiting, I wish to ensure that she has no need to make any alterations."

"Quite right," came the reply. "Though I fear we must travel to London for your fitting. Madame Delacroix is making a most awkward business over your bridal gown. She's refusing to travel here until her account is settled."

"Shouldn't we settle it, then?"

"We will, on your marriage—as I've assured her numerous times. But not only has she refused to accommodate us, she's encouraged every other modiste in town to do likewise. It's monstrous!"

"What, that we've not settled her account?"

"No!" Aunt Kathleen cried. "It's monstrous that I—a blood relative of the future Duchess of Dunton—am being treated thus!"

Arabella said nothing and reached for the teapot. Doubtless the rumors about Dunton's debts had reached the ears of London's tradesmen and women. But there was little point in discussing the matter with her aunt. The last time she asked about her fiancé's creditors, she had earned her a sharp slap with Aunt's fan. She still sported the bruise on her upper arm, just beneath the sleeve—administered in such a position as to be invisible to others.

"What are you doing?" Aunt Kathleen asked.

"I want tea."

"You're not some commoner who serves at the table! Charles—pour my niece's tea."

"Very good, ma'am."

Arabella suppressed a sigh. Was there no part of her life over which she had any control?

The footman poured a measure of tea into a cup, then handed it to her. At least he hadn't added any milk, which, judging from the odor coming from the jug on the table, had suffered the same fate as the eggs. His gaze met hers, sympathy in his eyes.

How dare he! Did he—a mere servant—deign to express such an emotion? Was she so pathetic a creature as to command the pity of a nobody?

"Where's my sugar?" she demanded. "I take two spoonsful. Don't you *know* that by now?"

His expression morphed into the cold politeness of the impeccable servant.

"Forgive me, Lady Arabella," he said, in a tone that conveyed anything but contrition. He tipped two measures of sugar in her tea and stirred it. She acknowledged the action with a nod, then sipped the tea.

Too sweet.

She loathed sugar in tea. But a dark little corner of her soul rejoiced in having someone obey her command. She might be a prisoner of her situation, but there was a twisted comfort in knowing that others were bound by stronger chains—at least in the breakfast room.

Breakfast concluded, and there was still no sign of Dunton. But his absence had become something she craved—respite from the anticipation of his attentions. If he were cavorting with whores before their marriage, how would he behave once he'd secured her hand and her dowry?

Arabella allowed herself a wry smile as she exited the breakfast room. At least Dunton's creditors would stop plaguing them once her dowry was released. Did he think her so much of a simpleton that she didn't know who all those men were—hammering on the door at his London lodgings at all hours, demanding payment? Their flight from London to hole up in this godforsaken manor, with its overgrown garden and empty larder, was merely delaying the inevitable. It wouldn't be long before his creditors followed them to Ilverton.

Which raised the question…

She stopped and glanced out of the window overlooking the garden. She hadn't meant to stop there—it had just been a coincidence. But there he was, in his bronzed, semi-naked glory, working the land, driving his shovel into the earth, his body exuding a raw, primal power.

How had Dunton secured that gardener's employment if he lacked the funds?

She let out a sigh. "What am I doing?"

Was being a duchess worth losing control over her destiny? Would she ever be able to make a decision for herself again, other than how many sugars she took in her tea?

Yes. There was the garden. The unkempt mess she'd seen from the carriage on the driveway when they first arrived. Ilverton Manor was suffocating—a mausoleum filled with rotting wood and musty furnishings, not to mention the vermin that scuttled beneath the floorboards and behind the wainscoting. Whereas the garden she could mold into shape, and it would become her place of respite from the world, from life—and from *him*.

Lost in her thoughts, she wandered along the hallway until she reached the main doors, where a footman stood in attendance. He stiffened as she approached, then met her gaze.

Don't show me pity—I could bear anything but your pity.

"Well?" she demanded. "Aren't you going to open them?"

He blinked, smoothing his features into the bland expression of a servant, the same expression that her maid wore when Arabella admonished her—the mask all servants donned in the company of a master, or mistress, they despised.

He bowed and opened the door. Sunlight illuminated the hallway, picking up dust motes that swirled in the air, floating aimlessly and freely.

Sweet heaven—am I comparing my life unfavorably to that of a dust mote?

Tilting her chin, she swept past the footman and stepped out into the summer air, relishing the warmth of the sun on her skin. Doubtless Aunt Kathleen would admonish her for venturing outside without a parasol, but Arabella's spirits lifted at the notion of committing an act of rebellion, no matter how small.

It wasn't as if she were committing a transgression. She'd insisted on the work to the garden. It was only right she review its progress from time to time.

Much of the overgrown part of the garden had already been cleared, revealing the landscaping. As she'd suspected, the garden consisted of two tiers—the outer edge forming the upper tier, with a square, sunken section in the center, accessed by a single flight of steps. Several more shrubs had been planted on the upper tier, forming a symmetrical pattern.

She caught sight of the gardener carrying a pile of branches and leaves through an archway at the far end, beyond which smoke was rising. Near the steps, he'd driven his shovel into the ground. She approached it and ran her fingertips over the handle, the wood polished smooth through years of use. Beside the shovel was a pile of wooden-handled tools, a thick notebook—open at a page depicting a sketch of a garden—a hessian bag, and a man's shirt and jacket, neatly folded. As she glanced toward the archway, she heard the crackle of a fire. The smoke thickened, punctuated by the occasional wisp of burning leaves, caught by the rising air before they disintegrated into ash.

The gardener reappeared, wiping his hands on his breeches and retracing his steps. He looked up and caught sight of Arabella. Rather than showing deference, he stared at her, boldly, his gaze traveling over her body, and the ghost of a smile played on his lips.

"How dare you stare at me!" she cried.

Amusement danced in his eyes. He lowered his gaze to her neckline, and the tip of his tongue flicked out and caressed his lower lip.

"Do you not speak?" she demanded.

"I do."

"Yet you continue to stare."

"A man can be forgiven for lookin' when such a sight is before him."

Arabella tempered the tiny pulse of excitement.

"You've no right to speak to me!"

His grin broadened, showing even white teeth. "You're the one who asked me to speak."

"No, I didn't—I only asked whether you did speak," she said. "And

I'll thank you to address me properly."

He raked his gaze over her body again, and she fought to temper the pulse that had thickened in her center.

"I'll address you properly, ma'am—but I doubt you'll thank me for it."

"It's Lady Arabella to you."

"Then, *Lady Arabella to you*—you can't blame a man for looking."

"You impertinent knave!"

He let out a low chuckle, which sounded almost like a growl. *Heavens*—even his laugh sent a ripple of sensation through her body!

"I'm only teasin' you, ma'am—sorry, *Lady Arabella*. Have you come to see the garden? The duke tells me it's for you."

"It's his wedding gift to me."

Why she felt the need to tell him that, she didn't know. But if she meant him to be impressed, he showed no sign. Instead, he arched an eyebrow in a gesture that carried an air of amusement—or disdain.

"Is that so?"

"Yes," she replied. "It would serve you well to remember my position—as well as yours."

"I'm always willin' to recall a woman's *position*," he said, his voice deepening, "particularly in relation to mine."

He cocked his head to one side, and the uncomfortable heat in her center began to spread through her veins. Whatever the meaning of his last words, they carried an air of…depravity.

Delectable *depravity*.

Sweet heaven! Her body had reacted on her observing him from a distance, but at close proximity, his potency threatened to overwhelm her. She drew in a breath to temper the sensations threading through her body, but her senses were assaulted by the scent of him—the heady, spicy cocktail of wood, smoke, and fresh sweat.

The scent of man.

No! This will *not* do!

She closed her eyes in an attempt to compel her body to quieten the maelstrom swirling inside, curling her hands into fists to stem the tremors in her body as fear threatened to engulf her...

Fear of the unknown, fear of her body, which seemed to have a will of its own...

...and fear of her own desires—the raw, base need in her soul to surrender to the depravity.

No!

"Anythin' the matter, your ladyship?"

His voice, laced with amusement, broke through the fog of need, and she opened her eyes to see him staring at her, his eyes filled with a lust to match her own—and something far worse.

Recognition.

He recognized her desire for what it was—like a stallion recognizing the scent of a mare in heat.

Stop it!

She stepped back, and his eyes widened with concern. Before his concern turned into pity, she gestured toward the garden.

"I want the rosebushes clipped into a symmetrical pattern after you've planted them," she said.

"You'll never force a rosebush to conform to your niceties, your ladyship. I can plant them in a symmetrical pattern, but if they're to thrive, they must be allowed to grow as nature intended."

"Not if the garden is to conform to aesthetics," she said. "Or are you so ignorant of your trade that you refuse to obey instructions? I hardly think it proper to let *anything* run wild."

"Do you speak of rosebushes, or prospective duchesses?"

"I should have you whipped for insulting your better!" she cried.

The warmth in his eyes turned to frost. "You're no better than I, madam," he said. "An idle, pampered creature, engaged to a man nearly twice her age, merely because he has a title. Do you even love him?"

Arabella caught her breath. "Who are you to ask such a thing?"

He shrugged. "It's a simple enough question—do you love the man or not?" He turned the shovel over in his hands, as if inspecting the handle. "I care nothing for your feelings, but perhaps *you* should, seein' as you'll be surrendering your freedom and your person to him."

Her arrow may have found its target, but his missile buried itself deep into her heart, releasing the uncomfortable truth.

Then his expression filled with understanding, as if he recognized the pitiful creature that she was. An object—chattel—to be used according to the whims of the man who owned her.

Curse him! Curse them all!

She drew her hand back, then slapped him across the face.

Her palm stinging, she tilted her chin to convey her superiority, and glared at him.

A flare of anger ignited in his eyes, and he lifted his hand to rub his cheek.

"You get one strike for free, woman," he growled, "but try that again and you'll suffer the consequences."

A dark little nugget pulsed in her center with a secret thrill at the prospect of *consequences* being administered at his hands, and she raised her hand again.

With the speed of a striking snake, he caught her wrist and pulled her hard against him.

Sweet Lord—he was magnificent! Rather than cow her with the whining words of a duke, he claimed her with the rough hands of a beast. His body was iron-hard, yet he molded himself against her as if they were one. She tilted her head backward, and a low whimper escaped her lips as she looked into eyes the color of storm clouds.

Then he lowered his mouth to hers.

His tongue probed against the seam of her lips, demanding entrance, and, with a whimper, she surrendered. He plunged inside like an invading army, then the soft, velvety weapon swept across her mouth with a gentleness that belied the hard body that had imprisoned her in its grip. Her defenses crumpled at the tender caresses—as if he cherished every last drop of her. Then he curled his tongue around hers, encouraging her to respond. With slow, tentative movements, she probed his tongue with hers, shifting from side to side to engage in the dance.

A long, slow growl of approval reverberated in his chest, and her heart swelled at the notion of his taking pleasure from her touch. She curled her tongue around him, and he darted the tip back and forth, beckoning her toward him until, fueled by need, she kissed him in return, running the tip of her tongue along the roughened skin of his lips.

Little mewls of pleasure swelled in her throat, and she felt something, hard and hot, pressing against her belly. The heat coursing through her body began to converge, to form an ache in her center. She shifted her hips to ease the ache—the raw need that her body's instinct told her only he could satisfy. Then she let out a low moan, surrendering to pleasure.

He broke the kiss and pushed her back.

She let out an involuntary cry of frustration as the pleasure faded, leaving only the ache.

Then he let out a laugh.

"Lady you may be, but you're like all women when it comes to bein' in need of a good rutting."

Shame and humiliation doused her, like ice-cold water. But it wasn't shame at her own wantonness—it was shame in having responded to his tenderness.

A tenderness that did not exist.

What a fool she'd been! Instead of recognizing her plight, he'd sought to humiliate her. Like all men, he cared nothing for her except as an object to quench his lust—or to ridicule.

Hot tears stung her eyes, and she wrenched herself free.

"You—bastard!" She swung her fist, but he sidestepped, and she lost her balance and crashed to the ground, her skirts flying up, exposing her legs, right up to the scars on her thigh.

His eyes widened as his gaze fell on her legs.

Could her humiliation get any worse? Now, as well as viewing her as a wanton, he'd seen her deformity—the scars. Aunt Kathleen had threatened her with a beating if she were ever to reveal them.

Arabella grasped her skirts, covering herself, blinking back tears. Then he offered his hand.

"Forgive me, miss," he said. "Let me help you up."

She slapped his hand away. "Don't touch me!" she cried, struggling to her feet. "You should be horsewhipped for forcing your disgusting attentions on me!"

"You were willing enough," he said. "But your secret's safe. Nobody saw us."

"How *dare* you speak in such a familiar manner!" she cried. "There is no 'us.' I want you gone, this instant!"

"Only the duke can order me gone."

"I'll speak to him when he returns," she said. "At the very least, I want you out of my sight for the rest of the day."

"I've work to do."

Stubborn creature! Why wouldn't he do as she bade?

She glanced behind him at the column of smoke rising from the bonfire, and an idea took shape. If he refused to take heed of her words, she would seek satisfaction by other means.

"Very well," she said. "But you need food—I won't have you say we're ungenerous to the staff. Go to the kitchen. Tell the cook I sent you."

He arched an eyebrow.

"Must I repeat my request?"

"Very well, seein' as you've asked so politely."

He inclined his head, then set off for the kitchen, whistling a merry tune.

What a *beast*, to take such amusement from her distress!

But, as she smoothed her hair into place, she smiled at his retreating back.

He'd had his amusement—now she would have her vengeance.

Chapter Four

Lawrence pushed the lump of cheese around the plate, but no matter from which angle he looked, it was still as unappealing as a cowpat. The least the cook could have done was scrape the green bits off. The bread wasn't any better, with a texture guaranteed to dislodge a tooth.

Lawrence pushed the plate aside, and the cook sighed while the butler watched him from the head of the table, a glass of ale in his hand.

"Forgive me, Mrs. Broom. I'm not that hungry."

"I believe it's I who should be asking your forgiveness, Mr. Baxter," she said. "You've worked ever so hard these past days, and we can't give you a decent meal. What must you be thinking?"

"That you're a good woman seeking to do her best under trying circumstances," he replied. "Doubtless the master of the house enjoys finer fare."

The cook let out a laugh. "Mrs. Green's so mean with her housekeeping that we *all* have to make do with scrapings."

"*Lady Smith-Green* to you, Mrs. Broom," the butler said.

"Oh, stow it, Mr. Head!" the cook cried. "She might have airs and graces, but she's as common as the likes of you and I, for all that she's Lady Arabella's aunt."

"Lady Arabella?" Lawrence asked. "Her *aunt's* the housekeeper?"

The cook let out an explosive noise of contempt.

"She's not the sort to sully her hands with anything remotely akin to *work*. But she holds the purse strings, and we must make do with what we're given."

"Mrs. Broom, it's not our place to gossip about our betters," the butler said, pushing his ale aside. He pulled out his pocket watch. "I can't sit here idling. His Grace is due back for dinner."

The butler stood, and the cook followed suit. Then he gave Lawrence a pointed look.

Cursing the hierarchy that existed even below stairs, Lawrence rose to his feet. After the butler left, he resumed his seat, and the cook relaxed into hers.

"Mr. Head means well," she said. "He takes his duties a little seriously, that's all, especially seeing as the master's a duke. A fine position, that is—butler to a duke's household."

Lawrence glanced around the kitchen, which was smaller than that at the King's Head. Hardly indicative of a ducal palace.

"Is this the duke's ancestral home?" he asked.

"Bless me, no!" The cook laughed. "That'll be Middlewich Hall—near York. Sold to clear his debts, it was."

"*Sold?*"

"By Millican's Bank—do you know them? The master's great-grandfather entailed the estate, but the entail only lasted three generations. All that's left is the title—and this run-down place."

"How do you know such things?" Lawrence asked.

"My nephew's a clerk at Millican's—he's gone to London. A clever lad, Jonny is, though I say so myself. It's him who's shown me how to put a bit by each month to save for a little cottage of my own. Though whether that'll happen now..." She hesitated, then tilted her head to one side, regarding Lawrence with a thoughtful expression in her eyes. "They paid you yet?"

Lawrence shook his head. "I'll be paid on completion."

"If you've any sense, get them to pay you something now, lest you find yourself out of pocket. The master's only employing you to keep Lady Arabella sweet. He cares little for this place, and I suspect he'll abandon it once he's got his hands on her fortune."

She folded her arms, then sighed. "I should feel sorry for her, seein' as she's a woman in a man's world. I often see her running off to the stables to hide from the duke—and sometimes I see such misery in her eyes. But then she lets loose with that sharp tongue of hers, threatening to have us beaten or dismissed. A harpy like that deserves everything that's comin' to her. I've never met such an unpleasant creature in my life. Not even my sister, and she's a right one, I can tell you. The way she speaks to poor Jonny sometimes makes me want to take my fry pan and—"

"The duke's not a kind master, then?" Lawrence asked, unwilling to hear what the cook would do to her sister with a fry pan.

"Far be it for me to gossip, but there's no young women in the household—excepting Lady Arabella's maid. And do you know why?"

Lawrence shook his head.

"Because, for all his stuffiness, Mr. Head is kind enough to deter any women in danger of...*unwanted attention* from joining the staff here. His Grace doesn't accept refusal from anyone—especially not a woman he takes a fancy to." She shuddered. "We had to let a lass go when she was found to be..." She blushed and made a random gesture in the air.

"I understand," Lawrence said, his gut twisting in revulsion.

"Luckily, Mr. Barnes at the King's Head was in need of a scullery maid. He's a right kind soul, is Mr. Barnes—and *Mrs.* Barnes, for I'm sure the idea was hers. Mr. Barnes might have his name over the door, but it's Mrs. Barnes who rules that household. And why not, I say? It's us women who do the work—except yourself, Mr. Baxter, of course. I've seen you work ever so hard in the garden. Yet poor Susie had to bear the consequences of the master's actions. But she's a parlor maid now, with the bonniest boy you could imagine. You may have seen her?"

Lawrence nodded, recalling the thin young woman toiling in the guest rooms with a baby in tow. How many other bastards had Dunton fathered?

"Susie's not the first," the cook continued. "There's a rumor about some Society miss in London, a friend of Lady Arabella's—if that haughty creature could secure any friends! Doubtless there'll be others." She paused, guilt in her expression. "I shouldn't speak of the master so, but there's no harm in warning decent folk, is there? I wouldn't want no daughter of mine working here. Do you have a daughter, Mr. Baxter?"

"Yes."

"And your wife?"

Lawrence drew in a sharp breath. "She died six years ago."

The cook's face creased in distress. "Oh, bless me, Mr. Baxter, I'm that sorry! You're carrying grief and here's me rattling on. You poor man—widowed with a child."

"Three children."

"*Three* motherless mites! And they're all alone while you're here?"

"A friend's taking care of them while I'm here."

"Where might they be—if you don't mind my asking?"

"At Brackens Hill," Lawrence replied. "My friend's finding us a house there."

"Aye, I've heard of it," she said. "That's a long way to go to leave your children."

Lawrence nodded, the familiar ball of guilt unfurling in his stomach. "I cannot bear to leave them, but I'm doing it for them. *Everything I do is for them.*"

"Of course," the cook said, her voice softening—as did the voice of any woman of a certain age when faced with the notion of a man on his own with children to support. By the count of five, she'd be recommending candidates for a second wife.

One...two...

She leaned forward.

Three...

"You're a good man, Mr. Baxter."

Four...

"But children need a mother. A fine, hardworking man like yourself—there's plenty sensible, practical women who'd do for you. My niece, for one—if she wasn't already walking out with young Luke."

"Luke?"

"The ostler at the King's Head. Lovely lad, he is—dotes on my Sara. His sister is Lady Arabella's maid, worse luck for her. There's a young girl in the village—the baker's daughter. Ever so polite, and uncommonly pretty. Tilly, her name is. Her pa sends the boy to deliver the bread, but I could ask him to send Tilly instead on Thursday."

There it was—before he'd reached the count of five, she'd not only determined that Lawrence needed a wife, but she'd selected the most suitable candidate, and was on the brink of having the banns read.

Lawrence glanced at the stale slice of bread, and the cook blushed.

"That came last week," she said. "The bread's fine when fresh. Tilly bakes it herself, you know. A wife needs to cook, does she not?"

Heavens! This must be how the condemned man felt. The skin around Lawrence's throat itched almost as if he could feel the vicar's noose around his neck.

"I should be getting on, Mrs. Broom," he said, rising.

"Won't you stay a while longer?" she asked. "You've eaten hardly a thing. Or perhaps a glass of ale? We're not supposed to give it to tradesmen, but what Mr. Head don't know won't hurt him. At least, unlike the bread, or the cheese, the ale won't go off."

"I wouldn't want you to go to any trouble on my account," Lawrence replied. "I've a lot to get done if I'm to get those shrubs in before sundown. I prefer to take my ale in the evening, after work—not in the afternoon, instead of it."

"Lord bless you!" She laughed. "You're a fine man. I don't doubt you'll have all the young girls hereabouts clamoring at your door before you return home."

Thanking the cook, Lawrence rose and exited the kitchen.

What had she said?

If you've any sense, get them to pay you something now, lest you find yourself out of pocket.

Surely Dunton would pay him? Though the man had a reputation for taking what he wanted from doxies without payment—perhaps he applied that principle to tradesmen as well, which explained the lack of edible food in the place.

It was almost enough to make Lawrence pity her. That haughty creature…

The woman with a body ripe for the taking, who'd yielded in his arms when he kissed her.

Did he invade her thoughts in a similar unwelcome manner to that by which she'd invaded his?

Was she, perhaps, waiting for him in the garden?

A wicked voice whispered of his desire to see her again—to see those blue eyes darken with need. But when he returned, she was nowhere to be seen.

Neither were his tools, or his notebook. He'd left them beside the pair of rosebushes that he'd set out for planting.

A thickset man in a footman's livery appeared at the archway to the back garden, behind which the bonfire still crackled, sending a plume of smoke into the air.

That fire should have died down by now—that final pile of clippings wouldn't have taken long to burn.

"You there!" he cried. "Have you seen my tools?"

A sneer crept across the footman's lips.

"I left my shovel here—and a rake," Lawrence added, gesturing toward the soft earth that showed the mark where he'd driven the shovel in. "They were here, together with my jacket."

"Oh."

Oh? Was that all he could say? Why did he look so damned pleased with himself?

"And my notebook," Lawrence added, indicating the size with his hands. "It was so big—contains all my plans."

"Oh."

"*Oh?*" Lawrence repeated. "Are you indulging in some sort of game? Have you…"

His voice trailed away as his gut twisted with anticipation.

Surely he hasn't…

"What were you doing in the back garden?" Lawrence asked.

The man folded his arms.

"Tell me!"

"I was followin' orders."

Lawrence caught the man's sleeve. "What orders?"

"I obey orders, I do. Which is more than I can say for others."

The footman glanced toward the bonfire.

Shit!

Pushing him aside, Lawrence sprinted toward the archway, beyond which the bonfire still burned, crackling and spitting in the afternoon air, the rising heat distorting the air, which rippled and danced.

Protruding from the base of the flames was the head of his rake. Of the handle, there was no sign—it must have long since turned to ash.

"No!" Lawrence ran toward the fire, the heat searing his skin.

"Stay back!" the man cried. "You'll burn yourself!"

"You should have thought of that before you threw my belongings onto the fire!" Lawrence replied.

He reached for the rake, and a spike of agony tore through his hands as he touched the metal, which was already distorting with the heat of the fire.

"Fuck!"

"There's no call for that kind of language, mister."

"Pompous arse!" Lawrence retorted. "You'll pay for this!"

He circled the bonfire in search of the rest of his belongings. The head of the shovel lay charred at the base, on top of which he caught sight of wisps of charred fabric—all that remained of his jacket.

Then his gut twisted with a ripple of nausea as he caught sight of his precious notebook containing years of work—or what remained of it.

"Dear God—*no!*" he cried. "Do you have any idea what you've done? That's my life's work you've tossed onto the fire! My drawings—my research. All my plans! What am I going to do?"

"You're going to leave," the footman said. "I've been told to escort you off the estate."

"What about my fee?"

"You're not to be paid. Them's the orders."

Orders…

Fighting the swell of despair, Lawrence fisted his hands, focusing on the pain in his right hand to fuel a new emotion—dissipating the hot despair until only one emotion remained.

Pure, ice-cold fury.

Her orders…

Bitch.

"Where is *she*?" he asked.

There was no need to ask who *she* was. The footman's eyes widened in recognition.

"I-I don't rightly know, mister."

"Never mind—I'll find her myself."

"Now, don't you go and…" the footman began, but, in a swift, smooth movement, Lawrence swung his arm down and back, then drove it forward, smashing his fist into the underside of the man's chin. The footman made no sound, except for a small sigh, then he crumpled to the ground.

Through the crackling of the fire, Lawrence could swear he heard a sharp intake of breath.

"I know you're there!" he cried. "Come out where I can see you!"

Silence.

"The least you can do is face me after what you've done—or should I say, instructed another to do!"

He lowered his gaze to inspect the blistered skin of his fingers where he'd tried to retrieve the rake. Then he turned it over to see the broken skin of his knuckles where they'd connected with the footman's jaw—an infinitely more satisfying injury.

Then he heard a rustling of foliage, and he glanced up to see a flash of pink silk disappearing behind a hedge.

Not content with getting a servant to carry out the deed, she chose to relish the sight of his despair on seeing his life—and hopes—turn to ash.

A bitch, and a coward.

No doubt she'd lived her spoiled, indulged life dealing out her particular style of cruelty on those she considered beneath her, and believing she could escape unpunished. But not this time.

What had the cook said?

I've often seen her running off to the stables to hide from the duke.

He gritted his teeth in a grim smile.

This time, Miss Haughty, you'll not be able to hide.

———⋙⋘———

AS THE STABLES came into view—a building that looked in a worse state of repair than the house—Lawrence slowed his pace, taking care not to make a sound. His quarry would be easier to catch if she believed she'd eluded him.

Where was she?

Let the prey reveal itself.

That was what his da had said when they'd gone hunting rabbit. Lawrence smiled to himself at the notion of that haughty creature skinning a freshly killed cony. It would serve her right to have her hair mussed up, hands deep in guts and gore—faced with the choice of starvation or survival.

A man can but dream.

He settled himself in a secluded position at the corner of the building and waited.

At length, she appeared. Like a rabbit—albeit a particularly spiteful rabbit—she emerged, tentatively at first. A delicate slippered foot appeared from behind the stable door, followed by pink silk skirts—then the rest of her.

She was close enough for him to discern her expression. But rather than vindictive triumph, he saw only sorrow in her eyes. A horse's head appeared at a stable door, and she curved her mouth into a smile.

A tender enough smile to breach his heart and break his resolve.

"Hello, boy," she said softly, lifting her hand to rub the animal's nose.

Lawrence's chance had come. He strode forward and caught her arm, and she let out a shriek, her eyes bright with fear.

"How dare you touch me!"

"How dare *I*?" Lawrence let out a harsh laugh. "After what *you've* done? Were you a man, I'd horsewhip you in the village square."

"You wouldn't dare!" she spat. "You're nothing but a common laborer."

"And what are *you*?" he sneered. "Nothing but a spoiled wench who vents her spite on those she considers beneath her, so she can feel better about her pathetic life!"

Her eyes widened, and for a moment, he thought he saw moisture in them, before they flashed with fury.

"You're nothing!" she cried. "*Nothing*—do you hear me?"

"Is that why you burned my belongings?"

"I never touched them."

"Spiteful mare! Your servant may have destroyed my things—my tools and my papers. But it was at *your* direction—just what I'd expect from your sort."

"My *sort?*"

"Yes, Lady Arabella," he said, thrusting his face close to hers. "A pampered miss with no knowledge of the world, nor understanding of hard work or kindness."

"I see," she said coldly, only a slight tremor in her voice betraying her fear. "You hate me because I'm better than you."

He let out a laugh. "I don't hate you, madam," he said. "You don't matter enough to hate. You're nothing—a woman who seeks gratification from inflicting misery on others merely to satisfy your own joyless existence. If I feel anything for you—it's *pity*."

Her eyes widened in horror, then she blinked and they flashed with defiance. A little pulse of need threaded through his body. What might it be like to take such a woman as his own—to tame that spirit in his bed?

But she was not for him.

Or was she?

He pulled her close and caught the faint scent of smoke—evidence of her crime—together with the sweet, sharp undercurrent of the most delicious scent known to man.

The raw scent of female desire—a scent that not even the most accomplished harlot could fake, nor could the haughtiest lady disguise.

He pushed her against the stable door, and a fire of need ignited inside him at the expression in her eyes. Her cheeks were flushed, her pupils dilated until her eyes were almost black—yet, deep within, sparks of desire flashed like stars, beckoning to him.

Sweet heaven! All that passion imprisoned by years of decorum and poise—most likely beaten into her by a governess, or that aunt of hers. And now, before him, her passion swelled, bursting to be let loose from her stays.

Then she arched her back in an almost imperceptible gesture—but nevertheless, an unmistakable gesture of pure need.

She wanted him.

He caressed her neck, relishing the feel of her smooth porcelain skin against his work-roughened fingers. Her lips parted and she let out a small whimper—her body's cry of need.

Then he dipped his fingers beneath her neckline, running the tips across the top of her breast, which seemed to swell at his touch. He slipped his hand in and cupped her breast. Her eyes closed, and she leaned toward him, as if in offering.

"Oh..." She let out a soft whisper filled with wonder.

Bloody hell—he'd never witnessed such pure need. Of her innocence, there could be no doubt—the surprise in her voice told him she'd yet to experience pleasure at a man's hands. But the little pip beading against his palm spoke of a passion waiting to be unleashed.

Oh, to be the one to unleash it! Would that lecherous duke to whom she was about to shackle herself know how to elicit her pleasure? Would he even care?

He gave her breast a gentle squeeze, and she let out a little mewl as her nipple hardened further.

"Do you feel it?" he whispered. "Your need?"

She nodded, closing her eyes, as if she feared being overwhelmed by sensation.

Then he lowered his head and brushed his lips against hers. She parted them almost immediately, and he smiled to himself at her offering.

"I shall only kiss you if you ask," he whispered.

She tilted her face, seeking his lips, but he withdrew, and she let out a cry of frustration.

"No, my lady. You must *ask*."

"I-I can't..."

"Then you shan't have your reward."

She opened her eyes, and he drew in a sharp breath to temper the surge in his cock. She was ready. Were he to toss up her skirts and bury himself inside her against the stable door, she'd be screaming his name within a heartbeat.

But a man should never take—no matter how much the woman desired it.

"Ask," he demanded, his voice a low growl.

Her eyes flared once more, then she shifted her legs, a small gasp escaping her lips as she pressed her body against his hardness.

"Do you want me?" he asked.

He held his breath in anticipation. Then she nodded, slowly.

"Yes."

Her whispered word was so quiet he could almost have imagined it. But it was enough. He claimed her mouth, sliding his lips over hers, and his manhood surged as she responded. She reached up and fisted her hands in his hair. Little whimpers of need resonated in her throat, as if she had endured a desert and was now desperate to quench her thirst.

He ought to have relished her surrender—the victory he'd secured. But the desperation in her kiss elicited only guilt.

To think, this might be the only passion she'd experience in her life.

The kiss grew more desperate, her whimpers of need increasing, and he shushed her like he would a fevered child, caressing her face with soft sweeps of his fingers, to reassure her. His anger had all but gone as he recognized her anger and spite for what it was. Desperation—and a deeply rooted need.

A need to be free.

"Let me free you," he whispered.

Almost at once, she stiffened. Snapping her head back, she withdrew, and her eyes, once unfocused with passion, cleared into bright, hard contempt. She reached up, bending her fingers into claws, and raked her fingernails across his face.

Thick, sharp pain sliced across his cheek, and he jerked back with a cry.

Bloody hell!

His stomach churned at the metallic stench of blood, and he lifted his hand to his cheek, where his fingers slipped against thick, warm liquid.

"Sweet heaven, woman—what was *that* for?"

She stood before him, hair in disarray, a feral expression in her eyes, and—curse his body—his cock rose at the sight of such wild abandon. Then she lowered her gaze to her hand, where he caught sight of the red smear on her fingernails.

"You—*animal!*" she cried. "Violator of women! You've lusted after me from the beginning."

"I did nothing that you didn't beg for, woman—and you know it," he growled, pressing his hand against his cheek.

Fuck—that hurt!

"First you destroy my possessions, then you assault me. I shan't leave here until I have satisfaction."

"You'll *never* have satisfaction from me, you, you...*peasant!*" she cried. "I could have you hanged!"

"Don't be a fool, woman."

"Fool, am I?" She lifted her head and screamed. "Help me!" she cried. "For God's sake, help me! Save me from him!"

"Stop that!" he said. "I'll not harm you—it was you that begged me."

"I did nothing of the sort," she said. "You—you're a debaucher of women, a violator of maidens."

"I've violated no one."

"Who do you think they'd believe?" She spoke more calmly now, the coldness returning to her tone. "A stranger, a nobody? Or the future Duchess of Dunton?"

She lifted her head once more and cried out, filling her voice with terror.

"Help me, someone! He's after me—*please!*"

Lawrence's heart sank as he heard footsteps.

"Where are you, miss?" a voice cried.

"The stables!" she replied. "Be quick! I'm so frightened!"

Then she turned to face him, a cold smile on her lips. "What say you, you *uncouth peasant?*" she sneered. "Care to pit your word against mine? Leave, now, and you can save your thick neck."

She'd bested him—*curse her*—and she knew it.

But he'd be damned if he let her see her victory come to completion. Mirroring her cold smile, he stepped toward her, tempering the flare of guilt as the fear returned to her eyes.

"I'll go," he said, "but I curse you for the harm you've done me. We mayn't live in a fair world, but I pray, one day, you will reap the rewards of the choices you made today."

She stepped back. "Choices—what choices?"

"Do you think your fiancé will relish hearing about your supposed violation?" he asked. "He'll view you as sullied goods and punish you for it."

"H-he'll punish *you*—not me."

"You sound unsure of yourself, madam," he said. "We live in a man's world. You might exert your power over me by virtue of our difference in rank, but never forget the power your betrothed can exert over you by virtue of your difference in sex."

"Wh-what do you mean?"

"I mean, madam, that you will never own me. But your fiancé—from the moment you submit to him at the altar—will own every part of you, *until death do you part.*"

Her fear thickened the air, but Lawrence was beyond reason.

"Do you know what, Lady Arabella?" he said, smiling coldly.

"Wh-what?" she whimpered.

"I wish you joy of him. So, tell the footman what you wish—tell and be *damned*, Lady Arabella."

She glanced about as if she feared Dunton's arrival. Then the footman came into view, running toward them.

"Your ladyship!" he panted. "Are you in danger?"

She glanced at Lawrence, moisture shining in her eyes, and his resolve almost melted as a tear splashed onto her cheek.

"I-I'm quite well, Thomas," she said. "I…" She glanced around, as if in desperation.

"You said *save me from him*," the footman said. "Has this fellow harmed you?"

"N-no. I was frightened by"—she glanced toward the stables—"the horse. Yes—the horse."

"The horse?" The footman glanced toward the animal, which stared placidly out from its stall.

"I went inside the stables and was almost crushed by one of the horses. This"—she gestured toward Lawrence—"this…*man* pulled me free."

The footman narrowed his eyes. "Is that true, sir?"

Lawrence nodded.

"Very well—but I'll have to tell the master."

"There's no need for that, Thomas," Lady Arabella said. "I only want you to get rid of *him*."

"I'm going nowhere until you've paid me," Lawrence said.

"I thought you'd say as much," the footman replied. Then he reached into his jacket and drew out a pistol. "Get yerself gone, or I'll shoot."

Damn it, Lawrence *needed* that money. But there was little point arguing the matter if all it earned him was a bullet in the head. He had no wish to leave his children fatherless as well as motherless.

He'd have to rely on Fate to exact vengeance upon her—by having her live out her days as Dunton's wife.

"Then I'll take my leave of you, your ladyship," he said, "and I wish you all the happiness that you deserve in your impending nuptials."

He gave a bow, exaggerating the gesture in mockery, before taking his leave.

How the devil would he be able to settle his account at the King's Head?

But the lack of payment was the least of his concerns. Without his tools, and his notes, what the bloody hell was he going to do to survive?

Chapter Five

You don't matter enough to hate.

As she returned to the house, Arabella wiped her eyes and suppressed a sob.

How *dare* he!

How dare he look into her eyes and *know* her—know that while she might be the lady on the outside, on the inside she was nothing.

No—worse than nothing. She was a prisoner of her position in Society. Helpless, unable to do anything. Not even able to command her fate.

But she could command the fate of others.

I showed you—peasant!

Yes, she'd shown him.

Why, then, could she feel nothing but shame and self-loathing? After the brief burst of triumph as the fire had flared, the flames licking around his possessions, the realization had stuck her. It wasn't his freedom, or life, that had turned to ashes in that moment.

It was hers.

Tears splashed onto her cheeks, and she lowered her gaze to her fingertips. In striking out at him, she'd only succeeded in striking out at herself. Three parallel lines were scored across her heart, to match those on his face.

Aunt Kathleen's form came into view.

"There you are!" she huffed. "Where have you been? Just *look* at you!"

"In the garden, Aunt."

"Don't speak with such an insolent tone! What have you done to get yourself into such a state?" She wrinkled her nose. "Oh, you *stink*! Have you been near that gardener fellow despite my telling you not to fraternize with his sort?"

Arabella opened her mouth to explain, then closed it again.

Tell and be damned, *Lady Arabella.*

"Let me look at you, child."

A bony hand grasped Arabella's chin and thrust it upward, and she let out a soft groan at the ache in her neck.

"Aunt…"

"I said silence! You look like you've been dragged through a bush."

She squeezed her chin, and Arabella let out a low cry of pain as tears spilled onto her cheeks.

"And that's quite enough of that," her aunt said. "Women of our rank should not be given to such outbursts. Such histrionics belong in the schoolroom."

"I can't help it if—"

"Yes, you can!" Her aunt thrust her face close, her poisonous eyes glittering with contempt. "Who do you think you are, disgracing the family name like this?"

"It's *my* family name, not yours."

"Don't take that tone with me, young lady! Remember your position. You'd be nothing without me, do you hear? After all I've done for you—the sacrifices I've made—you repay me with this? You're on the brink of securing our triumph, yet you threaten it, behaving like a guttersnipe! Get yourself inside, before somebody sees you."

"Who's to see me out here?"

"Your betrothed, for one thing," her aunt said. "Do you think he'll maintain his interest if he sees you like this? With a blotchy face and puffy eyes? Your appearance dictates your future."

"I thought that was my fortune," Arabella said bitterly.

Slap!

Her aunt struck her cheek, then gripped her wrist and led her inside.

As soon as they'd passed the footman guarding the main doors—who, though he tried to stare straight ahead with nonchalance, couldn't help a glance in their direction—Arabella wrenched her arm free.

"Do not defy me," her aunt warned.

"I'll do what I like," Arabella said, forcing a frost into her voice. Then she tilted her head to one side and gave her aunt a cold smile. "What do you think the duke will do once he's secured my hand? Do you think he'll have further use for you? *I* certainly won't."

"You'll still need me to teach you decorum."

"I'll need no one," Arabella said. "Isn't that what you've always told me? Isn't that why I have no friends?"

"You'd have plenty of friends if you associated with the right sort."

"What of Juliette Howard?" Arabella asked. "She was my particular friend until last Season."

"I've told you before not to speak of that whore!"

"What did Juliette do to cause such offense?" Arabella asked. "Dunton himself was enamored by her until she disappeared. I always thought he'd offer for her."

"He'd never offer for someone with her background—daughter to a common shopkeeper. But she got what she deserved in the end—banished to the country to live out her disgrace. That's all her sort deserve."

"Her sister Eleanor secured the hand of a duke," Arabella said.

"By spreading her legs, no doubt," her aunt sneered. "How else could that ungainly little imbecile have snared a man?"

Arabella winced at her aunt's vicious words directed at a young woman who, though beneath her in station, had seemed perfectly harmless, if a little reserved.

"Aunt…" she began, but Kathleen pushed her up the staircase.

"I'll have no more of your insolence," she snarled. "Your fiancé understands my worth, and he'd punish you for disrespecting me. Once you're married, he can treat you how he wants, with the full endorsement of the church and the law. So, if you wish for an advocate in your married life, you'd do well to give me the respect I deserve. Now, go upstairs and make yourself presentable before he returns. It'll be the worse for you if he chooses not to wed you. You won't want to suffer Miss Howard's fate."

Banished to the country to live out her disgrace.

In truth, Juliette Howard's fate seemed less abhorrent with the passing of each day.

Aunt Kathleen hailed a passing footman.

"Fetch Lady Arabella's maid—*now!*"

"Yes, ma'am." The footman bowed and scuttled off as Arabella's aunt marched her toward her chamber, opened the door, and pushed her in.

"Calm yourself, child, and make yourself presentable. Then I'll decide how to punish you."

"But I've done nothing wrong."

"Don't answer back!" Aunt Kathleen snapped. "I see there's much I must do with you before your marriage—though I'm sure your fiancé is more than capable of taking you in hand."

Arabella's gut twisted at the notion of Dunton *taking her in hand.*

"Ah, *there* you are, girl," Aunt Kathleen said as Arabella's maid appeared. "See if you can fix…*that.*" She gestured toward Arabella. "Make the best of her, or I'll have you punished also."

The maid curtseyed, then waited until Arabella's aunt had gone before rushing toward Arabella.

"Oh, miss! What's happened?"

"Nothing," Arabella said. Despite the girl's expression of sympathy, she might be like the rest of the servants creeping about the place—ready to spy on her to ingratiate themselves with her aunt, or worse, with Dunton.

"Is it the gardener? Has he done something to distress you?"

So—her maid *had* been spying on her.

"No, Connie. I'm tired, that's all."

The maid placed a light hand on her shoulder, and Arabella's heart threatened to crack at the pity in her eyes. The last thing she wanted was to be *pitied*—not by that insolent man in the garden, and certainly not by her maid.

"I only want to see you happy, miss."

Arabella brushed the maid's hand aside. "I *am* happy," she retorted. "What nonsense you speak, Connie. Fetch my evening gown. I wish to change for dinner."

"It's not yet six o'clock, miss, and—"

"I didn't ask what time it was," Arabella said. "I told you to fetch my gown."

The maid's smile disappeared. "As you wish."

Arabella sat at dressing table and stared at her reflection.

She looked like a farm girl who'd been cavorting in the hedgerow. No wonder her aunt had been so angry!

"Connie, fetch me some water," she said. "I must wash my face."

"Very good, miss. And perhaps some of that tincture for your skin. You don't look at all well."

"Do you mean to insult me?" Arabella snapped.

The maid cringed, then shook her head. "I spoke only out of concern, Lady Arabella. Forgive me if I gave offense."

She bobbed another curtsey and exited the chamber, leaving Arabella with her reflection and her conscience.

"Oh, Connie, there's nothing to forgive," she whispered. "*You've* committed no sin. Whereas I..."

Unwilling to face her image, she turned toward the window.

Shortly after, Connie reappeared carrying a small phial and a pitcher of water. Arabella resumed her position but closed her eyes, relishing her maid's gentle ministrations while Connie dabbed her face with a cloth that gave off the faint scent of lavender, then ran a brush through her hair in a soft caress—her touch gentler than Arabella deserved.

Were their positions reversed and Connie was the mistress, Arabella would have sought retribution for her harsh words—scrubbing her face a little too hard, then driving the hairbrush into her scalp, running through the tangles without mercy. And, had Connie treated her with such roughness, she might have weathered it. But the kind, gentle touch—kindness she didn't deserve—threatened to breach her defenses.

When Connie finished, Arabella opened her eyes and studied her reflection. Gone were the blotches on her cheeks—concealed cleverly under a layer of powder. Her hair shone, the intricate array of curls catching the light as she moved her head.

Her maid had worked a miracle. Gone was the sorry creature who'd had a taste of passion before tearing it apart with her hands. She had been replaced by Lady Arabella Ponsford—Society beauty and duchess-in-waiting.

We don't thank the staff—it gives them ideas above their station.

Her aunt's words echoing in her mind, Arabella gave a curt nod, then stood. Connie curtseyed then exited the chamber, leaving her alone.

Alone—and friendless.

But, as Aunt Kathleen said, she had no need for friends. Why would she, when she had a houseful of paid subordinates at her beck and call? She could live out her life in the manner to which she had been born—unimpeded by the need to open her heart to another living soul.

Her future as a duchess was all she needed.

Being *happy* was not a part of that.

Chapter Six

What the bloody hell am I going to do?

"What did you say, my lovely?"

Lawrence glanced up at the comely face of the woman who'd warmed his bed the night he arrived at the King's Head. Her full lips curved into a smile, and he almost forgot the pain.

Almost.

She dipped her fingers into the salve and smeared it over his hands.

He flinched. *Fuck*—that hurt!

"Sorry, my darlin', but you'll be as right as anything in the morning, especially if your Millie warms your bed tonight."

He held up his hands. "There's little I can do with these."

She pursed her lips into a perfect rosebud. "A shame to womankind if those expert fingers of yours cannot be put to use," she said. "But it wasn't yer fingers that gave me such a pleasin' time when ye came here. Yer tongue will please me just as well—and I've a fancy to riding that proud cock of yours."

She leaned forward, offering her lips for a kiss, but he turned his head aside.

"Forgive me, Millie," he said.

"Did I not please ye the other night?"

"You pleased me well enough, Millie, but..." He shook his head. "I've not the appetite for pleasure at the moment."

Millie began to wind a strip of cotton around Lawrence's fingers.

"Curse that woman," she said. "Miss High-and-Mighty Lady Arabella has much to answer for."

Lawrence drew in a sharp breath. Doxies were known to be astute—but could Millie read his innermost desires that easily? Did she know that even the prospect of savoring that fiery creature—no matter how unlikely that may be—had ruined him for other women?

"Lady Arabella?" he said, aware of the tightness in his voice.

"Aye," Millie replied. "As bad-tempered a harpy as I've had the misfortune of encountering, I can tell ye. I'd like to see her driven out of the village—and that duke of hers. She's worse than him—bein' a woman and all that."

"You hate her because of her sex?"

Millie secured the bandage with a knot. "No, my lovely, I hate her for what she's done to you—burnin' your tools like that, then sending you packing without payment. A fine, hardworking soul such as yourself shouldn't have to suffer at her hands."

"It's the way of the world, Millie."

"Aye," she said, "which is why I make my customers pay me in advance before I service them."

Lawrence sighed. "I've no money to pay you."

"Ah, bless you, lovely—I was going to offer you my arms for free."

"It wouldn't be right," Lawrence said, "and comely as you are, I have no appetite for pleasure."

She kissed his hand, brushing her lips against the bandage.

"There!" she said. "Your Millie will kiss the pain away. And ye needn't worry about settling yer account here. Mr. Barnes is a generous man."

"I won't take charity," Lawrence said.

"Male pride!" Millie let out a snort. "Them that are undeserving will take what they will, whereas those in need refuse an offer of help. I'll never understand men like you."

The chamber door was knocked upon, and a man appeared.

Thickset with a thatch of graying hair on his head, ruddy cheeks and bright blue eyes, the innkeeper nodded in greeting.

"Mind if I have a word, Mr. Baxter? It's about your account."

"Mr. Barnes," Millie protested, "can't you see he's—"

The innkeeper raised his hand—a hand marked by callouses, the trophies of a life of hard work and toil. He gestured to Lawrence's bound hands.

"Fixed you up right and proper, didn't they?" he said. "Them folk up at the big house. Funny how them with the most are the least inclined to pay."

"Lady Arabella burned all Lawrence's things, Mr. Barnes," Millie said.

The innkeeper's eyes widened. "Is that so?"

Lawrence nodded. "I'm sorry, Mr. Barnes, I've nothing to pay for my room. But I can work for my keep."

The innkeeper eyed Lawrence's bound hands, doubt in his expression.

"Millie says they'll be better in the morning," Lawrence added. "I could tend to your garden if I'd not lost my tools."

"He's a fine worker, Mr. Barnes," Millie said.

The innkeeper smiled. "It seems as if our Millie's taken a shine to you—and I trust her judgment. Very well, if you wish to earn your keep, a day or so helping out in the stables should suffice, provided your hands have healed."

"I can weather a little pain in the pursuit of honoring my debts," Lawrence said.

The innkeeper's face broke into a gap-toothed smile. "I daresay you could, with your physique. Are you a fighting man, perchance? We've a few bouts in the yard every Friday if you fancy it. There's good money to be had—more if you can fell your opponent. I reckon you'd flatten Jakey Bates good and proper—and he's needing a good pummeling."

Lawrence shook his head. "The only adversaries I deal with are unruly gardens. I can wield an axe if you've any wood needing chopping. Though you'd have to provide the axe now I've lost mine."

"You mean now that bitch destroyed it," Millie said, loathing in her voice.

"I daresay I can find ye something to do in the garden," the innkeeper said. "My Alice is always nagging at me to clear the back corner, but those brambles are so bleedin' persistent—they come back every year."

"You need to remove the root system," Lawrence said. "If you merely cut them at the base, they'll grow back with even more persistence than before."

"And you can get rid of them for good?"

Lawrence nodded. "They find a way back eventually, but I can hamper their assault. There's a tincture you can paint them with, but I'll not be applying potions in a garden—they can poison the earth and impede the growth of other plants. Tending to a garden is about taking care of the plants and creatures that live there."

"Your passion does you credit," the innkeeper said. "Very well—if those hands of yours are up to it, perhaps you can see to the brambles. We've some old tools in the store doing nothing. You can take them home with you when you're done. They're nothing special but will help you get back on your feet."

Lawrence shook his head. "Honest work I can accept, Mr. Barnes, but I can't take charity."

Millie let out a huff, and the innkeeper rolled his eyes.

"Stubborn fool!" he said good naturedly. "Are you so awash with friends that you don't need any more?"

Lawrence let out a bitter laugh. "I have but one friend."

"Who might that be?"

"His name's Ned—Ned Ryman. He works at the inn in Brackens Hill."

Millie's face broke into a smile, and a flicker of female desire shone in her eyes. "Oh, *that* Ned! He's a right charmer, he is."

"He's kind, certainly," Lawrence said. "His niece is looking after my children while I'm here. And he's looking for a home for me in Brackens Hill. I'm down on my luck, you see."

Which was the understatement of the decade, seeing as he'd been evicted from his former home for rent arrears, turfed onto the street with three children clinging to his breeches, and had rendered himself penniless to travel to Brackens Hill to make a fresh start in the hope that a man he'd befriended at an inn would take pity on him.

Some *fresh start* that had turned out to be—losing what little possessions he had within a week of embarking on his future.

"You've two more friends right here," the innkeeper said. "Isn't that right, Millie?"

"That's right," she said. "Any friend of Ned is a friend of mine. Perhaps you've little cause to trust anyone if your life's been hard. But it's only by taking a leap of faith and trusting the unknown that we can find our true friends—them that stick by you in adversity, not just during times of prosperity."

Lawrence stared at her, and she laughed.

"You needn't look so surprised, lovely. A whore's best placed to have an insight into human nature, seein' as she experiences the very best and the very worst of it. Often in the same night."

He squeezed her hand, flinching at the ache in his fingers. "Then I accept your friendship with gratitude and pleasure."

"Excellent!" the innkeeper cried. "I'll make sure my Alice gives you a hearty breakfast tomorrow, then you can start your day helping Luke in the stables."

"I don't know how to thank you, Mr. Barnes," Lawrence said.

"You can thank me by prospering and ensuring that you're never defeated by the cruelty of others." Then the innkeeper nodded. "I'll see you tomorrow, young man. Take care of him tonight, Millie."

Millie's eyes flared with desire, but Lawrence had spoken the truth. He was in no mood for pleasure.

And he could hardly surrender to Millie's ministrations when his mind was filled with desire for another woman—even if he loathed that woman with every fiber of his soul.

<hr />

MILLIE'S SALVE WAS akin to witchcraft. Other than a slight soreness on the skin, Lawrence's hands had almost completely healed from yesterday's ordeal.

Anything a man failed to understand, or find a plausible explanation for, he attributed to witchcraft. Which, most likely, explained why so many women had been persecuted in the past. A man felt threatened by a woman with greater intelligence than he.

Might *she* be at risk of persecution for being more intelligent than her fiancé?

He let out a sigh and continued to brush the horse's pelt. Lady Arabella plagued his waking thoughts as well as his dreams. Last night she'd visited him, her furious passion unleashed as he'd taken her into his arms—only to morph into a ball of flame, screaming in triumph until he woke up, shaking, to the sound of a cock crowing.

Curse her!

The horse let out a snort.

"Sorry, boy." He stroked the animal's nose. "I shouldn't be wasting my time thinking about that spoiled creature when I've you to keep me company."

The animal's ears pricked up.

"Heard something, have you?" Lawrence moved toward the stable door and looked out.

Three riders approached the inn—two side by side, a third trailing behind. Lawrence recognized Dunton's portly figure atop a black gelding. The man seemed unsuited to the saddle, ready to fall off at any moment, and the woman beside him seemed equally ill at ease. But the third rider steered her mount as if they were the same creature.

He caught his breath as they drew near.

The third rider was Lady Arabella Ponsford.

Unable to help himself, Lawrence stepped outside to get a closer look.

The road ran west to east, and the morning sun shone directly on the riders, the horses' pelts glistening in the sunlight. A number of villagers darted to and fro, going about their business, stopping as the riders passed. The women dipped into a curtsey, and the men removed their caps and bowed, or touched their forelocks in submission.

The duke gave a cursory nod, and the woman beside him tilted her head, sticking her nose in the air to affirm her superiority.

As to the third rider…

Lawrence caught his breath as he noticed her looking directly at him. Her sapphire eyes widened as he met her gaze, and he smiled to himself at the fear in her expression.

You've every cause to be afraid of me, madam.

She glanced toward Dunton, curling her hands around the reins. Her mount shifted sideways, responding to the movement. Her lips parted, and she blanched.

She wasn't afraid of Lawrence. She was afraid of *them*.

Hate her he ought to—but he couldn't help the spark of compassion at the thought of Fate having placed her under Dunton's ownership.

He could never hate her.

"Instead, I pity you, Lady Arabella Ponsford."

Though he spoke in a whisper, she startled as if she'd heard. Her mount shook its head and reared up. With a cry, she grasped the reins, struggling to maintain control.

"Arabella!" the older woman cried. "Compose yourself in public."

Lady Arabella tugged at the reins until her mount quietened. Moisture glistened in her eyes. Then she wiped them in a sharp, angry gesture and, before Lawrence could react, steered the horse toward him, forcing him into the side of the road. He lost his balance and fell into the ditch that ran alongside.

Shit.

Quite literally. The stench was enough to turn his stomach.

He clambered out, holding his breath to avoid expelling his breakfast. *Ye gods*—he was covered in the stuff.

"Arabella, leave that creature alone—it's beneath you. Come here at once."

"Yes, Aunt."

She steered her mount toward her companions.

"What was that about?" Dunton asked. She leaned toward him and muttered something. Then Dunton turned and stared at Lawrence before curling his lips into a sneer. "Quite so," he said. "The ditch is where he belongs."

Then they resumed their path along the road disappearing at the far end.

Spiteful creature! First she'd ruined him, now she humiliated him—taking pleasure from both acts. But, despite her cruelty, he found himself wanting only one thing.

To see her smile—not the cold smile of calculation, but a genuine smile of pleasure.

How might those beautiful eyes look, illuminated with joy?

But, given the future she had consigned herself to, joy would forever elude her.

Chapter Seven

The bonfire crackled, distorting the air with ripples of heat as smoke rose into the sky. Flames licked over the book, curling around the pages like a caress, until they twisted and distorted, then finally surrendered, disintegrating into ash.

But her triumph was replaced by self-loathing and a deeply rooted throb of fear, a thick, advancing tide. And in the background…

The shadow of death.

Bella!

Her name, uttered in a shrill scream, crackled in the air as the fire raged before her, angry red wraiths reaching out with clawlike fingers…

"Mama!"

She thrust out her hands to fend off the inferno, then threw back her head and screamed. Pain exploded in her mind, and she fell back. The ground met her body with a jolt, and she opened her eyes.

The flames had gone—replaced by the cold blue light of the dawn.

"That's quite enough of *that*," a sharp voice said.

Arabella blinked, and her vision cleared.

She was in her bedchamber. Aunt Kathleen stood beside the bed, in her dressing gown, reams of lace rippling in the air as she moved.

"F-forgive me, Aunt," Arabella said. "I was dreaming."

"I don't care. You could be heard halfway across the house. Most unbecoming."

"But..."

"Don't answer back!"

"But I always have that dream," Arabella protested. "I've told you before. It ends with a burning building, and a voice calling my name—like a memory reaching out. Then it slips away."

"There's nothing to remember, child," her aunt said. "Your parents were killed in a fire, and your cousin sent you to me to take care of you. And I've been taking care of you ever since. Rather than waste your time trying to remember *that*, you should remember everything I've done for you and be grateful."

"I can't help having bad dreams."

"Yes, you can, Arabella. It's a matter of self-control—a quality expected in a woman of your rank. You must act with decorum in private as well as in public. What do you think the duke would do if he knew of your nighttime ravings? He'll not want a bride who suffers from insanity."

"I'm not insane!" Arabella cried. "How can you—Ouch!"

She let out a shriek as her aunt slapped her across the face a second time.

"I *said*, that's enough! Even if the duke didn't hear you, the servants are about. And you know what *they're* like."

Arabella flinched at the contempt in her aunt's tone. "Tell me what they're like, Aunt."

"They gossip about their betters. And your reputation is vulnerable until you're safely married. The lowest of the low will relish the slightest drop of gossip about their betters, because it gives pleasure to their pathetic lives." Aunt Kathleen turned toward the door. "Isn't that right...*you*."

Connie stood in the doorway.

"Well?" Aunt Kathleen prompted.

The maid curtseyed. "Yes, Lady Smith-Green."

"You sent for my maid?" Arabella asked.

"Of course I did!" Aunt Kathleen gestured to Connie. "Come here, girl—see to it that your mistress doesn't disturb the household again."

"Yes, ma'am."

The maid approached the bed, holding a beveled glass filled with white liquid.

"What's that?" Arabella asked.

"It's milk," Aunt Kathleen said. "To settle your stomach."

"Ma'am, shouldn't we—" Connie began.

"That's enough, girl! Do as you're told, or I'll have you whipped again."

Again?

Connie flinched, then pressed the glass into Arabella's hand. "Please drink this, miss," she said. "It'll help you sleep."

"B-but it's morning," Arabella protested.

"It's early yet," Aunt Kathleen said, "and the duke's taking his rest. He's not long returned from his outing, and I doubt he'll want to be disturbed. That girl"—she gave Connie a look of contempt—"can bring you breakfast in your chamber. We need to ensure you're fully recovered before the duke sees you."

Arabella shifted her gaze between her aunt and her maid—two women with the same purpose. But that purpose was driven by two different emotions. In her aunt's expression, she saw determination and self-interest. In her maid's, she saw terror.

She took the glass and swallowed a mouthful of milk. The sugar her maid must have stirred in couldn't completely disguise the bitter taste of laudanum. She hesitated and looked up, and Aunt Kathleen raised her eyebrows in expectation. Accepting the futility of defiance, Arabella tilted the glass and drained the contents.

"I'm glad to see you can sometimes respect the wishes of your elders and betters."

Elder Aunt Kathleen may be. As to better…

The one consolation from marrying Dunton was that Arabella

would outrank her aunt and therefore be free of her. That was worth any inconvenience she must suffer now—including a dose of laudanum intended to keep her quiet. And, in truth, oblivion would give her respite from her dreams.

But nothing could give her respite from her conscience.

Chapter Eight

It was worse than he'd feared.

Far worse.

Clutching his tools, Lawrence stared at the building before him.

"What do you think?"

Lawrence glanced at Ned, with his mop of brown curls, warm amber eyes, and overly optimistic smile.

"Is that…"

"Your new home, yes."

Saints alive!

"I doubt you'd want to know what I think," Lawrence said.

"Indulge me."

"It's fucking awful."

Ned's smile faded.

A pang of guilt twisted Lawrence's gut. He wasn't in a position to turn his nose up at anything, given that he had nowhere else to go. Neither was he in a position to admonish Ned, given all the man had done for him.

"It's not much, granted," Ned said, "but the rent's minimal, and there's plenty of room in the garden for your children. Might help tire them out—if that's possible." There was no mistaking the exasperation in his tone.

"They been much trouble?" Lawrence asked.

"Nothing my Sophie can't handle—though even *she's* in danger of losing her patience. A lively trio, ain't they? Especially that young Roberta. Pretty lass when she's not rolling around in the dirt—but she's more trouble than the boys."

"I'm sorry."

"There's nowt to worry about," Ned replied. "A bit o' spirit's good in a little 'un. I can't be done with children who sit on their arses all day. Runnin' around's good for them, though I doubt Mrs. Chantry will agree. She's a stickler for obedience—her cane warmed my arse many times when I was a lad."

"Mrs. Chantry?"

"She runs the school at the other end of the village."

Lawrence glanced about, but no other buildings were visible. "It looks like *everything's* at the other end of the village from here."

"Don't be down," Ned said. "This was the only empty place in Brackens Hill, and you can't take a room at the inn. The Oak's no place for children, and besides, Mr. Colt always wants payment in advance."

Payment Lawrence couldn't afford.

"I've nothing bad to say about Mr. Colt," Ned continued. "He's a fair employer—I get a shilling a week more than the manager at the Stag Inn in the next village." He glanced at Lawrence's tools. "Those look the worse for wear—are they the same tools you had before?"

Lawrence shook his head. "These were a gift. I lost mine."

"That's careless."

"I was careless in trusting my employer," Lawrence said. "I should have taken a lesson from Mr. Colt and taken payment in advance."

Ned let out a chuckle. "Your work weren't up to scratch?"

"The lady of the house took against me and turned me out without paying."

"And your hands?" Ned gestured to the bandages. "You got into a brawl with her?"

"Not in the way you mean." Lawrence sighed, though his body

tightened at the prospect of wrestling Lady Arabella into submission. "I burned them trying to retrieve my belongings after she'd ordered her footman to throw them on the fire."

"Fucking hell." Ned sighed. "There's no understanding some folk. She ought to be whipped raw. Do your hands pain you?"

"A slight soreness, that's all," Lawrence said. "They gave me a salve at the King's Head."

"Ah, yes." Ned grinned. "I know old Tom Barnes well—he'd have seen ye right. And Millie—did you see Millie when you were there? I've never seen a finer pair of teats in my life."

Ned raised his hands, cupping them as if holding a pair of invisible oranges.

"Just right for my hands, they are—and tasty morsels for a man when he's hungry after a day's work. Did you take your fill?"

"The first night, yes."

Ned licked his lips. "Lovely! Did she do that thing she does with her tongue?" He closed his eyes as if reliving the memory. "I can feel it now—the way she parts a man's legs and licks all the way along his—"

"I should take a look inside," Lawrence said.

Ned let out a laugh. "If you say so. I only hope if I take a wife, she'll let me teach her some of Millie's tricks. A wife should know how to please her husband, aye?"

"I wouldn't know," Lawrence said. "A widower with three children is hardly likely to find a wife."

"Don't be sayin' that!" Ned slapped Lawrence on the arm good naturedly. "There's plenty lasses hereabouts who'd jump at the chance of a man like you, though you'd need a strong woman to cope with them three."

Ned was right. Few women could manage such unruly children, even if they'd nurtured them from birth. But to take on three children in the prime of their mischief—that was too much to ask from even the most stout-hearted woman.

When did children grow out of the phase where everything they touched shattered into shards? Or, in the case of Bobby, did they *ever* grow out of that?

Lawrence gestured toward the cottage. "Thank you," he said. "All I need now is a spot of work to pay the rent."

"You'll not be short of work here. The vicarage garden's needing clearing. And my Sophie heard from a lass who works in a big house in the next county—the new owners are needing some work doin' on their estate. We'll see you right here, Lawrence. We look after our own at Brackens Hill—even incomers like yourself. Now, come and look at your new home, then you can take a bite of supper at mine."

"I mustn't trouble you," Lawrence said. "I should get the children settled here right away."

"Best not just yet," came the reply. "You'll want to tidy up the place first. Come and see."

As they entered the cottage, Lawrence heard scratching, followed by a patter of tiny feet. He blinked, his eyes adjusting to the darkness in the hallway, and caught sight of two small, furry forms scuttling along the floor, giving him a glimpse of their tails before they disappeared through a hole in the floorboards.

Lawrence shuddered. What other creatures occupied the place? And though the children preferred to be *grubbing about in the dirt outside*—according to Miss Tewkson, the schoolteacher who'd declared that she'd *never come across such nasty little beasts in twenty years of teaching*—not even Bobby, who surpassed her brothers in boldness, would wish to share a bed with a nest full of rats.

Ned gave a wry smile. "Welcome to Brackens Hill."

Chapter Nine

The rush of water grew louder, mingling with the voice of the wind tearing through the trees. Arabella shivered as she steered her mount along the path. The wind carried with it a bite of cold, even though summer had just begun.

"I'm glad you came for a ride, my dear," her fiancé said. "I love a good, hard ride, myself."

Arabella's stomach churned at his voice, heavy with innuendo.

He steered his mount alongside, and she shuddered at the stench of cigars, stale brandy, and cheap perfume.

"Must you ride so close?" she snapped. "You're crowding my horse. This path is too narrow—one of us could fall into the river."

"A husband can ride as close to his wife as he likes."

"You're not my husband yet."

He caught her wrist.

"Even a *prospective* wife must learn obedience."

"Let me go," she said, swallowing the ripple of fear. "Would you show such a lack of decorum toward your future duchess?"

For a moment, his gaze darkened. Then he smiled, his fleshy face puckering.

"Of course, my dear." He patted her hand before releasing it. "This coquettish behavior of yours is quite charming—I like a filly with spirit."

She rubbed her wrist, and he smiled. "The greater the challenge, the sweeter the reward, no? You'll yield in the end." His smile broadened. "But don't yield too easily. A little resistance in a woman can increase the pleasure when the conquest is complete."

"A man must earn his conquest," she said. "No woman would yield to the undeserving."

"How sweet you are in your innocence, my dear!" He laughed. "But affection will come in time. My affection for you remains as it ever was."

Of that, she didn't doubt. But Dunton's affection began and ended with her dowry and her title. He certainly harbored no affection for *her*.

In fact, there wasn't a single living soul who harbored any feeling for her other than a casual dislike.

Except perhaps one.

A secret thrill coursed through her at the thought of the burning hatred she'd seen in the eyes of the man in the garden…and the raw, masculine scent of him as he'd taken her in his arms and claimed her with a kiss—a kiss so savage and primal that her body had been driven almost wild with need.

He might have loathed her, but he'd wanted her also.

And, heaven help her, she wanted *him*.

She urged her mount forward.

"Eager to rid yourself of my company?" Dunton's thick, nasal voice cut through her mind, dissipating the memory of the voice of another—the deep baritone roughened by a country accent.

"My horse is restless," she replied.

"Another mare in need of a damned good riding," he muttered, and she caught his words before the wind carried them away.

Ahead, the river curved around in a tight arc. The ground sloped downward, and the river narrowed and steepened, the water growing restless, forming a boiling, swirling mass, tumbling over rocks to form waterfalls, plunging ever forward.

She urged her mount into a trot, steering around the boulders in the path.

"Don't stray too far, my dear," Dunton said, and she glanced back to see him following her.

Was this what her life would be like—to be always at his beck and call? Why was it that he was permitted to disappear of an evening and return the next morning reeking of whores, yet she was denied a moment's respite from his company during a ride?

Propelled on by a flash of rebellion, she leaned forward in the saddle, urging the animal into a canter.

"My dear!" Dunton cried. "You must remain by my side! Your aunt would have you obey me."

Bugger Aunt Kathleen.

Arabella giggled to herself. What would her aunt think if she cursed in her presence? Lately, the urge to break free and behave like a guttersnipe was too strong to resist. In fact, the urge had only beset her since...

No! Don't think of him. He hates you. He'd as soon see you dead in a ditch.

Or drowned in the river.

The path turned a corner, and Arabella's mount slipped on a loose stone. The animal dipped its head and stumbled toward the river. She clung to the reins and squeezed her legs against the pommel but could not stop the momentum.

With a cry, she toppled forward and tumbled through the air toward the riverbank. Then she landed with a jolt that sent a shudder through her bones and began slipping toward the water. She tried to gain purchase on the side of the bank, and cried out as a spike of pain tore through her wrist. Gritting her teeth, she dug her fingers into the bank while the river boiled and swirled mere inches from her feet.

"Help me!"

She looked up. At the top of the bank, the grass grew in clumps, beyond which the trees swayed in the wind, silhouetted against the sky. Of her horse there was no sign.

"Dunton! Where are you?"

She almost sobbed with relief as her fiancé's face appeared over the top of the bank.

She felt herself slipping once more and kicked out with her legs to steady herself, but to no avail.

"Dunton—help!" she screamed. "I can't swim!"

But he merely stared at her.

"Don't just stand there!" she cried. "*Do* something!"

The bank shifted beneath her, mud and stones loosening under her grip. She scrambled to maintain her hold, but continued to fall. Then the bite of cold assaulted her body as she slid into the water. She drew in a sharp breath, and the world disappeared as the water swallowed her completely. She kicked out against the assault and surfaced, gasping for air, before the water claimed her again. The current swirled around her legs, entangling them with her gown and binding them together to prevent her escape.

Fighting for her life, she kicked out and resurfaced, her lungs bursting with pain. She sucked in the blessed air, looking around, seeking something—anything—to cling to.

The river pulled her along, then widened out. Ahead, a low branch stretched across the surface. If she could reach it, she'd be safe. Then she would deal with Dunton and his cowardice. Reputation and propriety—and Aunt Kathleen—be damned. She would *never* marry him.

"You hear that, Dunton?" she screamed. "I'll never marry you!"

But there was no answer.

She raised her arms. The branch—and safety—was only a few feet away.

Then she saw it—a rock jutting out from the surface. Sharp and angular, like the blade of a flint knife, it filled her vision as the current pulled her toward it. She opened her mouth to scream but choked as water poured into her mouth. Then the water dashed her against the rock as if she were a rag doll. Pain exploded in the side of her head and plunged her into oblivion.

Chapter Ten

There was nothing so satisfying as an honest day's work with a fair wage at the end.

Lawrence drove the hoe into the ground, then stretched and surveyed his handiwork.

To the untrained eye, the vicarage garden merely looked a little neater. The weeds—particularly the ground elder, which had taken a stranglehold on the borders, its roots spreading beneath the surface to smother every other living thing—had finally surrendered to his tenacity and were now smoking on the bonfire.

Next year, the garden would be ablaze with color. The new plants in the borders would bloom throughout spring and summer—a myriad of colors in a carefully planned pattern, yet still retaining the appearance of wildness, as if Mother Nature, though unwilling to be fully tamed, had embraced a little order in her world.

The vicar's wife approached, carrying a pitcher and glass. With mild features, soft brown eyes, and a kind smile, she was the antithesis of the last woman who'd employed him.

"Mr. Baxter, I thought you'd like something to drink," she said, "seeing as you've been working so hard."

Lawrence eyed the pitcher. "Is that…?"

"Fresh lemonade," she said. "I thought you'd prefer it to tea, as it's such a hot day. Not like yesterday with that dreadful storm. Were you caught out in it?"

"I don't mind the rain, Mrs. Gleeson."

"No, I suppose a man of your trade is more resilient than most. Mr. Gleeson detests the rain, and he got caught in the downpour on his way to visiting Mrs. Richards. Do you know her?"

"The widow next door to the inn?"

"That's her. You'd have seen her at church on Sunday, but when you're new to a village such as ours, it must feel very overwhelming."

"Overwhelming?"

"Aye." She nodded. "Everyone knows *everyone* here in Brackens Hill—and Mrs. Richards knows more than most. She likes to keep appraised of local news."

Which was the polite way for saying that she was a gossip. But Mrs. Richards was harmless enough—a congenial woman of a certain age who loved company. She had already seen her best days, and, as she was widowed with no children, her prospects were never going to improve. But she maintained a cheerful disposition.

Unlike that haughty harpy.

Lawrence sighed. Why did his thoughts always turn to *her*? Doubtless she'd have forgotten about him and turned her attention to her trousseau—or whatever a spoiled heiress concerned herself with before her wedding.

"I hope you don't find Mrs. Richards too tiresome," Mrs. Gleeson said, returning him to the present. "She does rattle on—she forgets that we've heard her stories several times. I swear she's told me the tale of the chicken that escaped and made its way into her bathtub at least six times."

"No, I like her," Lawrence replied. "She told me about the chicken when I visited her. I even met the culprit, but I doubt her feathered friend will repeat the escapade now the coop's secure. There was a hole at the back."

"And you fixed it? There's kind! Ned Ryman said you were a goodhearted young man. And hardworking too, I can see."

She placed her hand on his arm. "Forgive me for being forward, but Ned told me you'd suffered misfortune and loss, though he wouldn't say what—and I wouldn't dream of asking. But we'll look out for you—you're one of us, now you're here."

"Thank you, Mrs. Gleeson," Lawrence said. "And I appreciate the work you're giving me."

"It's I who should appreciate *you*, Mr. Baxter. I could never keep that border so tidy, not with my rheumatics. It's too much for one person, and Mr. Gleeson's too busy tending to his flock. We might consider a kitchen garden round the back if you're wanting a bit more work?"

"I can't take charity, Mrs. Gleeson."

She rolled her eyes. "The pride of the male sex!" She let out a huff, then laughed good naturedly, and he smiled at the memory of Millie's exact words. "You'll be doing me a favor. I've always wanted a little kitchen garden, but I seem to have the knack for killing every plant I touch. My sister gave me a beautiful houseplant when she visited over Christmas, and it lasted less than a fortnight, even though I watered it every day."

"Then it would be my pleasure, Mrs. Gleeson, though I cannot accept payment."

"Yes, you can," she said. "If not for yourself, take it for your little ones." She cocked her head to one side and gave a wry smile. "Are they settling in here?"

Lawrence grimaced. Bobby had already been sent home twice from school for misbehavior. Her twin was no better—Mr. Colt had come knocking on his door two nights ago, dragging a red-faced Billy by the scruff of the neck, with a tale of how the boy had been caught drinking the dregs of the tankards in the bar. As for Jonathan, Lawrence's youngest poked his tongue at every adult he came into contact with.

"They're taking time to settle," Lawrence said. But instead of dipping her head and glowering at him over her glasses—like Mrs. Chantry from the school—the vicar's wife merely smiled, understanding in her eyes.

"Poor little things," she said. "Torn from their home—and their mother...?" She raised her eyebrows.

"She's not here," he said. "She didn't come with us to Brackens Hill."

The last thing he wanted was sympathy over being a widower—or a suggestion that he console himself by courting one of the girls in the village.

She sighed. "That's a shame, you poor man. Well—perhaps if you're finished, you'd prefer to take your lemonade inside? Mr. Gleeson should be home soon—he's visiting the vicar in the next parish. Mr. Coles, his name is—a very pleasant man, if a little young. He was curate before the previous vicar took a chill during the winter and passed, and he's finding the responsibility as vicar a little overwhelming. He's come to rely on Mr. Gleeson for guidance. Not that Mr. Gleeson minds, of course."

She rattled on, scarcely drawing breath. Mrs. Richards had a rival for the title of the most talkative woman in the village. But an invitation to share good-natured, if inane, chatter was balm to the soul, for it bore the marks of friendship and acceptance.

"Ah!" she cried. "Here he is now. My love—we're in the garden!"

The vicar approached, raising his hand in greeting. "Mr. Baxter, how goes the garden? I trust you're not too wearied from the work—or my wife's chatter."

"Simon!" Mrs. Gleeson scolded. The vicar drew her into an embrace.

"Forgive me, my love," he said. "You know how I like to tease."

Lawrence's heart tightened at the obvious affection between the couple, nurtured through years of a happy union. With Elizabeth, he'd never had the chance to nurture affection, much less love. He'd liked her, but marriage with the burden of responsibility was different to courtship. They'd had to scrape a living, their difficulties only increasing when the twins were born. Then she'd fallen pregnant again and been taken from him in childbirth, leaving him widowed, in debt, with three children to feed.

Now, to his shame, when he tried to picture his wife, he was unable to recall her.

Perhaps it was for the best they hadn't had the time to grow to love each other. Perhaps those pampered fools in Society had the right idea. Marry for practicality and comfort—not for love. For with love came heartbreak and despair.

And with trust came betrayal.

"What news from Drovers Heath?" Mrs. Gleeson asked.

"A mysterious young woman has been found," the vicar replied.

"What woman?"

"Nobody knows," the vicar said. "She was seen floating in the river. Were it not for the keen eyes of a lad from Drovers Farm, she might never have been found. You know what the river's like."

"Good grief!" Mrs. Gleeson's eyes widened, and she placed her hand over her breast. "You mean a *body's* been found? Lord have mercy!"

"Heavens no," the vicar said. "She's alive. The boy's been lauded a hero—he dived in and fished her out. But the young woman has lost her memory—she cannot even recall her name. Dr. Carter's taking care of her until it can be decided what to do with her."

"She's not a stray dog, Simon."

"Very well—until her family comes to claim her."

"Assuming she has a family, poor lamb."

"I'd spare your sympathy," the vicar said. "I've never seen such a foul-tempered creature! If she has family, they ought to be pitied."

"Simon!" Mrs. Gleeson cried. "How can you be so uncharitable?"

"You've not endured her company. She's been ordering Mrs.

Carter about as if she were a servant, and has found fault with everything, calling everyone who tries to help her a vile peasant. She struck Dr. Carter when he tried to examine her—so Mrs. Carter said."

"I'm sure that's not true. Charlotte Carter is prone to exaggeration."

"I saw it myself—a bruise below his eye and a deep scratch on his cheek, poor man. The woman has the voice of a lady, but the mouth of a harpy."

Vile peasant...

Where had Lawrence heard that before?

He rubbed the fading marks on his cheek from where *she* had scratched him.

Surely not...

It would be too much of a coincidence.

"A *harpy*, you say, reverend?" Lawrence asked.

The vicar nodded. "I must beg forgiveness in my prayers tonight for such uncharitable thoughts. The face of an angel, but the disposition of a demon. In fact..." He tilted his head to one side. "I say, Mr. Baxter—are you all right? You look as white as snow."

"I-I'm quite well," Lawrence said. "Might you describe the young woman?"

"You know her?" the vicar asked.

"Does she have dark hair?" Lawrence continued. "Almost black—thick black locks that curl at the ends. And blue eyes—the most intense blue eyes that reflect the color of a summer sky, but in anger glower with fire even as they darken?"

Mrs. Gleeson placed a hand on his arm. "You look quite ill, Mr. Baxter. Simon, my love, perhaps Mr. Baxter might like a glass of your brandy. Would you fetch it?"

"Yes, of course." The vicar nodded, then retreated toward the vicarage. As soon as he disappeared inside, Mrs. Gleeson spoke.

"Forgive me, it's not my place to ask," she said, "but this young woman—is she the reason why you look so uneasy? Is she..." Her voice trailed off and her eyes widened. "*Sweet heaven...*" Mrs. Gleeson lowered her voice. "Does she have any bearing on what you spoke of earlier? Perhaps you should go to Drovers Heath. Then, if you do recognize her—whoever she might be—you can reunite her with her family. Her husband—children..."

A blush spread across her cheeks.

"Oh dear—I hope you'll forgive my husband anything he said untoward about the woman if she's your...family. Having seen so much poverty and suffering in his work, he has little time for those he deems ungrateful. He can take you to Drovers Heath if you don't know the way—or young Ned could take you in his cart. And if she is your family, you'd want to be reunited, won't you?" She patted his arm.

Sweet Lord—they thought the woman was his *wife*?

My wife...

A wicked idea formed in his mind—the idea to restore the balance of justice.

What if this mysterious woman was *her*—the woman who plagued his waking thoughts and besieged his dreams? The woman who had insulted, humiliated, and ruined him?

Perhaps providence had presented him with a chance.

The chance to exact revenge on Lady Arabella Ponsford.

Chapter Eleven

Why were there so many people? And their incessant chatter—voices slicing through the air, bodies crowding her, menacing, filling the room.

A woman entered the chamber—the woman with the large nose with the wart on the end and thick lips who'd poked her awake yesterday. Or was it the day before? She carried a tray bearing a bowl from which steam arose.

An aroma filled the air—a not-unpleasant smell of…

Of what? As hard as she tried, the word wouldn't form in her mind.

"Come now, young lady," Mrs. Wart-Nose said in an overly sing-song voice. "Why don't we take a little broth? It's beef."

Beef—*that* was the word.

"We might feel better if we drink it this time, rather than let it go cold."

We?

Why did she say "we" in such a condescending tone, as if speaking to a witless child?

Perhaps I am witless.

Words that should come easy failed to materialize in her mind, leaving her dumbstruck and unable to ask their questions.

"Don't we like beef broth?" Mrs. Wart-Nose continued. "We can't afford to be overly choosy when our health is at stake."

Perhaps I don't like beef.

What did beef taste like?

She closed her eyes and reached out with her mind, scrabbling at the thin ribbon that led to the precious piece of her past. But, like a coin dropped into a well, it sank, giving a final flicker as it reflected the sunlight before disappearing into the darkness.

Mrs. Wart-Nose smiled, revealing yellowing teeth.

"Have we remembered our name yet?"

"Of course I remember. It's…"

Her name hung in the air—a soft blur. She willed it to snap into focus, but the harder she strained, the blurrier it became.

"Never mind, child." The woman patted her arm.

"Don't touch me, you hag!" She balled her hand into a fist.

"That's quite enough of *that*, young lady. I'll not tolerate such behavior."

The door opened, and a man stood in the doorway. The doctor—yes, that was it. And his name was…

It was on her lips, if only she could recall it.

He approached the bed, and she winced at the sight of him—the bruise below his eye and a line of scratches on his cheek.

"It's time for our medicine." He held up a phial.

Now *he* was patronizing her.

"It's *my* medicine, not *ours*," she said.

"Very well—it's time for *your* medicine."

"Don't speak to me like I'm a child!" she snarled. "Leave me alone—you shouldn't be in my chamber."

"I'm a doctor," he said. "Like it or not, you're my patient."

"And we'll speak to you in any manner we see fit," Mrs. Wart-Nose said, "seeing as we took you in, and little thanks we're getting for it. Look what you've done to my Gerald when he's been nothing but kind toward you!"

"Wh-what I've done?"

The man touched his cheek. "Charlotte, my dear—we must make

allowances. The young woman's been through an ordeal. I'm sure she meant no harm. We all strike out when we're frightened." He smiled and resumed his attention on her. "Have you remembered your name yet? Or where you're from?"

"Wh-where I'm from?"

"Can you describe your home, if you can't recall its name? There's a number of villages upriver."

"Why upriver?"

"You were found floating downriver, so it makes sense to make inquiries in the opposite direction. I think—" He broke off.

"My dear, are you all right?"

The river...

Icy fingers rippled over her flesh, curling around her body like chains, binding her arms, swirling and forming a maelstrom of angry, dark liquid. She tried to draw breath, but the chains bound her too tight. Then the fingers gripped her shoulders, and she let out a cry.

"Forgive me, my dear," the man said. "It must be very distressing."

"Is she having a seizure, Gerald?"

"No, Charlotte, I believe the poor child was reliving the moment she almost drowned."

She blinked, and a hot tear splashed onto her cheek. "D-drowned?"

"Don't you remember? We told you yesterday."

She closed her eyes, willing the memory to surface—a man approaching her, his thick body blocking the sunlight, hands reaching for her throat as she struck out in fear.

"No, I don't." She glanced about the room, with its dull white-washed walls and bare floorboards. "I need to go home. Why haven't you taken me home? I can't stay here—this place is horrible."

"Well, I've never heard anything so uncivil!" the woman cried. "After all we've done for you! If it were up to me, I'd turf you out to fend for yourself. It's plain to see why nobody's come to—"

"Charlotte, that's enough!" the man interrupted. "Go see to the children. Leave our guest to me."

Children—*ugh*. So that explained the cacophony earlier—the high-pitched shrieks and uncouth gaiety.

The woman scratched the wart on her nose. Then she set the tray beside the bed and exited the room.

The man placed the phial on the tray, then leaned forward. "May I?"

"May you what?"

He gestured toward her head. "I'd like to inspect your wound."

She reached for her forehead, but rather than skin, her fingertips met cloth.

"Careful," he said. "You had a nasty bump. The bones seem sound, but it'll be tender for a while." Then he hesitated. "You'll not strike me again? We want to help—you must try to trust us."

He placed his hands on her head, running light fingertips along her forehead, and she winced at the pulse of pain.

"Very good," he said. "I think we can remove the bandage tomorrow."

"And then?"

"We'll see about getting you up and outside. You want to be well when you leave."

"I doubt Mrs. Wart-Nose cares whether I'm well or not."

The doctor's smile slipped. "My wife may have been uncivil toward you, child, and for that, I apologize. But that's no reason to treat her with disrespect. Where would you go if we hadn't taken you in?"

"Home."

"And where's that?"

She paused, focusing on an image—a red-bricked building, an unkempt hedge, and a column of thick gray smoke spilling into the sky...

Then the image faded, consumed by the smoke. Another tear spilled onto her cheeks. But the sympathy she'd first seen in the doctor's gaze had now gone.

"Exactly," he said, with a sharp nod. "I'll not turn you out—yet. But the time will come when we must decide on your future—that is, if nobody comes to claim you."

To claim me...

She shuddered. Was she the property of another?

You will belong to me—utterly and completely...

A heavy voice, thick with lust and laden with threat, pushed into her senses, and her gut twisted with fear.

Where had she heard those words?

She glanced about, pain thickening behind her eyes. But the figure was a product of her imagination. The room was empty save her and the doctor.

"You're distressed," he said. "It's to be expected—you've suffered a severe concussion. But you'll soon recover. For now, you must rest. You can take some of my wife's broth later." He picked up the phial and shook a few drops onto a spoon. "Are we going to do as we're told?"

She tried to shake her head, then groaned as pain flooded her senses. He held the spoon to her lips, and she swallowed, wincing at the bitter taste. Then, with a firm but gentle hand, he pushed her back onto the pillows.

"Sleep now," he said. "The best remedy is rest."

She opened her mouth to reply, but the words never came. The world slipped sideways, and she slid, once more, into oblivion.

Chapter Twelve

"Remind me why we're doing this?" Lawrence glanced at his friend, who steered the cart toward the cluster of buildings that ran either side of the main street at Drovers Heath.

"You know why, Ned," he said. "If it's *her*, then Fate's given me a chance for justice."

"That's *vengeance*, not justice," his companion replied. "If it looks like horseshit, and smells like horseshit, then it's horseshit—no matter how many flowers you sprinkle over it."

"I can't see the harm," Lawrence said. "It's not as if I'll be holding her captive."

"Not in chains, perhaps, but if she's lost her memory, you'll be imprisoning her by deceit and filling her mind with false memories."

Ned steered the carthorse toward a small, neat building, a climbing rose framing the front door, where a coach-and-four waited.

"Whoa there!" Ned drew the cart to a halt. "This is Dr. Carter's house."

The carriage with a crest painted on the side, a driver, and two liveried footmen looked as out of place next to the tiny building as Mrs. Chantry would in a brothel.

Lawrence grinned to himself. Perhaps that prim schoolmistress needed a good, hard shag to loosen her character—then she wouldn't be so ready to look down her crooked nose at him and his children.

"The children…"

He recalled their faces that morning—Bobby's resolute look as she stuck out her lower lip and declared she didn't want a mother; Billy's intelligent eyes sparkling with the notion of the mischief he'd make. And Jonathan…

Lawrence's resolve almost faltered as he recalled the eager expression in the sensitive little boy's eyes.

"What did you tell your children?" Ned asked.

"That I may have found them a mother."

Ned sighed. "The loss of a mother is not something a child can easily recover from."

"Jonathan never knew Elizabeth," Lawrence said. "The twins don't remember her—heavens, I knew her so little that I struggle to recall her now."

"Not something to be proud of."

"Perhaps not," Lawrence said, "but I'm not one for sentiment."

"What if they grow attached to her?"

"Ha!" Lawrence let out a bark of laughter. "Once you've seen her, you'll understand how improbable *that* is."

"Then why do it?"

"Because she wronged me, Ned, and she must pay. Too often the likes of them can do what they want, and the likes of us suffer for it. It's about time one of them learned a lesson on what it's like."

"I only hope you know what you're doing."

"I'm gettin' myself a housekeeper and cook," Lawrence said, grinning, "and she's gettin' a taste of her own medicine."

"*If* it's her."

Lawrence eyed the carriage. Why did that crest look so familiar?

"Out of my way!" a voice cried—a very *familiar* voice.

The front door opened and a young man in a vicar's dress appeared in the doorway, before being thrust aside by a portly figure dressed in ostentatious finery.

The vicar stumbled against the door. "Your Grace, don't you want—"

"Don't presume to speak to me! It's not her. I've had a damned waste of a journey, and now you plague me with questions."

The man strode toward the carriage, turning to glance toward the cart.

Lawrence froze. But the Duke of Dunton showed no sign of recognition. Doubtless, to him, the lower classes all looked the same.

A footman leaped to the ground and opened the carriage door. Dunton climbed inside, the carriage tilting under his weight, before righting itself with a wobble. The footman resumed his position, and, with the crack of the driver's whip, the carriage lurched into motion and rolled away.

So—the woman wasn't Lady Arabella.

Perhaps it was for the best. But Lawrence couldn't suppress the shiver of loss, driven by the memory of kissing that wicked mouth of hers and holding that lush body in his hands.

"Ned, we should go."

His friend snorted. "Conscience got the better of you?"

"Ah—Mr. Baxter, I presume," the vicar said, approaching the cart.

"Y-yes." Lawrence nodded.

"Reverend Gleeson wrote to say you'd be coming."

"Yes, but…"

The vicar gestured toward the door. "Shall we?" When Lawrence made no move, the vicar frowned. "Aren't you anxious to be reunited with your wife?"

"What of the man who just left? Did he think she was his…wife?"

"His sister. He spun some tale about her eloping with the gardener, but he seemed hesitant, as if concealing something. Then he caught sight of her through the parlor door and realized it wasn't her." The vicar cocked his head to the side and frowned. "I could swear he recognized her. But he said not. He wouldn't even see her. It was as if he were desperate to leave as quickly as possible."

And well he might, given that Dunton would consider the house beneath his dignity to enter. Come to that, so would Lady Arabella.

Pity it wasn't her—there'd have been some small satisfaction in knowing that she had to suffer the discomfort of a house so far beneath her dignity.

Then his conscience pricked at him. His obsession—and there was no other word for it—was eliciting a mean-spirited side to his nature.

"Come in," the vicar said, "and you can see if she's your wife. It's a mercy she didn't drown in that river. Dr. Carter wasn't certain she'd regain consciousness at first."

"We should go," Ned said.

"What about your friend's wife?" the vicar asked.

Lawrence frowned at Ned. They had to at least make a pretense of looking at the woman, whoever she was. It was too late to turn back.

He climbed off the cart and followed the vicar inside.

Unlike his home at Brackens Hill, the house was clean and bright, filled with light rather than dust and cobwebs. Muffled voices came from behind a door, then it opened, and a woman burst into the hallway. With wisps of hair peeking beneath her cap and wearing a bone-white lace-trimmed apron over a pale blue gown, she looked every part the efficient doctor's wife. No doubt the state of the cottage was down to her touch—a loving wife who undertook her housekeeping duties with vigor and enthusiasm.

She let out a huff. "I swear, vicar, the Almighty has given me a test beyond the endurance of the stoutest of men. Do you know what that unpleasant harpy—"

She broke off as she caught sight of Lawrence.

"This is Mr. Baxter," the vicar said. "Come from Brackens Hill."

"Oh! Begging your pardon, Mr. Baxter." She glanced toward the door through which she'd just come, a flare of hope in her eyes. "Are you come to…"

"No, I'll not take any more of that disgusting medicine!" a sharp voice cried. "Get it away!"

Sweet heaven! There was no mistaking that voice.

The woman behind the door was Lady Arabella Ponsford.

"Mr. Baxter? Are you all right?"

The vicar's eyes shone with hope.

No—not hope. Relief.

"You *know* her," the vicar said.

It wasn't a question.

A fork in the road stretched before Lawrence. Withdraw and leave her to her fate, or…

Or what? Leave her in the care of people eager to be rid of her? When their patience ran out, where would she go? Dunton had abandoned her to the mercy of the Carters—mercy that was, by the expression on Mrs. Carter's face, rapidly diminishing. With no means to support herself she'd end up begging on the streets—or in service, if some wealthy family took pity on her.

And a life beholden to the charity of others was not to be borne.

By executing his plan, he was not only meting out justice for the wrongs she'd done him. He was giving her a better life than the alternatives.

"Yes," he said, nodding. "That's my—my Bella." Then he grinned. "Speaks her mind, doesn't she?"

"A little too much, if you ask me," Mrs. Carter said.

"Mrs. Carter, you shouldn't speak ill of the young woman," the vicar said. "It's not your place to criticize her behavior—it's her husband's. Isn't that right, Mr. Baxter?"

Lawrence nodded. "I apologize for any trouble she's caused."

Mrs. Carter smiled. "You're a fine young man. She's a lucky lass to have you. Would you like to be reunited with her?"

"No—I won't, I say," Lady Arabella yelled from the room, "you *vile peasant!*"

Lawrence suppressed a snort. "Forgive me—she has a wicked tongue sometimes. Rest assured, I'll teach her the error of her ways."

"I'm glad of it," Mrs. Carter said, and she opened the parlor door.

"Why have you come back?" an angry voice demanded.

"I've good news, my dear," Mrs. Carter said. "Your husband has come to take you away."

This was met with a sharp intake of breath, followed by silence.

Lawrence entered the parlor.

There she was—Lady Arabella Ponsford—reclined on a sofa. She looked up, and bright sapphire eyes met Lawrence's gaze without a flicker of recognition. Undeterred, he opened his arms and passed the point of no return.

"Thank heaven!" he cried. "I've found you—my Bella!"

Chapter Thirteen

My Bella...

A huge man stood in the doorway.

Not huge—he was a *giant*.

He towered over the vicar, his shoulders spanning the doorframe. She cast her gaze over his form—the chest over which a rough-spun shirt strained to fit, the thigh muscles discernible beneath his breeches, and thick boots that were scuffed and soiled.

With a mane of unkempt, dark blond hair, and a nose that bore a kink as if it had been broken, he looked like a Viking fresh from a bloody battle.

And he'd come for *her*.

Excitement—tinged by fear—curled in her belly, and she drew in a sharp breath as he entered the room.

He extended a hand—large enough to wield axes and snap necks—then uncurled it to reveal a calloused palm.

So uncouth, so rough...

More *beast* than man.

She met his gaze, and eyes the color of sharp steel regarded her with a hungry expression, as if he longed to devour her.

What might it be like—to be *devoured*?

He stepped toward her.

"Get away!" she cried. "I don't know you!"

"He knows you, miss," the doctor replied. "He knows your name."

She shook her head. "I-I've never seen this…"

She longed to say "peasant," but something in the giant's eyes sent a twist of fear through her. A Viking warrior would not take insults likely, unlike the weak-bellied doctor and his overly starched wife.

The Beast's forehead crinkled into a frown. "Don't you remember me, Bella? I'm your husband."

"H-husband?" Her voice came out in a squeak. He took another step, and she let out a scream. "Don't touch me!"

"That's enough, love…" the Beast began.

"Do *not* address me with such familiarity—I don't know you!"

"But he knows *you*," the doctor's wife said.

"You're only saying that because you want rid of me."

"Well, seeing as you say as much, I—" the doctor's wife began, but her husband raised his hand.

"That's enough, Charlotte."

"The young woman has a point," the vicar said. "If she cannot remember this man, then he must prove his claim on her."

Her gut twisted with fear. "What do you mean, his *claim*? Am I to be handed over like chattel?"

"If you're his wife, he has that right, given your vow of obedience," the vicar said.

"Obedience?" The word left her lips in a squeak.

The giant watched the exchange, his gaze flicking between the occupants of the room, a curl of amusement on his lips. Then he resumed his attention on her.

"I'm your Lawrence," he said.

"Lawrence!" she scoffed. "What kind of a name is that?"

"That name's fallen from your lips on many occasions," he said. "I've missed hearin' you say it—in a soft whisper, in anger when you're unable to control your temper, or"—he licked his lips, his eyes darkening—"screamed at night, when unable to control your—"

"Ahem!" the vicar said. "There's ladies present, Mr. Baxter."

Ignoring the thread of heat in her blood, she shrank further back.

"Your name is Baxter?" she asked.

"And you're my Bella," he said. "Bella Baxter. It's time to stop this nonsense, now." He grinned, and a sparkle of mischief glimmered in his eyes. "Or perhaps you're teasin' me in anticipation of punishment?"

"P-punishment?"

His grin broadened. "Oh, Bella, would you embarrass these good folk?"

"Nevertheless," the vicar intervened, "we cannot, in all conscience, hand this young woman over until we're certain. I must insist."

Relief flooded through her. "Thank you, vicar," she said. Then she lifted her chin and met the Beast's gaze.

But rather than defeat, she saw determination.

Ye gods—what if she *were* his property?

The determination in his eyes turned to triumph. "I can prove she's my wife."

Her stomach clenched in apprehension.

He leaned toward the vicar, and though he spoke in a whisper, she caught his words.

"She has a series of scars on her right leg—from just above the knee, all the way up to her"—he hesitated and licked his lips—"the top of her thighs, near her"—he lowered his voice—"her *intimate area*."

"Well, I never!" the doctor's wife cried, her cheeks reddening.

But the doctor remained silent, turning to her with an expression in his eyes that could only be described as relief.

"Gerald, what is it?" the doctor's wife asked.

Scars on my leg?

Four pairs of eyes stared at her skirts.

Very well. If the Beast wished to indulge in some ridiculous charade, then she'd expose his lies.

"Would you like some privacy, miss?" the doctor asked.

"No. I intend to put a stop to this nonsense with you all as witness.

Then you can turn this person away."

Summoning her dignity, she rose from the chaise longue, then approached a screen at the far corner of the parlor. Concealed behind it, she lifted her skirts. The skin of her lower legs was pale and smooth, with no sign of a blemish other than a yellowing bruise on her shin.

Then she saw it—the puckered skin just above her right knee. She raised her skirts further to reveal a scar that covered her leg from the knee to the top of her thighs. She ran her fingertips over the marks, where the flesh was smooth and hard in places and roughened in others, a myriad of shades, from dark red—almost purple—to light pink, to white.

What in the name of heaven had happened to cause such an injury?

She closed her eyes, willing the memory to surface. Surely the sight of the marks of her history should elicit something! But other than the faint crackling sound, and the acrid smell of smoke in her nostrils, no memories came to the fore. Not even the memory of pain—she poked the scar, but there was nothing other than the faint sensation of touch.

Then she lowered her skirts, her hands trembling.

The Beast had spoken the truth. Which meant…

Sweet Lord! It meant that she belonged to him.

She stepped out from behind the screen.

The vicar nodded, satisfaction in his eyes. Beside him, the doctor and his wife grinned with joy.

As for the Beast…

He opened his arms and approached her in the manner of a powerful animal seizing its prey.

"Come to your husband."

Chapter Fourteen

"This cart stinks!"

Lawrence glanced over his shoulder and suppressed a laugh.

Lady Arabella—no, from now on she was *Bella*—sat among the straw in the back of the cart, her mouth creased into a grimace of discontent.

Sweet heaven, she was a beautiful creature! He'd not believed it possible for her to be even more alluring than when she'd been dressed in all her finery in Dunton's garden. But in that ill-fitting gown—courtesy of Mrs. Carter's charity—her hair a mess of jet-black curls, sky-blue eyes glittering with fury, she was exquisite.

And the spirit with which she'd resisted him as he led her out of the cottage and onto the cart had warmed his blood and stirred his cock. How he'd enjoy taming her!

"It's never bothered you before, Bella, love," he said. "You've endured far worse, and will do so again."

"Why should I?" she demanded—the question that had fallen from her lips several times already.

"Because you're my wife and vowed to obey me," he said—the reply he'd given each time.

"It's so bumpy," she continued. "I'm bruised all over."

"Then sit in the straw, love, like I told you. It'll cushion your arse, and you'll have an easier ride. We'll save the hard ride for later."

She flushed with indignation and stuck her chin in the air. Such an act might look appropriate on a lady—but with her dressed in a tattered gown, covered in straw, it was nothing short of comical.

The cart hit a rut. She squealed and lost her balance, and Lawrence couldn't suppress a snort of laughter. Giving him a glare, she righted herself, pushed her hair from her face, then sat back in the straw, curling her hands around the edge of the cart to steady herself.

"That's my good girl."

She wrinkled her nose but said no more. At length, he resumed his attention on the road.

Ned continued to steer the cart, the horse responding to his hands on the reins as if they were of one mind. The road veered toward the river, and the rush of the water mingled with the wind in the trees. Lawrence glanced to the back of the cart. Bella sat, her back against the edge, eyes closed, moving gently from side to side with the motion of the cart. She seemed to have fallen asleep—or the laudanum Dr. Carter gave her had finally taken effect.

At least they'd have some respite from her tongue. Battle would resume when they reached Brackens Hill.

"You didn't have to place her in the back," Ned said.

"Neither did you have to hit that rut."

"I didn't do it on purpose."

Lawrence laughed. "You're too good a driver for that."

"I don't know why you're griping. It got her to settle, didn't it? She'd have fallen off otherwise."

They continued in silence. Each time the road veered toward the river, Lawrence shuddered at the notion of what she must have endured. He might loathe her, but nobody—not least a woman—deserved to be torn to pieces in the river. Neither did they deserve to be abandoned by those who were supposed to love her.

Dunton didn't love her—unsurprising, given their sort never married for love. They entered into contracts, marrying for money or rank. Then they foisted their children onto nursemaids and nannies, governesses and schoolmasters, only viewing them occasionally to inspect them for cleanliness and decorum.

Cleanliness and decorum—something his children knew nothing of.

What would she make of them? And what would they make of her?

His conscience pricked him again at the thought of his children—three motherless pups. What made him better than Lady Arabella and her sort? His children had been deprived of a parent's love as much as any nob's child. He'd foisted them onto neighbors and paid subordinates at every opportunity, trying to convince himself it was for their benefit so he could work to keep food in their bellies and a roof over their heads.

He'd have failed in that had Ned not found him a home at Brackens Hill. And now, he was repaying his friend by involving him in his scheme.

"I won't keep her forever, Ned."

"You shouldn't keep her at all. If not for her sake, think of your little 'uns."

"I *am* thinking of them," Lawrence said. "If they're unhappy, then I'll stop. If I promise that, will you promise not to betray me?"

Ned resumed his attention on the road. After a moment, he sighed and nodded.

"I'll not betray you—you're too determined to have her reap the consequences of her actions. Just mind you're prepared to reap the consequences of yours."

"I'll face my retribution when it comes, Ned," Lawrence said. "And, no matter what, I'll always put my children first."

"Then we'll say no more on the matter." Ned grinned, revealing a row of teeth with a gap in the middle. "If Lady Arabella—"

"Bella," Lawrence said. "Bella…Baxter."

Ned nodded. "If *Bella* is to pay for what she did to you, I can think of no better punishment than to take those three tykes of yours into her care. My Sophie told me yesterday that Mrs. Chantry's been complaining about them again. The twins started a fight with sticks in the middle of class, and your Jonathan tipped a bottle of ink on the floor."

Which explained why they'd been unable to sit still at supper last night—that miserable old sow Mrs. Chantry seemed to measure her success as a teacher not by how much her charges learned, but by how often she disciplined them. Still, a reddened arse harmed no one. He'd received plenty himself as a lad.

But woe betide Bella if she took it upon herself to discipline his children. If that haughty minx laid so much as a finger on them, he'd teach her a little marital discipline in return, false wife or not.

Oh yes—she'd earn back what she'd cost him. Not with coin, but through a bloody good dose of hard work.

Chapter Fifteen

The warm aroma of straw thickened in the air—the scent of the countryside. She inhaled, and the acrid note of manure caught in her throat.

Something nudged her shoulder. The memory floated before her—a long brown face with a white mark across the forehead and big, thickly lashed eyes. Her horse, perhaps.

Do I have a horse?

The creature nudged her again.

"What are you doing?" she murmured.

"Come on!" a voice said. "This isn't the time to be lazin' about."

She opened her eyes, lifting her hands to shield them against the sun, and sat up.

She was in the back of a cart, in a pile of straw.

Where am I?

Who am I?

Another poke—in her back this time.

Cursed animal! She whirled around.

"Will you stop…" Her voice trailed away as her gaze fell on a man.

Not a man—a beast. A giant with dirty blond locks framing his face, forming a halo as they caught the sunlight. Another man stood next to him—smaller in stature, but equally rough in appearance.

Then she remembered.

The giant was the man from the doctor's cottage. He'd called her *Bella*.

And—Lord save her—he was her husband. He'd proved it when he mentioned...

Her cheeks warmed as she recalled what he'd said about the scars on her leg near her *intimate area*.

The Beast grinned, revealing dimples in his cheeks, then offered his hand.

"Come on—let me help you down."

Bella stared at the hand, then back at the man. His smile slipped and he cocked his head to the side.

"Must I remind you of your vow of obedience?"

"Lawrence, I hardly think—" the other man began.

"Stow it, Ned! She's got to learn. A disobedient wife's no use to a man."

Though she heard laughter in the Beast's tone, his eyes narrowed. Swallowing the ripple of apprehension, tinged with an unfathomable smattering of excitement, she took his hand. Her skin tightened as he closed his fingers around hers, the rough callouses of his palm abrading her skin. Then he pulled her toward him, and she stumbled out of the cart. He squeezed her hand, and she caught her breath at the fizz of need.

"Best tidy yourself up, love," he said. "You got into a right state in the back of that cart. We're living in a respectable village now."

She glanced about. The cart had stopped at a fork in the road. One direction was wide enough to fit a cart, but overgrown. The other led to a smattering of dwellings—small, unremarkable houses forming rows either side of the track. Beyond, a spire rose, pointing toward the sky, surrounded by trees. A shot sounded in the distance, and a cloud of birds rose from the trees, squawking and scolding at the world, before circling then settling back into the trees.

Halfway along the road—if a filthy track with a gully running through the middle could be called a road—a sign jutted out from one of the buildings, swinging in the breeze, depicting a thick-stemmed tree topped by a crown. Raucous laughter filled the air and two men stumbled out of the building. One spat on the ground, then they thrust their hands in their pockets and ambled along the road.

At the far end of the road, a couple on horseback rode toward them. The men stopped to remove their caps and bowed, but the riders passed without acknowledgment.

How uncivil!

The Beast tugged at her sleeve.

"Tidy yourself up, love!" he whispered. "That's the squire and his missus—Sir Halford and Lady Merrick."

She lowered her gaze to her dress—Mrs. Carter's ill-fitting gown, given with little grace and accepted with even less.

"I can't help it if this…*rag* isn't suitable," she said, aware of the petulance in her tone.

"Heaven help me, lass, that bump to your head's made you soft." He reached toward her, and she flinched, but he caught her sleeve and pulled her close. "You're a right mess with all that straw. Let me."

He brushed her gown with his hands, wiping off strands of straw.

"There's naught I can do about the horseshit, but their sort don't expect the likes of us to smell as sweet as them. But if they catch you looking like that, they'll think we've been rutting in a stable."

She caught her breath. "R-rutting in a *s-stable?*"

He grinned. "Later, lass. You're insatiable for me as always." He held her at arm's length and grinned. "There!" he said. "You almost look presentable."

Almost? Insufferable savage!

The elegantly dressed couple approached them—the squire in a close-fitting dark-blue jacket and cream breeches, and his wife in a deep-purple riding habit complete with a hat set at a jaunty angle and a feather on the brim.

Compared to them, she was a peasant.

Is that what I am—a grubby peasant?

The Beast and the other man—Ned, was it?—bowed their heads.

"Good day to you, Sir Halford," the Beast said. "And Lady Merrick."

The man reined his mount to a halt. His wife followed suit, tilting her nose in the air as if she'd encountered a bad smell.

"Baxter, isn't it?" Sir Halford said.

"That's right, sir."

"And you're a friend of Mr. Ryman here."

"Aye, that's right—Ned's been a good friend, findin' me a place here, thank you, sir."

"Good—very good. You're renting Ivy Cottage, are you not?"

"Yes, sir." The Beast bowed his head again. Then he gave her a nudge.

Why did he insist on poking her at every opportunity?

"What is it?" she snapped.

"It's Sir Halford and Lady Merrick," he said through gritted teeth. "Forgive my wife's disrespect, Sir Halford—she's taken a nasty bump to the head."

Lady Merrick turned her attention to Bella, lowering her gaze to her feet, then following a line along her body—the dress covered with pieces of straw and the tangled mass of curls. Then she wrinkled her nose and looked away.

"Pretty little thing," Sir Halford said. "And she hurt her head?"

"Aye, sir," the Beast said. "She's been known to wander off—but she always comes home."

"A woman should remain at her husband's side, Mr. Baxter."

"She's generally obedient, sir."

"I'm glad to hear it," Sir Halford said. "A husband should never be too free with his indulgences. A little marital discipline can work wonders in establishing a happy home."

"I'll remember that, sir, thank you."

Who were these men to speak as if she were not among them?

Couldn't she—or any woman—be permitted to speak for herself?

Another nudge, and the Beast leaned toward her and lowered his voice. "Wife, you're disrespecting Sir Halford, and embarrassing me. Where are your manners?"

Did he expect her to *curtsey*?

The firmness with which he clenched his jaw spoke of grim determination. A ripple of fear—accented with a wicked hint of anticipation—threaded through her at the notion of *a little marital discipline*. How might he respond if she tested his patience?

But now was not the time.

"*Wife.*" The Beast's voice came out in a low growl.

"Lawrence…" his friend said.

"No, Ned. She must learn."

Bella gritted her teeth. There was no reason why she should curtsey to these people. In any case—how did one curtsey?

A memory flashed before her—a young woman in a dark gown covered with a crisp white apron, bobbing before her, down and up like a cork in a pond.

She bent her knees. The hem of her gown dipped into the mud at her feet, and she glanced up in shame. What they must think of her!

Her feet caught her hem, and she stumbled forward. Tears stung her eyes at the furtherance of her humiliation. Could life get any worse?

Then a strong pair of arms caught her.

"There, love! I've got you."

She glanced up and met his gaze. Clear gray eyes stared back at her, a glimmer of desire in their expression. Then the desire was replaced by guilt. He righted her and resumed his attention on Sir Halford.

"Rest assured I'll take good care of her."

Was he trying to convince Sir Halford—or himself?

The squire nodded, then squeezed his horse's flanks and continued on his way, his wife in his wake.

"Well, Ned, it's time I took Bella home," the Beast said.

"Aren't you wanting me to drive you in the cart?"

"We can walk."

"Suit yourself," Ned replied, his voice wavering with what sounded like anger. "Mind you do the right thing." He climbed onto the cart and drove it toward the inn.

"Come on, Bella, love." The Beast offered his elbow. "Best we get you home. It looks like rain, and you'll not be able to do your chores if you catch cold."

Before she knew it, she'd slipped her arm through his, as if it had always belonged there, and they set off along the track.

"Chores?" she asked.

"Surely you remember your chores?"

"I don't even remember *you*."

"I'm your husband."

"No—I mean—what do I call you? What's your name?"

"Can't you recall it? It's Lawrence Baxter. But you usually address me as husband."

"Usually?"

He grinned once more and flicked his tongue out to lick his lips. "Sometimes, when we're alone, you call me sir—or *master*."

She suppressed a shudder.

"You're a *beast*."

He laughed, and she fought the urge to slap the crudeness from him. "Beast I may be, love, but I'm your husband, and there's been enough nonsense for one day. If you catch a chill, I've not the time to tend to you and the children, so it's best if you do as I bid."

What did he say?

"Ch-children?"

"Aye, that's right. Perhaps you'll remember your children, if not your husband."

"I have *children?*"

"Yes, love."

"H-how many?"

"Why don't we keep the questions until we get you home?"

"So, a wife's supposed to be silent while the men around her discuss her and her fate? How beastly!"

Rather than the flare of anger she'd expected, he merely chuckled.

"You'll see, Bella my love," he said. "You'll see."

Chapter Sixteen

*S*WEET HEAVEN—THIS WAS a nightmare.

Before her stood—if *standing* were an appropriate term for something that looked as if it might blow over at any moment—what could only be described as a hovel.

A squalid little place with windows caked in dirt, rotting timber, a chimney that leaned sideways, and a gate falling off the hinges.

And she was expected to live in *that*?

She glanced about, summoning a grain of hope that the building before her was a stable, or a gatehouse, and that the main dwelling was further along the track.

But there were no other buildings.

The only saving grace was the garden surrounding the building—a neatly trimmed lawn, borders filled with shrubs surrounded with fresh earth, as if they had just been planted…

She caught her breath at the flash of a memory—or perhaps a dream—of a man, stripped to the waist, sweat glistening on his bronzed body while he drove a shovel into the earth.

"Bella?"

A huge hand caught hers. Instinct drove her to curl her fingers around his and her fingertips over the callouses on his palm—the evidence of hard toil. A primal urge flared before she bit her lip to suppress it.

Whatever or whoever she might be, she was *not* a wanton.

He gestured toward the building. "What do you think? I've made a lot of improvements."

"You mean—it was once *worse* than this?"

"Don't say that, love. It's better than our last home. Don't you remember?"

She shook her head. Perhaps there was a reason why her memory was yet to return. Her life was so dreadful that her mind, in an act of kindness, had obliterated it.

But now it was before her, in all its horror.

"Come on, love," he said.

"Sweet Lord!" she cried. "Can't you say anything other than *come on, love*? Is your command of the English language so restricted?"

He chuckled and steered her toward the door. "Come on, love—your palace awaits."

Curse him! He was goading her.

But she wouldn't rise to it. Summoning as much dignity—and courage—as she could muster, she entered the cottage.

A narrow hallway awaited her, with a door either side and a tiny staircase at the end. The Beast led her through the first door, into a parlor—or something resembling a parlor. It was a small, low-ceilinged room filled with mismatched furniture—a sofa that looked on the brink of collapse, a leather chair with scuff marks on the arms, and a threadbare rug. A sliver of light struggled across the room, picking up a host of dust motes that swirled angrily as she moved about. The walls, covered in stains, were bare, save for a set of candle sconces, and cobwebs clung thickly to the corners of the ceiling, spreading out in tendrils to conquer the upper part of the walls.

"Sweet Lord!" she cried.

"I know," he said. "It's luxury compared to our last home. But nothing's too much for my Bella."

Was he jesting?

"Is this *it*?" she asked, wrinkling her nose at the odors—the cocktail of damp, dust, and something that indicated the existence of a dead rodent beneath the floorboards.

"No, that's not it, of course!" He laughed. "There's two bedrooms upstairs, together with my study. "And"—he puffed out his chest with pride, reminiscent of a strutting bird showing a prospective mate a particularly delightful nest—"we've a privy at the bottom of the garden so you can see to your needs in the fresh air."

See to your needs.

"Must you be so coarse?"

"Better that than refer to your takin' a piss."

She shuddered, but he merely laughed, then led her out of the parlor.

"The kitchen needs a little work," he said.

After showing her that cesspit of a parlor, if the *kitchen* was the room he'd singled out as needing a little work, what state must it be in?

"But," he added, "with your resourcefulness, you'll easily manage your chores in there."

Chores.

There it was again, that dreadful word, and all the implications that came with it.

"What do you mean..." she began, but a volley of shrieks interrupted her.

Footsteps clattered on the stairs, and the building seemed to vibrate. Then two pairs of feet appeared at the top of the staircase, followed by the bodies of two...

Two what?

Feral creatures—wild beasts in rough-spun smocks, dark breeches, and thick boots—descended the stairs. One of the creatures lost its footing and slid the rest of the way, landing in a heap at the bottom.

"Bugger!"

"Ha ha!" the other cried in a singsong voice. "Bobby's landed on her arse!"

"Piss off, Billy!"

"Piss off yourself. Or I'll stick a spider in your breeches."

Dear God Almighty—what fresh horror is this?

"It's our children, Bella, love," the Beast said.

Heavens—she'd spoken aloud.

Surely these urchins couldn't be *her* children? Wouldn't she have remembered having to endure a life with such unpleasant, filthy creatures?

"Stop it!" the Beast roared.

The creatures stopped arguing. Two pairs of bright blue eyes stared at Bella. Then both children tilted their heads almost in unison as they cast their gazes over her. They looked identical with their tangled masses of dirty blond hair and faces caked in dirt, the only difference being that the one who'd slipped onto the floor had slightly longer hair.

"William, Roberta, stop playing the fool," the Beast said. "Look who's back?"

Roberta? Surely one of those urchins wasn't a *girl*?

"Hello, Mama," they chorused.

"Very good," the Beast said, turning to Bella. "You remember the twins, don't you?"

She shook her head.

"Oh, love!" he cried. "That's so disappointing. I'd have thought our children would have restored your memory, given how much you'd longed for them—not to mention how vigorously our efforts were to start a family."

"Don't be so crude!" she said.

"It's never bothered you before," he replied. "You've always had a ripe tongue, Bella, love. You curse enough to make a sailor blush."

"I do *not*!"

"You'll remember soon enough," he said in the good-natured tone that was beginning to needle at her.

Did nothing discompose him?

"Two children..." She shook her head. "I can't have two children. This must be a horrible dream..."

"Now, Bella, you must stop this nonsense. We don't have two children."

The urchins stood, nudging one another as they jostled for position.

"Then—they're not my children?"

"You misunderstand me, love. It's—"

He broke off as a high-pitched wail came from upstairs.

"What's *that*?" Bella cried.

"Not again!" he huffed. "William, go upstairs and set him free."

"But we're pirates, and he's our prisoner."

"Just *do* it."

One of the urchins stuck out its tongue—bright pink against the grime on its face.

"Do it *now*," the Beast growled.

A crash echoed from above, followed by screeching, then a small, red-headed whirlwind descended the stairs with a wail.

"Papa—Papa! Billy tied me up, and Bobby put a frog in my bed!"

"Jonathan, don't tell tales, you nasty sneak. Not in front of our"— Bobby glanced at Bella—"our *mother*."

"Mama!" The whirlwind let out a cry, then flew toward Bella. Before she could prevent it, the creature flung its arms around her legs. "Mama, you're back! What's for supper?"

The Beast caught the child by the shoulders. "Let your mother catch her breath."

"But you said we should—"

"Yes, and you've given her a lovely greeting, son. But she's a little tired. She can't cook supper tonight." He glanced at Bella and raised his eyebrows. "Unless she wants to?"

"I do *not* want to," Bella said.

Who the devil did they think she was—some sort of housemaid and cook?

The Beast sighed. "Never mind—we'll make do. I can fetch something from the Oak for tonight."

"The Oak?"

"The Royal Oak—the inn in the village. Perhaps a bit of mutton stew? You can resume your chores tomorrow."

"Chores again!" Bella scoffed. "What do you mean, I can resume them tomorrow? I've never heard anything so ridiculous!"

"I've no objection to your resuming your chores tonight, love, but I thought you'd be tired from your journey."

"I *am* tired!"

"Then you can start tomorrow," he said, "once you've walked the children to school."

"Once I've *what?*"

He let out another laugh. "It's an easy enough task, and, tell you what, I won't ask you to make breakfast tomorrow—how about that?"

"You'll prepare breakfast?" she asked.

"Heavens no!" He laughed again. "What self-respecting husband would prepare breakfast? We'll make do tomorrow without it. But the day after tomorrow, we'll be hungry, won't we, children?"

"Yes!" two voices cried in unison, but the red-headed creature let out another wail that sliced through the air. Bella winced at the pain in her head. So much noise!

"I'm hungry!" the red-headed creature cried.

"Don't be such a baby," one of the other children sneered.

"Stop it, Roberta," the Beast said. "Don't tease your brother. He's missed your mother, haven't you, Jonathan?"

The creature nodded once more and reached for Bella again. She recoiled at the sight of his dirt-covered hands and the notion of where they might have been.

She glanced about the hallway, at the walls that closed in around her, and her chest constricted as she struggled to draw breath. The hallway shifted out of focus, and her legs began to give way. But before she pitched forward, two strong arms took hold of her. For a moment, a ripple of need threaded through her body.

But she ignored it.

"Let me go, you vile peasant!"

"As my wife commands," he said, his voice thick with amusement, and he released her. She slid to the ground, landing legs akimbo. As she hit the floor, a puff of dust erupted from the carpet, and she convulsed into a volley of coughs.

However dreadful a nightmare might be, it came with one consolation—freedom through the inevitability of waking up.

But this...

This was reality, from which there was no escape.

Chapter Seventeen

The look on Lady Arabella's face was almost reward enough to atone for her sins.

Almost.

A wicked little voice in Lawrence's mind had whispered of the pleasure from seeing Miss High-and-Mighty curtsey before a country squire. But that pleasure had been surpassed, first by the disgust in her eyes when she caught sight of Ivy Cottage, then by the unbridled horror as she set eyes on the children.

Then the guilt that had lingered in the back of his mind came to the fore when that horror turned into distress. During their prior altercations, her emotions had been limited to anger and pride. But now, lying in a heap on the floor of a house she'd not deem fit to stable a horse in, let alone be mistress of, her pride surrendered to misery.

The children stared first at her, then at him. They'd played their parts with aplomb—perhaps too well. But children could not be blamed for the consequences of their actions, not when they'd done what he asked—treat the stranger he brought home as their mother.

He extended his hand to her, but she slapped it away and scrambled to her feet.

"I can help myself," she snarled.

"Excellent," he replied. "Then you're best starting in here."

He led her into the kitchen, suppressing a laugh as she let out another cry of disgust.

"Here is your realm," he said. "You'll have it tidied up in no time. I'll bring something tomorrow for you to cook—how about a bit of scrag end?"

The panic returned to her eyes. "I *cook*?"

"That's what I've been saying, Bella."

"What do I cook with?"

He gestured toward the iron range beside the window. "With that."

She approached the range almost tentatively, as if approaching a nest of vipers. "I don't know what that is."

"It's a little dirty, I'll admit," he said, "but that's how we got this place so, cheap seein' as it's not been taken care of. You'll have it shining in no time once you've cleaned it up."

"I-I clean as well?" She teetered on her feet, and he caught her arm.

"Steady, love, we'll have none of that. You'll not be able to do your chores if you can't stand upright."

She wrinkled her nose again at the mention of chores—oh, how he loved that word!

"You needn't look worried," he said. "We'll help, won't we, children?"

"Yes, Papa," the children chorused.

"I'm not one of those husbands who expects his wife to do everything. You'll not be expected to clean the children's room—they're old enough to look after that themselves." He nodded. "See how generous I can be?"

He fought the urge to laugh at the expression on her face.

"Let's show you upstairs—with luck, that'll help you remember."

"*That's* an element of luck I can do without," she said.

"Oh, how you amuse!" He chuckled. "What do you think, children? Isn't Mama amusing?"

"May we go outside, now?" William asked. "We want to play in our den."

"Run along, then."

With a clatter of footsteps, the children ran through the kitchen to the back, jostling against each other before slamming the door behind them. Excited voices and laughter faded into the distance.

Lawrence offered his arm and led Bella up the staircase, pausing at the turn of the stairs to show her his study—a tiny parlor into which he'd crammed a desk and chair—before they reached the landing at the top with two doors leading to the bedchambers.

He pushed open the first door. A table lay on the floor in pieces, together with strands of rope. William and Roberta had been playing at pirates since Christmas, when he'd fashioned them swords out of a spare piece of wood as gifts, with Roberta declaring herself as the captain. William staged the occasional rebellion, culminating in swordfights at which she usually beat him. But the two of them often took it upon themselves to declare Jonathan as a Spanish princess, take him captive, and tie him to a chair, and he'd broken free, smashing a table in the process.

Lawrence ought to admonish them, but he'd never had a brother or a sister—and he couldn't begrudge them the simple pleasures of playing make-believe with a sibling.

The woman beside him let out a snort of disgust as she cast her gaze about, seeing not the fruits of imaginative play, but the evidence of socially unacceptable behavior.

"What a mess!" she cried. "Surely I'm not expected to sleep here."

"No, it's the children's room," he said. "There's two beds, see? William and Jonathan share the larger bed by the window. Roberta's is in the corner."

Her pretty little nose wrinkled with disgust, and Lawrence tempered his indignation. What right had she to turn her nose up at him and his family?

Her eyes narrowed as she approached Roberta's bed. "There's something moving beneath the blanket."

"Don't touch it."

Ignoring him, she reached for the blanket, pulled it back, then let out a scream.

"What devilry is this?" she cried.

A small frog hopped across the bed.

Lawrence let out a laugh and picked the creature up.

"How could you?" she cried. "What a disgusting thing to do."

"What, take a defenseless creature to safety? He's more afraid of you than you are of him—unless you're a coward."

"I'm no such thing!" she retorted. "Just get rid of it, will you?"

He pushed open the window and placed the creature on the sill. With a croak, it leaped from his hand and disappeared outside.

Lawrence fought back a ripple of guilt at the stricken expression in her eyes.

"Come on, love," he said brightly. "There's one room left—our bedchamber."

She drew in a sharp breath, but complied as he steered her toward his chamber.

For a brief moment, he felt a sense of apprehension—as if he were a bird that had worked tirelessly for days fetching twigs and weaving them together to form a nest to present to his mate, and it now lay vulnerable, awaiting her approval.

He couldn't afford to furnish it like a fancy gentleman, but the room was tidy, and the bedspread, though a little moth-eaten, gave a splash of color. He'd made an effort—which was more than most men did for their womenfolk.

What the fuck am I doing?

He shook his head, dispelling the notion that he cared one jot about her opinion. But he couldn't stop the stab of hurt as her eyes widened, not with wonder, but with horror.

"Th-there's no other room?" she asked. "A-and the—the…" She approached the bed, then stopped and turned to face him. "There's only one bed in here."

"We've no need for more," he said, grinning. "We've achieved much in that bed."

"Such as?"

Was she jesting? Surely she'd grasped his meaning. But the confusion in her eyes spoke of her innocence.

"The fruits of our labors are, at this moment, playing in the garden outside," he said. "But you always said you wanted at least six children, so we can resume our efforts. The bed's sturdy enough—which is just as well, given how much you like to—"

"Oh!" She let out a shriek, and he fought the urge to laugh.

"Does my wife recall her marital duties?"

Her lower lip wobbled. "A-am I expected to…" She gestured toward the bed, and a tear splashed onto her cheek.

You're a cad, Lawrence Frederick Baxter—an utter cad.

Bloody hell—it wasn't often that his conscience referred to him by his full name.

But there was a point beyond which even he wouldn't travel. As his wife, she'd be his for the taking, and the world would approve of the taking. But she wasn't his wife.

"This is a comfortable room, Bella," he said. "The best in the house."

"That's not much to boast about, given the state of the rest of this hovel," she scoffed. "Best in the house indeed! That's like comparing horse dung to dog excrement—only marginally less repugnant."

Bloody harpy! Just because he hadn't been born into luxury, didn't give her the right to sneer at him.

"It's only filthy, love, because you've not cleaned it," he said. "You wandered off before we moved here."

"W-wandered off?"

"We thought you'd abandoned us."

She glanced around the bedchamber again, settling her gaze on each item as if trying to force her memory to return.

"Is that how I ended up in that river?" she asked. "They said I'd fallen in—th-that I might not have survived. But I can't recall it."

Another tear fell.

Harpy she may be, but she had been through an ordeal she'd been lucky to survive.

He took her arm, and she stiffened as he pulled her into an embrace.

"It's all right, love."

She remained stiff and unyielding in his arms.

Perhaps he should say something comforting. Wives were supposed to love fancy speeches.

"You *did* survive, Bella," he said, "and we're all glad of it."

She let out a sigh, then yielded, almost as if, having been hardened to a lack of consideration, she was unable to withstand a few words of kindness.

Almost as if she'd never heard a truly kind word in her life.

Don't be getting soft.

But the voice inside his mind could go to the devil when there was a female body in his arms.

Soft and slight, yet round in all the right places—a delectable arse he longed to run his hands over, and those lovely teats pressed against his chest.

His cock hardened, but if she felt it, she gave no sign. Her chest rose and fell in a sigh, and she shifted position, her thighs moving against swollen member.

Sweet heaven—he was on the brink of spending!

Then she lifted her face and parted her lips—an instinctive offering. What lush pink lips—his for the taking. Then he lifted his gaze to her eyes, and the vulnerability in their expression broke his heart and doused his lust.

What the fuck am I doing?

Uncouth beast he might be—she'd called him as much. But he was not a man to take a woman unwilling, no matter how her body responded to his touch.

His cock twitched, almost in reproach at being denied the pleasure of her body, and he placed a chaste kiss on her forehead, then pushed her back.

"I'll be off now to the Oak, to fetch a bit of supper," he said. "I'll not be long."

He almost sprinted down the stairs. Once outside, he breathed in a lungful of fresh air to subdue his raging cock.

This wasn't how it was supposed to play out. She was to cook, clean, and keep house for him until he considered she'd worked off her debt. That was all.

The last thing he wanted to do was bed her, much less harbor any affection for her.

Chapter Eighteen

"How do you like the stew, love?"

The man across the table—no, she must think of him as her husband, no matter how distasteful the notion—tucked into the stew with gusto, shoveling it into his mouth.

She stabbed a piece of meat with her fork and bit into it. The texture resembled the soles of an old boot and presented a very real risk of loosening a tooth. Hunger overcame revulsion, and she swallowed, wincing as it slid down her throat. She followed it with a large gulp of water. She'd have preferred wine, but he'd said they couldn't afford something so fancy, and she'd never stoop so low as to drink ale.

She lifted her fork for another bite, then set it down. One mouthful was enough.

"It's your favorite," he said, nodding toward her bowl.

"Then I dread to think what else you'll place before me at the dinner table."

He laughed. "Isn't Mama amusing, children?"

The urchins watched her, wide eyed, as if she were some otherworldly creature they'd never seen before.

"It's rude to stare!" she said.

"It's also rude to not finish your meal, Bella, love, when there's others less fortunate."

She pushed her bowl aside. "Then the less fortunate—if such people exist—are welcome to *that*."

"We're unlikely to have this again for supper—cost me a packet, that did. But Ned said he'd send his Sophie round tomorrow with a bit of scrag end for you to cook."

"Must you speak with your mouth full?" she said. "I can see everything you're eating."

He grinned and opened his mouth once more, revealing partially chewed meat. Her stomach churned and she looked away.

"Beast!" she hissed. But her retort was met with laughter.

When she'd taken in a deep breath and turned her attention to the table once more, she caught sight of three little mouths wide open, like chicks begging for food—only they, too, were filled with pieces of stew.

"Children!" the Beast cried. "Not at the table—you'll upset your mother."

His admonishment might have carried more meaning had his voice not been filled with laughter.

The twins closed their mouths and continued chewing, but their brother burst into a fit of giggles, spraying half-chewed food onto the table.

Bella leaped from her seat, knocking her chair over. "This is intolerable!" she cried, her eyes stinging with the weak tears she'd fought to control ever since he'd shown her that bedchamber earlier and made all those crude remarks.

"Quite right," the Beast said. "Apologize to your Mama, Jonathan."

The child shook his head and poked out his tongue.

"There's no way I can be mother to that vile creature," she said. "It's the spawn of the devil—and the devil is *you*!"

The child's eyes widened, then he started to wail. The twins began to protest, and the girl—or, at least, the one with the longest hair that claimed to be a girl—wrapped her arms around her brother. "Ignore her—she's a witch."

"Yes," the other twin said. "She's not our—"

"Stop that!" the Beast roared, rising to his feet. His eyes had darkened to the color of coal, but a spark of fury flashed inside their depths. He balled his hands into fists, the knuckles whitening.

He was a man not to be crossed.

And, as her husband, he owned her.

The girl regained her composure first. "Papa—"

"Get to bed, Roberta," he said. "You too, William. Take care of your brother."

"Yes, Papa," they said in unison, and all three children climbed off their chairs and exited the kitchen.

The Beast closed his eyes and inhaled, slowly, as if composing himself.

Was he readying himself to beat her? Husbands beat their wives if they deemed it proper. And while it was most certainly *not* proper to beat her after forcing her to endure such a dingy cottage and a disgusting meal, he might think otherwise.

And he was so big—so strong—that she'd never be able to fight him off.

But when he opened his eyes, the anger had gone.

All she could hear was the sound of his breathing, punctuated by distant voices and the occasional sniff from the child she'd admonished.

No, not admonished—she'd called him a *vile creature*.

Vile he may be, but he was a child.

He was *her* child—even if she couldn't recall him.

"I didn't mean to call..." She made a random gesture in the direction in which the children had fled.

Dear Lord—he was her son and she'd forgotten his name again.

"Jonathan," the Beast said.

"Jonathan. I didn't mean to call him a..."

"A *vile creature*."

Her words seemed harsher on his lips, and she flinched. "I'm sorry."

"No matter—Jonathan's a forgiving soul."

"But I'm his mother."

He opened his mouth to reply, then closed it again. "That you are," he said. "Now, it's late and I've had a long day fetching you back. Time to retire. You can clear the table in the morning."

He cocked his head to one side and stared at her, as if expecting a reply. As if expecting to be thanked.

Curse him! Couldn't he take her apology with the good grace it demanded?

At length, he let out a chuckle.

"No matter—you can thank me later," he said. "Come on. *Bed.*"

Bed...

She caught her breath at the wicked pulse deep inside.

"The sofa in the parlor's plenty comfy," he said.

Relief flooded through her. While she'd relished the brief moment of tenderness in his arms earlier, the thought of his claiming her with that huge body of his was too much. What did husbands do with their wives? Would he mount her like a stallion took a mare? He must have done so in the past. He'd seen her... What had he called it? Her *intimate area.*

Her cheeks warmed with embarrassment at the notion of someone—*anyone*, let alone this beast of a man—seeing her naked body.

"Y-you don't mind sleeping on the sofa?" she asked.

He threw back his head and laughed. "Heavens, love, no matter how you try my patience, I cannot be angry with you for long. No—*you* take the sofa."

He pushed open the parlor door. "You've always found trouble gettin' to sleep in the bed," he said. "That is"—he grinned, showing his teeth—"when we've used the bed to *sleep* in."

"Don't be crude."

"I'll be as crude as I like in my home."

"I won't sleep on the sofa."

"There's nowhere else, love."

"Then I'll leave!"

"Where would you go?"

She opened her mouth to say "home" then closed it again. Like it or not, this *was* her home.

Grinning, he untied his neckerchief, then wound it around his fists.

"Your wanderin's got you into trouble before," he said. "I don't want you falling into the river again. And I don't want any more gossip in the village about your wayward ways."

"My..."

"Yes, love," he said. "What are people to think when a family comes to their village and the wife immediately runs off and returns half-naked in a gown that's not her own? I'll not have my good name—or yours—ruined by wagging tongues."

"Y-you mean they think I'm a..."

She couldn't bring herself to utter the word.

"What are folk to think? There's plenty such women selling their wares hereabouts."

"Are you calling me a whore?" she cried.

"You shouldn't take such names to yourself, love," he said, "but what's a man to think when his wife runs off? Now, must I secure you to prevent any more nighttime wanderings?"

"There's no need to bind me," she said. "I'll not leave."

"There's my good girl."

"Don't presume to speak to me in such a—"

"Now-now," he chided, wagging his finger as if she were a child. "It's best if you save your efforts for tomorrow—you've a busy day ahead."

He took her hand, and she caught her breath at the crackle of need. Then he led her into the parlor.

"There's a blanket over the armchair you can use," he said. "You shouldn't be too cold—but if you'd like me to warm you up, you only need come upstairs and ask."

She withdrew her hand and snatched the blanket, wrapping it around herself as if to hide her body from his gaze. With a chuckle, he bade her goodnight, then exited the room. His footsteps creaked on the stairs, then a door opened and closed in the distance.

The exhaustion that had lingered in the background finally overcame her, and she sat on the sofa, sleep claiming her even before she lay back.

Chapter Nineteen

A MAN WITH a clear conscience slept as soundly as a corpse—or so Ned had told him on the journey back to Brackens Hill.

Which means that sleep will elude me for the coming weeks.

Lawrence hadn't intended to sleep tonight anyway, with Lady Arabella in the house.

No—not Lady Arabella. She was Bella Baxter, and she'd already begun to believe that. Why else had she called him *husband* earlier?

But if he'd been concerned that his conscience would plague him too much, those concerns were lessened every time she opened that foul mouth of hers.

Vile creature indeed!

She could insult him as often as she liked, but woe betide those who insulted his children. Little Jonathan—with his sensitive nature—took every admonishment to heart.

Poor soul—though Elizabeth's passing had been nobody's fault, the boy didn't deserve to suffer from the knowledge that his entry into the world had brought about her demise. He needed a mother more than the twins.

Lawrence sighed, and the candle flickered in the air before calming.

There was always so much to be done! More so now his precious documents had been destroyed—courtesy of Miss High-and-Mighty. Some sketches and notes he could recall, but others were lost. Perhaps over time the memories might resurface to be committed to paper—tiny fragments to piece together.

Was that what it was like for her? Would her memory return in pieces, or all at once? Dr. Carter had said that memory loss in such cases—when a person had been on the brink of death—was often permanent. He'd said that her only hope was for Lawrence to present her with something familiar—a treasured personal possession or shared memory.

A personal possession like…

He reached into his jacket pocket and pulled out its contents—a torn petticoat, a necklace with a pearl pendant, and a ruby brooch.

The petticoat he'd give her tomorrow for mending—add it to her list of chores. The necklace, a delicate gold chain, looked thin enough to snap. The pendant—though its value was likely far in excess of anything he could afford—seemed too small for a woman of her rank. Perhaps it had sentimental value.

Then he snorted. For an object to have sentimental value, its owner needed to be in possession of a heart. But, nevertheless, he'd return it to her tomorrow also. He wasn't entirely cruel, after all.

The brooch was different. The ruby was enormous—he'd never seen the like. Any fool could tell it was a fine piece—valuable enough to attract attention and unwanted questions.

Ned might know someone who could sell it discreetly on his behalf—all manner of travelers must visit the inn. And it'd fetch a pretty sum—think of the tools and books he could buy!

It would be stealing.

His damned conscience again!

He turned the brooch over, running his thumb over the delicate filigree work surrounding the jewel. The back was plain and smooth, save for a gold clasp in the center and the initials *A.P.* engraved at the bottom.

Arabella Ponsford.

He pulled open a drawer in his desk, dropped the brooch inside, then closed it. Then he opened the notebook on the desk and flicked through it until he reached the sketch he'd been working on for the garden of a big house in the next county that a wine merchant—Trelawney, his name was—had recently moved into. It was an opportunity to undertake a large design project, and Lawrence's work in redesigning Dunton's garden would have demonstrated his experience and capabilities and shown his suitability for the project—had *she* not had him dismissed and destroyed his notes.

Curse her!

He picked up a pencil and added a path to the sketch, together with a row of rosebushes and an armillary sphere. Then he held the sketch at arm's length to admire it.

Clichéd and unimaginative—shrubs placed in a symmetrical pattern with a focal point in the center. Just like every other bloody garden in the world. He might as well have drawn a pile of horseshit.

He ripped out the page, crumpled it up, then tossed it over his shoulder.

He needed inspiration—but he'd been otherwise occupied with Miss High-and-Mighty.

Then he sighed. He really needed to stop calling her that. *Bella.* Her name was Bella. At least now she was here, she could mind the children while he was out. Poor Ned and his niece were reaching the limits of their endurance.

The thought of Bella enduring a day with those rascals lifted his spirits, and he flipped the pages of his notebook until he came to a blank page and began his sketch again. This time he placed the features at irregular intervals, moving the focal point to one side to draw the eye away from the center.

Much better. Any piece of art needed to contain an element of surprise—hidden corners and pathways that were unnoticeable at first glance. Something to provide interest for its inhabitants—particularly ladies who were so easily bored.

A muffled cry came from outside the study. Roberta tormenting her twin again, no doubt. Last week she'd hidden a spider among his underclothes. Smiling to himself, he continued.

Then the cry came again—a low wail of anguish.

Little buggers.

He rose and exited the study as another cry came.

But it came from downstairs.

Spoiled madam—perhaps the blanket was too scratchy, or the sofa too hard.

"No! leave me alone—please!"

His skin tightened at the fear in her voice, and he descended the stairs and pushed open the parlor door.

She lay on the sofa, the blanket on the floor—she must have thrown it off. Then she cried out, her breath misting in the air.

"Burning! It's burning!"

Perhaps her conscience visited her in her sleep, and she was reliving the moment she'd burned his possessions.

"The fire!"

He placed a hand on her forehead. Her skin was cold. Then he took her hand, and she snatched it free.

"Don't touch me!" she cried.

"Bella, you're freezing." He reached for her again, and she thrust out her arm to fend him off.

"No, I beg you have mercy, Your Grace!"

"Bella!" he cried, giving her a shake. Her eyes snapped open, at first unfocused, then they cleared and focused on him.

"Wh-who are you?" she asked. "Y-you're not…" She shuddered, and her gaze darted about the room, as if she were searching for her tormentor. At length, she stilled, and he drew her into his arms.

"Who was it?" he asked. "Who did you see?"

"I saw…" Her brow furrowed in concentration. "He…" Then she

shook her head.

"What did he look like?"

"A-a man. A lord. It was so vivid! B-but I can't remember. I try to picture him, but it's slipping away."

"Did you know him?"

"I-I thought I did."

"Do you know *me*?"

Sapphire eyes glazed with tears focused on him. Then she nodded.

"You're my husband. Lord save me—you're my husband."

She pulled free from his grasp, and his gut twisted at the disgust in her voice. He reached for the blanket, but before he could wrap it around her, she snatched it off him.

"Did *you* try to touch me?"

"No," he bit out.

"Good. Now leave me." She wrapped the blanket around herself, then settled on the sofa once more, turning her back to him. "Close the door on your way out."

Insufferable, haughty creature—dismissing him as if he were a servant!

But perhaps he should be thankful for her vile disposition. It helped to assuage his guilt.

CHAPTER TWENTY

A THICK CLOUD of smoke filled the air, moving in an ever-tightening circle, pulsing in and out. She reached up to fend it off, and it morphed into a cloud of birds, swirling, squawking, and cackling.

"Leave me be!"

The laughter increased, and she pressed her hands over her ears.

"Please—stop!"

A hand grasped her shoulder and the cloud dissipated, leaving three little demons standing before her.

No, not demons...

Urchins.

"That's enough, Jonathan!" a deep voice cried in the distance. "Leave your mother be."

"You said to wake her!" the smallest cried, before sticking his thumb in his mouth.

Your mother...

She rubbed her eyes and sat up. Sunlight stretched across the parlor, illuminating the children's faces and their eyes—three identical pairs of bright blue eyes...

Eyes like hers.

Then the memory of last night came to the fore—three pairs of eyes staring at her across the kitchen table.

The urchins were *hers*.

"Come, on children!" the voice cried once more, then *he* appeared. The Beast. Her husband.

She clambered into the recesses of her mind, seeking the memory—but his name refused to break into her consciousness. Only hers.

Bella.

And the children's…

"Jonathan," she said, looking at the red-headed child, before turning to the twins. "William and"—she stared at the girl—"Rowena?"

The girl scowled, and her brother poked her with his elbow. "Ha-ha!" he cried in a singsong voice. "She's already forgotten you!"

"Shut up!" the girl cried.

"Roberta—manners!" the Beast said, though his voice contained an undercurrent of laughter.

Jonathan grinned and jumped up and down. "She remembered *me* first!"

"Do you remember my name?" the Beast asked.

She stared at him, then shook her head.

"Lawrence," he said. "It's Lawrence. Not *the Beast*."

Heavens! Could he read her mind?

"Bella, love, it's time to get up," he said. "You'll not get your chores done if you spend the day idling on the sofa."

Chores. That hateful word again!

He pulled a piece of paper out of his pocket. "You needn't look so worried," he said. "I've written you a list."

She rose, and his gaze settled on her dress. Her cheeks warmed at the flare of desire in his eyes.

She snatched the paper and read it. "Clean the kitchen, wash the windows, stoke the fire…"

Was he jesting?

"Oh—I've forgotten to include the mending," he said. "You tore your petticoat when you had your…accident, and we can't afford a new one."

"Don't I have another?"

For a moment, she saw discomfort in his eyes. "We lost your clothes when we came here," he said. "But don't worry—Ned's niece has said she'll give you some of her old gowns. Isn't that kind of her? And she's going to ask around for donations. Mrs. Gleeson's always collecting."

"Who's Mrs. Gleeson?"

"The vicar's wife. She'll see you right."

"Am I to be subjected to the charity of others?" she asked. "Do you mean to humiliate me?"

"Bella, love," he sighed, "folk hereabouts are being very kind. We're outsiders, and they owe us no favors. Let's not make enemies before we've made any friends. You never complained about taking charity when we had nothing."

"We have nothing now!" She gestured about the parlor. "Just look at this...hovel!"

"It just needs a clean and a tidy-up," he said. "You'll know what to do."

"But I've never done any—"

"Yes, you have, love, and you've never complained about it before." He gestured to the list. "I've done what I can to help."

"By writing instructions for me to do all the work!" she cried, curling her fingers around the list. "Why should *I* do it all?"

"Because you're my wife," he said. "But I tell you what—I'll take the children to school before I start work. How's that?"

She glanced at the piece of paper. "Take the children to school? That's not even on the list."

"I didn't think I'd have to remind you about *that*."

"Then you'll come back and help with this?"

"You can't expect me to do *women's* work. How will I put food on our table if I'm to be fancying about the house making a fool of meself? Talk sense, woman."

"Talk sense, woman!" Jonathan echoed, and he burst into laughter.

Tears stung Bella's eyes, but she bit her lip to stem them. The last thing she wanted was to further her humiliation by crying in front of them—despite the provocation.

Her husband—Lawrence—met her gaze, and for a moment, she saw tenderness in his eyes. Then he blinked and the amusement returned.

She glared at the child. "I *am* talking sense, *Jonathan*."

"That's settled, then," Lawrence said. "Children, go find your shoes."

The children scrambled out of the parlor, yelling and laughing.

Bella pressed her hand against her forehead. The pains that had tormented her since her accident had lessened, but a dull ache throbbed behind her eyes. But there was no use telling *him* that—he seemed to think her sole purpose was to serve him.

Isn't that what any husband expects of his wife?

For a brief moment, the memory of her dream broke through—a portly man dressed in finery, with sour breath and a spiteful disposition, his lust-filled eyes small in his fleshy face…

"Bella!"

She startled and stared at the clear-eyed man before her. Uncouth beast he may be, but there was an honesty in his roughness. He carried no pretense at finery. No—his uncouthness was on display, rudely invading her consciousness.

"Are you all right?"

He moved closer, his body filling the space—the same body that had held her close when she woke from her nightmare. It was the body of a laborer—a beast—built for toil. Yet, in that briefest of moments, it had been capable of such tenderness.

She must have married him for a reason. Had he wooed her with offerings of courtship and stolen kisses?

He reached toward her, but, fighting the need to be in those strong arms, she pushed him back.

"Yes, I'm all right."

"Good." He nodded, and the tenderness in his eyes disappeared. "Aren't you going to thank me?"

"What for?"

"The list."

"If you think I'd thank you for such a…" she began, but he raised his hand.

"No man wants a harpy for a wife," he said. "Remember your vow of obedience."

She dipped into a mock curtsey. "Thank you, *husband*," she sneered.

He laughed. "Oh, Bella—you always were a handful! I'll take the words, but not the manner in which they were spoken. But mind you get those chores done."

"Will you beat me if I don't?" she challenged.

Hunger flared in his eyes. "I rather relish the prospect of taking you over my knee—as I'm sure you do, you insatiable wanton." He licked his lips, and she caught her breath at the wicked little pulse of pleasure deep inside her body.

"A-an insatiable wanton?" she said, her voice tight.

"That's my Bella," he said, grinning. "And there are few women who can measure up to your skills when it comes to pleasin' me."

Ugh.

He chuckled and stepped closer. "That's something we can explore later," he said, licking his lips. "But now, let us seal our bargain with a kiss."

Her stomach fluttered with anticipation—then, with a clatter of footsteps and a cacophony of shrieks, the children returned.

"Take good care of that list, Bella, love," her husband said. "I can't be wasting paper writing out another one. Come on, children—say goodbye to your mother."

"Goodbye, Mama!" they chorused.

They exited the parlor, and she heard the front door open and shut, their footsteps and voices fading into the distance.

She glanced at the list. Heavens—there were more than ten items! How would she even begin?

Chapter Twenty-One

A CART APPROACHED from behind and Lawrence tightened his grip on Jonathan's hand. His youngest child always had a tendency to spot danger, which would have been a quality to celebrate if he didn't always veer toward it with enthusiasm.

Enthusiastic was how Lawrence justified the boy's behavior to the schoolmistress. Though Mrs. Chantry, who looked down her long nose at his family, preferred to say *disruptive*.

The cart rolled by, and the wheel hit a puddle, splattering Jonathan's breeches. The boy stopped to wipe himself, smearing mud over the material.

"You look like a mud pie!" William cried.

"He won't have to wash his breeches," Roberta said. "Not now the woman's here."

"Roberta, I've told you before—you must call her Mama," Lawrence said.

"Is she our mama?" Jonathan asked.

"She is while she's staying with us," Lawrence said. "She's to keep house, clean, and cook for us. That's what mothers do."

"That's not what Tommie's mother does," Roberta said. "Mrs. Chantry says she entertains men. She says she's a—"

"I don't *care* what Mrs. Chantry says!" Jonathan cried. "I like Tommie. He's nicer than *you*." He gave Roberta a push.

"Stop that, you little worm!" Roberta said.

Jonathan poked out his tongue. "I don't like her."

"You can't say that about your sister," William said. "You have to like her, even if she puts frogs in your bed."

"I meant *her*."

"Mrs. Chantry?" Lawrence asked. "You're not supposed to like your teacher—just learn from her."

"No. *Her*."

Ah, well. He could be forgiven for that. Bella wasn't exactly likeable—more the opposite.

"How long is she staying with us?" Roberta asked.

Until she's paid her debt.

"What's a debt, Papa?" Jonathan asked.

Bugger. He'd said that aloud.

"It's when you have to pay someone back," Roberta said.

"Like when Bobby put that spider in my bed," William said. "I paid her back by stuffing a worm down her shirt. Bobby hates worms."

"I don't."

"You do!" William said. "You screamed and called me a bugger."

"Bugger!" cried Jonathan.

"I *beg* your pardon, child?" a female voice asked.

They had arrived at the school, where Mrs. Chantry stood at the entrance.

Bugger.

Mrs. Chantry folded her arms and met Lawrence's gaze. Cold blue eyes stared at him. But unlike Bella's eyes, which conveyed a spirit begging to be tamed, the teacher's eyes lacked warmth—as if she existed to suck the joy out of everything.

But, as a teacher, she knew best.

"I'm sorry you had to hear that, Mrs. Chantry," Lawrence said, tipping his hat. "Jonathan, apologize at once."

The boy tightened his grip on Lawrence's hand. "I-I'm sorry, Mrs. Chantry."

She narrowed her eyes. "Given that you uttered the profanity outside school premises, I'll let it pass unpunished. But any more such behavior will be dealt with severely." She shifted her gaze to Roberta and William, before resuming her attention on Lawrence. "That goes for all of you—do you understand?"

"Are you including *me* in your admonishment?" Lawrence asked.

"Children learn their habits from those whom the Almighty has entrusted with their moral development."

"Their *what?*"

"Parents, Mr. Baxter," Mrs. Chantry said. "The risk to the child's moral development is tenfold if one of those parents is absent—particularly if it's the mother."

"We have a mother, Mrs. Chantry!" Jonathan cried.

The teacher's eyes widened.

"I thought you a widower, Mr. Baxter. Have you married again?"

The key to maintaining a story was to stick to the facts as much as possible and avoid questions that couldn't be answered truthfully.

"I've not married again," Lawrence said. "Bella—" He glanced at the children. "She went missing."

"She went missing?"

"She's back home now."

The teacher drew in a sharp breath, her face morphing into an expression of horror that would have been credible were it not so exaggerated.

"What is the world coming to?" she said. "What makes a woman act in such a manner? I daresay there was a man involved. Some women are weak and fall to temptation." Then she drew in another sharp breath and arched her eyebrows. "You *are* married, aren't you? Otherwise, your children…"

"My children are not bastards, Mrs. Chantry."

The woman clutched at her breast. "Such unseemly language—and, within sight of the church!"

"I hardly think the church will crumble at a few curses."

"But your children's souls are at risk, Mr. Baxter." Mrs. Chantry gestured to said children. "Get inside unless you want the strap. If your father—or that *mother* of yours—cannot teach you proper discipline, then I must do it for them."

The children rushed inside with a clatter of footsteps, as if the devil were on their tail. Or standing in the doorway threatening them with a strap.

"Mrs. Chantry, I—"

"Never fear, Mr. Baxter." She placed a hand on his arm. "I understand a man often feels the need to curse, for which he repents on a Sunday. But I advise you to take a firmer hand to your wife. A disciplined home is the best environment for impressionable young minds. You must lead by example if your wife's in need of correction."

Lawrence touched his cap. He was no match for an educated woman who used fancy words to make her argument. Children needed an education if they were to thrive in a world that punished those born with nothing.

"Thank you, Mrs. Chantry," he said. "I believe my wife already understands the consequences of her behavior."

Judging by the look of horror in Bella's eyes as he'd left her with the list of chores ten minutes ago, she understood the consequences, all right.

Chapter Twenty-Two

Why was it that every time she tried to sweep dust out of a room, it merely swirled around the air, like a cloud of stubborn crows, then settled back where it had begun? But not before filling her nostrils with an acrid scent and clinging to her hair.

She inhaled to let out a cough once more, and her nostrils tickled.

Not again...

She covered her mouth with her hands before she convulsed with a sneeze. Then she removed her hand and studied her palm. A film of sticky dust caked her skin.

Sweet heaven—that came out of her nostrils.

Fighting nausea, she rushed outside, like a drowning man in a filthy pond seeking air before succumbing to death.

Death would be better than *this*.

The air wasn't that much better outside. It carried the scent of—of what? Horse manure? Cow dung? Rotting meat? Something unsavory—rivaled only by the stench coming from beneath the floorboards.

Stains covered her gown—from when she'd tried to wipe the dust off her hands, and from a dark brown substance that she'd picked up, thinking it was a pile of raisins, then promptly gagged at the odor.

It felt like she'd been working without respite—save for a visit to the privy, which she had no intention of enduring again—for a full day. Yet when she checked the cracked, dust-coated clock over the fireplace, she'd been working less than an hour. Her hands burned from when she tried to wash the apron she'd found in the kitchen, and the heels of her feet chafed from rubbing against the insides of her shoes.

Falling into a river seemed a vacation in comparison.

She held up her hands—hands that, according to him, had been used to years of toil. The skin glowed red, as if lit from inside, and her whole body felt as if she'd been run over by a carriage.

Footsteps approached, and she darted back into the kitchen. There was only one way her humiliation could get any worse—and that was to be seen by others.

She sat at the table and pushed aside the dirty plates from last night's meal. Cleaning those was item seven on the list. She pulled out this list and read it again.

She'd only completed—no, attempted—the first two items. Perhaps she could try the third.

Stoke the fire.

Whatever stoking was. She'd seen a pile of logs at the back of the building, but there were no identifiable means with which to light them.

Damn you…

She hesitated. What was his name? Lawrence.

Damn you, Lawrence. You've told me what to do, but not how. I can't remember.

She scrunched up the paper and winced at the soreness in her palm.

"Damn you!" she cried. "I can't remember!"

She placed her head in her hands and succumbed to the tears, each shuddering breath sending an ache through her lungs.

"I don't know what to do!" she said. "Sweet Lord—won't anyone help me?"

Rap-rap-rap!

She glanced up and drew in a sharp breath.

A young woman stared at her through the window. She knocked on the glass again. "May I come in?"

Bella rose and backed away. But the woman had already seen her. Hiding in the shadows would only give her more to gossip about.

I don't want any more gossip in the village about your wayward ways.

She cringed as she recalled her husband's words.

The kitchen door opened, and the woman appeared, carrying a sack. Bella let out a shriek and leaped back.

"Don't be cryin' out, ma'am," the woman said. "Didn't Mr. Baxter say I was comin' over?"

The woman—hardly a woman at all; she looked barely out of the schoolroom—glanced about the kitchen, then smiled.

"I'm Sophie," she said, as if that would explain her presence. "Ned's niece," she added.

Bella stepped back. "Who's Ned?"

"My uncle."

"I understand *that*, given that you said you're his niece," Bella said. "I'm not a simpleton."

The girl's smile slipped. "Uncle Ned said you might want some help. He said you'd had an accident and lost all your clothes. I've brought some of mine. May I put them on the table? My arms are achin' real bad."

Bella glanced at the table—another dirt-covered surface she'd been unable to conquer. But the girl seemed not to notice. She placed the sack on the surface, then pulled out a gown and held it up.

"What do you think? It'll do for you until you can make your own."

"Make my own?" Was she expected to *make* clothes?

"You're taller than me," the girl continued. "But we can let out the hem."

"Let out the hem?"

"I can show you."

"Are you saying I don't know how to…to"—Bella gestured toward the gown—"*let out a hem?*"

Compassion replaced the irritation in the girl's eyes. "Oh, forgive me," she said. "You must have forgotten, on account of your accident. Hit your head real bad, Uncle Ned said. Mr. Baxter must have been so worried about you. I'm sure he's glad you're home."

Perhaps he was—but only because he needed a housemaid, scullery maid, nursemaid, cook, and…

"Are you needing a bit of help?" the girl asked, interrupting Bella's thoughts.

"Do you think I'm incapable of—" Bella began, but the girl interrupted.

"If you've hit your head, it can take a long time to recover. Uncle Ned said you'd lost your memory and might need some help." She rolled her eyes. "Men think the work a woman does in the home is the easiest thing in the world—yet it's not something they can take a hand to. They'd rather sit in idleness waiting for their women to sweep the floor around them. And they think they have the worst of it. Granted, they earn a living to keep food on the table, but their work stops as soon as they return home. A woman's work never stops. Men are—"

She broke off and sighed. "Forgive me for rattling on—I hope you won't take offense. Your husband's a hardworking man, Mrs. Baxter. I'm always seein' him toiling away in some garden or other."

"In a garden?" Bella asked.

"He's a gardener, isn't he?"

Bella blinked back tears. "I-I don't know."

"Oh, sweet Mother Mary!" the girl cried. "Can't you remember? You're still not recovered, and he's left you all on your own. No wonder you look in such a…"

Her voice trailed off, but she had no need to continue when Bella could see, from her reflection in the window, exactly what state she looked in.

"You might wear an apron when doing the housework," the girl said. "It'll keep your dress clean. Now—what can I do to help? It's often difficult to know where to start. Perhaps you can begin by writing a list of everything needing doing."

Lists—lists... Why did everybody talk about damned lists!

The girl's eyes widened. "Have I upset you, Mrs. Baxter?"

Bella held up the paper, her hand trembling. "I have a list—he wrote it—but I'll never get it done before he returns. I don't even know how to start. I..."

She caught her breath as a tide of despair battered at her soul.

The girl took the list and read it.

"I've tried," Bella said. "I really have—but I ache everywhere, and my hands..." She held them out, palms upward. "Are they supposed to look like that?"

"Heavens!" the girl cried. "How did that happen?"

"I was trying to wash an apron. I found a cake of soap, but the more I scrubbed, the more it hurt. Then, when I soaked my hands, it hurt even more."

"You used the lye soap on your hands?" The girl shook her head. "That'll burn your skin."

"Soap doesn't burn," Bella said.

"Expensive soaps don't—they've some at the Oak for guests who're willing to pay for it. I could ask Uncle Ned to get you some if that's what you're used to."

"I don't know what I'm used to," Bella said. "All I know is that *he* wants the house cleaned and his dinner on the table."

"Let me help," the girl said.

"I can't."

"Why not? Do you have so many friends that you're not in need of one more?"

Friends. Do I have any friends?

Bella focused her mind on the past, searching for a memory. But, other than a flash of bright silk and a blurred shape, together with a sharp voice issuing thinly veiled insults, no memories came to the fore.

"I have no friends."

"Then," the girl said, taking Bella's hand gently, taking care not to touch her burning palm, "let us start as friends. I always think, once in a while, it's good to start anew."

"Thank you…" Bella cursed herself. What was the girl's name?

"Sophie, Mrs. Baxter. My name's Sophie." The girl smiled—not a smile of mischief, or wickedness, but a genuine smile from one who offered friendship with no expectation of anything in return.

It was the kind of smile Bella had no recollection of ever receiving—or giving.

"I hope we'll become friends, Mrs. Baxter."

The girl—Sophie—was right. Sometimes it was best to start anew.

Bella smiled and squeezed her hand.

"So do I," she said, "and call me Bella."

Chapter Twenty-Three

As Lawrence trudged along the path, he caught sight of two flickering lights—large, rectangular, luminous eyes watching him from ahead.

The windows of Ivy Cottage, illuminated from within, as if they guided him home. The light stretched across the garden, picking out the leaves in the shrubs, and the edge of the fence he'd erected with Ned's help.

"Papa—look!" Jonathan tugged at his sleeve. "Doesn't it look pretty, Papa?"

"Don't be so foolish!" Roberta said. "It's like all houses. Somewhere we have to sleep while we're waiting to go outside again."

Lawrence couldn't help smiling. Roberta was her father's daughter, all right. Already stronger and braver than her twin, and with a keen interest in plants, she'd helped him clear the garden around Ivy Cottage. And the most intelligent of his children—if a parent was permitted to admit the superiority of one child over another. She had a bright future ahead.

Or would, had she been born a boy. As a girl, she'd have to set aside her ambitions and succumb to the duty of all women.

Which reminds me…

"Come on, children!" he said brightly as he reached the cottage and opened the front door. "Let's see what Mama's been up to."

The hallway was empty.

"Bella?" he called out.

Silence.

"Bella!"

"Mama, where are you?" the children chorused.

Perhaps she'd taken flight.

"What's that smell?" William asked.

"It smells good," Jonathan said. "I like it!"

"You like *everything*," Roberta said. "You're such a baby! People won't like you any more just because you like them."

"Don't like *you*!" Jonathan gave her a push.

"That's enough," Lawrence said. Though he had to admit, the aroma had a certain appeal. It smelled suspiciously like...

Cooking.

He pushed open the parlor door. A fire flickered in the hearth, and the candles at either end of the mantelshelf were almost out.

What the devil was she about? They couldn't afford to waste candles and logs in an empty room. Clearly, she had no appreciation of how much things cost.

"Papa—come and look!"

He followed the children's voices into the kitchen.

Ah—that explained the aromas.

A pot sat on top of the range, and next to it, a loaf of bread.

He picked up the loaf, which was still warm to the touch. It was on the small side, and somewhat hard—it barely yielded when he squeezed it—but it was better than nothing.

And in the pot...

He lifted the lid to reveal a thick brown stew that simmered gently. He stirred it, revealing pieces of meat, potato, smaller pieces of onion, and the occasional carrot.

"Bella!" he called out again, but there was no answer. "Children—go upstairs and remove your shoes, then return to the table. I'll find your mother so she can serve supper."

"She's not our—" Roberta began, but William poked her in the ribs.

"Yes, she is—remember what Papa said."

She pulled a face, then exited the kitchen, followed by her brothers.

"Don't push me!" William cried, followed by a shriek from Jonathan.

"Children!" Lawrence roared.

Heavens! He'd been toiling in the vicarage garden all day, and now he had to deal with their bickering? That was what wives and mothers were for.

A female scream echoed from upstairs.

Ah—the children had found her.

"Come on, Mama!"

"Sleepyhead! Mama's a sleepyhead!"

"Mama, I'm hungry!"

The clatter of footsteps resumed, and the children ushered Bella into the kitchen.

Lawrence almost lost his composure. Hair unkempt, with blotches of soot on her cheeks and a dark smear across the front of her gown, she resembled a chimney sweep.

"Bella, where have you been?" he asked, struggling to contain his laughter.

"She was on my bed!" Jonathan cried out. "That's *my* bed. You're too big for it."

She glared at Jonathan, and the room fell silent, as if awaiting a tirade of fury. But she merely sighed and shuffled toward the range, where she lifted the lid of the pot and gave it a stir.

He hadn't expected such a rapid transformation. The haughty demeanor had gone, replaced by the cowed attitude of a servant.

At last, Miss High-and-Mighty, you're experiencing what you force your maidservants to endure every day.

He pointed to the pot. "Is that our supper?"

"No," she said. "It's the contents of the privy."

Jonathan let out a giggle, cut short as William shushed him. Bella turned and faced Lawrence, her eyes glittering with venom.

Her fire hadn't *completely* died.

Good. He liked her spirit. As did his cock, which had twitched with need as soon as he heard her footsteps, and now strained in his breeches. Eyes flashing, plump lips parted, as if ready to receive his kiss, she straightened her stance and returned his stare.

A wife was supposed to submit to her husband's authority—but where was the pleasure in that?

He gestured to the children. "Sit, while your mother serves us."

He caught a flash of anger in her eyes, before she spooned stew into bowls then placed them on the table. The last bowl she set at the empty place, spilling some of the contents on the table.

"Ha-ha!" Jonathan sang. "Mama's made a mess! You'll have to clear that up." The twins tittered with laughter, and she glared at them.

"Why, you…" she began, but Lawrence interrupted.

"Wife—not at the table."

"I *beg* your pardon? You expect me to put up with—"

"*I'll* admonish the children."

"Why must you—"

He raised his hand. "That's enough," he said. "Children, don't laugh at your mother. I've not been working hard all day to endure such noise. A man should expect a peaceful home when he enters it."

Bella's eyes flashed, but she either thought better of arguing, or was too tired to respond. Instead, she picked at the stew in front of her, while he shoveled forkfuls into his mouth.

Bloody hell—that was delicious.

"Did you make this?" he asked.

"You ordered me to cook for you, did you not?" she retorted.

"Well, it's proper tasty, thank you."

A flicker of pride shone in her eyes.

No—that wouldn't do. She was proud enough already.

"Where's the bread?" he asked.

She rolled her eyes, then rose from the table, returning with the bread and a knife. She raised the knife and smiled coldly at him. The blade reflected the candlelight, curling into an evil grin.

I've no doubt you'd as soon plunge that knife into my heart, wife.

She cut the loaf into slices.

"Help yourself," she said. "I presume you're capable of *that*, unless the process of entering his home renders a man completely useless."

Roberta gave a snort.

"What's so funny?" William asked.

"*She's* right. Boys are useless."

"Don't say *she*—it's rude!" Jonathan cried. "Isn't it, Mama?"

Bella turned to the little boy, and her mouth curved into a smile.

Lawrence's breath caught at the expression in her eyes—a softness he'd not seen before.

Then she resumed eating, and the moment was gone.

"This bread's tough!" William cried, chewing on a slice.

"Dip it in your stew, silly," Roberta said.

"Mind you chew it," Lawrence said. "You want to keep your teeth."

Bella's smile disappeared. "I'd like to see *you* bake bread."

"That's women's work," Lawrence said. "A man shouldn't sully himself with women's work."

"Why? Because men are incapable?"

Roberta laughed again.

Curse her! Was she trying to enlist his daughter against him?

"Have you finished your supper, children?" Lawrence asked. In response, they pushed three empty bowls across the table. "Good—get ready for bed. Your mother will be along later to tuck you in."

"I'll what?" Bella asked.

"You always tuck them in," Lawrence said. "And read them a story. Doesn't she?"

Roberta hesitated, but the boys nodded. Then the children scraped back their chairs and clattered their way upstairs.

"I suppose you've not made anything for pudding," Lawrence said.

Rather than scowl, Bella gave a smile of triumph. "That's where you're wrong, oh munificent *husband*."

She stacked the bowls while he sat back and watched, then she cleared the table, casting him the occasional glance as if she expected him to help.

Bugger that—she had a debt to pay.

Then she opened the range and pulled out a pie.

He wrinkled his nose at the warm aroma of apples.

"You baked a *pie*?" he asked.

"Didn't you say I always cook for you?"

"Yes, but I didn't expect..." He shook his head. "Never mind. Serve me a slice."

"A *please* wouldn't go amiss."

"Why?" he asked. "You're my wife."

"Unfortunately, I am," she said. "If you lack manners, that's your misfortune—but you should set our children an example."

"Our children?" he said. "But they're..."

They're not yours.

He checked himself. "Very well—serve me a slice, *please*."

The irony was not lost on him that she, of all people, saw fit to lecture another about manners.

She cut a slice, placed it on a plate, and pushed it toward him before cutting a smaller slice for herself.

He shoveled a forkful of pie into his mouth and let out an involuntary groan. The apples were firm, yet soft, their natural sweetness complemented by an exotic taste he couldn't quite place. It was delicious.

Then he caught the pride in her eyes.

No—that won't do.

He pushed back his chair and beckoned to her. "Wife, remove my boots."

Her eyes widened. "What?"

"It's what you do when I come home. Normally you do it before supper, but I'll let that slide tonight."

"Oh, you will, will you?"

"It's never bothered you before."

"Or perhaps it did, and you were too ignorant to listen to my protests."

He laughed. "That's my Bella—feisty before she yields. I do love that in you."

"And what is there in *you* to love?"

"The pleasure of serving me."

She eyed his boots. "I'll suffer it this once," she said, "if only to ensure you don't cover my floor with muddy footprints."

"*Your* floor?"

"It's my home as well as yours, is it not?"

In response, he stretched out his legs. She kneeled at his feet, grasped one boot at the ankle, and tugged until it worked free. Then she removed the second boot and placed them on the floor beside the range.

"Bella?"

She glanced up, and his body surged at the image of her at his feet, eyes wide, mouth parted, as if in readiness to serve him.

Was there ever a sight more arousing? He squeezed his thighs together to temper his rising cock. Then she lowered her gaze to his groin and, blushing, drew in a sharp breath. Her tongue flicked out and moistened her lower lip.

Like it or not, she was aroused.

"Like what you see?" he asked.

She scrambled to her feet, almost losing her balance. He reached toward her, and she fended him off. "Don't touch me!"

"Why the sudden coyness, Bella?" he teased. "Most nights you're beggin' me to touch you—and more besides."

"You're a boor!"

"I'm *your* boor," he said. "Come here."

She backed away. "I'm tired," she said. "All I want to do is sleep."

"Then ask permission to retire and I'll grant it."

"I shouldn't have to…" she began. Then she let out a huff. "I'm too tired to care," she said. "Very well—please may I retire, oh lord and master?"

"You may." He gestured to the table. "I'll excuse you from clearing up the supper things."

"Thank you." Her mouth twitched into a smile.

"You'll just have to add them to your list of chores for tomorrow."

"I'll *what*? After what I've had to do today—you expect me to do it all over again?"

"What—throw a few pieces of pork into a pot and bake a pie? Hardly a day's hard toil."

"What would you know of hard toil?" she sneered. "And to think—we made the pie special. With cinnamon, as a treat, to—"

"Cinnamon?" So that explained the exotic taste. Exotic and *expensive*—the foolish, spoiled madam! "What the devil have you done?" he asked. "Do you have any idea how much that costs?"

"It was a gift," she said. "I—"

"*Nothing* is a gift, Bella," he said. "Everything must be paid for. Though I wouldn't expect someone like you to understand."

"Someone like me? What do you mean?"

Bugger—he'd almost betrayed himself.

"I-I mean someone incapable of keeping house."

"Incapable?" she said. "Do you have any idea what I've endured today? No—I suppose not, because I'm a woman, and women don't matter in your eyes. Neither do children, from what I can see."

"You're criticizing my children?"

"There you go again! *Your* children—as if I had no role to play. Am I just a broodmare? An unpaid cook and housemaid?"

"That's marriage, Bella, love."

She stepped toward him, thrusting her face close. "That's not marriage—it's indentured servitude!"

He gripped her shoulders, and her eyes widened. Then, unable to resist the torrent of desire in his veins, he pulled her toward him and crushed her mouth to his. For a moment, she struggled, then she gripped his arms, digging her fingertips into his flesh, and pulled him hard against her body.

Sweet Lord—she was delectable! All fire and passion simmering beneath the surface of that lush body. It was a body made to accommodate him—with soft curves and plump, ripe breasts made to fill his hands.

He slid his lips against hers. She parted them, and he slipped inside, relishing the taste of sweetness and spices. She was a delectable meal on which he'd gladly feast. And she was ready for him. She trembled against him, softening to mold against his form. He lowered his hand to cup a breast, and a low growl escaped his lips as her nipple beaded against his palm.

What might it be like to taste it—to taste her?

His mind filled with the image of her spread before him on the kitchen table, offering her sweetness. He pushed her against the wall, and she let out a mewl, shifting her legs with an instinct born of pure female need to receive him. He only need lift her skirts and he'd be buried inside her in a heartbeat…

What the fuck am I doing?

He broke the kiss, closing his mind against the sight of her—lips swollen, face flushed, hair in disarray, like a twopenny whore who'd taken her pleasure in the bushes.

She was not his to take, no matter how greatly he desired her.

She stilled, then her eyes fluttered open. Dark with desire, they were the color of a deep ocean, until they cleared and filled with horror.

He released her and retreated, willing the ache in his groin to subside.

No matter how much he hated her—and he *did* hate her—he had no right to take her innocence.

"Forgive me, Bella," he said. "I didn't mean to touch you. I'll not do so again."

Regret rippled across her expression, and she lifted her hand and wiped her forehead. He caught a flash of redness on her palm.

"What's that?"

"Nothing." She turned her palm inward. "May I retire now?"

"Bella, I—"

"For heaven's sake!" she cried. "Just leave me be, you vile beast!"

Vile beast—it hadn't taken long for that evil tongue of hers to lash him once more.

"Very well," he said. "But take care not to disturb me. I have much work to do before I can retire. *I* can't languish on the sofa all evening."

"Devil take you!"

She turned her back and exited the kitchen. Moments later, he heard the parlor door open and slam shut.

He climbed the stairs to his study and settled at his desk. Then he picked up his pencil and began adding to the sketch for Mr. Trelawney. He winced as the pencil rubbed against a callous on his palm, and he stopped to examine the flesh. It was bright red where he'd rubbed it against the shovel—the marks of hard toil.

That was the lot of folk of his class, unlike those of hers…

Though her palms had seemed very red. But she'd concealed them when he asked. Out of pride, no doubt.

He set the pencil aside. There'd be time to work on the sketch tomorrow. Mrs. Gleeson was holding a garden party, which meant his presence was not required, and it was days yet before he was due to start work on Sir Halford's garden. Besides, there was enough work to do here—those beans, for a start, needed sowing in the kitchen garden. And he could keep an eye on her—make sure she wasn't shirking her duties.

He leaned back, glanced about the study, then froze.

Something was different.

What was it? The books were in the same order on the bookshelf—alphabetical order of the author, just how he liked it.

Then he saw it. The dust lining the walls was no longer there—neither were the cobwebs that had occupied the corners of the ceiling. The gold embossing on the spines of the books gleamed in the candlelight. As for the window overlooking the garden—the smears of dust and debris had gone. He could actually see out where the moonlight bathed the garden with a soft blue glow.

The study had been transformed. Even the floorboards had been cleaned and polished—he ought to have noticed the faint odor of wax earlier.

What else had she done?

He rose and exited the study, looking—really *looking* for the first time—at the hallway. The floor had been swept—that pile of rabbit droppings William had brought in was gone—and the windows washed.

Perhaps she'd not been so idle after all.

He tiptoed down the stairs and opened the door to the parlor, wincing as it creaked on its hinges.

The fire was almost out, the dying embers casting a dull orange glow. But even in the fading light he could discern the transformation. The rug beside the sofa now bore a discernible pattern of reds and greens. And the table beneath the window had been polished and bore a cracked vase of pale pink blooms.

Bloody hell—she'd cut his best roses.

But, in doing so, together with everything else she did today, she'd transformed Ivy Cottage into a home.

No wonder she was exhausted.

He crossed the floor and kneeled beside the sleeping woman on the sofa. In the stillness of repose, her expression was that of an angel—serene and beautiful.

You're a bastard, Lawrence Baxter—do you know that?

"Yes," he breathed, his gut twisting with guilt. "I'm an utter bastard."

She stirred, and, unable to fight the impulse, he took her hand. She curled her fingers around his, and his heart ached at the gesture so simple, yet it conveyed such trust—a wife seeking comfort from her husband.

But he wasn't her husband. He was the blackguard who'd deceived her.

Better him than that vile man Dunton, who'd seen her as a possession, then saw fit to abandon her, alone and afraid.

You can't justify your own transgressions merely because they've been surpassed by another's.

Her eyes fluttered open.

"Lawrence."

His heart ached to hear his name on her lips.

She lifted her head. "Is there something you need? Or—the children?"

She tried to sit, but he placed a hand on her shoulder and pushed her back.

Why must his conscience plague him so? Lady Arabella Ponsford was a harpy. He *hated* her.

Didn't he?

You don't hate her. In fact, you...

"No!"

Her eyes widened. "Lawrence, what have I done?"

He shook his head. "It's nothing you've done, Bella. It's me—I-I'm afraid I've not been..." He hesitated. "There's something I must tell you, Bella. Forgive me, I should have said it before—but I was afraid."

"Afraid? I can't imagine *you* being afraid."

He lifted her hand and brushed his lips against her knuckles, bracing himself for her rejection. But instead, she curled her fingers around his and smiled.

Sweet heaven—she was beautiful enough in the throes of anger, all fire and passion. But the quiet smile she gave him rendered her breathtaking.

"What did you want to say to me?" she asked.

May God forgive me.

He kissed her knuckles again.

"Thank you," he said. "I wanted to say thank you."

She smiled again and blinked, slowly, her eyes heavy-lidded with fatigue. He placed his hand on her forehead, caressing the skin with his fingertips.

"Sleep now, love."

She closed her eyes and her chest rose and fell in a sigh. Moments later, her body settled into the quiet rhythm of sleep.

So—he could add cowardice to his list. A blackguard and a coward.

But he could, at least, show himself to be a better man than the Duke of Dunton.

Chapter Twenty-Four

Bella poured water into the teapot, then set it aside to brew while she slid into her seat at the kitchen table.

Her limbs ached, and her palms itched.

Today had been wash day. Her palms always itched after wash day, despite the salve Sophie gave her. It was her least favorite day of the week—if any day could be called *favorite*, given that from Monday to Saturday they were much the same. She rose before dawn and set the fire in the range—fighting back the wave of terror that gripped her as the flames danced around the coals. Then she dressed the children, before the endless cycle of cooking and cleaning began, snatching a few minutes' rest where she could indulge in a little embroidery—something she'd discovered she had a talent for—before they returned in the evening demanding to be fed, followed by more cleaning, until finally she dropped onto the sofa, welcoming the oblivion of sleep.

Except Sunday.

On Sundays, she was permitted a little respite. She rose later than usual because her husband brought her a pot of tea in the parlor—which, as he never hesitated to remind her, made him more considerate than other husbands. He then disappeared outside to tend to the kitchen garden, after which he returned inside to don his best suit before waiting in the parlor while Bella helped the children put on their best clothes. Then they set off for church to be preached to on the merits of wholesome living, the benefit of hard toil, and the rewards to be gained in heaven for the morally virtuous.

Reverend Gleeson loved to lecture on the benefits of moral virtuosity, during which he'd tilt his head and stare out at the congregation over his glasses. His gaze would wander about the church, settling occasionally on a congregant, as if his words on morality had been uttered for their benefit.

Each time his gaze settled on Bella, her cheeks flamed, as if betraying her guilt. But for what, she couldn't fathom. Memories of her past remained resolutely out of reach—save the occasional flare of terror that gripped her each time she tended to the fire. An accident she'd sustained as a child, her husband said. As to the rest of her life—her marriage, her children—at times, a memory pushed into her mind, only to recede again.

All she knew was that she'd had a tendency to wander about, a reputation that the village gossips relished. Mrs. Chantry, that poisonously pious woman at the school, had called her a *hussy*.

Which would have made her laugh had it not been the opposite of the truth. Wasn't a hussy supposed to have intimate relations with all manner of men?

She didn't even have relations with her husband—not that she recalled what *relations* were, or whether she enjoyed them. Other than kissing her—and what a kiss that was; she could still recall the wicked warmth pulsing in her center—he barely touched her.

In short, he didn't *want* her. Which made the envious glances from the women in the village all the more unjustified.

Envy, according to Reverend Gleeson, was a sin that women had a greater propensity for. Women, with their restricted lives and limited intellect, were tempted to look beyond their world, into the lives of others. In his view—which, according to him, was also the Almighty's view—a woman could only achieve redemption if she accepted her lot.

How she wanted to stand up and declare his pontifications to be nonsense! They were words spoken by men to subjugate women. But the other women in the congregation—except perhaps Sophie, Bella's only friend—nodded their bonneted heads, thereby perpetuating their fate, and the fate of their daughters.

Which was why Roberta's unruliness was something to be celebrated, despite what that hag Mrs. Chantry said about the girl.

Bella glanced across the kitchen table at the daughter she still had no recollection of, save the past month. Roberta pulled a face, and, with a sigh, Bella lifted the lid from the pot, releasing the aroma of lamb stew.

Her husband leaned forward and frowned.

"There's not much there, Bella, love. We don't want to be seen as poor hosts."

She gritted her teeth. "Perhaps you shouldn't have invited Mr. Ryman for supper if you didn't want to be seen as a poor host."

"It reflects on you, love, seein' as you're the woman. Couldn't you have added more potatoes?"

"I've had much to do today, Lawrence," she said. "You're lucky I've had time to cook anything, given the state of those trousers of yours—they'll have to be soaked for days."

Jonathan burst into laughter, spitting out his drink, before letting out a volley of coughs.

Lawrence glanced at Mr. Ryman and shook his head. "See what I have to endure, Ned?"

Mr. Ryman narrowed his eyes. He might be Lawrence's friend, but he always filled Bella with discomfort. She could never quite identify it, but he seemed to look at her as if she had no business living at Ivy Cottage.

Did he object to her having his niece's gowns? Perhaps he felt she was incapable of taking care of them as Sophie had. She'd tried her best to mend the tear in the gown she was wearing today—but she was unable to match the color of the cotton. But it was the best she had, except her Sunday dress, which she'd set to soak that morning to remove a stain on the skirts.

"Leave her be, Lawrence," Mr. Ryman said. "There's plenty enough to go round—unless young Jonathan eats it all." He turned to the boy. "I swear you've grown a full ten inches since I last saw you."

The boy jumped up and down. "You're funny, Mr. Ned!"

"He's grown half an inch," Bella said. "I measured him. We're marking his height on the doorframe to the children's bedroom, aren't we, Jonathan?"

Mr. Ryman's eyes widened. "*You* measured him—then marked the walls?"

What was it that he didn't like about her?

"Why shouldn't I?" she asked.

"Bella," Lawrence growled. "Ned's your guest. And he's hungry."

Curse him! Always giving orders. She ladled stew into a bowl and pushed it toward Mr. Ryman.

"Thank you, Mrs. Baxter."

Dislike her he might, but at least he had manners.

She served the rest of the stew, filling her husband's and children's bowls before ladling the remains into hers.

"You've left hardly any there for yourself, Mrs. Baxter."

"Leave her be, Ned," Lawrence said. "She's probably not hungry after sittin' at home all day."

"I can answer for myself, husband," she retorted.

He gave Mr. Ryman a see-what-I-have-to-put-up-with look before resuming eating.

"It's a pity your niece was unable to visit, Mr. Ryman," Bella said. "Sophie's my only friend here. She was so kind to me when I arrived."

"She's a good girl, is Sophie," Mr. Ryman replied. "But she's too busy courting to spend time with her old uncle."

"Courting?" Bella asked. "Is it that young man from the big house—the gardener's boy?"

"Aye, Sam, his name is. Sam Cole."

"He's a good worker," Lawrence said, between mouthfuls of stew. "Knows a thing or two about plants. He'd be a great help if I secured that job for Mr. Trelawney."

"He's very taken with Sophie," Mr. Ryman said. "I favor the match."

"Does Sophie want the match, Mr. Ryman?" Bella asked.

"I think so."

"Shouldn't you ask her, before deciding her fate?"

"Bella," Lawrence growled, but their guest raised his hand.

"It's a fair question, Mrs. Baxter. She seems sweet on him, though she has no mother to advise her, poor lass—only her old uncle."

"She's a fool if she doesn't accept him," Lawrence said. "And he'd be a fool if he didn't offer for her. She keeps house for you beautifully, Ned. You're a lucky man."

"As are you, Lawrence," Mr. Ryman said. "Sophie tells me your wife is skilled at sewing."

"A wife needs to do more than sew on a button, Ned," Lawrence said, laughing. "My Bella here could learn a thing or two from your Sophie."

Mr. Ryman scowled.

"Oh, *could* I?" Bella said, folding her arms. Why did the men always belittle a woman's efforts?

"Bella, stop your nonsense and pour the tea. It must be right brewed by now."

Oh Lord—she'd forgotten the tea!

She pushed back her chair, wincing as it scraped against the floorboards.

"Careful!" Lawrence said. "That's the floorboards needin' another wax." He turned to Roberta. "Mind you don't pick up any bad habits from your mother."

"Ha-ha!" William cried. "I wouldn't be a girl if you gave me a hundred sovereigns!"

Roberta stuck out her tongue.

"Roberta," Lawrence said, "I hardly think—"

"You're quite right, Billy," Bella said. "A hundred sovereigns isn't nearly enough to compensate for being a woman in *this* house."

Lawrence opened his mouth to reply, and she glared at him.

Go on—I dare you. One more word and you'll regret it.

His eyes widened, then he closed his mouth again.

Turning her back, she lifted the lid of the teapot and stirred the contents. Titters of laughter and whispers filled the kitchen, but she was too tired to bother herself with whatever nonsense the children were indulging in. When she returned to the table, her husband and the children were eating their stew with an air of nonchalance. Only Mr. Ryman looked uncomfortable.

Something was afoot.

"There's no need to pour the tea," Lawrence said. "Finish your stew first."

Surprisingly considerate of him—he usually demanded his tea at every opportunity.

She picked up her fork, her skin tightening at the feeling that several pairs of eyes were on her. Then she took a mouthful of stew.

The acrid taste flooded her senses, and she spat it out with a cry.

Someone had dumped a packet of salt into it.

The children burst into laughter, and Lawrence threw his head back, roaring with mirth. She curled her hands into fists, suppressing the urge to take a griddle pan to his head.

Was she nothing but an object of ridicule? Mr. Ryman was the only one who seemed unamused.

She wiped her mouth and pushed her bowl aside. Then her husband reached across the table and caught her hand.

"Bella, love—it's just a bit of harmless fun."

"All part of a woman's lot," she said bitterly. "I trust your Sophie will have better luck than I, Mr. Ryman."

Their guest colored and said nothing.

"There's no need to bring Ned into it, love," Lawrence said.

"You started it!" she cried.

"Bella…"

She snatched her hand free and forced a smile.

"No matter, husband," she said. "I know my place."

He nodded, then smiled at Mr. Ryman. "See, Ned? A good woman knows her place. And a hot-tempered woman only needs to cool off, then she's right again."

"I thank you for your correction, husband," Bella said, picking up the teapot. He tensed as she poured tea into each cup. When she set the pot down again, he relaxed and leaned back.

"That stew were proper tasty, Bella, love."

She smiled back, picking up the milk jug. Then she leaned over and tipped its contents over her husband's trousers.

"Shit!" He leaped back, his chair clattering on the floor.

"Oh, husband," she said, shaking her head. "Such unseemly language. How can you set such a poor example to our children?"

"Shit!" Jonathan cried.

"Jonathan!" Lawrence tugged at his trousers while milk soaked into the material, dripping onto the floor to form a puddle at his feet. "Bloody hell—they're ruined."

"Bloody hell!" Jonathan echoed.

"Stop that!" Lawrence said. "Bella—what the devil did you think you were doing?"

She met his gaze. "Why, husband—I thought you needed a little cooling off. Your temper tonight is hotter than mine."

"You've ruined my trousers!"

"Then I must rinse them."

Bella approached the sink, already filled with water to wash the dishes. Then she dipped a saucepan into the water and returned.

"Don't you dare," Lawrence growled.

"Go on, Mama!" Jonathan cheered.

"Very well." She jerked forward, and the water flew through the air in an arc before it landed on her husband. His mouth opened and shut, as if he struggled to speak. Then he shook his head, sending droplets of water flying.

The children burst into laughter, and Mr. Ryman, despite being splashed with water, let out a chuckle. "You have to give your wife credit for giving as good as she gets."

"Wait until I get my hands on you, woman!" Lawrence cried.

"You'll have to catch me first!" Bella held up the saucepan. "And I'm armed!"

He convulsed, and, for a moment, she thought he was going to burst with rage. Then his mouth twisted into a smile, and he leaped toward her. She turned and fled from the kitchen.

"Get her!"

A clatter of footsteps followed her. She pushed open the front door, then darted to the right, skirting around the side of the house to the garden, where she could hide in the children's den—the last place he'd expect to find her, given the unsavory items they collected.

Before she could reach the den, an excited voice cried out, *"There she is! I said she'd be in the garden!"*

Three small figures headed toward her. The first collided with her, wrapping its arms around her waist, followed by another, and another. She lost her balance and crashed to the ground, falling face down in the mud, taking the children with her.

With a cry, the children leaped to their feet.

"Mama! Are you all right?"

"Don't be silly—she's fallen down."

"Are you hurt? Don't be angry—we didn't mean to hurt you!"

Roberta's plea tore at Bella's heart, and she shivered at the fear in her daughter's voice.

She rolled onto her back to find her children standing over her. Roberta and William's faces were streaked with mud. But Jonathan was caked—his was indiscernible beneath a thick layer of mud, save for a red mouth and a bright pair of eyes.

Like a mole—a mole topped with hair the color of carrots.

She bit her lip to stem the tide of mirth, while her body shook.

"Mama?" Jonathan's eyes widened, and Bella descended into a volley of laughter.

"Oh, Jonathan—you look so…" She drew in a shuddering breath. "You look like a mole!"

Jonathan screwed up his eyes, his mouth creasing as he let out a wail, and Bella sat up and pulled him into her arms.

"Oh, my precious boy!" she said, shaking with laughter. "How dull life would be if I didn't have you." She glanced up at the twins. "All of you."

"What's all this?" a deep voice asked. "Children, go back inside. Mr. Ryman's all on his own."

Bella's laughter died as her husband came into view. She gave Jonathan a squeeze of affection, then kissed the top of his head.

"Run along," she said. "Leave your clothes in the kitchen and I'll give them a rinse tonight."

"Yes, Mama," the boys replied.

Roberta hesitated.

"What is it, Bobby?" Bella asked.

"Don't be angry with her, Papa," the girl said. "I like her when she laughs."

"I'm not angry," he said. "I could never be angry with"—he hesitated—"your mother."

Roberta skipped inside, yelling at her brothers to remove their muddy clothes.

Bella looked up at her husband. He offered his hand, and she stared at it.

"Shall we call a truce?"

"How can I trust you?" she asked.

"You can't."

She sighed. "I suppose I shouldn't expect anything more from you."

She took his hand. He pulled her up, then lost his balance, and they crashed to the ground. He let out a laugh, and she found herself caught up in his mirth, and they lay on the ground, shaking with laughter while he continued to hold her.

She tipped her head up to face him, and her heart fluttered at the expression in his clear gray eyes—she had never seen such joy in him before. Their laughter died, and, for a heartbeat, they simply stared at each other.

Then he lowered his mouth onto hers.

His kiss was gentle—lips caressing hers, coaxing her to yield and soften in his arms.

And soften she did, relishing his strength and the feel of his body enveloping hers. He stroked her lips with his tongue, and she parted them, inviting him in, relishing his taste while he teased and caressed her mouth. Then he withdrew and placed a trail of tiny kisses along the seam of her mouth, before nuzzling the tip of her nose with his.

Sweet heaven, how could such a large man—such a *beast*—show such gentleness, elicit such pleasurable sensations?

Was this what it was like to make love?

He would have no need to ask—after all, in the eyes of the law and the church, she was his for the taking. Perhaps he waited for an invitation.

But how could she invite him when she knew not what to say?

But her body knew. She had only to listen to the needs of her flesh—the needs that had plagued her at night from the moment he'd touched her breasts, where the little peaks at the center had hardened, bringing forth such a pleasurable sensation…

She arched her back, and he let out a low growl.

"Lawrence…"

"Bella," he said. "My Bella…"

Then he stiffened and drew back, slowly climbing to his feet, and helped her up.

"We should tidy ourselves up," he said. "Who knows what the children are doing to Ned in there? Come on."

Then he thrust his hands into his pockets and returned to the cottage.

Blinking back tears, she followed.

Why had he rejected her? Was it because Mrs. Chantry was right, and that she was a hussy? Yet he must have wanted her before, or else they wouldn't have the children.

She fingered her necklace—the delicate chain with its pearl pendant. Something she'd had since a child, Lawrence said, though she couldn't recall it—or anything from her past.

What had she done in the past that he found her so repugnant? Was it to do with the nightmares that plagued her—visions of flames engulfing her while a woman's plaintive screams filled her ears…

Why couldn't she remember?

Chapter Twenty-Five

"Bloody hell, Lawrence—you need to stop this."

Lawrence glanced across the desk at his friend. There was no need to ask what Ned meant by *this*. While they indulged in a bottle of ale in his study, the source of *this* slept downstairs in the parlor.

"Stop what?" Lawrence asked.

Ned rolled his eyes. "You're a scoundrel, but I never took you for a simpleton. You know what I'm talking about."

"She's better off than—"

"No!" Ned slammed his bottle on the desk. "Don't use that excuse! You think that because she was at risk of a life of abuse at the hands of some duke, that gives *you* the right to abuse her?"

"It's hardly abuse."

Ned's eyes flashed with fury. "I almost caught you rutting her in the garden!"

"I stopped myself."

"No matter—she's already ruined."

"Nobody need know."

"Don't be a child!" Ned scoffed. "You think folk won't make up their own minds about what she's been up to? You know what young Tommie's mother has to deal with—a respectable widow, but just because she earns a bit teaching some of the farm laborers to read, the wagging tongues in the village say that she runs a brothel. Them that gossip in High Society won't be any better." He shook his head. "I knew I should have stopped you when I first realized what you were doing. I bloody *knew it!*"

"Then why don't you put a stop to it now?"

"Because it'd destroy her—and I'm not doin' your dirty work. You have to tell her before it's too late."

It's already too late for me.

Lawrence couldn't imagine not having her in his life. The children had never been cleaner. Jonathan, while still timid, seemed happier. William, though still full of mischief, at least did what he was told—most of the time. As for Roberta—for the first time in months she gave more than monosyllabic answers when he asked her a question. And though Bella had taken to putting all sorts of nonsensical ideas into her head, such as why women should have the same opportunities in life as men, he had to admit that his daughter—in fact, all his children—were a joy to be around.

As for *her*…

Lady Arabella Ponsford had a vile temper. But Bella Baxter…

Bella had a temper, but rather than coming from a meanness of the soul, it came from a desire for justice—justice for her, justice for women, and justice for his children. Many said that the fiercest creature in the world was a female protecting her young. The children might not be Bella's, but she protected them with a ferocity that warmed his heart.

Which only made his deception worse. Bella Baxter was the better person—but she didn't exist. She was an imposter—as if Lady Arabella Ponsford had been killed and replaced by another.

And he'd been the one to kill her.

He set his ale aside. *Fuck*—it must be strong. An excess of liquor always did elicit uncomfortable truths.

Or had his conscience finally awoken?

Either way, he'd made an almighty mistake.

"Bella's happy here," he said.

"A lame excuse," Ned replied. "How can she be happy with her lot when she didn't choose it? She's uttered no vows of obedience, no pledge to serve you."

"Neither does any servant, Ned. Do you think them that had to obey Lady Arabella's orders were willing? No—they had no other choice."

"But *she* has a choice," Ned said. "Like it or not, she's different to the likes of us. You can argue about the fairness of that till your cock drops off, but it's not for us to change the world, or to run about in mobs cutting off the heads of folk that have more than us out of resentment."

"That's a big leap from a man wanting justice to a revolutionary."

"Not from where I'm sitting."

"So, I should send her back to that worthless lecher who'll treat her as nothing more than a possession?"

"How does that differ to the way *you're* treating her?" Ned asked. "She's a possession—living in a cottage rather than a mansion. Or perhaps you consider yourself the better man because you *know* what you're doing to her is wrong."

"I do know it's wrong, Ned," Lawrence said. "I've struggled to reconcile myself with my conscience these past weeks."

"Which makes you worse than the duke," Ned said coldly. "He's been brought up to expect to have ownership over others. He's like the fox—an animal that kills livestock because it knows no better. But *you*"—he jabbed his finger at Lawrence's chest—"you're like a murderer—you know it's wrong, yet still you do it."

Lawrence leaped from his seat, curled his hand into a fist, and rammed it into Ned's chest.

"I'm not a murderer!" he cried. "She's safer with me than she ever could be with that man. I won't send her back to him—he'll never care for her, much less love her! Whereas I…"

He trailed off.

Bloody hell—where had *that* come from?

Ned sat back, rubbing his chest.

"*Fuck*, that hurt. I don't know why you won't take part in the bouts at the Oak. You'd make a packet."

"I'm a gardener, not a knucklehead."

"And you're a fool who's waded into water too deep for him."

"What do you mean?"

Ned frowned. "Why did you say the duke wouldn't love her?"

"Because their sort don't know the meaning of the word."

"Whereas you do?" The anger in Ned's eyes disappeared. "Bloody hell, man—what have you got yourself into?" He shook his head. "I should have known—I've seen how you look at her. Even my Sophie's remarked on it."

"Sophie?"

"My niece is a bright girl," Ned said. "And seein' as nobody in the village will have much to do with Lady—with Bella, she's taken a liking to her. Always a friend of the misfit, is my Sophie—the first to take pity on a bird with a broken wing."

"And what does she say?" Lawrence asked.

"Rather a lot about you. Even more about her."

"Such as?"

"She says you work her too hard, and that while *Bella* knows little about running a home, she tries harder than most, despite her fears."

Lawrence leaned forward. "What fears?"

"She's terrified of fire," Ned said. "The day after you brought her here, when my Sophie came round to help, she near screamed the place down when she opened up the range to stoke the fire. But you must know that, seein' as she's laid fires and cooked for you every day since."

Yes, she had. She'd undertaken every chore he'd written out for her. Not always uncomplainingly, but she'd done them: washing his clothes, sweeping the floors, putting food on the table—granted, not always the most appetizing of dishes, but at least she'd tried.

As for the fires, he'd often seen her kneeling beside the fireplace, tending to the fire, her eyes illuminated in the orange glow of the flames with what looked like wonder.

But perhaps it was terror.

His chest tightened at the merest thought of her being afraid. Why hadn't she told him?

Because you're the last person she can turn to. You're the cause of her misery.

"Oh, Bella…"

Ned let out a mirthless laugh. "You've got it bad. Perhaps that's your retribution for having abducted her—guided by your cock rather than any sense of justice."

"I've not touched her, Ned."

"Not for want of lust. I bet you fist yourself to sleep every night with her name on your lips. Not that I blame you. She's comely enough—but not for the likes of us."

Lawrence opened his mouth to protest, then closed it. There was little point in lying. Many a night he'd woken, his cock hard and ready at the thought of her—stroking himself until he spent into his hand, crying her name. Then he'd mopped himself up, overcome with shame and the fear that she'd ask why his sheets were stained.

But she never asked. In her innocence, she'd have no idea of his depraved activities—or how greatly he wanted to spend inside her.

He was a beast—an uncouth, vile beast who lusted after the lady he'd taken captive.

But when he'd held her in his arms not one hour ago, their laughter echoing around the garden, he'd finally admitted to something other than lust.

Love.

Ned let out a chuckle. "I might have something—or someone—to solve your problem. Remember Millie?"

"Millie?" Lawrence asked, feigning nonchalance. There was no forgetting Millie, with her skills at bringing a man to pleasure.

"You know full well who I mean," Ned said. "She's staying at the Oak for a few days—on her way to visit her sister. She asked after you."

"Did she?"

"Aye—even while she was giving me a little...*comfort*, she asked whether you'd be visitin' her. She's very discreet, is Millie, and she wouldn't charge an old friend."

Lawrence shook his head. He'd long ago lost his appetite for any woman other than Bella.

He should have realized that way back—even when she was Lady Arabella, triumphant from having destroyed his livelihood, he'd fallen under her thrall the moment he kissed her.

"I can't, Ned," he said. "But I should speak to Millie—I wouldn't want her recognizing Bella. And I wouldn't want Bella seeing us—I can't have her upset."

"Bloody hell," Ned sighed. "You *have* got it bad. Come to the Oak tomorrow—I'll take you to Millie."

"Thank you," Lawrence said. "You're a good friend—better than I deserve."

"Oh, I think you're getting what you deserve, judgin' by that lovesick expression on your face," Ned replied. "You were always one to say that a sinner reaps their rewards eventually. Perhaps you're beginning to understand that lesson yourself."

Chapter Twenty-Six

Bella shifted her basket from one arm to the other, wincing at the ache in her shoulder.

"I said you'd bought too many potatoes," her companion said.

"William's fond of my potato pie, Sophie, and when they're being practically given away, I can't leave them be."

"Isn't Mr. Baxter generous with the housekeeping?"

"He gives me what he can."

Sophie grinned. "I'll bet he does. I overheard Mrs. Gleeson saying you were the luckiest woman in the county—and she's a vicar's wife!"

"Sophie, you mustn't speak of such things," Bella said, glancing about. "The women of the village say enough about me as it is."

"Take no notice. They're only jealous because you've caught yourself such a virile husband."

"Sophie!" Bella cried. Though she had little understanding of what Sophie referred to, she knew enough to understand it wasn't a topic on which a young woman should speak. "I trust Sam's not been taking advantage of you."

Sophie colored. "Sam's a good man—he wouldn't do nothing to dishonor me, but seein' as we're betrothed, I see no harm in having a bit of a kiss and a cuddle." She lowered her voice. "The way a man pushes his tongue into your mouth—I'd never have thought it'd be so…"

"Pleasurable?" Bella suggested, tempering the little pulse of need at the memory of Lawrence's kiss.

"I'm quite envious of you, having a man to kiss you every day like that. It must be wonderful."

"It is," Bella said.

Or it would be if he kissed me every day.

"And then, at night..." Sophie continued. "I know it's not proper to speak of such things, but I never knew my mother, and my aunt passed when I was young. There's only Uncle Ned, and I can hardly ask him. I hope you don't mind."

Bella glanced at her friend—the eager young girl betrothed to an amiable, soft-spoken young man. Sophie had a life of fulfilment and love ahead, with a man who adored her.

She and Bella were of similar age—perhaps a year apart. But next to her, Bella felt like an aged aunt watching a young girl through envious eyes.

"Does it hurt much?" Sophie asked. "Mrs. Chantry said I'd bleed like a pig on my wedding night."

"She said *what*?"

"Will I bleed every night? I mean—I know I bleed every month, but it doesn't hurt, least not at the time, though my body aches before."

"I-I don't know," Bella said. "I can't remember."

"But surely each night when Mr. Baxter..." Sophie trailed off. "Oh, forgive me! I know I shouldn't speak of it, but I'm"—she lowered her voice—"I'm frightened. Sam's a big lad. I don't know if I..."

Bella took her hand. "Do you love Sam?"

"More than anything."

"And does Sam love you?"

"Oh yes!" Sophie cried, her eyes glistening. "Only the other day, he walked nearly three miles to fetch me buttercups from the meadow beyond the river, just because I said I liked them. He even fell in the river on the way there."

Bella shuddered at the memory of water engulfing her—the cold seeping into her bones, her skirts binding her legs, pulling her down, until an explosion of pain plunged her into darkness…

"Bella?"

She blinked and resumed her attention on her friend.

"Will Sam hurt me?"

"No, Sophie dearest," Bella said, caressing the girl's hand. "Sam won't hurt you. He's a good, kind young man. Lawrence says he's working hard so he can take care of you after you're married. But you must be honest with him, as you're being with me. If you fear anything, you must tell him—if you can trust him."

"Oh, I can trust him," Sophie said, her eyes filled with love. "Just like you can trust Mr. Baxter."

Bella looked away.

How she longed to trust her husband—longed to speak of her fears and to bury herself in those strong arms of his. But save the briefest flash of compassion in his eyes, she saw nothing but deception—as if he could never fully reveal himself to her.

And if he couldn't trust her with himself—his *true* self—how could she trust him?

They continued along the road, nearing the inn on the opposite side. A flame-haired woman emerged from the inn, dressed in a bright-green gown. She raised her hand to shield her eyes from the sun and glanced about, as if looking for someone. With plump red lips and a rosy complexion, she was the most beautiful creature Bella had seen.

Then her gaze fell on Bella, and her lovely face creased into a frown.

"Sophie, do you know that woman?" Bella asked.

"That's Amelia," Sophie replied. "She's staying at the Oak for a few nights. Never mind her—come and have a look at Hall's. They've got some new ribbons in the window that'll do very well for my wedding gown."

"*How* do you know her?"

"Uncle Ned's been visiting her." Sophie colored and lowered her voice. "She's one of—*them*. Take no notice." Then she slipped off toward the building opposite the inn bearing the sign *Hall's Haberdashers*.

Bella glanced at the woman.

Them.

A small, innocent-sounding little word that carried with it a whole host of sins.

Working women, some called them. Mrs. Gleeson, with her more charitable turn of phrase, referred to them as *fallen women*.

Whores. That was what Mrs. Chantry said—a word uttered in hushed whispers by the village gossips. A handful of them occupied rooms at the inn, providing travelers with comfort—or so Mr. Ryman called it. Of course, the travelers paying to enjoy such *comfort* were not derided. No—the derision of the world was reserved for the women.

They were no different to wives—they lived in a world ruled by men, and serviced men's needs. What did it matter whether the man dropped a few coins into his wife's hand for housekeeping at the beginning of the day, or dropped a few coins into a doxy's hands after a night in her bed?

It was an act that men and women had shared or thousands of years.

Except she and her husband.

Stop it, Bella—you're being melancholy.

And envious.

But she envied Sophie. Who wouldn't envy such a bright young woman with her young man so obviously in love with her? And, as she stared at the doxy standing beside the inn, Bella found herself envying her also. She envied the confidence Amelia exuded as she acknowledged the admiration of the men who walked past—the butcher's boy whose eyes were as wide as saucers; Reverend Gleeson, who, despite his piety, couldn't disguise the desire in his eyes; and the man who approached the woman, arms outstretched…

Sweet heaven!

It was Lawrence.

He called out, his deep voice treacherously familiar, and the woman turned toward him, her lips curving into a beautiful smile.

"My Lawrence!" she cried. "I've missed you. My bed's in need of a good warmin'."

Bella's chest tightened at the joy in his eyes, and the smile he rarely turned on her.

She fisted her hands, fighting the urge to swing her basket at her deceitful husband. But what would that achieve? Further humiliation as the population of Brackens Hill witnessed his desire for another?

Sophie's attention was firmly on the ribbons in the window. Bella grasped her arm and pulled her inside the shop. Then she stared out of the window, making a pretense at studying ribbons while Sophie squealed in excitement at the wares on display.

Lawrence was still talking to the doxy. Then he took her by the elbow and glanced over his shoulder, and they hurried inside the inn.

Together.

"Mrs. Baxter, is there anything I can help you with?"

Bella turned to see Mrs. Hall standing beside her.

"N-no, I'm just with Miss Ryman here."

"Ah yes, Miss Ryman. How are the wedding preparations going?"

"Very well, Mrs. Hall," Sophie said. "I just need some ribbon to trim my bonnet. Uncle Ned said I can choose anything I want."

"How about *you*, Mrs. Baxter? Will you be needing a ribbon?" Mrs. Hall glanced at Bella's gown, and sympathy shone in her eyes as she studied the frayed neckline and the poorly concealed mend on the sleeve.

"Do buy one!" Sophie said. "If you took that pink one, we could make a sash for your gown. You want to look pretty for my wedding, don't you? Mr. Baxter would like that."

Bella glanced at the ribbon. Such a rich shade of pink—the same color as the roses she'd brought inside from the garden that had long since faded. But a woman with three children to feed had no business wasting her housekeeping on ribbons.

"I can't..." Bella hesitated, aware of two pairs of eyes on her.

I can't afford it.

What would Lawrence say if she wasted his money on such frivolities? It wasn't as if a ribbon on her gown would make him appreciate her—not when he had all the women of the village eyeing him with appreciation, including that painted beauty at the inn.

"I can't indulge in such frivolities," she said, tilting her chin.

Sophie's eyes widened. "There's no need to be so uncivil to Mrs. Hall. Her family's lived here for hundreds of years, whereas you—"

"That's all right, Miss Ryman," Mrs. Hall said, placing a light hand on Bella's arm. "Mrs. Baxter meant no harm, did you, dear? It must be tough living in a new place where everybody knows everybody else, and they're all eager to poke their noses into your business. We don't all have to like the same things, do we?"

"No," Bella said, glancing at the ribbon.

Mrs. Hall plucked the ribbon from the display and clicked her tongue in annoyance.

"Oh, that Rosie!" she said. "I told her to put the new ribbons on display—not *this*."

"It's very pretty," Sophie said.

"Aye, but there's no more of it. I asked Rosie to discard it." Mrs. Hall held it out to Bella. "I don't suppose you'd have a use for it, would you, Mrs. Baxter?"

"Mrs. Hall, I couldn't possibly—"

"Yes, you *could*, dear," Mrs. Hall said. "I was only going to throw it away. You'll be doing me a service."

Bella glanced at Sophie, then shook her head.

"Have you chosen, Miss Ryman?" Mrs. Hall asked.

Sophie nodded.

"Rosie!" Mrs. Hall cried. "Come out and tend to Miss Ryman, would you?"

"Yes, Mama!" Moments later, a thin girl appeared, a reel of lace in her hands, and led Sophie to the back of the shop.

"Now, Mrs. Baxter, I insist," Mrs. Hall said. "Please take it. I know how hard it is coming to a new place. When folk don't know you, tongues start to wag. But I wouldn't want you thinking badly of Brackens Hill. Folk aren't used to strangers, that's all." She held out the ribbon. "Please."

Could the humiliation get any worse? Mrs. Hall had all but told Bella the village thought her a wanton—and now she believed her to be a case in need of alms, like one of Mrs. Gleeson's waifs, for whom she collected rags every Saturday.

"I-I won't take charity, Mrs. Hall."

"It's not charity when it's a gift, is it?" Mrs. Hall said. "Don't you want to look pretty for your friend? When she was in here last, she said you were going to embroider roses on her wedding gown. She showed me a handkerchief you'd embroidered—you've a real knack for choosing the right colors. I'm sure you'll make her look real pretty, and I say you deserve a little reward for it. Were you perhaps a seamstress before you married?"

Heat rose in Bella's cheeks. "I-I can't remember, Mrs. Hall."

"That's a rare shame." Mrs. Hall patted Bella's hand. "I daresay that husband of yours hasn't seen fit to tell you. Men—they're all the same! They think we women chatter too much, yet they say nothing."

She glanced up. "Ah! All done, are we, Miss Ryman? Very good. Rosie—tidy up those gloves, would you? When Sir Halford visited yesterday, Mr. Hall couldn't find any in his size, for the mess in the storeroom."

"Yes, Mama." The girl disappeared into the back of the shop.

Mrs. Hall pressed the ribbon into Bella's hand and curled her fingers around it. "There!" she said. "All ready? My—you've a lot of potatoes in that basket of yours, Mrs. Baxter. But what with those three tykes of yours, I daresay they'll have eaten the lot before the morning."

"Thank you, Mrs. Hall," Bella said, slipping the ribbon into her pocket. "I had thought I had only one friend here in Miss Ryman—but perhaps I have another."

"Of course you do, my dear. Now run along—those potatoes won't cook themselves."

As Bella left the shop, she glanced toward the inn. But there was no sign of her husband. Weighed down by the basket in her arms, and trying, with little success, to ignore the greater burden on her heart, she made her way home, buoyed by the hope that he'd be there waiting for her.

But the cottage was empty.

Chapter Twenty-Seven

"I NOW PRONOUNCE you husband and wife."

Bella blinked back tears as the newlyweds turned toward each other—Sophie, in her white muslin gown with roses embroidered on the sleeves, and Sam, in a dark brown jacket and matching breeches, his ruddy face filled with joy as he embraced his bride.

They were both so beautiful. And so happy! Bella had never seen such joy.

She placed her hand on her lap, inches from her husband's, willing him to take it. But he lifted his hand and adjusted his necktie.

Curse him—why did he have to look so handsome? His usual rugged demeanor—unkempt hair, crumpled suit, and the film of dirt that was always under his fingernails after a day's toil—was alluring enough, for it exuded a masculinity that set her heart fluttering. But decked out in his best jacket, his hair freshly combed, smelling of soap and woody spices, he was breathtaking.

No wonder every woman in the village wanted him.

And no wonder they all thought she wasn't good enough for him—the wayward wife with the past that nobody, not even her husband, spoke of.

She turned her hand, palm upward, and traced the callouses on her skin from her chores.

Chores... She'd hated them at first, but now she took comfort in them. Chores gave her a purpose—something she could take charge of. And they were something to take pride in. If she swept the floor, it became free of dust, and if she washed the windows, they became clean. They did as she bade.

Except the fire—the angry flames that sprang from the tinder, curling and crackling with a life of their own, eliciting a deep-set fear that threatened to overwhelm her as they pulsed back and forth. Each day, she fought to conquer the flames, telling them she would not be cowed.

Until recently, when her husband had begun to light the fires for her. Why, she couldn't fathom, seeing as he did little else around the house. But he insisted, wearing her resolve with something akin to guilt in his expression, until she relented.

She glanced up to see him looking directly at her, that same guilt in his eyes. Then he resumed his attention on the happy couple at the front of the church.

Was I once as happy as Sophie is now?

"Bella?"

A large hand enveloped hers.

"What did you say?" he asked.

She let out a sigh. "I was only wondering whether I was as happy on our wedding day as Sophie is now."

His eyes flared, and the guilt in them thickened. The children shifted in their seats, and three heads turned in their direction, watching their father, as if they feared his response.

"Weddings are happy occasions," he said. "Mine was no different."

Mine? Why did he respond in such a manner?

Had he been forced to marry her? Perhaps because…

Sweet Lord—had their wedding been out of necessity, like countless marriages where a woman ruined herself to catch a man, and the man was threatened into matrimony at the muzzle of a pistol?

She glanced about the church. Was that why they thought her a hussy?

The ceremony over, Bella rose and took her husband's proffered arm as they filed out of the church, the children in tow.

"May we explore the churchyard, Mama?" Roberta asked.

"No, Roberta," Bella's husband said. "It's not done to clamber over gravestones. It's disrespectful to the dead."

"The dead won't care," Jonathan said. "They're too busy being eaten by worms."

"Would a worm eat *you* if I stuffed it down your shirt?" William asked.

"Children!" Bella cried. "Leave the churchyard be. Why don't you go and speak to Thomas? He's all alone with his mother. Perhaps he needs a friend."

"Don't like Thomas," Willian said. "He pushed me at school yesterday."

"You pushed him back twice as hard, Billy," Roberta said.

Bella sighed. "Then it's time to make up and be friends again."

"*He* started it."

"That doesn't matter," she said.

"Why?" Jonathan asked.

"Because it's lonely not having any friends. Perhaps Thomas pushed your brother because he was unhappy, and it was the only way he could show how unhappy he is."

"Why didn't he just tell us?" William asked.

"Sometimes it's difficult to tell others how we feel," Bella said. "We can only talk to people we love and trust—and who love and trust us in turn. If Thomas behaves badly, we should try to understand why. Perhaps he's hurting."

"Like when I fell out of the tree and hurt my leg?" Roberta asked.

"No, Bobby," Bella said. She placed her hand over her heart. "Perhaps he's hurting *here*. Just because we can't see where he hurts, it doesn't mean he's not in pain."

A small hand took hers, and she looked down to see Jonathan

staring up at her.

"Are *you* in pain, Mama?"

"No, my love," she said, giving his hand a squeeze. "But perhaps Thomas is—and you can help him."

The boy nodded, then ran toward Thomas, his siblings in tow.

The newlyweds emerged, amid cheers from onlookers, then climbed onto a cart decorated with ribbons and flowers. Sophie tossed her posy into the air, and a volley of eager hands thrust upward until a young girl—Rosie Hall—caught it with a squeal of triumph.

"That'll be Mr. Hall needin' to save every bit of spare cash if their Rosie's next down the aisle," Lawrence said.

"Must you say such things?" Bella retorted. "If you have nothing kind to say, you should keep quiet."

His eyes widened. "I only meant that daughters are expensive."

"And sons aren't?"

"Bella, love, you know what I meant."

"I know perfectly well what you meant," she said, pulling herself free. "Women are a burden, to be cast aside when we're no longer wanted."

"Bella, what nonsense is this?"

"Do you really wish to know? I—"

"Mrs. Baxter!" a voice cried, and she turned to see Ned Ryman approaching. "Am I interrupting anything?"

"No," she said bitterly. "Nothing of any importance."

"Good." He glanced at Lawrence and frowned. Then he took Bella's hands. "I want to thank you for all the help you gave my Sophie. Her gown looks right pretty, it does. And I'm glad to see that Lawrence here isn't so mean with your housekeeping that he refuses *you* something pretty. That ribbon looks lovely. Sets off the color of your gown just perfect."

He tipped his hat, then returned to the throng to embrace the bride and shake the groom's hand.

Lawrence narrowed his eyes and glanced at her gown.

Bella placed a protective hand over the sash. "It was a gift," she said. "I-it didn't cost anything. I know we can't afford it."

Once again guilt flickered in his eyes. "You think I'm such a poor husband that I'd begrudge my wife something pretty?"

She opened her mouth to reply.

No—because you want another woman.

Then she closed it again. Why ruin such a happy day? And what would the revelation that she knew of his infidelity achieve?

She glanced around the company and caught sight of Mrs. Chantry, eyes on her, nose wrinkled in a sneer. Her breath caught in her throat as she fought to suppress a sob.

"Bella?"

Why must he speak so tenderly? She could better weather his teasing, for at least then she could fight back.

"I know what they say about me," she said. "That I'm a hussy—a wayward wife who only cares for herself."

He pulled her into his arms, and she fought the instinct to yield.

"That ain't true," he said. "You care a great deal for others—you take care of my home, my children."

There it was again—*my* home, *my* children. As if she had no right to be here.

His lips touched her forehead, his breath a warm caress, and her body tightened with the need to be cherished.

"Come on, Bella, love," he said. "Let's go."

"Aren't you spending the evening with Ned?"

"No, I want to take you home."

A flicker of hope swelled in her soul, which his next words extinguished.

"I need to turn in early if I'm to get to the Oak before dawn tomorrow."

"The inn? What business do you have at the inn?" she asked, wincing at the sharpness in her voice.

"I'm visitin' a big house about their garden," he said. "I'm hirin' a horse to ride over. It could mean a lot of work—a tidy sum of money if they'll hire me. I thought I told you."

"No," she said. "You didn't."

"Oh, well, there's no mindin' that. It'll mean I'll be out from under your feet for a few days."

"A few *days*?"

"Don't be complaining," he said. "Chances like this don't come often. The last time I had a chance like this, I…" His voice trailed away, and his expression hardened for a moment.

Then he smiled and patted her hand.

"Never mind that now," he said. "Time we returned home. Children, come on!"

WHEN THEY ARRIVED at Ivy Cottage, he pushed open the door, then stood back to let her in.

"Mercy me, it's getting right cold out there!" he said brightly, shedding his jacket. "Children—go upstairs. I want those clothes folded neatly to save your mother doing it. If anything's soiled, leave it out to wash. Don't stuff it in the closet—I'm talking to *you*, Jonathan."

"Yes, Papa!" they chorused, clattering up the stairs. Bella entered the parlor and crouched beside the fireplace, which she'd laid that morning, and reached for the tinderbox. Then she struck the flint, the spark igniting the tinder, before holding it at the bottom of the fire, waiting for the kindling to catch.

A flame sparked into life, and her chest constricted, the fear rising. Then a hand caught hers.

"Let me."

"I can light a fire, Lawrence."

"I know, but you must be tired. It's been a long day."

"No more tired than you," she said. "Don't you need to prepare for your trip tomorrow?"

"That doesn't mean I can't help you."

The flames began to curl around the logs, then, with a crack, a spark flew out. With a scream she jerked back and collided with a solid body.

Strong arms wrapped around her. Then he rose and steered her toward the sofa.

"You rest there, Bella. I'll see to the fire."

"But…"

"Must you be so stubborn, woman? I'm doin' this so you don't get hurt."

She sank onto the sofa while he poked and prodded the fire until it burned and crackled merrily.

"There!" he said, standing back. "Now you can have a bit of a rest while I finish work on my designs."

He exited the room, leaving her alone.

I'm doin' this so you don't get hurt.

"You're too late," she whispered, placing her palm over her heart.

CHAPTER TWENTY-EIGHT

"M RS. BAXTER, I want a word."

Mrs. Chantry stood at the school entrance, her expression resembling a crow ready to pick over a carcass.

"What about?" Bella asked.

"Your children, of course." Mrs. Chantry beckoned to the interior of the building. "Inside. Now."

"Would you speak to my husband like that?"

"Your husband's not here, is he?" Mrs. Chantry wrinkled her nose as if Bella exuded a bad smell.

Lawrence had been away for two days, leaving Bella friendless in Brackens Hill now Sophie had moved to the next village with Sam. With a sigh, she followed the teacher inside to where her children waited in the classroom.

William stuck his thumb in his mouth. Roberta sat, arms folded, defiance in her eyes, fidgeting as if trying to find a comfortable position. Jonathan poked Roberta in the ribs as Bella entered.

"What have you done?" Bella said.

"Ha-ha!" Jonathan sang. "Bobby's in trouble again!"

"Go and jump in a ditch!"

"Roberta Baxter!" Mrs. Chantry cried. "Didn't I tell you what would happen if you spoke again in my presence?"

Roberta opened her mouth to respond. Mrs. Chantry stepped toward her, and the little girl cringed.

"Mrs. Chantry, please explain what's going on," Bella said. "What have you done to my daughter?"

"*I've* done nothing," the teacher said. "*She's* refusing to tidy up the classroom."

Bella suppressed a laugh, remembering the battles she'd engaged in, and lost, with the children about tidying their bedchamber. "Is that *all?*"

"Isn't that enough?"

"Do the other children refuse to tidy up?"

"I don't require *them* to do it."

"Why not?"

"Because the other children are boys. Roberta is a *girl!*"

"So, you expect my daughter to clean up after everyone because she's a girl," Bella said. "That doesn't seem fair."

"It's perfectly fair, Mrs. Baxter. Your daughter will have a home of her own to keep clean, and a husband to obey. Or do you want her to fail in that as in everything else?"

"In what way is my daughter a failure?"

The teacher snorted. "*All* your children are failures. Especially that little brat." She gestured toward Jonathan. "He can't even read. He *refuses*—as I discovered only today."

"You've discovered it *today?*" Bella asked. "That doesn't say much for your teaching skills."

"He's been lying to me, and his brother and sister have been part of that deception."

"Children, is this true?" Bella asked.

Jonathan's cheeks flushed, and he looked away.

"Don't ask *them*," Mrs. Chantry said. "They're incapable of telling the truth, the vile little beasts."

Vile…

Swallowing her guilt at having used that word herself, Bella took a step toward the teacher.

"Please explain what gives you the right to describe my children as *vile*."

"They refuse to listen. They're unruly, disruptive..."

"In what way?"

"They won't stop asking questions."

"Isn't school a place to ask questions?" Bella asked. "To learn?"

"Children don't learn by asking questions—they learn by being told what to do."

Bella let out a laugh. "You can't tell children what to do!"

"You can, Mrs. Baxter, if you set a good moral example—in which you're sorely lacking."

Bella curled her hands into fists. "What right have you to speak so?"

"Someone has to say something about those brats," Mrs. Chantry said, "not to mention their slattern of a mother."

"Slattern!" Jonathan cried.

Roberta gave him a push. "Shut your mouth!"

"Desist, you brat!" Mrs. Chantry advanced on Roberta, hand raised. But before she could strike, Bella grasped her wrist.

"Don't you *dare* touch my children," she said through gritted teeth, "unless you're prepared to get what you mete out in return."

"Are you threatening me?"

"I'm defending my daughter against a bully," Bella said. "Children, wait outside."

"But Mama..." Jonathan whined.

"Outside!" Bella yelled. "Now!"

The children slid off their seats and exited the classroom.

Bella released the teacher's hand. "Leave my children alone."

"With pleasure," Mrs. Chantry said. "They're no longer welcome in my school—at least then I'll not have to deal with their whore of a mother."

"*What* did you call me?"

"You heard," the teacher sneered. "The whole village is talking about how you abandoned your husband. Ran off with a lover, no doubt, to satisfy your base urges. Then, fool that he is, he took you back when your lover grew tired of you."

"That's a lie!" Bella said. "Nothing but vile gossip you've heard—or peddled yourself. I suppose it's impossible for you to entertain the notion that the *husband* could ever be at fault?"

"A wife's duty is to keep her husband satisfied, and maintain the moral standards of the home," Mrs. Chantry said. "You, Mrs. Baxter, have failed on every count. Perhaps you're not satisfying your husband. Have you thought of that?"

"I have no knowledge of what I may or may not have done in the past," Bella said. "I only recall being pulled out of the river and subjected to the attention of strangers—until one stranger claimed to be my husband and brought me here. I don't know whether I committed the sins you accuse me of. But I do know that I'm not *satisfying my husband*, as you call it. I know that he spends his time with painted women while I remain at home cleaning up after him. Is it therefore any wonder that I object to Roberta being expected to suffer the same fate? Why should she—or any girl—submit to a man only to be cast aside when he takes a fancy to another? I chose that life by pledging obedience to my husband—but I don't want my daughter making the same mistake, unless she knows that the man of her choice will appreciate, love, and cherish her."

The teacher's eyes widened. Then she shook her head. "A woman's place is—"

"A woman's place should be wherever she wants it to be, Mrs. Chantry," Bella interrupted. "It is not to sit quietly at home while men—and women like you—blame her for the sins of others."

"If your husband's carrying on with a doxy, then he's succumbed to *her* wiles."

"So, you blame the doxy rather than the man who breaks his

vows." Bella said. "Doxies would not exist if men didn't want—"

"That's enough, you slattern!" Mrs. Chantry snarled. "With such unsavory views, it's no wonder you can't keep your husband!"

Before Bella could reply, a deep voice spoke from behind.

"I'll thank you *not* to insult my wife."

Lawrence stood in the doorway.

CHAPTER TWENTY-NINE

LAWRENCE ARRIVED HOME to find the cottage empty, the aroma of fresh bread and roast mutton in the air.

Where was Bella? She needed to be the first to hear the good news. Mr. Trelawney had agreed to hire him, provided he could finish the designs to satisfaction. He hadn't felt this elated since...

Since he'd been hired by Dunton to landscape his garden.

And look how *that* ended.

"Bella! Children!"

There was no sign of them. Even if the children had been in the garden, he'd have heard their continuous buzz of noise and laughter.

Perhaps they were still at school, though they should be home by now—it was past six.

Thrusting his hands in his pockets, he set off for the village, retracing his steps toward the inn until he reached the fork in the road that led to the school.

He found his children sitting on the wall outside the schoolroom.

"What's going on?" he asked.

"Mama's inside," Roberta said. "Mrs. Chantry wanted to see her."

Lawrence sighed. "What have you done?"

"Nothing!" Jonathan cried. "Mrs. Chantry's a witch, and she smells!"

"You shouldn't say such things," Lawrence said. "Is that why your"—he hesitated—"your mama is speaking to her?"

"She's shouting at Mrs. Chantry!" Jonathan replied. *"You* never shout at Mrs. Chantry."

"That's because she's your teacher."

"Told you," Roberta whispered at her brother, giving him a sharp nudge.

"What's happened?" Lawrence asked.

Jonathan opened his mouth, then shut it again. "Nothing."

With a sigh, Lawrence entered the building. There was no need to search for Bella—her sharp voice echoed from one of the schoolrooms, and he cringed at the memory of hearing Lady Arabella admonishing a servant.

Then Mrs. Chantry's voice filtered through the door, and he froze.

If your husband's carrying on with a doxy...

How dare the woman say such a thing!

Then Bella rose her voice in her defense of doxies, laying the blame at the feet of errant husbands.

He allowed himself a smile. Millie—who'd loathed Lady Arabella—would have liked Bella, even if Bella was the reason he'd rejected her advances.

As he reached the door, he heard Mrs. Chantry's voice.

No wonder you can't keep your husband...

Shaking with fury, he pushed open the door.

Bella and Mrs. Chantry stood facing each other. The teacher, a heavily built woman, dominated the space, but Bella held firm, her body rigid with determination.

"I'll thank you not to insult my wife," he said.

Bella stiffened and turned toward him, her face flushed. "L-Lawrence..."

He held out his hand. "Come here, Bella."

She stared at it, then met his gaze, and his heart ached to see the sorrow in her eyes.

Where was the firebrand—the harpy?

"Mrs. Chantry, why did you refer to my wife as a..." He could hardly bring himself to utter the word.

"Are you blind?" the teacher replied. "We've heard the stories. Not that we blame *you*."

"What stories?"

"Lawrence, no," Bella said. "Not here. The children—"

"Are outside and can't hear us. What stories, Mrs. Chantry?"

"A-about your wife."

"My wife?" He stepped toward the teacher, and she moved back.

"Perhaps I was mistaken," Mrs. Chantry said. "I-I heard your wife had abandoned you—and you came to Brackens Hill with your children, but no mention of a wife. When they first came to school, they said they didn't have a mother—that she was dead."

Bella drew in a sharp breath.

Shit. Had the day of reckoning arrived?

"Then," the teacher continued, "she turns up showing neither remorse nor repentance. What was any reasonable person supposed to believe? When a woman abandons her husband and children, there's only one reason. She ran off with a lover."

She turned her spiteful gaze to Bella. "She won't even deny it. And to think, she's living among respectable folk here—who knows what influence she'll have on us? I've seen the influence she's had over your children! It's not virtuous. It's not—"

"Will you stop, you damned harridan!" Lawrence roared.

"Well!" the teacher exclaimed. "I've never heard anything of the like."

"Then it's time you did, Mrs. Chantry," he said. "My wife went missing through no fault of hers—not that it's anyone's business but mine. She had an accident that took her memory and nearly took her life. We're strangers to her, Mrs. Chantry—can you understand how frightening that must be? Yet she's cared for me and our children without a single word of complaint. *That* is what it means to be virtuous, and I'll thank you to show her the respect due to her, not just as my wife and the mother of my children, but because she's a better woman than you—nay, a better woman than any in the whole damned village!"

He took Bella's hand and lifted it to his lips.

"Insult my wife, Mrs. Chantry, and you insult not only me, but every virtuous woman in the kingdom. And now you've taken up enough of my time. I've been away from home and have missed my family. I don't want to spend another moment apart from them. I don't expect you to apologize, for I fear you lack the grace, but if I hear you've been gossiping about my wife, you'll regret it."

"Is that a threat, Mr. Baxter?"

"No, Mrs. Chantry," he said. "It's a promise that you'll reap the consequences of your sins—a lesson I'm sure you teach the children in your charge every day. Do I have your promise that you'll desist from gossiping about my wife? I won't leave this room until I do."

The teacher glanced at Bella, then, at length, she nodded.

"Good. I expect to hear that my wife's treated with more respect in the village from now on."

He led Bella outside to where the children sat waiting.

"Lawrence, I—"

"There's no need to say anything, Bella," he said. "I'm only ashamed."

"What for?"

"For not realizing folk were gossiping about you."

"Nothing else?"

"Perhaps I've not voiced my appreciation enough, for all you do."

She nodded, her eyes glistening, and looked away.

"Is something the matter?" he asked.

She shook her head and sighed. Then she forced a smile. "So, I've worked without a single word of complaint?"

He let out a chuckle. "I didn't think it right to tell Mrs. Chantry about the time you threw a pan at my head. I didn't want her thinkin'

I'd married a harpy."

"Or a sla—"

"Don't take names to yourself, love. I meant what I said. And I want to know if Mrs. Chantry is uncivil toward you."

"I can weather her insults," Bella said. "But the children…"

"Mama, what's for supper?" Jonathan asked.

Bella glanced at the little boy and smiled. "Roast mutton," she said. "Mr. Ryman brought round a hindquarter yesterday—said he got it cheap."

"Should I be jealous if another man's calling on you?" Lawrence teased.

Her smile died. "Why did you come by the school? It's not on the way home from the inn."

"I went home first, but you weren't there," he said. "I didn't want to wait a moment longer before telling you."

"Telling me what?" she asked, her voice tight.

"It's good news," he said. "Mr. Trelawney wants me to prepare a proposal for his garden. If he gives me the job, it'll mean a fair bit of work, but it could be good for us. You wouldn't mind a bit more money for your housekeeping, would you?"

"There's more to life than money, Lawrence."

"What about you, children?" he asked. "You'd not say no to some new toys from Midchester. We could go there for a treat."

"Oh yes, Papa!" William cried. "I'd like a *horse!*"

"You're too small, silly," Roberta said. "You'd fall off."

"Not a real horse—a toy horse, like the one I've seen Charles Merrick with. His papa buys him anything he wants. He told me so—at least, he did, until his nanny told him not to speak to me."

"You'll have to wait before you've picked every toy in the land," Lawrence said, laughing. "It's not certain that I'll be hired yet. I need to finish the designs."

"I thought you had finished them," Bella said. "You spend enough time in your study."

"Papa goes to his study to avoid having to help tidy up," Roberta said.

"No, he doesn't!" Jonathan cried. "He does it because he's a man. You're a girl, which is why you and Mama should tidy up."

"You should *all* help your mama," Lawrence said.

"Then why don't *you*, Pa?" Roberta asked.

Their arrival at Ivy Cottage spared him the necessity of responding.

Five minutes later, they sat at the dinner table while Bella dished out supper and sliced the bread.

Lawrence picked up a slice, dipped it into the gravy, then tasted it. *Delicious.*

Since when had she become such an accomplished cook? The roast mutton was tender and flavorsome, and the bread was soft inside with a crispy crust—just how he liked it. And the children loved it, judging by how quickly they emptied their plates.

He almost choked in astonishment when Jonathan offered to help Bella clear the table. But she waved the children off with a smile, and they fled from the kitchen to play outside, their shrieks of laughter echoing around the garden.

Bella pushed her bowl aside, rose, and busied herself about the kitchen, making a pot of tea and taking a dish of stewed apples out of the range. She placed one onto a dish and set it in front of him before pouring his tea. Just how he liked—with a dash of milk and a spoonful of sugar.

"Thank you, Bella," he said. "There's nothing more a man wants on coming home than a fine meal cooked by his wife."

She nodded, but the smile he'd been hoping for didn't materialize.

"I'll be seein' Ned later tonight, so I won't be gettin' under your feet." Perhaps she'd smile at that.

Instead, she frowned. "At the inn?"

"Of course—I'm in the mood for a mug of ale."

"*Must* you?"

"You wouldn't begrudge a man an evening with his friend, would you?"

She let out a sharp sigh.

"It could be good for us if Mr. Trelawney hires me," he said. "I could afford to build us a greenhouse for next year. We could even move somewhere larger—a house with two parlors, perhaps, or another bedchamber."

Next year...

What a foolish notion! He'd only meant to keep her for a month or two, and she'd been here longer than that already. Each day he woke, praying that her memory would remain buried—not because he feared retribution, but because he couldn't bear the thought of losing her.

How had she burrowed her way into his affections?

By rising to the challenges she'd faced, even though it must have terrified her—tending to strangers and coping with chores she'd never done in her life.

By her own resilience and spirit, she'd secured a place in his heart. And that heart would break if he lost her.

"Mr. Trelawney would be a fool not to hire you," she said.

"*If* I can produce designs to his satisfaction," Lawrence replied. "Or rather, his wife's. He's a merchant—a working man. But she's a lord's daughter, as he let slip. Ladies are not to be trusted."

She leaned forward, her sapphire eyes fixed on him. "Why can't ladies be trusted?"

"Because they look down on those of us who must earn our living. A lady will change her mind on a whim with no thought for the effect on others. And when she finds something not to her satisfaction, she'll go out of her way to destroy it. Not in the name of justice, but out of spite."

She shrank back. "I've never heard you speak with such hatred,

Lawrence. I take it you've suffered at the hands of a lady?"

He nodded.

"Did you seek retribution for her sins?"

"I did."

"And did you find it?"

"No." He sighed. "I only learned that in seeking retribution, I became the very thing I intended to punish."

"Was *I* there?"

He took her hand. The once-smooth skin of her fingers was covered in callouses—the trophies of physical labor.

"It matters not," he said. "What matters is that I do right by you now."

"If you can complete your designs in a manner that satisfies a lady and her whims."

He nodded. "Aye—if I can."

"*I* might have an understanding of a lady's whims," she said.

His gut twisted in apprehension. "Y-you?"

"I'm no lady, but I can appreciate beauty of form. Perhaps I could help with your designs."

"I wouldn't want to trouble you with that, love," he said. "You've enough with your chores."

"I was able to embroider roses on Sophie's gown as if I've been doing it all my life."

"Embroidery's not the same as designing a garden, Bella."

"Perhaps not in the execution," she said, "but to create a pleasing image requires the same eye for color and form—particularly if a lady is to appreciate it."

"No, Bella, it's out of the question."

"I want to help."

"I know," he said, patting her hand. "You've good intentions, but they'd come to naught. I must solve the problem myself."

"Why?"

"It's *my* dream to be a garden designer," he said. "Nobody else's."

Her eyes flashed, and for a moment, as she glanced about the kitchen, he feared she'd take a fry pan to him. But she merely withdrew her hand.

"I'll leave you to fulfill your dream," she said. "Excuse me while I take a turn in the garden. Don't bother to clear the table—I'll resume my chores when I return."

She rose and exited the kitchen.

Chapter Thirty

"Mama, look, Papa's cleared the supper things!" Bella stared at the kitchen. The plates and bowls had been neatly stacked beside the range, and the table wiped clean.

There was no sign of her husband. He must have gone to his study to work on the garden design.

My dream. Nobody else's.

She sighed and made her way to the parlor. She placed a log onto the fire, suppressing the ripple of fear as the flames swelled around it. Then she sank onto the sofa.

The children followed. Jonathan climbed onto the sofa beside her and took her hand.

"Don't be sad, Mama," he said. "You might leave us if you're sad. I'll work harder in school, then Mrs. Chantry won't be so angry with me all the time."

"What makes you think I'd leave?" Bella asked. "Has Mrs. Chantry said anything?"

The boy shook his head.

"What, then?"

He opened his mouth to reply, but Roberta gave him a push. "Jonathan's playing the fool."

"Mrs. Chantry's said nothing," Jonathan added.

"She told me you can't read," Bella said. "Is that true?"

He colored and lowered his gaze.

"There's no shame in being unable to read at your age. You're only…"

She hesitated—why couldn't she recall how old her children were?

"I'm six, Mama."

"Yes, of course."

"He *can* read," William said.

"Then why refuse to read in class?" Bella asked.

"Because I can't read *now*," Jonathan said. "I've forgotten. At least—I know what the words look like, but when I try to read, I can't *see* them."

"Did you tell Mrs. Chantry this?"

"She thinks I'm playing the fool. I can read the sign outside the school, but I can't read in class. Tommie says I'm going blind, and I might be dying. He said his Papa couldn't read, then he got pains in his head, then one day he dropped dead and never woke up."

"And you think that might be happening to you?"

Jonathan nodded. "My head hurts when I try to read. I'm frightened."

"He cries in the night," Roberta added.

"Why didn't you tell me?" Bella said, her heart aching at the distress in the boy's voice. "Or your father? Didn't you think we'd want to help?"

"Papa says I must grow up to be strong. He'd be angry if he knew. And you…" He shook his head. "I didn't want to tell you."

"If you can't tell your mother, who can you tell?"

"But you're not—*Ouch!*" Jonathan cried out as Roberta kicked him in the shin.

"Bobby, don't do that!" Bella said. She glanced about the parlor, and her gaze settled on a pile of books in the corner. She rose and picked one up. "Can you read the title?"

Jonathan narrowed his eyes.

"Lady's"—he tilted his head to one side—"maid?"

"There!" she said. "You *can* read. Try the first page."

She opened the book and handed it to him. He stared at the page and shook his head.

"The writing's a little small," Bella said. "Move the page closer."

"That makes it worse." He held the book at arm's length. "It gets better when I do this, but the writing's so small I can't read it."

Of course!

Why hadn't Mrs. Chantry noticed? Was she such a poor teacher that she refused to see what before her?

Am I such a poor mother that I also refused to notice?

The boy closed the book and threw it on the floor. Then he flinched. "Don't be angry with me, Mama!"

Bella drew him into her arms. "I could never be angry with you, Jonathan."

"*Is* he dying?" Roberta asked.

"No, Bobby. Your brother needs spectacles, that's all."

"How do you know that?" William asked.

"My papa was the same. He could read signs from afar, but he could never write letters without needing his spectacles..."

Bella's voice trailed off as the image flashed before her—a man with deep-set blue eyes and a shock of thick black hair, looking at her over the top of wire-framed spectacles, a soft smile on his lips and love in his eyes.

My papa...

She closed her eyes and reached out with her mind. But a burst of flames obliterated the image, and she startled, the memory of her lungs burning and the thick stench of smoke in her nostrils.

"*Can* Jonathan have spectacles, Mama?" William asked. "Won't they cost money? Papa might refuse."

Bella sighed. The housekeeping money Lawrence gave her was barely enough as it was.

"*I* could ask Papa if you don't want to," Roberta said.

"No—I'll ask him when he's returned from the inn," Bella said.

Softened by ale and having enjoyed the company of doxies, he might be more disposed to be generous—especially with the prospect of the money he'd earn working for Mr. Trelawney.

If Mr. Trelawney existed.

She reclined on the sofa and rubbed her temples.

"Is *your* head hurting, Mama?" Jonathan asked. "Can't you read either?"

"Don't be silly!" Roberta said. "She just read to you."

"I'm tired, that's all," Bella said. "Could you be quiet for a moment?"

The children rose and exited the parlor, and she leaned back and closed her eyes.

Moments later, a clatter of feet approached the parlor, and she heard Roberta's excited voice.

"Mama! Look what I've found!"

She opened her eyes to see her daughter standing before her, her body vibrating with excitement. Then a hard object was pressed into her hands.

"Look!"

It was a brooch—an enormous ruby set in gold with delicate filigree work around the edges. She held the brooch up, and light reflected off the planes of the gem, which seemed to pulse with life—blood red with deeper tones in the center.

She'd never seen anything so magnificent. It must be worth a fortune!

She turned the brooch over in her hands, her gut twisting as she spotted the letters etched into the gold.

A.P.

What was the name of the doxy at the Royal Oak—that one she'd seen Lawrence with? Amelia, Sophie had said.

"Mama, what's wrong?"

She glanced up to see three pairs of eyes watching her. "Where did you find this?"

"In Papa's study," Roberta said. "Hidden in his desk. But I know where the key is."

"Roberta!" Bella cried. "It's wrong to steal."

"You think Papa stole it?"

"No—I meant *you*. You can't go into his study without permission."

"I was only looking for money for Jonathan's spectacles. Why do you think Papa hid it? Is it a gift for you, Mama?"

"It can't be," William said. "Mama's name doesn't begin with A. It's for someone else."

The ruby winked malevolently at Bella, and she handed it back.

"Put this back where you found it, Roberta," she said, "and don't mention it again—not to your father, and certainly not to me."

"We could sell it. It must be worth—"

"Just *do* it!" Bella said. "Why must you question everything?"

Roberta flung the brooch to the floor and ran from the parlor. William pulled a face and ran after his sister. Jonathan burst into tears.

Bella pulled the boy into her arms. "I'm sorry, sweetheart—I didn't mean to shout at your sister. I know she was only trying to help. Please don't worry. I'll get your spectacles—whatever it takes."

"W-will you ask Papa?"

"No," Bella said, gritting her teeth. "I'll find something else to sell."

She lifted her hand to her necklace, fingering the thin gold chain. She had no recollection of it, but Lawrence said it had belonged to her since childhood.

She glanced about the parlor—at the items she had no memory of. Nothing in it belonged to her. Even her gown had belonged to Sophia. Only her petticoat was hers—she'd been wearing it when they fished her out of the river. But she could hardly sell that.

The necklace was the one link to her past. But no matter how much she'd willed her memory to return, it remained out of reach.

Maybe the past was best left buried.

She thought of her husband—and the doxy at the inn.

Sometimes it was best knowing nothing.

Chapter Thirty-One

Lawrence trudged along the path home. Sir Halford might pay well, but Lady Merrick found fault in everything. Either the rosebushes didn't produce enough blooms, or the beans in the kitchen garden refused to grow to their full height.

His answer that he wasn't responsible for the frost that morning had been met with an equally frosty reply.

"Mr. Baxter, it's your *job* to ensure the weather is fair."

At which point he'd tried to argue the beneficial effect of frosts on the parsnips and was met with an accusation of deception.

Why was it that when faced with a problem, a woman sought someone to blame rather than a solution?

Except Bella. Though she'd been irritable of late. Perhaps Lady Arabella Ponsford was beginning to resurface?

You're being unjust.

Her shortness of temper was never directed at the children—she weathered their misbehavior with aplomb. Nor was it directed at the house, which was spotless each time he came home.

It was directed at him.

He pushed open the door and entered the house.

"A lady's maid is not just a servant to dress her when she asks," a voice said from behind the parlor door. "She must also act as a—a… What's that word, Mama?"

"Confidante," Bella voice said.

"What's a confidante?"

"Someone you trust with your secrets. Like a friend."

"Like Tommie. I can tell him anything," Jonathan said. "Do you have a friend?"

"There's Sophie," Bella said.

"She doesn't live here anymore. That means you have nobody."

"I have *you*, sweet boy."

Lawrence entered the parlor. His heart swelled at the sight of Bella and Jonathan curled up in front of the fire—mother and son spending a quiet moment together.

Only they weren't mother and son.

Jonathan spotted him first. "Hello, Papa. I'm *reading* with Mama."

Something about him looked different—more grownup, somehow. Was his little boy turning into a man?

Bella glanced up, and Lawrence's chest tightened at the beautiful expression in her eyes. She looked as if she belonged there, holding his child in her arms.

"What's that you're reading?" he asked.

"*The Lady's Maid: a Guide for Aspiring Young Women,*" Jonathan said proudly. "Did I get it right, Mama?"

"You did." Bella ruffled the boy's hair and kissed the top of his head.

"What do you think, Papa?" Jonathan asked.

"You read very well, though I wouldn't have thought a book about lady's maids is right for you."

"We're going to ask Mrs. Gleeson after church on Sunday if she has a copy of Johnson's dictionary we can borrow," Bella said.

The little boy pointed to his face. "No, I mean, what do you think about *these?*"

Then Lawrence saw it.

"Are those—*spectacles?*"

The boy nodded. "They're new! Mama took me to Midchester

today and got them special. Do you like them?"

Lawrence glanced at his wife. "Shouldn't Jonathan have been in school?"

"She told Mrs. Chantry I was sick!" Jonathan said. "Do you like my glasses? They cost a whole pound!"

"A *what?*"

"A pound!" Jonathan replied. "Twenty whole shillings—I've never seen so much money in my life."

"No," Lawrence said, fighting to temper his anger. "Neither have I."

"We brought gifts for Bobby and Billy too, didn't we Mama? A toy horse for William, and a toy boat for Roberta—it looks just like Nelson's ship the *Victory*. And we bought a gift for you. Mama insisted."

"In heaven's name!" Lawrence cried. "How much did this excursion cost?"

"Two pounds," Jonathan said. "I want to go again."

"I'm sure you do, seeing as you're not the one who'll have to pay for it," Lawrence said.

Bella lifted the boy off her lap. "Jonathan, why don't you take the book upstairs and read in your chamber until supper's ready?"

"Yes, Mama!" He skipped out of the parlor.

Bella stood, wiping her hands and smoothing back her hair. Lawrence approached her, and she tilted her chin, defiance flashing in her eyes.

How he'd longed to see her spirit again. But at what cost?

"Two pounds, Bella? *Really?*"

"It's for my son."

"He's not your…" He checked himself.

"What?" she snapped, placing her hands on her hips. "Not my responsibility? Whose responsibility is he, then? Did *you* notice he couldn't see close objects?"

"No—but I'm not the one who's spent money that we can't afford," he said. "It's no guarantee that Mr. Trelawney will hire me."

"*If* he exists."

"Are you accusing me of deception?"

"I'd like to know what you're accusing *me* of."

"Of having no sense when it comes to managing money!" he cried. "Don't you know that's how families get into debt—when they spend beyond their means on frivolities they don't need?"

"Jonathan is not a frivolity!" she said. "He needed spectacles. Can you swear *you've* never wasted money on frivolities?"

"Of course I haven't!" he replied. "What the devil are you accusing me of?"

"*I'm* not the one making accusations," she said. "But rest assured, I didn't waste any of your hard-earned money today. If you have no use for the gift we bought you, then I suggest you sell it, seeing as you care more for money than your family."

Her eyes flashed with fury, and he caught his breath. Infuriating she might be, but whatever straits she'd placed them in, he couldn't deny his attraction to her. Trembling with passion, she parted her lips—and he wanted nothing more than to claim that mouth of hers and bury his hands in her hair.

He fisted his hands as his cock sprang to life. To have her writhing beneath him, teeth bared, body trembling with life, while he claimed her for his own…! It was all he could do to stop himself from tossing up her skirts and fucking the anger out of her on the parlor floor.

Footsteps clattered on the stairs, and the children appeared.

"Time for supper," Bella said. Not pausing to glance back at Lawrence, she swept into the kitchen, where she served them in silence and picked at her meal. The children watched him, fear and accusation in their eyes.

Damn her—did she seek to spoil his children with trinkets and turn them against him?

But other than admonishing William for chewing with his mouth open, she said nothing, acknowledging Lawrence with a nod when he rose from the table to resume work in the study on what he'd begun to call *that fucking garden design.*

He still couldn't picture the garden. *Something different,* Mr. Trelawney had said. Something to transport his wife to another world. Foolish man—pandering to a woman. But the prospect of a hefty fee was enough to weather the whims of any woman, provided Lawrence could come up with a design she liked.

Tiredness overcame him, and he reached forward to extinguish the candle. Then he saw it.

A small packet on the corner of the desk.

He reached for it, unlaced the string, and opened the wrapping with the name *Beachamp's, Midchester* handwritten on the front. Inside was a neatly folded, cream-colored neckerchief. He lifted it to his face and brushed it against his cheek, relishing the softness of the silk and the faint aroma of roses.

He'd torn his best neckerchief last week when he dressed for church.

And Bella had noticed.

He moistened his thumb and forefinger, pinched the candle wick, which sizzled before the flame died, then exited the study.

Low voices came from the children's bedroom. Why weren't they asleep?

He crept to the top of the stairs. Their door was ajar, and he peered through the crack.

Bella sat on Roberta's bed, Jonathan in her arms, and the twins squashed either side of her. William clutched a small wooden horse in his hands, and Roberta had a toy boat tucked under her sleeve—their gifts from Midchester.

Had Bella bought anything for herself?

"When a lady is in need of solace," Jonathan said, studying the book in his hands, "she must not disturb her father or husband with her concerns. Instead, she will turn to her maid..."

"Very good, Jonathan," Bella said, turning the page. "You read well. Mind you take care of your spectacles."

"I will, Mama."

"Tell Mrs. Chantry she must ensure you look after them as well."

"Will she be angry with me for not going to school?"

"Leave her to me," Bella said.

"What if you're not there?"

"Then you tell me, and I'll go and see her."

"No," Jonathan said, "I mean what if you're no longer here—with us?"

"Why wouldn't I be?" Bella asked.

"Are you going to leave us?"

All three children stared at her, and Lawrence held his breath.

Bella smiled and shook her head. "Of course not."

"Papa said—"

"Take no notice of Papa," she said. "I suspect he was just tired after a long day. He works very hard for us, doesn't he?"

"So, you won't go away?"

Lawrence's heart ached at the anguish in his son's voice.

"I promise," Bella said. "What mother would leave her children?"

"I want you to stay forever," Jonathan said. "I love you, Mama."

Bella kissed his forehead. "I love you too, sweet boy. I love you all—more than life itself."

She looked up and froze as she met Lawrence's gaze.

Ashamed at being caught eavesdropping, he pushed the door fully open. Four pairs of eyes stared at him.

"Children, it's time you went to sleep and let your mama rest," he said. "I'm sure she's tired and wants some respite."

"Yes, Papa," they chorused. Bella climbed off the bed, tucked the children in, then exited the bedchamber.

Lawrence caught her hand. "Bella..."

"You were right," she said. "I do want respite—I *crave* it."

"Respite from what?"

She descended the stairs to the parlor. He followed and watched her tidy the room and set out the blankets on the sofa for the night—the sofa she'd been sleeping on since her arrival.

"What do you want respite from, Bella?"

She turned to face him, her eyes filled with tears. "Your deception."

Dear Lord—was her memory returning?

"D-deception?"

She nodded. "You've taken me for a fool. I-I don't know for how long—but I know it's the worst form of deception a man can undertake."

"What have I done?"

She reached behind the clock on the mantelshelf. "This," she said, holding out her hand—and Lady Arabella's ruby brooch with its huge gemstone, winking malevolently at him, like a huge red eye.

She ran her thumb along the monogram.

"A.P.," she said. "I know who A.P. is."

Shit.

He lifted his gaze to Bella's, and the breath caught in his chest.

The sapphire eyes filled with disgust and betrayal were not the eyes of Bella Baxter.

They were the eyes of Lady Arabella Ponsford.

Chapter Thirty-Two

Lawrence stared at the brooch.

"Have you been in my study?" he asked.

"Is that *all* you have to say, Lawrence?"

"That brooch was in a locked drawer."

"Oh, I *know*," she said. "Hidden away like a dirty secret."

Guilt flickered across his expression. "What were you doing in my study?"

"I didn't go there!"

"Then who did?" His eyes narrowed. "I'll wager it was Jonathan—I've told him not to disturb my papers, the little—"

"Don't you accuse him!" she cried. "It doesn't matter who found the brooch—what matters is that it was there, and whom it belongs to." She held it out. "Take it."

"But…"

"Just take it," she said. "I don't want it."

"Then what *do* you want?"

"I want you to admit what you've done, Lawrence. You owe me that, if nothing else."

He curled his fingers around the brooch. "I'm sorry," he whispered.

He closed his eyes for a moment, before opening them and meeting her gaze. The guilt and sorrow in his eyes threatened to crush her heart—this strong, virile man crumbling before her.

But no matter how pitiful he looked, he had betrayed her. He deserved neither compassion nor forgiveness.

"Is that all you have to say?" she asked.

"What more *can* I say?"

"You can tell me her name."

He frowned. "Whose name?"

Bella gestured toward the brooch. "The woman whose brooch that is."

"I-I don't understand."

"The..." She hesitated, unwilling to speak the truth, for in voicing it, there was no returning to hope that her husband's desire for another was merely the product of her imagination. "The doxy."

"What doxy?"

"Must I write it down for you? The doxy you've been carrying on with—the one at the inn! Amelia!"

"Amelia?" He glanced at the brooch, his eyes widening in surprise. "You think the A is for *Amelia*?" He let out a sigh, almost as if in relief. "I don't know an Amelia."

"Millie, then."

"Millie?" he said. "Surely you don't think she and I..."

The recognition in his voice was admission enough.

"I don't think," Bella said. "I *know*. I saw you at the inn. You embraced her, Lawrence. Can you say in truth that you've never desired her, never"—she drew in a sharp breath to fight the sob swelling in her throat—"never lain with her?"

For a moment, he stared at her, then his cheeks reddened and he nodded. "I did lie with her."

The air left Bella's lungs, and her limbs shook, as if her body had been waiting for the final admission before succumbing to despair.

He approached her, arms outstretched. "Bella, I—"

"Stay away from me! I can't bear it!"

Her legs crumpled, and a pair of arms caught her, pulling her against his broad chest. Oh, how she'd longed for his embrace! But not like this—not after he'd admitted to wanting another.

"I knew her before I met you," he said. "Like any man, I lay with other women as I entered manhood."

She struggled to break free, but he held her firm.

"Please," she said. "Let me go!"

"Not until you hear what I have to say," he said. "Do you know the moment when I lost all desire for Millie—and for other women? It was when I first kissed *you*."

"No…" she whispered, ignoring the pleas of her heart, which yearned to believe him.

"I swear it's the truth."

Tears stung her eyes. "How do I *know* you speak the truth?"

"You don't, love," he said. "I can only ask that you trust me. I heard Millie was staying at the Oak, and I went to see her—to tell her to leave you alone, that I wanted none but you. If the brooch was for her, wouldn't I have given it to her, rather than keep it in my desk?"

"You swear?"

He nodded. "Ask Ned, if you wish—he knows her well." He released her and took her hands, bringing them to his lips. "Bella, I swear on the life of my children, I have no desire for another woman. How could I even *look* at another when I have you?"

"Then why do you never want me?"

"Oh, Bella! You've no *idea* how much I want you."

He pulled her close and claimed her mouth. Her body came alive as the air filled with the musky, masculine scent of him—of fresh grass, smoke, and wood. She let out a whimper, and he deepened the kiss, drinking her cries while a low growl reverberated in his chest.

"Oh, woman," he growled. "Don't ever think I'm not touchin' you for want of desire."

His hardness swelled against the top of her thighs, and she arched her back, thrusting her hips forward, relishing the delicious sensation of him against that part of her where the ache begged to be eased. "Please."

He stiffened and broke the kiss. She glanced up to see him gazing back at her, his eyes black with desire. Yet in their depths, she saw guilt as he pushed her back.

"Forgive me," he said. "I-I can't."

"Because you don't want me?"

"Lord no, you can't imagine how much I..." He shook his head. "Believe me, it's *you* I'm thinking of, not me."

"Do you no longer love me, Lawrence?"

He blinked, and moisture shimmered in his eyes.

"Perhaps...you never loved me? Is *that* what you were going to tell me?"

He cupped her face in his hands, the callouses on his palms rough against her skin. "No," he said. "My feelings for you have only grown."

"Then what?" she whispered. "I-I cannot bear not knowing. Every day I try to remember and my mind stumbles around in the dark, trying to find a piece of my past—who I was, what I've done. You—our children... I've fought so hard to remember."

He caressed her skin, igniting a small ripple of need. "What can you remember, Bella?"

She closed her eyes. "Sometimes I see an image—a woman kissing me goodnight...a man who smells of cigars, smiling down at me...and flames." She swallowed her fear as the image rose in her mind. "Flames and smoke. Shouting, screaming—then roaring...until it goes dark, and the image is gone. Can you understand what that's like—to have my life taken from me? When *you* deceive me, it's like my life's been taken from me again. What if my memory never returns? I don't know who I was, or what I am—whether there are people who love me or hate me. What if I *am* what the gossips accuse me of? What if I did something so sinful, but I can't remember?"

He drew her in his arms again, and she cursed herself for revealing her fears. Shame engulfed her as she closed her eyes, bracing herself for his admonishment—or worse, his laughter.

But neither came. Instead, he rocked her to and fro, soothing her with soft whispers.

"You have not sinned, Bella," he said. "*I'm* the sinner—I've sinned against you, and I pray that you'll forgive me. I should have told you the truth about the brooch."

He placed a kiss on her forehead, then caressed her hair.

"I've something to tell you," he said.

"Then tell me, Lawrence," she said. "Tell me the truth—but please, don't break my heart."

He blinked and met her gaze, his eyes dark with desire—and guilt.

He placed the brooch in her hands and curled her fingers around it. "This brooch is yours, Bella. It was made for a lady. The daughter of a duke."

She stared at it, running her fingertips over the metalwork.

"You mean—it was made for another, but she had to sell it? Do you know its history?"

"No."

"And—you bought it for me?"

His brow furrowed.

"Oh, Lawrence! It must have cost everything you have."

"I-I couldn't afford to have it made for you special."

She eyed the monogram. "This brooch and I are the same, are we not—with broken histories. But why did you hide it?"

"I-I was saving it for a special occasion."

Guilt thickened his voice, and she placed her hand on his cheek. How could she have doubted him?

"A special occasion?"

He closed his eyes, his brow creasing as if in pain. Then he opened them again, his gaze clear.

"Aye," he said. "It's a special occasion when I finally come to realize how much I appreciate having you in my life. Starting now."

He took her hand and led her out of the parlor, upstairs to his bedchamber.

Her heart soared with hope. Was he going to make love to her?

"I'll sleep on the sofa from now on," he said. "It's the least I can do for my wife."

Then, after giving her a chaste kiss on the forehead, he exited the bedchamber, closing the door behind him.

Bella turned the brooch over in her hand, then set it on a table, slipped off her gown, and climbed into the bed. Alone.

How much I appreciate having you in my life.

Would it have killed him to say that he loved her?

Chapter Thirty-Three

"There you are! I've been looking for you."

Lawrence glanced up from clipping Lady Merrick's hedge, shielding his eyes from the afternoon sun. "That you, Ned?"

His friend's head appeared over the hedge. "What's all this about you bringin' Lady Arabella to the Oak tonight? Hirin' a private parlor, so Mrs. Colt says."

"Hush!"

Ned rolled his eyes. "Ashamed of what you're doin', are you? Don't you want me to speak her name—her *real* name?"

"It's not that," Lawrence said. "It's a surprise. Mrs. Colt should mind her own business."

"It *is* her business, seein' as she's the landlord's wife," Ned said. "Plannin' on tellin' her ladyship the truth tonight, are you? Softening the blow with a slice of Mrs. Colt's steak pie and a mug of ale?"

"No."

"What, then?"

"I'm treatin' her to a meal out. She deserves somethin' special."

"You're soft in the head, wastin' good money like that," Ned said. "A man shouldn't be sellin' his things needlessly—neither should his wife, though it'd serve you right."

"She's sold nothing of mine, Ned."

"That's not what Mrs. Richards says."

"Oh, this bloody village!" Lawrence cried. "Can a man not even take a piss without it being talked about? It's that Mrs. Chantry spreadin' her lies about Bella, I'll bet."

"Mrs. Chantry?" Ned shook his head. "No, Mrs. Richards saw her with her own eyes."

Lawrence's gut twisted. "With a *man*?"

"No, you arse! She saw her in Midchester, comin' out of a pawnshop—in broad daylight, too."

What the devil was Bella doing in a pawnshop?

What had she said when he'd argued about the cost of his son's spectacles? *Rest assured, I didn't waste any of your hard-earned money today.*

"Oh, Bella—what have you done?"

Ned let out a laugh. "Not so pleasant when you're the one bein' deceived, is it?"

"Bella wouldn't deceive anyone," Lawrence said. "Or, if she did, she'd have good reason—she thinks of others before herself. And I care not how much hirin' Mrs. Colt's parlor costs. My Bella's worth every farthing."

"Sweet swivin' saints, you've got it bad." Ned shook his head. "If you've fallen for her, it'll come to no good. She's not for the likes of you, and wasting your coin on Mrs. Colt's pie won't change that—no matter how good the pie."

"And you came to tell me that?" Lawrence asked.

"I came to say that, for your own sake, you must tell Lady Arabella the truth."

"Oh!" a female voice cried. "Ned Ryman, isn't it?" Lady Merrick approached. "The hedge looks very pretty, Mr. Baxter," she said. "Just how I wanted it."

About bloody time, seeing as he'd spent three days trying to fashion the damned thing into the shape of a cockerel.

"Are you here to see Halford, Mr. Ryman?" she asked.

"No, I came to see Lawrence. He's hirin' the parlor at the Royal

Oak for"—Ned hesitated—"for his wife."

"*Is* he?" Lady Merrick glanced at Lawrence. "Well, I suppose it's up to you how to spend your money. I hope that wife of yours knows how lucky she is."

"I'm the lucky one, Lady Merrick," Lawrence said.

"That young woman made the right decision when she accepted your hand. Few men are as considerate—excepting, of course, Sir Halford. In fact, as a reward for your generosity toward your wife, you can finish up early for the day."

Lady Merrick looked at him expectantly. Recognizing the prompt, Lawrence bowed his head.

"That's very generous of you, ma'am."

Ignoring Ned's pointed stare, he gathered the hedge clippings, set them in a neat pile in the corner of the garden, then set off for Ivy Cottage.

As he approached, animated voices came from the garden.

"You blackguard!" William cried. "I'll run you through with my sword!"

"Not so fast, Monsieur Nelson. The fair maiden is mine!" Roberta's voice.

"We will defend her to the death!" Jonathan said.

"Help—help!" Bella's cries pierced the air.

"Maintain your resolve, your ladyship. I, Admiral Nelson, will rescue you from the evil Bonaparte!"

Your ladyship…

Lawrence's blood ran cold. Had she remembered?

He broke into a run as Bella cried out again.

"Help me—I cannot bear it!"

"Take that, foul beast!"

"Die, you scoundrel!"

Clatters and cracks rang out, and Lawrence sprinted into the garden.

At the far end, tied to a tree, was Bella, struggling and wailing, while the children swung sticks in the air, shrieking as they came into contact.

"What the devil's going on?" Lawrence roared.

The party froze, and four heads turned toward him.

"What did the children call you, Bella?"

"Your ladyship," she said, her smile disappearing. "You deem it inappropriate that I should be titled thus?"

"She's Lady Emma Hamilton!" Jonathan cried. "We're rescuing her from Bonaparte."

"You're what?"

"I'm Captain Ralph Miller—and Billy's Lord Nelson."

"And I take it you're Napoleon?" Lawrence asked his daughter.

Roberta frowned. "I wanted to be Lieutenant Hardy, but someone had to kidnap Mama." She turned to Jonathan. "*You* can be Bonaparte next time. Just because you're the youngest, doesn't mean you always get your own way."

"When do I get my way?" Jonathan asked.

"At supper last night, you took the biggest piece of bread, and Mama always reads you a story first."

"That's enough, children!" Bella said, laughing. "Jonathan, please untie me."

"*I'll* do it," Roberta said. "They're sailor's knots. He'll only tighten them."

Lawrence watched as his daughter deftly untied the knots. As she coiled the rope up, Bella drew her into her arms.

"Clever girl!" she said. "It takes a brave sailor to play the part of the enemy."

"Don't you hate Bonaparte for being the enemy?" Roberta asked.

"One man's enemy is another man's hero," Bella replied. "When a man believes he's doing something good, we should try to understand, rather than revile him. Of course, there are men who knowingly commit acts of wickedness. I hope I never encounter such a man."

Lawrence's gut twisted with guilt. She might as well have been talking about him.

"You're home early, Lawrence," she said.

"I am," he replied. "It's a special occasion for which I want you to wear your best gown. And children?" He turned to three pairs of eyes watching their exchange. "Can you see to your own supper tonight? William, Jonathan—don't leave it all to your sister."

"Yes, Papa," they chorused.

Lawrence took Bella's hand. "Perhaps you might wear your brooch tonight."

"I couldn't—it's too fine."

"Nothing's too fine for you."

Her shy smile threatened to melt his heart.

"I'm content with…" She lifted her hand to her neck, then hesitated. "Of course I'll wear the brooch, if it pleases you. Well—I'd best set out my gown."

She stepped up on tiptoes and placed a soft kiss on the corner of his mouth before returning inside the cottage. As she reached the door, she lowered her hand from her neck, and he caught sight of her throat.

Her necklace was gone.

<hr>

"WHAT A DELICIOUS meal, Mrs. Colt," Bella said. "Thank you for taking such good care of us."

"No trouble, Mrs. Baxter," came the reply. "I pride myself in saying that my steak pie would stand up to anything served on any lord's table."

"I don't doubt it."

Bella smiled, her eyes glistening in the candlelight. How different she was to the creature who'd first arrived at Ivy Cottage—who'd turned her nose up at a good stew and found fault with the way Lawrence held his knife, the way he chewed his food, how he drank his ale…and probably how he took a piss.

The innkeeper's wife cleared the plates then left, with the promise of a glass of port each, on the house. Bella leaned across the table and took Lawrence's hands.

"Thank you," she said. "I should admonish you for your extravagance. Your money could be put to better use, but I've enjoyed tonight very much."

He lifted her hands to his lips. "Have you?"

"I felt like a lady, being served by others. Have we done this before?"

"No, love."

"Then I shall treasure tonight all the more." She glanced about the parlor. "Imagine what it must be like to be waited on like a lady, every day."

"Would you like that?"

She let out a sigh, a flicker of longing in her gaze. Then she shook her head. "What would I do if others did everything for me?" she asked. "If I dined like this every night, I could never appreciate it. Whereas tonight, I can savor the pleasure of a special occasion, and enjoy it all the more."

Lawrence's conscience clawed at him as she expressed such pleasure in indulging in a tiny crumb from the life he was denying her.

"Lawrence," she said, and his stomach clenched at the gravity of her tone, "there's something I've wanted to ask you. I think perhaps now is the moment."

Shit.

He closed his eyes, relishing the feel of her hands in his for what might be the last time if she were to ask…

"How did we meet?"

He opened his eyes. "What?"

"I can't remember," she said. "I've tried to picture it, but it's like its lost."

"Bella, I…"

"Please tell me," she whispered, her eyes glistening. "Tonight, you've made me so happy—it's a memory I'll carry with me forever. Can you not give me more memories—from times gone past?"

His heart ached at the plea in her eyes, and he uttered a silent prayer to the Almighty for forgiveness.

"I first saw you through the window of a mansion," he said.

"A mansion? What was I doing there?"

"You were lady's maid to the mistress of the house."

The fact that he'd lied hung in the air, but her mouth curved into a smile.

"That explains the book Jonathan and I have been reading," she said. "And you were…"

"I was working in the garden," he said. "I'd stopped to catch my breath, and saw you, looking out of the window." He sighed at the memory. "You were so still, yet I saw sadness in your eyes. I thought, then, you were the most beautiful thing I'd ever seen."

She colored and tried to withdraw her hands. "Lawrence, you don't have to—"

"No." He held her firm. "I had never seen anything so lovely—and I never have since. So I cut a rose from the garden and presented it to you. I told you that until I'd seen you, there was nothing more beautiful in my eyes than that rose."

"And what did I say?"

He glanced at her gown, the simple white muslin she'd trimmed with a piece of ribbon below the curve of her breasts.

"You asked me how I knew that the rose was your favorite shade of pink."

"And then?"

"I pledged to find you a ribbon that matched the color, so that after the rose faded, you'd have something with which to remember it forever."

"Oh, Lawrence." She let out a soft laugh. "What sweet words to fall from the lips of a man!"

"I meant every word," he said. "And I resolved, from that day, that you and I would be married."

"Am I so easily won?"

Her smile faltered, and he silently cursed the gossips in the village.

"There was never a woman more virtuous," he said, "nor a woman more deserving to be wooed like a lady."

She smiled. "How did you woo me?"

"I went to Midchester and bought as many pink ribbons as I could afford. Then I came and placed each one at your feet, and declared that from thenceforth, those ribbons, and my heart, would forever be yours."

"You spin a pretty yarn of courtship," she said. "Where are the ribbons now?"

"Some adorned your wedding gown and your bonnet; others you kept, to wear a different ribbon in your hair each day. But they're gone now. They were lost when we came here—and when I lost you."

Her eyes narrowed, and as she opened her mouth to reply, his breath caught in his throat. Would she ask about her accident?

But she merely shook her head.

"I'm sorry," she said quietly.

"What for, my love?"

"For losing them."

He dipped his head and kissed her knuckles. "There's nothin' to be sorry for, Bella, love. The ribbons may be gone, but my heart remains. And my heart is—and will always be—yours."

Her eyes widened at his declaration, but before she could respond, the door opened and Mrs. Colt entered with a tray bearing two glasses filled to the brim with a dark ruby liquid.

"My best port," she said. "Don't drink it too quick, mind. It's best savored and appreciated."

"Don't worry, Mrs. Colt," Lawrence said, glancing at Bella. "I know when something's deservin' of being appreciated."

And when someone deserved to be loved.

He might have spun her a tale tonight, but not everything he said was a lie.

For his heart was—and would always be—hers.

Chapter Thirty-Four

BELLA CLUNG TO her husband's arm as they returned home. The moon hung heavy in the sky, casting a cold blue light across the landscape and throwing sharp shadows across the path, where the first signs of frost glistened on the ground, tiny pinpricks of light.

The port, courtesy of Mrs. Colt's generosity, had warmed her blood when they set off from the inn, but now the chill of the night air penetrated her bones.

They rounded a corner, and the cottage came into view, its whitewashed walls illuminated by the moonlight, stark against the backdrop of the garden. A low, flickering light danced in the parlor window to welcome them home.

Lawrence pushed the door open and led her into the parlor, where the embers of the fire cast a dull orange light across the room. He placed a log on the fire, poking it until sparks ignited at the base.

"Come here." He pulled her close. "You're as cold as ice, love. Let me warm you up."

She relaxed in his arms, drinking in the scent of wood, earth, and smoke on his clothes.

"Better?" he whispered, his breath a warm caress on her forehead.

"Mmm..." She placed her head on his shoulder and sighed. "If only I could stay here forever—in your arms."

"We'd get nothin' done if we stood here all day, Bella."

Didn't he want to hold her? Why was he such a contradiction—

one moment melting her heart with tales of traveling miles to bring her ribbons as a token of his love, and the next rejecting her carefully worded plea to be loved?

If only she could be bold and ask him outright—even if she feared his response.

She withdrew from his embrace and approached the fire, holding out her hands to the warmth.

"Is anything the matter?" he asked.

"I'm tired, that's all," she said. "I've never eaten that late before—at least, not that I can recall."

"Then perhaps you should retire."

"To a cold bed."

"It'll soon warm up with an extra blanket or two, Bella—it's not bothered you before."

"No," she said flatly. "According to you, *nothing's* bothered me before."

"If it's warmth you're wantin', *I* can take the bed upstairs," he said, reaching for one of the blankets on the sofa. "I'll give you what you want."

"Oh, *will* you?"

"Here." He handed the blanket to her, but she swept it aside.

"I don't want a blanket!"

"Then what do you want?"

"Can't you tell?"

He stepped toward her, a flicker of desire in his eyes. Then he hesitated.

"A good night's sleep will see you right," he said. "I knew you shouldn't have taken that port."

"Sweet heaven!" she cried. "Have you always found me repulsive—or is it only since my accident?"

"Repulsive?" He shook his head. "What nonsense you speak!"

"Then why won't you touch me as a man touches his wife? That story you told me—of the ribbons, and owning your heart—was it a lie?"

He faltered and lowered his gaze, sending a spike of pain through her heart.

"I'm right," she whispered. "You don't want me—you feel nothing, while I—"

She broke off, unwilling to voice her need in the face of his indifference.

He shook his head. "No."

Her gut contorted with pain, and she stepped back, her eyes stinging with tears. "N-no?"

He drew in a deep breath, then spoke, his voice a hoarse rasp. "No, Bella, you're wrong—*so* wrong."

Then he looked up and she caught her breath. His eyes glowered with a base, raw hunger, reflecting the primal need that throbbed deep inside her—his desire calling to hers.

"I *want* you, woman," he said. "Don't say I feel nothin' when, from the moment I saw you, my whole body's been *burnin'* with want."

"Then why won't you touch me?"

She stepped toward him, and the pain in his eyes intensified. Hands fisted at his sides, he stood stiff, trembling as if he fought to control a madness.

"Don't come any closer," he rasped. "I'll not be able to control what happens if you do."

She reached toward him.

"Sweet heaven!" he said. "I cannot... I will *not* ruin..."

"Where's the ruination in an act between a man and his wife?"

He shook his head. "Bella, you know not what you offer."

"I do," she said, "and I offer it freely, willingly, and gladly." She took his hand, curling her fingers around his fist. "An offering of love."

Then he shuddered and let out a low cry. "May God forgive me."

He pulled her close and claimed her mouth, plunging inside as if he were a man dying of thirst. He swept his tongue through her with hungry strokes, deepening the kiss as he shifted against her, igniting a flame of desire. She shifted her thighs apart where the flame swelled and roared, and he let out a primal growl—the call of a beast ready to claim his mate.

He arched his back, and she felt him against her thigh, a delicious hardness moving closer to the center of her need.

He slipped a hand below her neckline, and her senses came alive as his calloused fingers claimed her breast, sweeping across her sensitized skin until they found what they sought—the hardened bud at the center. Then he flicked the nub, and she cried out as a fizz of pleasure shot through her body.

Then he grasped her gown, fisting his hand around the material, and lifted her skirts. Her skin tightened at the rush of cool air, and she shifted her legs further apart.

"Please…" she said. "I need…something… I know not what… *No!*" she cried out in frustration as he grasped her wrists and pushed her back. "Lawrence…" Tears splashed onto her cheeks at his rejection. "Please—don't stop!"

"Oh, Bella," he said. "I want to bury myself inside you so bad, but I've no wish to hurt you."

"You're hurting me *now*," she said. "Must you always push me away?"

"I'm not pushing you away, love, but it's your first…" He stopped and shook his head. *"Damn."*

"My first what?"

"I want you to feel only pleasure, Bella, but I fear it will hurt."

"I want this," she said. "I want *you*." She reached up and placed her hand on his cheek. "I trust you, Lawrence—my body and my heart are yours."

"Then your pleasure awaits."

He picked up the blanket, then spread it on the floor in front of the fire.

"Aren't we going to your bedchamber?"

"No, love," he said. "I fear we'd wake the children."

"Why?"

"Bloody hell," he muttered. Then he took her hand. "I've no wish for them to hear you screaming my name as you come undone."

"C-come undone?" Though his words were meaningless, a wicked pulse rippled through her.

He took her shoulders in his hands, and a small sigh escaped her lips as he caressed her throat with the tips of his thumbs. Then he lowered her neckline to reveal her breasts.

"Oh, Bella," he whispered. "You don't know how much I've been wantin' to do this."

The tip of his tongue flicked out to moisten his lips.

"We ate well tonight," he said, "but I find myself ready for another meal."

"Another... Oh!"

She cried out as he took her breast into his mouth and flicked her already beaded nipple with his tongue. His hot breath caressed her skin, and she arched her back.

He lifted his lips in a lazy smile. "Ah, there's nothin' as delectable to a man as his woman offering herself for him to feast on. But I mustn't spoil my appetite for the feast to come."

With a deftness that belied his huge, rough hands, he peeled off her gown. Then he removed her undergarments until she stood before him, naked save for her stockings.

She lifted her hands to shield herself from his gaze, and he caught her wrists.

"No," he said. "There's much pleasure to be had in lookin' at you—and there's pleasure to be had in being looked at, when it's your man doin' the looking."

His hungry gaze traveled across her body, lingering at the apex of her thighs and its thatch of curls where her flesh had grown hot and damp.

Sweet heaven, he was right. How could there be so much pleasure from merely being *looked at*? Or was it the *way* he looked at her, as if he needed her not just for pleasure, but because he couldn't exist without her?

Then he kneeled on the blanket, pulling her down with him. He cupped her breasts, and his eyes closed as he held them tenderly, as if he feared she'd shatter at his touch. For a moment, he grew still, a slow smile curving his mouth.

"What sweet, sweet breasts," he whispered. "Made to fit my hands—how I've longed to hold them, to worship them, and to taste them."

He opened his eyes, which shimmered silver in the firelight.

"I want to worship all of you," he said. *"Taste* all of you."

He drew in a labored breath, as if fighting to control himself. Then he pushed her back until she lay on the blanket before him.

She reached for the top of her stockings, running her fingertips across the scarred flesh at the top of her thigh.

"No," he said. "Leave them on."

Tears pricked at her eyes. Did he find her scars so repulsive that he wanted them to remain covered? She turned her head aside, but he caught her chin and coaxed her back.

"Bella—there's no shame in revealing your body to me."

"B-but my scars…"

Recognition rippled across his gaze, and he sighed.

"Sweet Bella, I've no wish for you to cover up your scars. They're part of you, and every piece of you is beautiful." He leaned forward and brushed his lips against the top of her stocking, peppering her puckered flesh with tiny, open-mouthed kisses. "Beautiful."

His voice was a low rumble reverberating through her body, and the moisture swelled between her thighs. But when she tried to squeeze them together, to ease the ache, he caught her legs.

"Oh no, love," he said. "Let me look. I like lookin' at your stockings—their softness over those lush thighs. And I like nothin' more than to look at *you*—my woman—all pink and sweet, when I've parted them thighs." His nostrils flared as he inhaled. "A man could go mad for wantin' with that scent of yours. All woman, you are, my Bella."

He flicked his tongue against her flesh.

"Oh!" she cried. "That tickles."

He kissed her thigh. "Does *that* tickle?"

"No."

"How does it feel?"

"Hot," she said, as the heat inside her center swelled, "a-and wet."

"Are you wet for me, woman?"

"I-I don't know…" Her breath caught in her throat as he nudged her thighs further apart, moving the trail of kisses further up her leg.

Her body jerked with the need to ease the ache, but he held her firm, his huge hands grasping her thighs, while he moved closer to the source of her need.

"I believe my woman is ready for me."

His voice whispered through her curls, and she lifted her head to see him kneeling before her splayed legs, his head of dirty blond hair between her thighs. Never before had she seen anything so wicked, so wanton.

So *debauched*.

"Lawrence…"

Overcome by shame, she whispered his name in a soft plea, and her voice caught in her throat. Then he looked up and met her gaze, his eyes filled with raw hunger.

The hunger of a beast ready to take his female.

Her shame at her nudity warred with the baser instinct to submit, and for a moment, they stared at each other. Then, at length, she caught a flicker of something else in his gaze, a spark of tenderness.

And love.

Closing her eyes, she lay back, yielding to him.

"Good lass."

She let out a whimper at the pulse of need elicited by his gentle praise. Then he dipped his head once more, and her skin burned where his tongue flicked out against her flesh.

"What a sweet scent," he said, his breath hot against her curls. "They say the enjoyment of a meal comes first from the lookin', then from the scent. Until there's only one pleasure to be had."

"Wh-what is that?" she panted.

"The tastin'."

He dipped his tongue into her curls and probed her flesh with the tip of his tongue, the soft, silken weapon moving slickly along the folds.

Sensations flooded her body—the heat radiating through her blood, the ache pulsing in her flesh, and the sharp waves of pure pleasure where he dipped in and out, murmuring his delight as he savored her. A great wave swelled in her mind—moving back and forth, each peak higher than the last, rising toward a crest…

"Mmm…" he rumbled, sending shock waves through her. "Delicious—the finest taste a man can devour is his woman, when she's ready."

"R-ready?" she said, her breath coming in shallow gasps.

"Oh yes," he said. "I could smell your need from the moment I parted them pretty thighs—and I can taste it now. It's when a man knows she's ready to take him inside her."

He dipped his tongue again, this time more insistently. The wave swelled toward the crest, and with it, a madness began to form—a craving that begged to be eased, intensifying until her whole body yearned for release…

Then he withdrew, and she let out a scream of frustration.

"No!" She reached out and fisted her hands in his hair, pulling him against her flesh. "Lawrence—don't stop, I beg you!"

But he withdrew and sat up. She lifted her knees and thrust her hips forward, no longer caring about the sinful wantonness with which she offered herself.

He reached for his shirt and began to unbutton it, his hands trembling. The first button came undone, but he struggled with the next.

"Oh, fuck it." Abandoning his shirt, he fumbled at his breeches, pulling at the buttons until he sprang free—thick and jutting.

Sweet Lord—he was huge! Surely he wasn't going to put *that* inside her?

He shifted toward her, his member bobbing as he moved until he'd climbed on top of her. He prodded the inside of her thigh, and she let out a whimper, her body tensing.

"You need to relax, love, when you take my cock," he said. "Trust me."

She nodded.

"No, Bella—you must say it."

"I trust you."

He slipped inside her curls to probe against her sensitized flesh. A flare of pleasure ignited, and she drew in a sharp breath, biting her lip, tasting blood.

"Woman, look at me."

She lifted her gaze.

"Do you want me?"

"Y-yes..." she whispered, bracing herself for the onslaught.

He gritted his teeth, sliding against her, each movement growing slicker. "Say it."

"I want you, Lawrence," she said. "Please!"

He moved his hips forward, and she felt her flesh stretching as the tip of him pushed inside her.

A low cry escaped her lips.

"Shh... Relax, love. Look at me."

She nodded and focused her gaze on him, willing her body to relax. Then she shifted her legs further apart, and he nodded his approval.

He leaned forward and brushed his lips against her mouth, coaxing her lips open with his tongue. She welcomed him in, and as his tongue slipped into her mouth, he thrust his hips forward.

She winced at the tight pinch, and he deepened the kiss, swallowing her whimper.

Pain throbbed deep inside her body—pain with the faint undertow of pleasure—until, at length, she felt her body stretch around him.

"That's it, my brave love," he whispered.

He withdrew, slowly, and she shuddered at the deep sensation. Then he eased himself back inside her. The sting lessened as pleasure overcame the pain, and she let out a long sigh as he sheathed himself in her once more.

"Do you my cock inside you, Bella?"

"Oh yes—it's…" Her voice trailed away as he withdrew again, and the wave swelled once more, but this time deeper, the sensations sharper, more intense.

"It's for you," he murmured. "Only for you. Take me—take all of me."

"Oh yes…" she breathed. "Please…"

He entered her again, and she let out a mewl of frustration as he withdrew once more.

"Does my Bella grow impatient?" he asked. "You must await your pleasure."

"I can't wait!"

He moved again, and she thrust her hips upward, taking him fully inside.

"Oh, sweet woman." He lifted his head, as if pleading to the heavens for respite. "What you do to me!"

He withdrew once more, then thrust his hips forward in a swift, sharp movement, slamming his hipbone against hers.

"Do you feel it, love?" he asked, his thrusts forming a steady rhythm. "Do you feel the pleasure from my cock?"

"Yes!" she cried, lifting her hips to meet each thrust. Then her whole body tightened, and she reached out, fisting her hands in the blanket. "Lawrence, what's... I don't know... Oh! It's coming—I can feel it. Lord save me, if we go together, I might die!"

He slammed into her once more, and the wave crested. Powerful surges tore through her senses, and she bucked against him, crashing against the wave again and again. She threw back her head and let out a long, low scream.

"Lawrence—oh, *Lawrence!*"

They continued to move their bodies in a frenzied, thrusting dance, while he roared out her name in deep, hoarse cries.

"Bella—my Bella!"

Then the wave receded, and she descended with it, the torturous pleasure receding, until a gentle pulsing remained while he continued to move inside her until, with a low cry, he collapsed on top of her. They lay together, entwined, the aftershocks of pleasure caressing her senses in soft ripples, until she drifted into a doze, his name on her lips.

"Oh, Lawrence—I love you."

Chapter Thirty-Five

I LOVE YOU.

There. She'd said it.

A woman still glowing from lovemaking, when her rational mind surrendered to the instincts of her body, spoke nothing but the truth.

His late wife might have uttered the words when called upon, but she'd never spoken them from the heart. And the doxies who'd serviced him over the years only loved the coin he gave.

A man knew when a woman's pleasure was genuine, when her body squeezed and rippled against his cock until it burst with pleasure. No woman could feign such pleasure, no matter how much she might moan and sob his name.

And no woman had given, or taken, such pleasure from a coupling as the woman in his arms now—the woman who had acted out of pure instinct, pure need.

The woman whose maidenhead he'd just taken.

The naked woman he now lay beside, fully dressed, save for his unbuttoned breeches from which his partially erect cock now jutted.

What have I done?

He'd treated her like a whore—stripping her, then fucking her on the floor.

And she had loved every bit of it.

She lay beside him now, stretched languorously on the blanket—a woman well pleasured, a smile of repletion on her lips.

He traced a line along her body, silhouetted against the glow from the fire—her shapely legs, the flare of her hips—until he reached her breasts, where he lingered. She arched her back, pushing her breast into his hand, and he flicked her nipple with his thumb.

"Mmm—that's lovely." She rolled onto her side and opened her eyes.

"Forgive me," he said. "I shouldn't have taken you like this—on the floor."

She frowned. "Did you not enjoy it? W-was I not good enough?"

"Heavens, love!" he said. "We came off together—it's better that way."

"I never could have imagined it would be so wonderful," she said. "Is it always like that?"

"Only with you."

"Will it be as wonderful again?"

He let out a sigh. *Would* he ever make love to her again?

"It *will* be wonderful," she said. "If it's with you, then anything will be wonderful."

She gave a contented sigh, and within moments, she'd fallen asleep, naked and relaxed against him. What greater expression of trust could she give him?

Did it matter, the manner of their meeting? No—what mattered was now. The woman he loved—and who loved him—was in his arms. Gone was the bitter, miserable creature, the spoiled princess trapped by an ogre. She had been replaced by Bella—his wife.

And he would spend the rest of his life treating her as she deserved to be treated.

Because he loved her.

<hr />

WHEN BELLA WOKE, the room was already light. A sunbeam stretched across the room. She shifted on the sofa and raised her hand, disturbing the dust motes that swirled in the sunlight.

"Lawrence..." she whispered, a smile on her lips.

Had last night been a dream?

She sat up and winced at the soreness between her legs. The memory returned—the delicious fullness deep inside her body when he'd pounded into her, and the shattering explosion of pleasure.

Heat flooded her cheeks as her gaze fell on the floor beside the fire.

"You're awake."

She glanced up to see her husband leaning against the doorframe, wearing only his breeches. He folded his arms, and her mouth watered at the way his muscles rippled with the movement—the barely concealed power of the male beast.

"I won't ask whether you slept well," he said.

"Why?"

"Because I held you in my arms all night. I carried you to the sofa just after dawn."

"While I was...n-naked?"

He grinned. "If I recall, I did a great deal more than *that* while you were naked."

"I'm at a disadvantage this morning," she said. "I am still naked."

"I can redress the balance," he said, unbuttoning his breeches.

"Lawrence—the children! They'll be up soon. What if they catch us?"

"Then they'll be witness to our love." He approached and took her hand, lifting it to his mouth. "We can resume our activities of last night once the children have left for school."

"What—here?"

He flicked his tongue out, hunger in his eyes. "I'm wantin' to enjoy you in every room in the house—the bedchamber, the kitchen..."

"The *kitchen?*"

"Where else would I feast on you but on the kitchen table?"

"Oh."

How sinful! Yet she pulsed with need at the notion of being served up on the kitchen table while he devoured her.

"Then there's the hallway—up against the wall, I think," he said. "And the garden…"

"O-outside? Is that not terribly wicked?"

"That'll make it more pleasurable. That is, if you're not too tender after last night."

He slipped his hand beneath the blanket, searching for her breast, which was already heavy with need, the nipple peaked for him.

"My woman's as hungry for me as I am for her."

"Lawrence!" she chided.

"Your body cannot lie, love, and the children won't be up for a while yet. Perhaps we might indulge in a morsel or two before breakfast. Then we can dine more fully throughout the day."

"Don't you have to work? Sir Halford Merrick's garden…"

"Is finished," he said. "Today, I need to work on the designs for Mr. Trelawney's garden."

"I can…" she began, then hesitated. He'd made it clear before how little he valued her opinion, or her offer of help.

"Yes, my love?" He caressed her breast, igniting a spark of need in her center.

"Lawrence!"

He leaned close and nipped her earlobe. "I love hearing my name on your lips." Then he brushed his lips against hers. "Might I ask something?"

"Anything."

"Would you help me with the design? You could come with me the next time I visit Mr. Trelawney."

"Me?"

He kissed her again. "Yes, love. You're clever, resourceful, with a heart as big as the world. I've been a fool not to have seen your worth until now. And if you can assist me with designing a garden suitable for a lady"—he licked his lips—"I can reward you."

"I'm no lady," she said.

He frowned, and once more she saw a flash of guilt in his eyes. "To me, you'll always be a lady."

She brushed her lips against his. "And you are my lord."

"Sweet heaven," he sighed. "What have I done to deserve a woman such as you? I shall never take you for granted again—and I'll spend the rest of our lives together showing you just how much I love you."

"Then, my love," she said, "that shall be reward enough."

Chapter Thirty-Six

Lawrence steered the horse along the tree-lined drive, until the manor came into view.

His wife drew in a sharp breath.

"Are you comfortable?" he asked. "I'm afraid it was rather a long ride."

"I'm quite comfortable," she said. "I wonder if I've ridden before—it feels familiar."

"Does something else trouble you?"

She gestured ahead. "That house—it's huge! Is Mr. Trelawney very rich?"

"He's earned his fortune, rather than inherited it."

"Then he's the same as you."

"No, love—he's far above me."

"Don't say such things, Lawrence. You're the best man that ever lived. Nobody is above you."

He gave her waist an affectionate squeeze, then urged their mount on, drawing to a halt at the main entrance. He dismounted, then helped his wife down, and she offered her lips for a kiss.

Could he be any luckier? Since their first time, they'd spent almost every moment alone loving each other, their bodies coming to pleasure together every time—and she gave him more pleasure than he could ever have imagined.

And with her drawings tucked into the satchel over his shoulders, she was about to transform his future.

No—*their* future.

"Ahem."

Mr. Trelawney's butler stood beside the entrance.

Bella let out a soft cry and lowered her gaze, blushing. Lawrence's cock twitched at the expression in her eyes—desire tempered by a frisson of guilt at being caught.

"Forgive me," Lawrence said. "It's Mr. Jenkins, isn't it? We're here to see your master."

"Mr. Trelawney's expecting you, Mr. Baxter, but not..." The butler glanced at Bella.

"I've brought my wife to explain the designs," Lawrence said.

The butler raised his eyebrows. "Very well. James!"

A footman appeared. "Yes, Mr. Jenkins?"

"Take Mr. Baxter's mount to the stables."

"Very good, Mr. Jenkins."

"Follow me, Mr. Baxter." The butler led them inside. Lawrence took Bella's hand as they followed him to a study on the first floor—a wood-paneled room with books lining one wall and a desk at the far end, in front of a tall sash window.

"Wait here," the butler said. "Mr. Trelawney will be along shortly." He glanced at Bella. "Perhaps you'd like some refreshment?"

"Some water, please, Mr. Jenkins," Bella said, "but don't go to any trouble. I wouldn't want to keep you from your work."

He raised his eyebrows, then broke into a smile. "It's no trouble, ma'am." He bowed and exited the room.

Lawrence motioned to his wife to sit, then he sat beside her. Footsteps approached—a steady, confident tread, unlike the butler's quicker, lighter pace.

Lawrence rose as the door opened to reveal Mr. Trelawney.

Dressed in a dark-blue jacket with a cream silk waistcoat and cravat bearing an embroidered pattern in matching blue, he looked every inch the titled gentleman. Only Lawrence knew him to be different.

"Baxter!" Trelawney offered his hand. "Good to see you."

Lawrence took the hand, once again noticing the callouses—trophies of hard work—on the man's palms, and Trelawney pumped it up and down enthusiastically.

"Bella, this is Mr. Trelawney," Lawrence said. "Trelawney, this is my"—he swallowed his guilt—"my wife."

"Forgive me," Bella said, rising to her feet.

"Please don't trouble yourself to get up, Mrs. Baxter," Trelawney said. "You must forgive my rudeness. I was expecting only your husband."

"My wife is here to discuss the garden designs," Lawrence said.

"You've completed your proposal?" Trelawney's face broke into a smile. "Excellent. May I see? Do sit."

He sat behind the desk, his frame silhouetted against the window.

Lawrence pulled four drawings out of his satchel and placed them on the desk. Trelawney leaned forward and picked up one, then another, his gaze wandering over each page.

Bella glanced at Lawrence uncertainly, and he took her hand, giving her a smile of reassurance. Silence stretched, punctuated only by the ticking clock on the mantel.

"Fascinating," Trelawney said. "However, one thing concerns me."

The air shifted, as if a frost had descended. Trelawney had a reputation for fairness, but he was not a man to fall out of favor with.

"Are these original drawings, Baxter?"

"Of course," Lawrence said.

Trelawney's eyes narrowed. "I don't take deceit lightly. These are different in every possible aspect to your other designs. Even the style of drawing is different."

"My wife drew them."

Lawrence caught his breath as the businessman known for his

sharp insight stared at Bella with renewed interest. *"Did she, now?"*

"I did, Mr. Trelawney," Bella said, "and I'd rather you didn't accuse my husband of deception."

"I wasn't accusing—"

"Not outright, perhaps."

"Bella," Lawrence warned.

She ignored him. "My husband is incapable of deceit, Mr. Trelawney," she said. "He's the most honest person I know. I've never heard him utter a single falsehood."

Bloody hell—must she be so passionate in his defense? He loved her for it, but her loyalty only served to magnify the severity of his crimes against her.

"Bella, love..." he began, but Mr. Trelawney raised his hand, a smile on his lips.

"Mr. Baxter, a man with so passionate an advocate for his wife should not temper her loyalty. Very well, Mrs. Baxter, perhaps *you* could explain the designs. This one, for instance—the arches in the hedge. What are they supposed to represent?"

"Y-you want *me* to explain?" she asked.

"You drew them, yes? Did you have a particular objective in mind when you created these images?"

"I was thinking of your wife."

"Do you know my wife?"

"N-no," she said. "At least, I don't think so. But my husband said you wanted a garden to make your wife happy. So I thought about what a woman might want from her garden—what she wants most in the world."

"And what does a woman want most in the world?"

"Freedom."

Trelawney frowned. "What are you implying, Mrs. Baxter?"

She colored. "Forgive me—I didn't mean she wanted freedom from *you*. I only meant that a woman's role is so confined. She keeps house, tends to the children, and has little opportunity to see the world."

"Go on," Trelawney said.

"So I thought that if a woman cannot see the world, then why not bring the world to her?"

"In a garden?"

"Why not?"

"Do you always answer a question with a question, Mrs. Baxter?" Trelawney gestured to the drawing. "What does this have to do with arches cut into a hedge?"

"It's not a hedge. It's the Colosseum."

"The *what*?"

"The Colosseum. It's in Rome, and—"

"I know where it is," Trelawney said, "but I wonder at *your* knowing."

"Because I've seen it," she said.

Lawrence drew in a sharp breath. She'd been to Rome?

"*Have* you, Bella?" Lawrence asked. "When was this?"

"I-I can't recall exactly. Perhaps with my mistress?"

"Your mistress?" Trelawney asked.

"I believe I was a lady's maid."

"You believe? Don't you *know*, Mrs. Baxter?"

Bugger. The last thing Lawrence wanted was for his prospective employer to think his wife soft in the head.

"I-I had an accident," Bella said. "I lost my memory."

"Oh, I'm sorry," Trelawney said. "Do you suffer pain?"

"Only from not being able to remember." She took Lawrence's hand and gave him a soft smile, her eyes filled with love. "I don't know how I would have survived had it not been for my husband."

"Nevertheless, it must be difficult for you, Mrs. Baxter. Have you been examined by a doctor?"

"Shortly after my accident," she said. "He said my memory might return gradually—a small piece here and there. Or it might return all at once, if I see or hear something familiar."

Lawrence squirmed in his seat. It was time to steer the conversation away from the restoration of Bella's memory. "Tell Mr. Trelawney about the other drawings, love," he said.

Before she could respond, the door opened and the butler appeared, a glass in his hand. "Your water, Mrs. Baxter."

"Oh no," Trelawney said, "that simply *won't* do."

Lawrence's stomach clenched with apprehension. "Is something amiss?" he asked.

"A glass of water in my study is hardly fitting hospitality for a guest," Trelawney said. "Is it, Jenkins?"

"But sir…"

"We'll take tea in the parlor in the west wing." Trelawney turned to Bella. "It overlooks the garden, Mrs. Baxter." He resumed his attention on the butler. "Please inform Mrs. Trelawney that we have guests."

"There's no need to trouble yourself—" Lawrence began, but Trelawney interrupted.

"There's *every* need. My wife would never forgive me if I didn't. Come—let us take tea."

Mrs. Trelawney—*oh, shit.*

How could I have been so damned foolish?

Mrs. Trelawney—only daughter of the late Lord de Grecy. And of all the people Lawrence had encountered since bringing Bella home, the most likely to recognize her.

⇛⇚

TRELAWNEY USHERED THEM into the parlor—a bright room decorated in pastel shades with a double aspect over the gardens. Shortly after, a woman entered the room—tall and slender, with delicate features and pale gold hair.

"Ah, Alice, my love," Trelawney said. "This is Mr. Baxter—the one I told you about. And his wife."

The woman glided across the floor, her silk skirts rustling, and offered her hand. Lawrence stared at it for a moment, then issued a bow before taking it, making sure the callouses on his huge, rough hands did not come into contact with her delicate porcelain skin.

She was exquisite—an ethereal faerie creature who looked fragile enough to disintegrate at the slightest touch.

"My husband's spoken much of you, Mr. Baxter," she said. "He's told me how knowledgeable you are about plants." Then she turned her attention to Bella. "And you're Mrs. Baxter?"

Bella then dipped into a curtsey. "Pleased to meet you, ma'am."

"The pleasure is mine, my dear," Mrs. Trelawney said. "But I prefer my guests not call me *ma'am*. It makes me sound like a matriarchal gorgon."

"That's very kind of you," Bella said.

Their hostess stared at her for a moment. "You look familiar, my dear. Have we met before?"

"P-perhaps," Bella said. "I was a lady's maid before I married."

"And now you're taking tea in my parlor?"

Bella glanced at Lawrence. "I-I'm here because I've sketched some designs for your garden."

Lawrence braced himself for Mrs. Trelawney's disdain. Instead, she smiled, her eyes sparkling in the sunlight.

"How *marvelous!*" she said. "I admire anyone capable of bettering themselves through their own efforts—particularly women."

"You do?" Lawrence couldn't help asking.

"Oh yes—a woman's always confined by the expectations of the world, is she not?"

Trelawney let out a laugh. "Perhaps now, Baxter, you can see why I proposed we take tea with my wife. I believe our wives share the same beliefs when it comes to a woman's role in the world. Alice, darling, you must see Mrs. Baxter's drawings." He led them to a round breakfast table beside the window.

"Sit beside me," Mrs. Trelawney said to Bella. "I hope we can become better acquainted."

Bugger—could this be any worse? Not that Lawrence minded Bella being valued for herself—but an acquaintance with an earl's daughter could only lead to trouble.

"Mr. Baxter, if you please," Trelawney said.

Lawrence placed the drawings on the table, and Mrs. Trelawney picked one up.

"Interesting," she said. "This one has a Grecian feel, with these columns among the shrubs. Do you intend them to be fashioned from marble?"

"Yes," Bella said, pointing to the page. "See the notes I've written there? It's only a pencil sketch, but I've noted what the colors should be—or, at least, how I envisage them."

"It reminds me of the Parthenon," Mrs. Trelawney said.

"The what?" her husband asked, and she rolled her eyes.

"You know, Ross. The Parthenon—where Elgin found those beautiful carvings and brought them to England."

"The ones you told me Lord Byron made such a fuss about?"

"So, you *do* occasionally listen to what your wife has to say." Mrs. Trelawney gave Bella a conspiratorial wink, then resumed her attention on the drawing. "I agree with Byron," she said. "Any treasure is best admired in a familiar environment. But something like *this*"—she pointed to the drawing—"brings the spirit of another land to us without desecrating its treasures." She nodded. "Yes, very clever indeed."

She set the drawing aside and picked up another. "Oh, the Colosseum! And it's to be fashioned from a box hedge?"

"I-I haven't thought about the type of hedge," Bella said. "I know so little about plants."

"That's where your husband comes in, I suppose." Mrs. Trelawney set the drawing aside. "How utterly perfect, don't you agree, Ross, darling?"

"I wouldn't presume to take liberties by disagreeing with you, Alice my love."

Rather than show offense, she gave her husband an indulgent smile.

"Mr. Baxter, I applaud your genius," she said. "Rather than attempt to undertake every aspect of designing a garden, you've called upon the talents of another to fashion the design, so that you may concentrate on your knowledge of plants. An excellent way to manage a business, is it not, Ross?"

"Again, I wouldn't presume…"

"Oh, Ross!" she said, giving him a playful slap. "Must you tease me so? You know as well as I that we can only succeed if we make use of our strengths and recognize when we must rely on the expertise of others in areas in which we lack the talent or expertise. Do you not agree?"

"If it pleases you, my love," Trelawney replied. "Well, I think that's settled."

"Settled?" Lawrence asked.

"Of course," Trelawney said. "The only question that remains is, when can you begin? And there's the matter of your fee, but that's not something to be discussed with ladies present."

"You like the designs?" Lawrence asked.

"We don't like them," Mrs. Trelawney said. "We *love* them." She glanced out of the window at the garden outside—the row of neatly clipped bushes that formed a straight, soulless line. "I can't wait to be rid of all that formality. To think—I'll soon have a garden that transports me to other worlds!"

"If Mr. Baxter thinks he can achieve it," Trelawney said.

Lawrence nodded. "I've a young lad—Sam, his name is—who's a hard worker."

"And our head gardener will be on hand to help," Trelawney said. "Jones isn't as young as he was, but he's at your disposal—and he has two under-gardeners for the heavy lifting. There's a mason in the village for the stonework, unless you have one to recommend?"

Lawrence shook his head. "My acquaintance isn't that extensive."

Mrs. Trelawney grinned. "I think that's about to change, Mr. Baxter. My husband and I will be the envy of our friends. You'll be the toast of the country—more so than Capability Brown himself."

"I hardly think so, Mrs. Trelawney."

"Nonsense!" she replied. "One can always tell an estate that's been subject to Mr. Brown's particular style of remodeling. They all look the same. But this..." She gestured toward Bella's drawings. "This will set our garden apart from the rest. You'll be the talk of Society. And I know of several families in want of a new garden."

"Now, Alice, don't make promises to Mr. Baxter when he's not even started work," Trelawney said.

"Why not? Whitcombe was saying last week that he wants to change the garden at Rosecombe now he's married that delightful Howard girl."

Bella stiffened. "Whitcombe, you say?"

"Yes, the Duke of Whitcombe," Trelawney replied.

"And..." Bella closed her eyes for a moment, then opened them again. "Howard," she said. "Eleanor Howard."

"Yes," Mrs. Trelawney said. "I quite adore her. Do you know her?"

Lawrence held his breath, but Bella shook her head. "I must have read the name somewhere, that's all."

"I'm sure you'll meet her," Mrs. Trelawney said. "She's a regular visitor here—though she's nearing her confinement, so I doubt Whitcombe will permit her to travel for much longer. He quite dotes on her."

"As does every man in love with his wife," Trelawney said. "Am I right, Baxter?"

Lawrence lifted Bella's hand to his lips. "I'll not disagree."

"Then that's settled," Trelawney said. "Baxter, perhaps you'll come with me to discuss disbursements."

"But my wife…"

"Is welcome to remain here with me," Mrs. Trelawney said. "In fact, shall we take a turn about the garden, Mrs. Baxter? We can discuss where each section of the garden should be located. There's a delightful spot close to the lake that might do for the Grecian area. And, of course, you must visit as often as you like while your husband is working on the garden."

Shit.

Shit. Shit. Shit.

Bella was bound to be recognized if this woman, Eleanor Howard, came to visit.

"Forgive me, Mrs. Trelawney," Bella said. "But with three children to look after, I cannot stay away from home."

"You may bring your children with you."

"I mustn't keep them from school."

"Then they're fortunate to have you for a mother, my dear," Mrs. Trelawney said. "There's nothing so important as a child's education. But I insist you come to stay when the garden's complete—as my guest of honor."

"I couldn't make such an imposition," Bella said.

"Why not?"

"You're a lady, and I'm…" Bella colored, and Lawrence's heart ached at the way she trembled.

"You've as much right to be my guest as anyone," Mrs. Trelawney said. "More so, for you have talent, and you radiate kindness—unlike some of the young women in Society. In fact…"

Her voice trailed off and she fixed her gaze on Bella. Then she shook her head.

"No matter," she said. "Well, that's settled, then." She rose, and the rest of the party followed suit. Then she held out her arm. "Mrs. Baxter, shall we take a turn while our husbands discuss business?"

Bella glanced at Lawrence, and he nodded. Then she took the proffered arm, and the two women exited the parlor.

"You've a special woman there, Baxter," Trelawney said. "My wife doesn't take to just anyone. Now, shall we?"

Lawrence nodded and followed Trelawney out of the room in the wake of the women.

He had eluded discovery.

For now.

Chapter Thirty-Seven

Bella grasped the weed at the base of the stem like her husband had shown her. Then she pulled. The plant resisted for a moment, then came free, bringing with it the root. She placed it on the pile beside the border, then rose to her feet and stretched, tipping her face upward to bathe in the afternoon sun.

The days were growing colder now summer had passed. But the occasional warm day enabled her to spend an hour or two in the garden. The trees were beginning to change color into the riot of reds and browns. And on a day such as today, when the sun bathed the landscape, there was no sight more beautiful than nature's palette.

Autumn was her favorite time of year.

Or was it?

Her past was still shrouded in fog, through which the occasional gap enabled the sunlight to filter through before it closed again.

But the past didn't matter anymore. What mattered was today. And today was the day to declare that autumn was her favorite time of year.

And to rejoice in her husband's return home after a week working on the Trelawneys' garden.

How she'd missed him! Only a few weeks ago she'd have welcomed the respite from his getting under her feet, adding to her chores with his endless stream of shirts to wash, the mess he made at the kitchen table, and the dirt he trod into the cottage with his boots.

But chores were a small price to pay for what he gave her in return—both in the bedchamber and out of it.

Her cheeks warmed as she recalled last night when, alone in their bed, the children sleeping peacefully next door, she'd slipped her hand between her legs, open and eager at the thought of his taking her. To her shame, she'd run her fingertips along the sensitized flesh, imagining his own fingertips, or his...

She drew in a sharp breath at the thought of the part of him that gave her so much pleasure. Such wicked, *delectable* pleasure...

She closed her eyes, and her skin tightened in anticipation, as if she could feel his fingertips tracing along her neck.

"Lawrence..."

A hand cupped her breast, and she arched her back against a solid, muscular body.

"Have you been needin' my touch as much as I've been wantin' yours?"

His voice, the low growl of a ravenous beast, vibrated through her bones. She whirled around in his arms and fisted her hands in her husband's hair, bringing their mouths together. "You're home!"

He grasped her and pushed her back against a tree, and she let out a mewl of pleasure, her body blooming at the feel of his primal strength. What could be more glorious than being at the mercy of her man—her beast—driven by a powerful urge to mate with his female?

He fumbled at his breeches, then a cold rush of air rippled across her thighs as he lifted her skirts before thrusting himself inside her, his breath coming in short, sharp puffs.

Pleasure came quickly. She let out a cry as he filled her completely, then wrapped her legs around his waist, drawing him deeper in while his breathing steadied.

At length, he tipped his head forward, resting it on her shoulder while she held him close.

"Bella, that's as fine a welcome as a man can hope for after a long journey! I've been missin' you so bad—when I saw you in the garden, I couldn't control myself."

"How long will you be home?" she asked.

"I go back in two days."

"So soon?"

"The garden's almost done, then you can come with me. Mrs. Trelawney has invited us to dine—and stay the night."

"That's kind, but we can't leave the children."

"Ned can watch them."

"No." She shook her head. "Dinner at a grand house? It's not for the likes of us."

"Don't say such things," he said. "You honor Mrs. Trelawney with your company."

Her heart swelled—to think, he loved her enough to say such things.

"Then," she said, "we must make the most of the time we have before you return."

He placed a kiss on her lips. "I intend to, my wild, wanton woman. A taste of pleasure in the garden is not enough. I'm wantin' to worship you so bad."

Could her life be any better?

⇝⇜

THE STENCH OF smoke choked her senses as harsh crackles split the night air.

"Bella!"

A woman's voice screamed in the distance as the smoke thickened. She turned toward the voice, but an explosion ripped into the air.

"Sebastien!"

"Mariah!"

The voices grew in urgency, but the roaring of the flames obliterated them.

"Mama!" she cried. "Papa!"

She rushed toward the screams, but the air burned her flesh, searing her with agony.

"Mama!"

Strong arms pulled her back. "I've got you, miss."

"Let me go! Mama—where are you?"

The flames danced in the air, bright demons filling the world. She raised her arms to fend them off, then an explosion shattered her into a thousand shards…

"Bella!" a deep voice cried.

A familiar voice—a voice she trusted and loved.

She opened her eyes to darkness. The flames had gone.

She was in her bedchamber, enveloped in a strong pair of arms.

"Hush, my love—it was a bad dream, nothing more. You're safe now."

She clung to him, seeking solace from his solidity. "Lawrence," she breathed.

"That's it, love. It's your Lawrence."

She caught a glint in his eyes—light reflected from the moonlight coming through the crack in the curtains.

"It was so real," she said. "The fire—the house, destroyed. And…they died."

"Hush." He rocked her to and fro, stroking her hair. "It's over now. It's not real."

"N-no," she said. "Don't you see? It *was* real. I remember."

He tensed. "You *remember?*"

"My mother—my father. And…" She caught her breath as tears stung her eyes. "And how they died."

"Can you remember anything else?" His voice carried a hard edge.

"No."

For a moment he remained still. Then he exhaled, the tension leaving his body.

"Poor love," he said. "How did they die?"

"An accident—a fire," she said. "I was there—I heard my mother screaming, and tried to find her, but a man picked me up and wouldn't let me go. He carried me out." She closed her eyes, capturing the image that had eluded her for so long. "So many people…standing around the building… Their faces glowing orange in the dark."

"And then?"

"I was sent away," she said. "They said it wasn't my home anymore."

"Because it had burned down?"

"No." She shook her head. "The building was saved. But with Papa gone, I couldn't live there anymore. They said I didn't belong there. So my aunt took me away."

"Where did she take you?"

She closed her eyes again, concentrating on the memory of the sharp-nosed woman with the cold eyes and bitter expression…

Then the memory faded.

"I can't remember," she said. "I only remember the fire."

"And your mother and father?"

"I remember a woman with kind blue eyes," she said. "And a man with glasses and a smile, wearing fine clothes and smelling of brandy." She nodded. "He was a gentleman. But they said I was alone now he was gone, and I had to leave."

"Why?"

"I don't know, but if I was a lady's maid, then I must have been sent into service. I must…" A cry escaped her lips. "I-I must have been my father's… I mean, my mother must have been his mistress, or a servant, if I was sent away. I m-must have been his bastard."

He let out a low hiss and tightened his hold. "Don't be sayin' that, love."

"Would you have married me, knowing I was a…bastard?"

He placed a kiss on the top of her head. "I care nothing for such things, Bella. I love you no matter the circumstances of your birth—whether you're the natural child of a gentleman, or"—he hesitated—"the legitimate daughter of a duke."

"How did I deserve such a man as you?" She relaxed against him and sighed. "I'm thankful for one thing."

"Which is?"

"That I'm not the legitimate daughter of a duke," she said. "If I were, I wouldn't have met you—and I cannot bear to imagine life without you."

"Oh, Bella," he said, his voice hoarse. "It's not you that ask should why you're deservin' of me—it's me who could never come close to deservin' you."

She tipped her face up, offering her lips for a kiss, and she caught the expression in his eyes reflected in the moonlight—in them she saw an emotion so powerful, she caught her breath at the intensity of it.

She saw guilt—as if he had sinned so badly that he was merely waiting for the inevitable condemnation to hell.

Chapter Thirty-Eight

"You've done a damned fine job, Baxter."

Trelawney unstoppered a decanter, filled two glasses with dark-red liquid, and pushed one across the desk.

"Regarding your disbursement, I've taken the liberty of speaking to Mr. Simms to open an account for you."

"Simms?"

"The banker. He has an office in Midchester, which is your nearest town, yes?"

"It is," Lawrence said, "but—a banker! They're not for the likes of me."

"Surely you didn't expect me to hand over your fee in a bag of clinking coins," Trelawney said. "I've banked with Simms for years, and he can give you a good rate of return. If your business expands, you'll need someone to deal with your financial affairs."

"My *what*?"

"Money, Mr. Baxter. You'll need someone to deal with your money."

"But I'm just a gardener."

"Not anymore," Trelawney said. "You're a businessman who, after our opening next week, will have a reputation for unique garden design."

Lawrence eyed the contents of his glass.

"The finest port in my cellar," Trelawney said.

"I wouldn't know, seein' as I know nothing about port."

Trelawney chuckled. "Neither do most of Society, though they'd never admit as much. Take it from me, out of everything I've imported, this is the best. Sweet to the taste, without the acridity of the younger vintages, and guaranteed not to give a shocking megrim the next day. Unless you drink it a bottle at a time." He pushed the glass toward Lawrence. "Go on—I don't give this to just anyone."

"Then I'm honored." Lawrence took a sip, and a rich flavor of sweet berries burst on his tongue.

"It's good, yes?"

"Yes."

"I'll give you a bottle to take home to your wife." Trelawney leaned forward. "Assuming she *is* your wife."

Lawrence's hand shook, spilling his port.

"I don't think I heard you properly, Mr. Trelawney."

"Did you not?" Trelawney leaned back. "I had a meeting with my lawyer yesterday. He shared an interesting tale."

"Your lawyer?" Lawrence asked. "What's that to do with me—or my wife?"

"He told me about a junior partner in his firm who'd been relieved of his position. Of course, a lawyer would never break a confidence in relation to his clients, but Stockton's an honest man, and I believe he had good reason to discuss the matter with me. The partner's name is Crawford."

"I've never heard of him."

Trelawney sipped his port. "Do you know what a trusteeship is?"

Lawrence shook his head.

"It's when assets are placed under the guardianship of others. The beneficiary of the assets has little to no control over them. Instead, the trustees are responsible for any decisions."

"Are you saying I should place my earnings in a—a trust?"

Trelawney arched his eyebrows. "You've not understood my

meaning."

Which came as no surprise—the man spoke in riddles.

"Mr. Crawford was a trustee of the fortune of an orphaned girl." Trelawney paused, as if expecting a reply, but Lawrence said nothing.

What the devil was he rattling on about?

"As an only child," Trelawney continued, "and a *female*, she couldn't inherit her father's title, nor his estate. But her father had the foresight to establish a trust in her name, which would be released on her marriage, or when she came into her majority."

"Majority?"

"When she reached the age of twenty-one," Trelawney said. "The father was, by all accounts, an excellent man—educated, well traveled. He doted on his wife and daughter—took them with him when he toured the continent. He was particularly fond of Rome, so Stockton said. Quite unlike his heir who is, I gather, something of a wastrel."

"His heir?"

"A distant cousin. On hearing about his inheritance, he couldn't claim the estate quickly enough, and he sent the child away. Of course, with a substantial fortune in trust, most would envy, rather than pity, the girl. And envy breeds great evil, does it not?"

"I wouldn't know," Lawrence said, swallowing the discomfort pricking at his skin. "I've never envied anyone in my life. I'm a believer in the rewards to be reaped from hard work."

"Then you're a better man than most. Better than Crawford and his client."

"What does Crawford, or his client, have to do with me?" Lawrence asked.

"The conditions of the trust stated that one of the trustees should be a partner in Allardice, Allardice, and Stockton. When Crawford became a partner, he took over the role from the elder Mr. Allardice, but he appointed his client as a fellow trustee."

Lawrence drained his glass. "Why are you telling me this?"

"Because Crawford's been exposed as a fraudster," Trelawney said. "Stockton told me he nearly ruined the firm's reputation when the full extent of his activities was revealed—trusts breached, clients overcharged, funds misappropriated. He came to reassure me that my affairs were in order."

"And you believe him?" Lawrence asked.

"Completely. He discovered Crawford's deception and acted swiftly. You see, when the beneficiary of the trust went missing, Crawford tried to release her fortune to his client. When Stockton discovered what he was up to, he promptly dismissed him. Crawford's currently residing in Newgate awaiting the assizes, and Stockton's taken over as trustee."

"So, the criminal was brought to justice and the fortune is safe."

"Perhaps, perhaps not."

Bloody hell—what was the man on about?

"Why are you tellin' me this, Mr. Trelawney?" Lawrence asked.

"Because I fear the client won't stop until he has his hands on the girl's fortune. They were engaged, you see."

Lawrence's stomach clenched. Surely Trelawney wasn't referring to…

"E-engaged?"

"She was set to marry him, at which point her fortune would transfer to him. But she disappeared. Without trace. After her disappearance, Crawford tried to seize her fortune. Now his plan's been thwarted, his client has only one course of action left."

"Which is?"

"To renew his efforts to find the young woman so he can marry her," Trelawney said. "Which brings me to the purpose of this conversation. She disappeared in June of this year—the seventh, to be precise."

Fuck.

"A coincidence, no?" Trelawney continued, his voice betraying no emotion. "The same date your...*wife* told mine that she'd suffered her accident in the river."

Trelawney fixed his shrewd gaze on Lawrence.

"Permit me to divulge the name of Crawford's client."

Lawrence reached for his glass, overwhelmed by the urge to drain it. But it was already empty.

Trelawney's expression hardened.

"The client's name is Dunton. The Duke of Dunton."

"A-and the young woman?" Lawrence asked, his breath catching.

"I believe you already suspect her identity," Trelawney said. "But let me remove all doubt. Her name is Lady Arabella, only daughter of the late Sebastien Ponsford, Duke of Southerton."

An invisible fist punched through the pit of Lawrence's stomach. He drew in a sharp breath and clutched at the arm of his chair.

Trelawney shook his head and sighed. Then he reached for the decanter and refilled Lawrence's glass. "What the devil have you done, Baxter?"

"Am I also bound for Newgate?" Lawrence asked.

"Have you committed a crime?"

"Not in the eyes of the law."

"A sin, then?"

"Everyone's committed a sin at some point."

Trelawney snorted. "You sound like the vicar in our parish. If he were to be believed, we must all prostrate ourselves before him on a daily basis, begging forgiveness to render ourselves worthy of consideration for the kingdom of heaven."

"And what do *you* believe?"

"That it's what we *do* that determines our worthiness," Trelawney said. "I must admit, your wife's playing her part well—not even my Alice recognized her. Now I know who she is, I can see the resemblance, but Lady Arabella was never someone we wished to become fully acquainted with."

"Why not?" Lawrence asked. "You dislike her because she's of noble birth?"

Hypocrite!

He cringed as his conscience berated him—wasn't that why *he'd* hated her at first? That and her behavior toward him—behavior that set him on a path of vengeance.

Now it was Trelawney's turn to look uncomfortable. "We're often led by first impressions," he said. "The sharp-voiced Lady Arabella, bedecked in scarlet silk, whom I was introduced to in passing at a ball, is an entirely different creature to the gentle Bella Baxter in her plain muslin, who spoke with such animation in defense of her husband when describing her design for the Colosseum. But if she's in hiding from Dunton, then it's only fair she be warned…"

Lawrence felt the heat rise in his cheeks as Trelawney's voice trailed away. "Dear God, no…"

Trelawney's knuckles whitened as he fisted his hands together. "She's *not* playing a part, is she? What she said about losing her memory is true."

Lawrence gripped his glass, his throat catching, as he fought to overcome his shame.

"Does she know who she is?"

"No."

"Bloody hell," Trelawney muttered, shaking his head.

"I only meant to keep her for a month," Lawrence said.

"Her accident was over *four* months ago!" Trelawney cried.

"I-I liked having her," Lawrence said. "And she grew to like being with me."

"She's done a damned sight more than that," Trelawney said. "My Alice tells me she's never seen a woman so much in love."

"Sweet Lord—does Mrs. Trelawney know?"

"Of course she doesn't!"

"Why do you say that?"

"Because you've still got your balls. If Alice knew what you'd done, much as she dislikes Lady Arabella—the *real* Lady Arabella—she'd have sliced them off and served them to her pug."

"What are you going to do?" Lawrence asked.

"Me? Nothing. I'll leave that to your conscience."

If Trelawney spoke the truth, then Dunton—the man who'd forsaken Bella, leaving her to the mercy of strangers—wanted her back. But Lawrence had no intention of giving her to a man who didn't love her—not when he loved her more than life itself.

"She's happy," he said. "*We're* happy. Do you think Dunton would make her happy?"

Trelawney wrinkled his nose. "True—Dunton only wants her fortune. But that's not your decision to make. You took her under deception, gave her no choice. In what way does that make you the better man?"

"I'm *not* like Dunton!"

"Aren't you? Many would say yours is the greater sin. In the eyes of the law, it *is* the greater sin."

Lawrence tightened his hold on the glass. Then, with a crack, it shattered in his grip. Shards bit into his flesh, and he winced as the liquor spilled over his hand, causing the cuts to sting.

But he relished the pain. It was the least he deserved.

Oh, Bella, what have I done?

"Take this." Trelawney held out a handkerchief. "A waste of a good port—and a good glass. Allow me." He grasped Lawrence's wrist and turned his hand over. Lean, strong fingers plucked shards of glass from his palm, then placed the handkerchief against the wounds.

"A waste of a good handkerchief, also," Trelawney muttered. "My wife embroidered the edge with my initials. Still—it's not the done thing to let a guest bleed over my Aubusson rug." The corner of his mouth curved into a smile. "That would be a waste of a good rug."

"I'm sorry."

"It's Bella you should apologize to."

"You mean *Lady Arabella*."

"I like Bella considerably more," Trelawney said. "And it's Bella who deserves the truth, for her sake, and yours. I'll not betray you—not when I can see how deeply you love her. But if you *do* love her, then you must tell her the truth. A sin kept hidden is never buried—it lies dormant, like a seed, until, when it's ready to grow, it breaks through the surface, at which point there's no absolution. And then…"

"Then what?" Lawrence asked.

"Then all hope for redemption is gone."

Chapter Thirty-Nine

Bella clung to her husband's arm as he steered her around the garden.

Today was a day of triumph. The other guests milled about, their chatter punctuated by expressions of admiration as they wandered among the marble columns and arched hedges.

And to think, they were guests at the big house, as if the Trelawneys considered them equals—friends, even!

She glanced up at Lawrence, her heart swelling with pride.

He seemed despondent—and had been the past week. Perhaps he feared the prospect of dinner with people who ranked so far above them.

"Is something troubling you?" she asked.

He let out a sigh and met her gaze.

"It is, isn't it?" she said. "You were silent for the whole journey over. Did you fear the Trelawneys wouldn't like the garden?"

"They like it."

She smiled. "I never doubted it—I know what a talented, hard-working man you are."

If anything, her words seemed to pain him more.

She took his hand. "Perhaps you're apprehensive over what is to come."

He drew in a sharp breath. What was wrong with him?

"There's nothing to worry about," she said. "I overheard one of the guests tell Mr. Trelawney that he'd like to commission you to redesign his garden. This could be the start of something wonderful—our future."

"Perhaps."

"I have every faith in you, my love," she said.

"I don't deserve you, Bella."

"Nonsense!" She laughed. "This garden's *your* creation. I only drew a few sketches. *You* brought it to life."

"It's not that," he said. "There's something I must tell you—but I fear you'll not like it."

"Do you love me, Lawrence?"

His eyes widened. "Of course I do! Are you in any doubt?"

"Then, my love, let us set any troubles aside and enjoy today, together."

He blinked, slowly, then let out a sigh. "What have I done to even begin to deserve you?"

"You've loved me, Lawrence," she said. "With your love, I can weather anything."

"*There* you are, Baxter!" a male voice cried.

A portly man in a charcoal-gray jacket and cream breeches hurried toward them.

"Good man, you must settle an argument between my wife and myself. She tells me that the shrubs surrounding the columns in the Grecian garden flower in the winter. But I said no plant could flower when it's so cold. Would you oblige us and settle our argument? I can take you to her now if I may be permitted to steal you from Mrs. Baxter."

He bowed to Bella. "Sir Henshingly Speakman, at your service. We live half a mile away. Our garden's smaller than Trelawney's, but I'd be much obliged if your husband could take a look at it—my wife's quite taken with the work you've done here."

Lawrence glanced at Bella, and she withdrew her arm. "Go, my love," she said. "I've a mind to find somewhere quiet."

"I'll join you as soon as I can," Lawrence said. He kissed her forehead, then followed Sir Henshingly through an archway and disappeared.

Bella let out a sigh of relief. The incessant chatter and cries of enthusiasm fostered her pride in her husband, but the afternoon was unusually hot for autumn, and her head ached. Each expression of enthusiasm cut through her senses like a knife, and while Lady Speakman was pleasant enough, she talked a little too loudly, a little too much, and on matters on which she had no knowledge.

A path led away from the main party, and she took it, making her way to a bench situated at the foot of a yew tree, half hidden in the shade. Drawing her shawl around her shoulders, she sat and leaned back, closing her eyes while she listened to the rush of the wind through the trees and the birdsong against the backdrop of distant chatter.

Occasional footsteps came and went as guests continued exploring the garden. Then another set of footsteps approached—heavier, more determined. They drew nearer, then stopped.

For a moment, she heard nothing, other than the sound of breathing. Perhaps another weary soul was looking for respite. Then a deep voice spoke, filled with contempt.

"I *thought* it was you."

Bella opened her eyes. A man stood before her.

Tall and broad-shouldered, he exuded power—a man used to being obeyed and revered. His jacket was tailored to perfection, and the waistcoat beneath shimmered in the sunlight, revealing the delicate, intricate embroidery adorning the material.

He stared at her from cold sapphire eyes, with the frank boldness of the aristocracy. Something about him looked familiar—the way his brow furrowed, the angle of the dark slashes of his brows.

Bella rose, then dipped into a curtsey.

His eyes widened, then he curled his lip into a sneer.

Her breath caught in her throat as an image flashed before her mind, of his bowing before her, then leading her onto a crowded dance floor, the same sneer on his lips.

"Do I know you, sir?"

He snorted. "You mean to ridicule me, madam?"

"Mrs. Trelawney has yet to introduce us. I'm—"

"I know perfectly well who you are," he said. "As you know me. Do you take me for a fool?"

"No, sir."

"Or perhaps you wish to insult my wife again?"

"Your wife? Is she here?"

"No. I thank the Almighty she's spared having to endure your company."

"She *knows* me?"

"Of course she does! What are you playing at, woman?"

Had she been in this man's employ—or his wife's? Had she disgraced herself by dancing with a man above her station?

"Forgive me, sir, I-I'm afraid I've lost my memory," she said. "Was I your wife's maid?"

He barked out a laugh. "That's imaginative, even for *you*. Or are you going soft in the head? Which would be a fitting punishment, given that you accused my wife of the very same thing."

"I accused her of what?" Bella asked. "You must be mistaken. I—"

"Desist, madam!"

He stepped toward her, and her gut twisted in fear. Who was this big, powerful man—and why was he so *angry*?

"I came here to ask why you're doing intruding on Mrs. Trelawney's hospitality, dressed in such a fashion? Are you indulging in some sort of deception?"

"I-I don't understand," she said, tears stinging her eyes. "I'm not deceiving anyone. I can't remember…"

"Stop playing the fool. You think you can garner sympathy from those you've wronged merely because you can summon a few false tears? Spiteful harpy I knew you to be, but—"

"Who the fuck are *you*?"

Bella turned to see her husband standing close by, his hands balled into fists.

"And who do you think *you* are?" the stranger said.

"I asked first."

"I am Montague FitzRoy, fifth Duke of Whitcombe."

Whitcombe...

Why did that name sound familiar?

Lawrence seemed unperturbed by the revelation. "Well, *Montague FitzRoy, Fifth Duke of Whitcombe*," he said, "I'd like to know what gives you the right to insult my wife."

The stranger glanced from Bella to her husband and back again, then let out a snort.

"You poor fool!" he scoffed. "I wish you joy of her."

"That's right kind of you," Lawrence said. "Nobody brings me more joy than my Bella."

"*Bella*, did you say?"

"Aye, that's right. Bella Baxter—my wife."

"Baxter..." The duke raised his eyebrows. "You're the gardener Trelawney wanted me to meet."

"Aye, but I'm not so sure if I'm wantin' to meet *you*."

"I *beg* your pardon?" The duke's eyes widened and his nostrils flared, as if the mere thought of a lesser being rebuffing him was inconceivable.

"You heard," Lawrence said. "Duke or no, you're no gentleman if you insult the woman I love."

"I should call you out for that."

"I've no idea what that means."

"It means challenge you to a duel. It's how gentlemen settle an argument when one has dishonored another—usually at dawn, with pistols."

"Doesn't sound very gentlemanly," Lawrence said. "And I should be the one callin' *you* out, seein' as you've dishonored my wife. We can settle it now if you like. With fists."

The duke wrinkled his nose, then he clicked his heels together, turned his back, and returned to the main garden without saying a word.

Lawrence drew Bella into his arms. "You're trembling, love."

"I-I don't know why that man said such things," she said. "What have I done to him?"

"Nothing that merits such treatment. Arrogant arse! Not like Trelawney at all—but then, Trelawney had to work for his fortune. That man—Whitcombe, or whatever his name is—probably hasn't had to lift a finger in his life."

"You heard what he said," Bella replied. "Mr. Trelawney must have told him about you—you shouldn't have spoken to him like that. What if he was going to hire you for his garden?"

"I wouldn't work for a man who insults you—not if he paid me a thousand pounds."

"But—"

"No, Bella. You mean more to me than all the money in the world." He placed a kiss on her forehead. "Let's get you inside—you should rest before dinner. It's been a long day."

"I can't attend dinner," she said. "What if that man's there?"

"He won't be, love. Trelawney assured me it was a family dinner. No other guests except you and I."

"But all those people here—they've come to see the garden, and to talk to you. If they're not staying for dinner, you should speak to them now—not waste time with me."

"Tending to the woman I love is the best use of my time."

They set off, and she lost her footing and stumbled against him.

"My poor love," Lawrence said. "Here, let me." He grasped her waist.

"What are you doing?"

"What any husband does when he wants to care for his wife."

He swiftly scooped her up into his arms and carried her inside.

⇒⇒⇒⇐⇐⇐

LAWRENCE HAD BEEN right. Dinner was a quiet meal, the two of them the only guests.

Bella had never tasted anything so fine in her life—soup that looked like cream, but with a savory taste that burst on the tongue, followed by fish, with a delicate flavor smothered in a buttery sauce. Then came the largest piece of beef she'd ever seen, which Mr. Trelawney carved from the head of the table, followed by what looked like a yellow snowball in a glass with a clean citrus taste, and, finally, apple tart.

Each course had been served by footmen wearing bone-white gloves, gliding around the table, placing each plate before them with smooth, elegant motions, as if engaging in a dance.

It was a wonder anyone could make so many dishes for one meal. She couldn't imagine the amount of clearing up needed—all those different plates and bowls, knives and forks that had been placed in such an intricate array on the table.

Her stomach full, Bella pushed her empty plate aside. At a nod from Mrs. Trelawney, the footmen approached the table and removed the plates.

"Thank you," Bella said.

The footman arched his eyebrows, then glanced at his mistress, who let out a laugh. "I'm afraid Henry is rather surprised by your behavior, Mrs. Baxter."

Bella's cheeks warmed. "I-I'm sorry. I didn't know I wasn't supposed to…"

"To what?" Mrs. Trelawney said. "Thank someone who's provided a service?" She smiled. "Few of our acquaintances deign to thank those they consider beneath them. I applaud your civility, Mrs. Baxter."

"But he's *not* beneath me," Bella said. "I'm no lady."

"Nobility," Mrs. Trelawney said, "*true* nobility, doesn't come from birth or lineage. It comes from how we treat others, particularly those with whom we do not seek to ingratiate ourselves. Too many men, and women, of our acquaintance lack true nobility, for all that they may be titled."

Such as that unpleasant man from the afternoon.

"Quite so, Alice, my love," Mr. Trelawney said. "Nobility is defined by honor, loyalty, and honesty. Don't you agree, Mr. Baxter?"

Bella glanced at her husband. Again, she caught a flash of apprehension in his eyes. Perhaps he felt as uncomfortable as she in such a genteel environment.

Her head still throbbed faintly from the afternoon, and she stifled a yawn. Then she caught Mr. Trelawney watching her, and her cheeks flamed with embarrassment.

"Forgive me," she said.

He smiled, his eyes sparkling in the candlelight. "There's nothing to forgive." He glanced at Bella's husband. "Baxter, care for a brandy while the ladies retire to the drawing room?"

Lawrence's eyes widened. "Oh—I-I thought…"

"Ross, my love," Mrs. Trelawney said, "for a man who considers himself a master at understanding the needs of his fellow man, you're showing a marked lack of observational skills. Can't you see how tired our guests are?"

"I'm not…" Bella began, but Mrs. Trelawney caught her hand.

"My dear, you look exhausted," she said. "I noticed how pale you were this afternoon. As much as I enjoy your company, I'm not so selfish as to require it if you wish to retire."

"You don't mind?"

"Of course not—we can take tea together tomorrow, before you return home."

"Baxter, you can still join me for a brandy," Mr. Trelawney said.

"Ross!" his wife chided. "I'm sure Mr. Baxter would rather tend to his wife than be subjected to a lecture on the intricacies of a superior cognac. Not everyone wishes to discuss the flavor profile of a liquor that burns the throat."

Bella stared at her hostess. How did a woman of her class dare to challenge her husband? But rather than show anger, Mr. Trelawney gave his wife an indulgent smile.

"Of course, my love," he said. "Forgive me, Baxter. I shall imbibe alone. But I trust you'll grant me an interview before you leave tomorrow."

The two men stared at each other, and Bella caught a flash of discomfort in her husband's eyes. Then he nodded. "I'd be delighted."

Mrs. Trelawney rose. The footman darted toward the diners and pulled back the chairs as they stood. "I'm rather tired myself," she said, "so I'll retire also, and leave Ross to his brandy." She turned to Lawrence. "Mr. Baxter, take care of your lovely wife."

"I will," Lawrence said, his voice catching. Then he offered Bella his arm, and the party exited the drawing room—Trelawney to his study, and the others to the bedchambers.

After bidding goodnight to their hostess, Bella's husband led her to her bedchamber.

"Sleep well, my love," he whispered.

"You'll not be joining me?"

"I'm in the chamber next door if you need me."

"I need you now." She curled her fingers around his. "I don't understand why they gave us a bedchamber each."

"It's what lords and ladies do."

"Then I never want to be a lady," she said. "I don't want to spend a single night without you in…in my bed."

"Nor I you, my love."

He pushed open the door and led her inside.

A fire was already blazing in the hearth. To think—these people had others to light a fire for them, burning away while they were elsewhere, as if they had no need to worry about the price of coal!

Bella approached the fire, stopping on the hearth rug to hold her hands out, letting the warmth seep into her skin. Her husband followed, and he dipped his head to place a kiss on her neck while he tugged at the laces of her gown.

"Mmm…" she murmured. "I wonder if Mrs. Trelawney takes as much pleasure from her maid undressing her?"

"I suspect Mr. Trelawney performs the service more often than her maid," he said, his hot breath tickling her skin. "They seem very much in love."

"But not as much as we are."

She closed her eyes, the loss of sight serving to heighten the sensations around her—the crackle of the fire, together with the sound of her husband's breathing, growing hoarser as he continued to unlace her gown. The aroma of wood and smoke filled her nostrils together with the deeper, muskier scent of man…

His fingers brushed across her skin as he removed her gown, and she shivered in anticipation. Then he swept her into his arms and carried her to the bed, where he peeled off her stockings, slowly, as if he relished the act. She inhaled, relaxing back into the bed. When she opened her eyes, he stood before her naked, the firelight shimmering across the planes of his muscles.

He was all man—and he was all hers.

And he was ready for her.

He climbed onto the bed and crawled on top of her. The hairs on his legs prickled the sensitive skin on the insides of her thighs, and she parted them in eagerness. He closed his eyes and inhaled, his nostrils flaring.

"Sweet Lord," he growled. "There's nothin' so fine as the scent of a woman who's ready for her man." He leaned down and brushed his lips against hers. "Does my women taste as sweet as her scent?"

Oh my…

A faint pulse of pleasure throbbed in her center, and she caught her breath. Then he placed a kiss on her chin, tracing his lips across her throat to the top of her breasts, where he stopped to flick her nipple with his tongue. He peppered her belly with soft, feathery kisses until he reached her curls.

"Shall I give you pleasure, my Bella?" he whispered, his hot breath rippling over her flesh.

She caught his hands. "No."

Disappointment flared in his eyes as she sat up. Then, twisting round, she pushed him back until he lay before her, his manhood jutting proudly.

She leaned over him and placed a kiss on his belly, tasting the salt on his skin. "It's time I gave *you* pleasure," she whispered.

Then she lowered her head and took him in her mouth.

He jerked and let out a low growl. "Devil take me, woman, you'll be the endin' of me!"

She ran her tongue along his length, and a deep groan bubbled in his throat, which grew deeper with each sweep of her tongue. Then he let out a strangled gasp, as if gritting his teeth, and tensed.

She released him, and he whimpered, fisting his hands in the bedsheet.

"Bella…" he groaned, as if in pain.

"Yes, husband?"

"You torture me, woman."

"How shall I atone?"

He jerked his hips, his manhood bobbing, and she climbed on top of him, parting her legs, relishing the feel of his hard length against her thigh.

"Sweet Lord, Bella—were you sent from heaven?" He tipped his head back, the tendons in his neck protruding, and his knuckles whitened as he tightened his fists. "I-I cannot bear it," he whispered.

"Oh, husband," she teased. "Do you wish me to withdraw and bid you goodnight?"

"No! Dear Lord, no!"

"Then be still, my love, while I pleasure you."

She crawled on top of him until she felt his tip nudging against her aching flesh. He let out another groan and tilted his hips upward.

"No, husband, you must be patient and await your pleasure."

"Wife..." he said, his voice strained through gritted teeth. "I-I can't..."

Slowly, she eased herself onto his length, relishing the deliciousness of having him inside her, until he filled her completely.

His mouth curved into a smile. "Ah...that's it," he whispered. "My woman—my beautiful woman."

Then she shifted upward before thrusting down, impaling herself on him.

"Oh, Bella!" he cried, "I..."

But before he could finish, she began to move, up and down, in a slow, steady rhythm. He opened his eyes and licked his lips, his gaze fixed on her breasts, which bobbed with each movement.

"Oh, goddess. Have I died and entered heaven, to be met with such a sight?"

Deep pleasure grew in her center, ignited by the delicious friction—receding each time she withdrew, then swelling higher each time she thrust forward. She increased the pace, chasing the pleasure, while her skin prickled with heat at the need in his hungry gaze.

Then she felt him shift inside her. A deep groan escaped his lips, swelling into a roar as she joined him in pleasure, shattering and rippling around him until she threw her head back, opening her mouth as she fought for breath. Air filled her lungs as she crested the wave, and she let out a long, low cry.

"Lawrence—oh, Lawrence!" At the peak, she screamed his name as myriad colors burst in her mind, shattering into a thousand stars.

"Bella!" he cried with one final thrust as she rode the wave, drawing every drop of pleasure until, at last, they crested together.

She leaned forward until she lay on top of him, chest to chest, their bodies merging to form a single creature, sticky with sweat, their hearts beating in unison. She clung to him, relishing the solidity of his hard, muscular body. Then she turned her head to one side, placing her ear against his chest while his heartbeat settled into the slow, languorous rhythm of a man well pleasured.

"Oh, Bella—I'm not deservin' of you," he said. "There's nothin' I can give you over what you've given me."

She caressed his skin, tracing the outline of his muscles with her fingertips. "There's one thing you can give me, my love," she said. "A child."

He stiffened. "A-a child?"

"Am I wrong to ask?"

"No, my love—there's nothing I want more. But—are you sure?"

She nodded against his chest. "Roberta wants a sister—as does William. And Jonathan has said he wants to complete the band of brothers."

"The band of brothers?"

"Nelson's band of brothers."

She traced the outline of his nipple with her fingertips. He drew in a sharp breath, and she felt his manhood twitch beneath her.

"William's the eldest, if only by a few minutes," she said, "so he's claimed Nelson's title. Roberta's Lieutenant Hardy. And Jonathan's Captain Miller."

"And there's a fourth member of the band?"

She let out a soft laugh. "My love, there's at least fifteen in Nelson's band of brothers. We're going to be very busy—but I doubt we'll consider our efforts a chore."

She tilted her head, offering her lips for a kiss. For a moment he hesitated, then he claimed her mouth, sweeping his tongue across her lips. He wrapped his arms around her and rolled onto his side, taking her with him.

She smiled and closed her eyes, nestling against him. "I love you," she whispered.

"And I you, Bella," he said. "More than life itself. Promise you'll never forget that. Promise me you'll remember that, whatever happens, I love you, and I always will."

He held her close until his breathing deepened, indicating that he'd fallen asleep.

Promise me you'll remember that, whatever happens, I love you, and I always will.

What had he meant by that? And why, as he said it, could she discern such despair in his voice?

Chapter Forty

"There's the chimney of Ivy Cottage above the trees—we're almost home!"

Bella turned to Lawrence, her face illuminated with her beautiful smile, and his heart swelled with love and pride—pride in the woman he loved more than his own life. And her love for him shone from her eyes.

Would they still shine with love when he told her the truth?

Tell her, Baxter. Tell her before someone else does.

Trelawney's voice echoed in his mind. He'd taken Lawrence aside after breakfast that morning, issuing a warning. Whitcombe—the imposing, arrogant creature who'd insulted Bella yesterday—had recognized her. It was only by virtue of the man "not wishing to sully his hands with a woman he despised," as Trelawney put it, that he'd said nothing in public. That and Whitcombe's friendship with Trelawney.

A friendship Lawrence had hoped to take advantage of, seeing as Trelawney had been recommending Lawrence's skills to all his acquaintances.

He sighed. Yet again, his hopes had been thwarted. But this time not at Lady Arabella's hand, but that of a man who despised her.

"My love?"

Concern clouded Bella's expression. She steered her mount alongside his and leaned forward, offering her lips for a kiss. How she managed to maintain her balance, he couldn't fathom. But in her former life she must have ridden all the time—and her body remembered.

Sooner or later, her mind would follow suit.

"Is anything wrong?" she asked.

"No, love." He forced a smile.

"Is it to do with what you said yesterday—about needing to tell me something?"

He nodded, and his gut twisted at the flicker of pain in her eyes.

"Then we'll discuss whatever it is once we've returned the horses to the inn and are settled at home. We can open that bottle of port Mr. Trelawney gave us, if you like. He wouldn't stop telling me how special it is. He must think a lot of you."

They passed the fork in the road leading to the inn, but Lawrence steered his horse toward Ivy Cottage.

"Shouldn't we return the horses first?" Bella asked.

"I'll do that once I've got you settled at home," Lawrence replied. "There's no need for you to overtire yourself. You're still suffering from your headache. And don't go denying it, woman—I can see how pale you are."

She smiled. "You take such good care of me. What would I do without you in my life?"

They rounded a corner, and Ivy Cottage came into view.

"My home," Bella said. "I'm ashamed to say I didn't like it at first—but now I love it. And do you know why?"

"No," he said quietly.

"Because you're there. You and the children. You're all I need to be happy."

Dear God, I hope so…

He lifted his gaze to the heavens as he uttered the silent prayer.

"Oh, look!" she cried. "An enormous carriage."

Lawrence lowered his gaze. A coach-and-four stood beside the front gate, with a driver and two footmen dressed in red and gold livery.

Very familiar red and gold livery.

His heart plummeted as a chasm opened up in the pit of his stomach.

"Bella, stop," he said. "I'll see who it is."

Ignoring him, she approached the coach and dismounted.

"Are you lost, sir?" she asked. "The inn's back the way you came."

"We're not lost, your ladyship."

She frowned. "*What* did you call me?"

As Lawrence dismounted, the carriage door opened. A footman jumped down from the back and set a block on the ground. Then a man climbed out, heaving his body through the door. He stepped on the block and stumbled against the footman. "Out of my way, damn you!"

Bella froze as the man righted himself and brushed down his jacket—a bright-blue silk, embroidered at the edges in gold thread. Then her eyes widened in recognition.

"Dunton!" she cried. "Your Grace—what are you doing here?"

Lawrence took a step forward. "Bella…"

A second footman climbed down from the coach and blocked Lawrence's path. "That's far enough," he said.

"Lady Arabella." Dunton issued a bow and offered his hand. Bella took it, then her face broke into a smile.

"I remember!" she cried, her voice filled with joy. "Sweet Lord—I can remember! Arabella… I've heard that name in my dreams at night. And now I remember. Arabella, Mariah…" She shook her head. "No! It's *Lady* Arabella—Arabella Mariah Ponsford. I'm right, am I not?"

"Yes, my dear," Dunton said, his fleshy face swelling into a leer. "And you're the future Duchess of Dunton."

She nodded. "Yes—that's it! A duchess—I'm a *lady*, a-and I'm to be a duchess."

She turned to Lawrence.

"Oh, Lawrence, isn't it wonderful? I-I can remember. I know who I am. I…"

"Mama! Papa!" excited voices shrieked from inside the cottage, then the door burst open and the children rushed out.

"Billy!" Bella cried. "Bobby, Jonathan—I can remember who I am. I'm—"

"Thomas!" Dunton roared. "Keep those brats away from my fiancée."

The thickset footman strode toward the children, fists raised.

"Stop!" Lawrence cried. "Lay a finger on my children, you devil, and you'll regret it."

"He's not the devil," Dunton sneered. "*You* are."

"Papa, who's that man?" Roberta asked. Then she turned to Bella. "Mama?"

Bella drew in a sharp breath. "Bobby…" she whispered. Then she frowned and lifted her hand to her forehead.

"Bella, are you all right?" Lawrence asked.

"Don't you *dare* speak to her!" Dunton snarled. He drew Bella toward him. "Are you well, Lady Arabella?"

"M-my head hurts." She closed her eyes, and when she opened them again, they glistened with tears. "I-I'm here with…"

She shook her head and glanced toward Lawrence.

"A-are we married? You said you're my husband. A-and the children…"

"Mama?" Roberta stepped toward her.

"Leave her be, Bobby, love," Lawrence said.

"Th-they're not my children, are they?" Bella shook her head. "How can they be my children? M-my accident was…"

"Four months ago," Dunton said.

"Th-that can't be true," she whispered. "No—w-we've been…" Her voice trailed off.

"Bella—" Lawrence began.

"Do *not* presume to address my fiancée!" Dunton boomed.

"Papa," Jonathan said, "is Mama leaving?"

"She's not your mother, you vile urchin!" Dunton said.

Lawrence's heart cracked as Jonathan let out a whimper and clung to his leg. "Papa, has this man come to take Mama away?"

Bella stared at Jonathan—the child she'd taken into her arms before they left for the Trelawneys' house and called him her most precious boy. But the love Lawrence had once seen in her eyes had been replaced by confusion.

Then the confusion turned into horror.

She lifted her gaze to Lawrence, her sapphire eyes hardening.

"I-I'm not Bella Baxter," she whispered. "I'm Lady Arabella Ponsford. Who are you?"

Then she let out a low cry.

"Y-you're the gardener. The one who…" She shook her head, and a tear rolled down her cheek. "Y-you said I don't matter enough to hate."

"Bella, I didn't mean it."

"You *did*," she said. "You said I'm nothing. To you, I'm *nothing*. Y-you said I inflicted misery on others to satisfy my own joyless life."

A dark ache swelled in his heart. "Oh, Bella, no…"

"Did you not mean it?"

"Bella, that was then," Lawrence said. "I—"

"No!" she cried. "Do me the honor of speaking the truth, for once. *Did* you mean it?"

Lawrence dug his fingernails into his palms to draw his attention from the raw ache in his heart.

"I see," she said quietly. "You're not man enough to voice the truth, but I see it in your eyes."

She tilted her head up, the emotion draining from her eyes, until the fire, the essence of his Bella, faded—doused by the ice-cold soul of

Lady Arabella. Though dressed in the same plain muslin gown, she now carried it like a lady. The woman standing before him now was not his Bella.

Nor had she ever been.

"Bella, please," he said. "Hit me, scream at me…anything to show me how you're feeling."

Her lips trembled. Any moment, she would crumple and cry, and reach out in her need for him.

Then she shook her head.

"No," she said. "You deserve no such consideration after what you did."

"What did he do?" Dunton asked. "Did he defile you?"

She glanced at Dunton, not quite disguising the fear in her eyes. "No," she said. "At least, in no way of consequence."

"Then come with me now, Arabella. This brigand has damaged your reputation. We must be married as quickly as possible to restore it."

"Don't go with him!" Lawrence cried. "He's deceiving you."

Her smooth demeanor crumpled, and she let out a bitter laugh.

"*He's* deceiving me? What about *you*? Reducing me to the life of a kitchen maid—and for what? Vengeance? Hatred? Pray tell me, Mr. Baxter, how would *you* define deceit?"

Dunton offered his hand, and she took it.

"Papa!" Jonathan said. "Don't let her go!"

Lawrence moved forward, but the footman raised a thick, fleshy fist.

"Now, mister—don't be making a fuss. It'll be the worse for you if you do, and you don't want them brats of yours without a father, do you? Who knows what might befall them?"

Lawrence's gut twisted as the footman leered, exposing a row of yellowing teeth punctuated by several gaps.

Dunton placed a possessive hand on the small of Bella's back. "Get yourself inside, my dear—you look like a common harlot."

"B-but I must collect my things," she said, taking a step toward the cottage. Then she hesitated.

"My dear?" Dunton said.

She shook her head. "It matters not. There's nothing of mine in the cottage. At least, nothing I care to take home."

Jonathan let out a wail, and Roberta took him into her arms.

"Mama!" William said. "Don't go!" He ran toward her, but the footman caught his arm, yanking him back. William gave a cry of pain, and Lawrence charged forward.

"Keep your filthy hands off my son!"

The footman let out a laugh, then released William, pushing him aside.

"Papa—please stop her from leaving!" the boy said.

"There's nothin' I can do, lad, if she's wantin' to leave us."

For a moment, Bella looked as if she was going to wrench free of Dunton's grip and rush toward the children, arms outstretched, professing her love for them. Then she turned away, and Dunton led her toward the carriage, pushed her inside, then climbed in.

The footman closed the carriage door then clambered onto the back. With a crack of his whip, the driver set the horses in motion.

"Papa!" Roberta cried. "M-make them stop—please!"

Jonathan wriggled free from Lawrence's arms and chased after the carriage. "Mama!" His screams of anguish ripped through the air and tore at Lawrence's heart. "You said you'd stay forever. You said mothers never leave their children!"

The driver cracked his whip again, and the carriage gained speed. Jonathan tripped and tumbled to the ground, shaking with sobs.

"Jonathan!" Lawrence ran to him and tried to scoop him up, but his son pushed him back.

"No, Papa! It's *your* fault!"

"Jonathan, I—"

"Bobby!" the child wailed, and Roberta ran over then embraced him, stroking his hair, as Bella had done. William joined her, and the three children sat in the middle of the lane, comforting each other.

"Children, I—"

"Go away!" Roberta said. "We don't want you—we want Mama."

"She's not your mother," Lawrence said. "She never was."

"Yes, she was," William replied. "And *we* love her, even if you don't!"

"I do love her," Lawrence said. "I love her more than anything."

"But n-not enough," Roberta said. "If you loved her enough, she would have stayed with us."

"Mama!" Jonathan let out another wail.

"Come on, Jonny," William said, "let's get you inside. Roberta and I can make you some hot chocolate, just like Mama did."

Between them, the twins helped their brother up. Roberta brushed the dust from his breeches, William took his arm, and they led him inside without even a backward glance.

Chapter Forty-One

Bella leaned back in the carriage, willing her headache to subside. But the pain only worsened as a cacophony of images and memories crashed into her mind.

A high-pitched scream of anguish cut through the memories, and she snapped her eyes open. Through the window, the trees whipped past as the carriage gathered speed. Then the voice screamed again.

"You said mothers never leave their children!"

She sat up and leaned toward the window. "Jonathan!"

A thick hand pulled her back. "Hush, woman! Don't make a scene."

"But—"

"They're nothing to you, my dear," Dunton said. "Some peasant and his spawn."

Bella stared at his fleshy fingers covered in bejeweled rings. Then she lifted her gaze, following the line of his elegantly fashioned sleeve toward the collar of his jacket, his silk necktie—and his cold, lust-filled eyes.

My fiancé...

Nausea overcame her, and she jerked backward, catching her breath.

"What's the matter now?" he asked.

"I'm going to be sick."

"Bloody hell, that's *all* I need..." he muttered. "Can you at least wait until we reach our destination?"

"Wh-where are we going?"

"We're going *home*," he said, his voice thick with exasperation.

Home...

Where *was* her home? Not the elegant, soulless London townhouse she'd lived in until her betrothal, nor the dark, neglected shades of Ilverton Manor. Perhaps the house she'd lived in with her parents had been a home—the elegant Jacobean mansion she'd forgotten until it had forced its way into her dreams.

She closed her eyes, and another image floated into her mind—a tiny, whitewashed building, the front door surrounded by a trailing rose; a parlor that carried the aroma of lavender, smoke, and wood; a kitchen with a range that had come to accept her rule; an array of children's toys adorning every surface; a garden filled with life, following the contours of nature, and...

And four souls she'd grown to love.

That was her home. Not a building in which she merely existed, but a place where she was needed, valued, cherished...and loved.

But it had been a lie—an act of vengeance played out by a man who despised her enough to deceive her into servitude. A man who had taken her freedom, her maidenhead—and her heart.

But she was not Bella Baxter, the pathetic creature ruled by her heart. She was Lady Arabella Ponsford, daughter of a duke.

And Lady Arabella was *not* weak. Lady Arabella was sensible enough to know that succumbing to the needs of her heart only led to misery and ruination.

She had already suffered ruination—she would *not* be conquered by misery.

She smoothed her features into the mask of the Society debutante, then wrinkled her nose and glared at the offending hand.

"Unhand me, Your Grace," she said. "Unseemly behavior is not to be tolerated."

"Unseemly behavior?" Dunton laughed. "You give a fine argument, madam, and I'd listen, had you not been wandering about the countryside like any slut. You looked quite content riding alongside that hobbledehoy."

"A temporary aberration," she said. "I was afflicted by memory loss, and was deceived by a…" She hesitated, her body tightening with need at the memory of a pair of slate-gray eyes filled with desire, and his gentle touch that soothed her body before igniting the fires of pleasure. "I was deceived by a *brute*," she said, channeling her bitter hatred into that final word.

He *was* a brute—and she would never forgive him. Not for behaving in the uncouth manner of a commoner, nor for attempting to wreak vengeance on her. No—she could not forgive him for deceiving her into believing, for a bright, glorious moment, that a little corner of goodness resided in the world.

And she could not forgive him for making her fall in love.

Dunton pulled her close, parting his lips for a kiss.

She turned her head away, fighting the ripple of nausea at the stench on his breath. Sweet Lord—had he been drinking liquor already?

"You forget yourself," she said coldly.

"Come now, Arabella," he said. "I've waited a long time for our reunion. And a woman must obey the man she pledged herself to."

"Her husband, yes," she said, "but you're not my husband."

"Not yet—but we can seal our union here and now."

"Do you wish to ruin me?" she cried. "Like you ruined Juliette Howard?"

"That little harlot spread her legs to trap me into marriage. She's nothing but a commoner's daughter—their sort are animals compared to us."

"Which is what you're doing now, by anticipating the wedding night," she said. "Are *you* an animal, Your Grace?"

He pulled her hard against his body, and her stomach churned as his manhood pressed against her thigh.

"A feisty mare, aren't you, beneath that cold haughtiness," he said. "But women are all the same—inside you're all whores, begging for a man's cock."

"Stop!" she cried. "Or I'll scream."

"Who would hear you?"

"If you defile me, I'll *never* marry you—ruined or not."

He hesitated, anger and lust flashing in his eyes. Then he loosened his grip.

She pulled herself free and shifted away from him.

"Forgive me, my dear," he said. "I was quite overcome by the violence of my affections. Your aunt will testify to the fact that I've thought of nothing but you from the moment you were lost."

"Aunt Kathleen?"

"She's been most anxious for your return." He raked his gaze over her form, then the sneer returned. "Perhaps it's best if I leave you in peace for the time being," he said. "I daresay you're riddled with lice, having lived in that hovel."

"Yes," she said, forcing her voice to remain calm. "I daresay I am. I'm anxious to take a bath, and"—she plucked at her skirts of the gown Sophie had given her, which she'd trimmed with pink ribbon, and smiled, ignoring the pain in her heart—"and to have this garment burned."

"Quite so," he said. "But once you've been restored to your true self"—he licked his lips—"*then* you shall be mine."

The urge to flee swelled within her. But where would she go? Back to the man who'd destroyed her faith and broken her heart? Or forward, to the world into which she was born—a world of duty, honor, and security?

What did she care if there was no place in that world for her heart?

Chapter Forty-Two

"Children, it's time to come inside."

The whispering from the den grew silent. Then William spoke.

"Read the sign."

Lawrence lowered his gaze to the lettering on the piece of paper pinned to the rosebush marking the den's entrance, scrawled in Roberta's hand.

Keep out. On pain of death.

"Supper's ready," he said. "You can't stay outside all night."

"We're not hungry!" Roberta cried.

"*I* am," Jonathan whispered, and Lawrence caught sight of movement among the bushes.

"Traitor!" Roberta said. "Get back here."

"I'm no traitor," Jonathan whined. "I'm—Ouch!"

"Come inside before I lose patience," Lawrence said. "Hiding out here won't make things any better."

"Neither will coming inside," William said.

"You'll catch a chill."

"What do *you* care?" Roberta sneered.

"I care very much," Lawrence said.

"Liar!" William replied. "If you cared, you wouldn't have let Mama go."

"She wasn't your mother, William," Lawrence said.

"You said she was!" Jonathan cried. "You told *her* she was—and she believed it."

"Well, she's gone now, son, and there's nothing I can do about it."

"You can bring her back."

Lawrence sighed. "I miss her too."

"Then go and rescue her from the bad man!" Jonathan said.

"Ye gods, boy—she's not Lady Hamilton needin' saving from Bonaparte's clutches, and you're not Lord Nelson!" Lawrence roared. "She went willingly—and she hates me."

"That's not our fault," Roberta said. "It's *yours*. Go away—if she doesn't want to be with you, then neither do we."

"There's a beef pie in the oven—and I've put some potatoes on, fresh from the garden. Come in or go hungry. It's your choice."

"Don't want pie!" Jonathan wailed. "I want Mama!"

Cursing, Lawrence trudged back into the kitchen.

They'd come when they were hungry—there was nothing better to stop children from sulking than a good pie on an empty belly.

Only they weren't sulking. They were grieving.

For the woman who'd made the pie.

He pulled out five plates from the cupboard and set them on the table. Then he caught his breath, staring at the fifth plate before returning it. Sighing, he approached the range to check the potatoes.

He stirred the pot, and the potatoes swirled around the water, bumping against each other. He pressed the back of the spoon against one to test it, but it was hard as a stone.

Shouldn't they be cooked by now?

He placed his hand on the range.

Warm, but not hot to the touch.

Curse the bloody thing! Why couldn't he get it to work? *She'd* never had trouble using it—except for the first few days after she arrived.

He shoved the pan aside. It slipped from his grasp and tumbled to the floor, landing with an explosion of water and potatoes, one of which rolled under the range.

"Bugger!"

Well, it could bloody well stay there. They'd have to make do without potatoes tonight.

Which left the pie—one of two he'd found in the pantry. She must have made them the day before they'd left for the Trelawneys', ready for supper on their return. But, given the luck he'd had so far, the pie would be uncooked also.

He opened the door to the range and reached for the pie.

Pain shot through his fingers as he grasped the pie dish, and he jerked back, falling to the floor.

Bloody hell, that hurt.

For a moment, he lay on his back staring at the ceiling, besieged by the memory of the day she'd slipped in the garden and fallen on her back—when he'd fallen on top of her, and they almost kissed.

He closed his eyes, willing the memory to linger—the soft scent of rose, the taste of honey on her lips, her beautiful sapphire eyes filled with love…

Then he opened his eyes to a ceiling smeared with smoke stains.

He'd promised to clean those stains for her, but he'd forgotten, dismissing the task as a frivolity. But that frivolity would have made her happy. Made her smile. More than anything, he wanted to see her smile. But he'd never see her smile again.

Would she smile for Dunton?

He shuddered at the thought of that vile man's hands on her. But in the end, she'd chosen Dunton. She had tilted her haughty little nose at Lawrence—and the children—before climbing into Dunton's carriage, sentencing herself to life in a golden cage.

He inhaled, and the rich, sweet aroma of spiced apples caressed his senses. Not beef pie, then. He must have picked up the wrong one. It smelled delicious, nonetheless.

He sat up and glanced at the range. The door was open, revealing a dark, gaping hole, like a toothless mouth. And beside it was the pie—upside down, surrounded by shards of pastry, its contents oozing over the floor.

"Fuck!" he cried. "Fuck, fuck, *fuck!*"

He struggled to his feet, glanced up, and froze.

Three faces peered through the kitchen window, silhouetted against the evening sky.

"Lawrence—are you all right?"

"Of course he's not, Uncle Ned!"

They disappeared, then the door opened and Ned walked in, followed by Sophie and Sam.

Sophie rushed toward him. "Are you hurt, Mr. Baxter?"

"I've had an accident with supper."

She glanced at the floor. "Yes, I can see that."

"Sophie, love, don't be tryin' to help him up," Sam said. "Not in your condition."

"I'm with child—not dying," she huffed.

Lawrence withdrew from her touch. "I can manage myself, Mrs. Cole."

"*Sophie*, please," she said. "We're among friends, are we not?" She glanced about the kitchen. "Where's Bella?"

"She's not here."

"I can see that also," she said. "Well, if we're quick, we can clear the mess before she comes down. Have you any bread or cheese? That'll do for us—save her the bother of cooking."

Lawrence shook his head. "I-I don't understand."

"You invited us for supper," she said. "Don't you remember?" She let out a laugh. "My Sam's always accusin' me of being forgetful because of my condition, but I swear a man's memory is worse than a woman's."

"Sophie, don't talk nonsense," Sam said affectionately.

"I speak the truth and well you know it, Sammy, love," she replied. "When Bella comes, she'll agree, I'm sure. Is she upstairs? I'm anxious to see her."

"No!" Lawrence cried. "For devil's sake, woman—can't you understand? She's gone!"

She turned. "Gone? What do you mean, gone?"

"She's left us."

"Bella? Has she taken the children?"

"No—they're in the garden."

Sophie shook her head. "No," she said. "Not Bella—I could understand if it was that Mrs. Duffy from the other end of the village—she's got a right wanderin' eye. Lord knows how many different men have fathered them kids of hers. But *Bella*? No."

"Oh, fuck," Ned growled.

"Uncle Ned!"

"She *knows*, doesn't she?" Ned said.

Lawrence nodded.

"Did you tell her, or did she find out?"

"She found out—and now she's gone."

"You fool," Ned growled. "You bloody, fucking fool!"

"Uncle Ned, what's—"

"I bloody *told* you, didn't I? I said this would happen if you continued to deceive her."

"For heaven's sake!" Sophie said. "Will one of you tell me what's happened to my friend?"

"She's back with her fiancé," Lawrence said, wincing at the bitterness in his voice. "She decided that a life of a duchess, with big houses and fancy clothes, was better than a life with them that love her."

"She *what*? You're making no sense."

"He speaks the truth, Sophie," Ned said.

"Uncle?"

"It's not my confession to make, Sophie, love. Go on, Lawrence—

tell my niece what you've done."

Lawrence's head throbbed and he pressed his fingertips against his temples—but the pain persisted.

"Bella... She's *not* Bella," he said. "She's Lady Arabella Ponsford. And she'll soon be"—he drew in a sharp breath as bile rose in his throat—"she'll soon be the Duchess of Dunton."

"You're jesting," Sophie said.

"Of course he is, Sophie, love," Sam said. "Aren't you, Mr. Baxter? What would a duchess be doin' with the likes of us?"

"I speak the truth," Lawrence said. "Bella had no idea who she was until this morning. She..."

He drew in another breath. *Sweet Lord*, this was hard!

"Sh-she lost her memory in an accident."

"I know," Sophie said. "She said how you were helping her to remember everything. But..."

The color drained from her face.

"I *remember* now!" She lifted her hand to her forehead. "I remember thinking how strange it was that you'd not mentioned a wife when you first arrived at Brackens Hill. Then, after you brought her here, you said she'd disappeared before..."

She shook her head. "I-I thought at first she'd run off with a man—abandoned you and the children—and you'd taken her back, until I saw that she really had lost her memory. But it was all a falsehood—a story to deceive us. And I believed her lies."

"She never lied to you," Lawrence said.

"I-I don't understand."

"Bella deceived no one, Sophie. It's I who deceived Bella. Made her believe..."

Horror sparked in Sophie's eyes.

"You made a lady believe that she was your wife—mother to your children? Why would any decent man do such a thing?"

"For Justice," Lawrence said, wincing. How weak that sounded!

"*Justice?*"

"Her fiancé, the duke, employed me in his garden. In a fit of spite, she burned all my possessions and refused to pay me. So when I saw a chance to make her work off her debt, I took it."

"Holy mother of God," Sam whispered.

Sophie stepped forward. Lawrence caught a blur of movement before pain exploded in his chin, his head snapping back with the force of her blow.

He staggered back, nursing his jaw. *Bloody hell*, that hurt!

"Sophie!" Sam said. "What the bleedin' hell do you think you're doing?"

She shoved her husband aside and advanced on Lawrence again. He retreated until his back came against the wall.

"How dare you speak of justice! There's no justice in what you did—only vengeance. Cold, calculated vengeance against an innocent woman."

"She wasn't innocent." Lawrence winced.

"She *was*," Sophie said, shaking off her husband's restraining arm. "I don't care what she's supposed to have done! No woman deserves to be abducted and deceived—'specially one who's lost her memory. Can you imagine how frightened she must have been? Alone in the world, ripped from all that she's known, and placed at the mercy of a man determined to ruin her for his own gratification."

"She had no loved ones," Lawrence said. "I saw her fiancé disown her with my own eyes—"

"So, you stole her for your own? That's not collecting a debt—it's *slavery*."

Slavery...

An ugly word, but was he so dissimilar to those who indulged in the flesh trade? What made his lies any different to the shackles that a slaver used to affirm his ownership over another human soul?

"Had you killed her with your own hands, you wouldn't have

committed a worse crime," Sophie snarled. "And your children—did you deceive them also?"

"No," he said. "They never knew their mother—she died bringing Jonathan into the world. But they came to see Bella as their mother."

"Why, you…" She raised her arm, and Sam caught it.

"Don't be distressin' yourself," he said. "Come away before you do any real harm."

"Why should you care for him after what he's done?" Sophie asked.

"I don't, Sophie, love, but I don't want you upsetting yourself. Think of our child."

Tears rolled down Sophie's face, and she let out a cry. "Bella…" She buried her head in her husband's chest while he held her in his arms, rocking her to and fro. The tender gesture of a gentle-hearted young man caring for his beloved clawed at Lawrence's heart. Their love was plain to see—a pure, abiding love founded on honesty, mutual adoration, and respect.

And for a shining moment, he'd deceived himself into believing that he and Bella shared such a love.

"Did *you* know about this, Mr. Ryman?" Sam asked. Sophie stopped crying and stared at her uncle.

Ned colored and nodded.

Sam let out a whistle. "Bloody hell."

"Sophie?" Ned approached her, but she raised her hand.

"Don't come near me, Uncle."

"I *told* Lawrence to tell her," Ned said.

"Why didn't you tell her yourself? Were you too weak?"

"It wasn't my place."

She nodded. "So, you *were* too weak." She turned to Lawrence. "*Both* of you, weak men, too afraid to say or do what's right if it risks making your pathetic lives less comfortable."

"Perhaps I *am* weak," Lawrence said. "I was wrong at first—I know that. Do you think I've not suffered in the knowledge that I've been doin' something so wrong? I'm still suffering."

"Well, forgive me for not carin' one jot about your suffering," she retorted.

"I suffer because I love her!" Lawrence said. "Maybe not at first—though it touched my heart when I first saw her to see her so unhappy with people who only valued her for what they could take from her."

"Makes them no different to you."

"I *cared*," he said. "I cared that she was condemning herself to a life of misery. I hated her at first—her vile temper, the way she considered the world beneath her. But as I came to know her, I realized that was an act she played to survive. She played the part well—the haughty lady, taking satisfaction from wielding power over others—but the loss of her memory freed her true self. The woman who emerged and blossomed into Bella—my Bella—was the purest soul on this earth. And when she smiled"—he hesitated, beset by the memory of her beautiful smile, her sapphire eyes illuminated with love—"it made my soul sing. Lady Arabella never smiled. But when my Bella first smiled at me, she captivated my soul. I resolved, then, to spend the rest of my life ensuring that she never stopped smiling." He shook his head. "How could I tell her the truth, knowing that if I did, her smile would die? I loved her too much to do that to her. I…"

His breath caught as he fought to withstand the agony in his heart.

"So help me God, I know I'm destined for hell, but I *love* her. I know she'll never forgive me, and I'll have to make peace with that. B-but I cannot bear the thought of her being in the hands of a man who will never value her, much less love her. She deserves to be loved."

He looked up, but tears clouded his vision, turning his companions into blurred shapes.

"*That* is why I suffer—not in knowing what I have lost, but in knowing what life awaits her. Even if she hates me with every fiber of her being, I shall always love her."

He flinched as Sophie approached him. Then she lifted a hand and placed it on his jaw where she'd struck him moments before.

"I understand," she said. "Love can catch you unawares. It can creep into your heart and settle there. It's the most joyous thing in the world, but with the sweet comes the bitter, for the loss of a loved one cannot be borne."

A sob swelled in Lawrence's throat, and she drew him into her arms.

"Sophie, love…" Sam said.

"Oh, shoo! Both of you, go and find the children."

"They're in the garden," Lawrence said. "They're refusing to come in."

"They'll come around," Sophie said. "Children are resilient. Despite what you've done, I can see you're a good father to them. They'll forgive you."

"And Bella?"

"Not even her memory coming back can destroy the love she bore you."

"She didn't—"

"Yes, she did," Sophie said. "She'll forgive you in the end. But you must reconcile yourself to one possibility."

"Which is?"

"That you will never be able to forgive yourself."

Chapter Forty-Three

"**H**OME AT LAST, my dear."

Bella glanced outside the carriage window. The familiar façade of Ilverton Manor loomed dark against the evening sky, and she bit her lip to stem the flutter of dread in her stomach.

Her headache still lingered, and though she'd been beset by fatigue throughout the journey, sleep had eluded her.

Dunton had spent much of the journey asleep, his snores rattling through the carriage, accompanied by the stench of sour wine and bodily odors not completely disguised by an abundance of cologne. Why had she never noticed it before? Unless she had and her mind had buried her revulsion, smothering it with the prospect of being his duchess.

Only, perhaps she no longer wished to be a duchess. Perhaps, instead, she wanted to be valued, appreciated—and loved.

At times, during the journey, Bella had been drawn to the carriage door, the handle only needing a single turn to open it, leading to—where? Freedom, perhaps, but not love. Her love had been built on a foundation of deception and betrayal.

"Did you not hear me, my dear?"

She turned to see her fiancé leering at her. "Wh-what?"

He took her hand, and she suppressed a shudder as he lifted it to his lips. "I was saying that we'll have the banns read on Sunday."

"Oh."

"And the following two Sundays after that. Then we can marry immediately—in three weeks."

"Three weeks?"

"It'll be the Society event of the year," he said, ignoring—or choosing to ignore—the horror in her voice. "Everybody must be there."

"Everybody?" She shuddered at the thought of the *ton* witnessing their union. Westbury with his overly assertive wife and her modern sensibilities. And Whitcombe...

Dear Lord, Whitcombe!

The man she'd set her cap at last Season—the man who, not two days ago, had called her *a spiteful shrew.*

"I-I'd prefer a quiet wedding," she said. "Surely there's no need for everyone to be there?"

"There's *every* need," Dunton said, a hard edge to his voice. "Your absence has been talked about. I'm anxious to show the world that our union brings me no shame."

"But...the expense!" she said. "A small affair, with a handful of acquaintances is all we—"

"Now, now, my dear." He patted her hand, his expression hardening. "I trust we're not going to indulge in a disagreement. Money's no object—or it won't be once we're married. You must trust my better judgment."

"Because you're a man?"

"Oh, how you amuse, my dear! Men possess a superior understanding to the fairer sex. You mustn't worry about matters such as *expenditure*. You'll have more important matters to concern yourself with, such as the duties of a duchess—which I'm sure you'll carry out to my satisfaction."

She tried to withdraw her hand, but he held it firm.

The carriage drew to a halt, and the door opened, revealing the thickset footman. Dunton climbed out of the carriage, which listed sideways under his weight. Then he pulled Bella after him and led her toward the main entrance of Ilverton Manor, where a row of servants stood waiting.

Bella smoothed her expression into the mask of Lady Arabella and approached the servants, who bowed and curtseyed as she glided past them and entered the building.

"Thomas, escort Lady Arabella to her chamber," Dunton said. "Make sure she's kept safe."

What did he mean by *safe*?

"Yes, Your Grace." The footman turned to Bella. "Come with me, your ladyship."

"I know the way to my chamber," she said.

"The master wishes me to accompany you."

There was little point in arguing when all she craved was the sanctuary of her chamber. She swept past the footman and climbed the staircase, aware of his heavy footsteps following her.

"I'll expect you at dinner," Dunton said. "Eight o'clock. Don't be late. Your maid will help you dress."

Ignoring him, she continued her ascent.

"My dear!" he cried, an edge to his voice. A thick hand grasped her upper arm, and she drew in a sharp breath at the squeeze of pain.

"The master asked you a question, your ladyship," the footman growled.

Quelling the tremor in her stomach, she stopped and turned. "Of course, Your Grace." Bella forced a smile. "I'll be there."

Dunton gave a self-satisfied smile. "That's better, my dear. I'm glad to see you're coming to your senses. Thomas, I believe you can release Lady Arabella. She knows her place—do you not, my dear?"

"Yes, Your Grace," she said coldly.

The footman released Bella's arm, then followed her to her chamber.

"I'll send for your maid, your ladyship," he said as they reached the door.

"There's no need—"

"Master's orders. You're not to be left unattended. For your safety."

"Then bring her to me at once, Thomas."

He ushered her inside, then closed the door behind her. Now alone, she let the façade disintegrate. The tears she'd kept at bay formed hot, fat droplets that splashed onto her cheeks. She held a fist against her mouth to suppress her cry.

"Lawrence…" A sob escaped her. "Why did you make me fall in love with you?"

The door burst open, and she jerked back, retreating further into the chamber until she collided with the bed.

Connie stood in the doorway.

"Lady Arabella!"

The maid stepped forward, arms outstretched. Bella's heart almost cracked at the concern in Connie's eyes—almost as if she cared for her—and she fought the urge to run into the girl's arms.

Then the footman appeared, towering behind the maid.

"Connie, bring me a fresh gown," Bella said. "And I require a bath. Immediately."

Her smile fading, the maid addressed the footman. "Thomas, can you bring hot water for Lady Arabella's bath, please? Quick as you can."

She curtseyed to Bella. "I'll bring you a fresh gown, Lady Arabella. Shall I choose one for you, or bring a selection?"

"Do I look as if I care, Connie?"

"Of course, Lady Arabella, forgive me. I'll be back directly."

The maid slipped through the adjoining door to the dressing room, while the footman remained in the doorway, his gaze wandering over Bella's form, a flare of lust in his eyes.

"Don't just stand there," Bella said. "I want my bath."

The footman's mouth curled into a grin.

"I want it *now*," she said, hardening her voice to disguise her fear. "Shall I tell my fiancé that you're refusing to obey my orders? He doesn't respond well to disobedience."

Fear flickered in the footman's eyes, and he bowed then retreated.

She ought to have been relieved to have found a method by which to control him—fear of Dunton and what he might do to those who defied him.

But it was a fear she shared.

BELLA APPROACHED THE bath and shed her garments. As she lifted her chemise over her head, she paused, tracing her fingertips along her neckline, searching for her mother's necklace.

But it was gone—sold to pay for Jonathan's glasses. The one possession—among all the fine jewels and gowns at her disposal—that she had truly treasured.

She let out a sigh. She'd been glad to sell it, for she loved the little boy…

Her heart clenched, and she drew in a sharp breath to temper the swell of sorrow.

No, she *didn't* love him—not *any* of them!

Yes, you did. You still do…

Ignoring the whispered voice in her head, she dropped her chemise and stepped into the bath. Wisps of steam and the aroma of lavender filled the air and, for the first time since her memory had so rudely crashed into her consciousness, the pain in her head began to ease.

She eased herself back, letting her body relax while the warmth from the water seeped into her bones.

How she'd missed a bath! The temperature of the water was just right—warm enough to soothe her aching body, but not so hot as to sting her skin. Connie must have taken pains to test the level of heat—

and to sprinkle the water with lavender petals. Just how she liked it.

Lying back in the bath with her eyes closed, the only sounds the ticking of the clock in her chamber next door and the gentle movements of her maid, Bella could almost believe she was in paradise—a brief respite from the need to submit to the whims of others for the sake of propriety, or to concern herself with chores.

It was times like this that would provide respite in the years to come. A duchess taking her bath was a creature to be left in peace—if only for a moment.

The door creaked open, and Connie's soft footsteps approached. But the maid knew better than to fill the silence with chatter. Instead, Bella heard a rustle of fabric as Connie kneeled beside the bath, then the splash of water as she began the ritual of bathing her mistress—first dipping the soap in to form a lather, then washing Bella's limbs with gentle, sweeping movements of her hands. Bella surrendered to her maid's touch, letting her arms relax while Connie moved the washcloth over her arm, massaging her shoulder and elbow with her fingertips.

"Oh, how I've missed this," she murmured. "Thank you, Connie."

The hand stilled.

"Y-you're welcome, Lady Arabella."

Bella's heart ached at the frank astonishment in the maid's voice. In all the years Connie had served her, she had never once given the maid a word of thanks.

"Oh, your poor hands!" Connie said, rubbing her fingertips over Bella's palms. "How you must have suffered! They're covered in callouses."

"No more than yours," Bella replied.

"But you're a *lady*. A lady cannot be seen with the hands of a laborer. I've an ointment for softening the skin. That'll get rid of those marks in no time. In the meantime, you can wear gloves—those lace ones I made you—then you won't have to see them."

Bella fought the urge to tell Connie that there were worse problems in the world than a few patches of roughened skin. Did her maid think her so frivolous that she'd faint at the sight of the evidence of hard work?

She opened her eyes and glanced at the bathwater, which had turned a faint shade of brown.

Her maid met her gaze, and the corners of her eyes creased with a smile of sympathy. "It's nothing to be ashamed of, Lady Arabella—and it's not your fault you were abducted. Nobody need know about the dirt—I won't tell."

Bella sat up, trembling. "That's enough, Connie," she said coldly. "You dare comment on my ablutions?"

The maid blushed, her eyes bright with tears. "N-no. Forgive me, Lady Arabella. I was just saying—"

Bella rose to her feet, sloshing water from the bath. "In my experience, it's better if a servant refrains from saying anything. Bring me a cloth, please, so I may dry myself."

"But—"

"Now, please."

"Very good, Lady Arabella," Connie said in her more familiar, toneless voice. She handed a drying cloth to Bella, then bobbed a curtesy before exiting the room.

Fighting the urge to call her back, Bella rubbed the cloth over her limbs, pausing at the scars on her thigh, which had always been a source of shame—ugly blemishes to be hidden, lest they ruin her prospects for greatness in Society...

Until *he* had told her that they were beautiful.

He had peppered them with kisses, running the tip of his tongue across the marks on the flesh, while she lay before him, thighs parted in offering. Then he'd traced a path to the top of her thighs with his tongue, toward that wicked, secret part of her, before dipping it into...

Stop it!

Tempering the swell of need, she finished drying herself, dropped the cloth onto the floor, and donned the chemise Connie had set out. Then she returned to her bedchamber, where the maid waited with a pale-blue gown.

Bella stood in silence while Connie dressed her. First came the stays, and each tug of the laces removed her further from the world she yearned for, followed by the gown, which slipped over her head with the rustle of silk. Then Connie steered her to the dressing table, where she brushed Bella's hair into a cascade of soft, dark waves framing her face.

"There!" the maid said, her reflection in the mirror smiling. "The lady is now restored to greatness. You're so beautiful, Lady Arabella—the duke is the luckiest of men to have secured your hand. Everybody says so."

In the past, such sycophancy would have elicited contempt, but now Bella felt only shame. Was that how the world viewed her—nothing more than a pretty thing for a duke to claim as his own?

That, together with her title and her dowry. Dunton did not value beauty alone. Juliette Howard—wherever she was—had learned that the day she gave herself to him, then was abandoned, carrying his bastard.

Were it not for her title, Bella might have suffered such a fate—pregnant with some man's bastard, vilified by the world, most likely selling her body to survive…

Any life was better than that. Even marriage to Dunton.

Connie picked up Bella's discarded gown. "Oh, you poor thing having to wear this—the hem's all frayed. I'll get rid of it, have it burned."

"No!" Bella cried. "A-at least let me take the sash ribbon. There might be something I can do with it."

"Are you sure?"

"Of course I am. Give it here." Bella snatched the dress and tore the ribbon from the bust line, rolling it up in her fingers. "I've taken a fancy to this particular shade of pink," she said. "I-I want it in the garden—if His Grace's gardener can find a rosebush to match."

"But…"

"Did I ask your opinion?"

The maid hesitated, and for a moment, Bella feared she'd penetrate the veneer to reveal the desperate creature beneath.

Then Connie shook her head. "Forgive my impertinence, Lady Arabella. Here—let me finish your hair, then you can rest until the dinner gong."

Bella sat in silence while Connie gathered tendrils of hair and twisted them into curls before pinning them in place. Before she finished, the chamber door burst open, and Bella's aunt appeared, her sharp-nosed features creased into an expression of disdain.

Connie dipped into a curtsey. "Oh, ma'am—you gave me quite the fright coming in like that!"

"How else should I enter a chamber in my home, girl?" came the reply. "Insolent creature!"

The maid cringed and lowered her head—almost as if she were a dog expecting a beating. "Beg pardon, ma'am."

"Yes, yes." Aunt Kathleen swept into the room and stood before Bella. She waited, expectation in her gaze, then let out a huff. "Well, child? Get up! Or have you lost all decorum?"

"Sorry, Aunt." Bella rose and forced herself to remain still while her aunt circled her, fingering her curls and peering at her face, as if she were a trader in horseflesh inspecting a mare.

"Has your mistress given you trouble, girl?" Aunt Kathleen asked.

"No, ma'am," Connie said.

"Good." Bella's aunt wrinkled her nose as she spotted the discarded gown. "Get rid of *that*," she said. "And anything else my niece had about her person."

"Yes, ma'am."

Bella fisted the ribbon and placed it behind her back. Connie moved to stand behind her then took her hand, coaxing it open with her slim fingers. Bella's heart ached at the betrayal—but what had she ever done to earn her maid's loyalty?

"Show me your hands, Arabella," her aunt said.

Connie snatched the ribbon, and Bella waited for the axe to fall.

"Well?" Aunt Kathleen stepped closer, and Bella held out her hands. "Palms *up*, if your please."

Bella turned her hands, and her aunt let out a snort.

"I feared as much. You've the hands of a commoner. We must ensure Dunton never has to look at them." She gestured to Connie. "Girl, find some gloves for your mistress."

"Yes, ma'am."

"Very good. Finish your duties, then go."

The maid bustled about the chamber, tidying the bed, then she slipped her hand beneath a pillow. Bella caught sight of a flash of pink ribbon as Connie met her gaze and gave her a quick, tight smile. Then the maid resumed her attention on the bed, smoothing the sheets, after which she bobbed a curtsey and left.

As soon as she'd gone, Aunt Kathleen raised her arm and backhanded Bella across the face.

Bella let out a cry at the sting of pain. She stumbled back and rubbed her cheek. "Aunt…"

"Silence, you slut!"

"*What* did you call me?"

"You heard! Do you have any idea the damage you've caused our family name—the name of Ponsford?"

"It's not even your name, Aunt. You're Lady Smith-Green—or, at least, that's what you want the world to know. Much better than plain old Mrs. Green, isn't it?"

"Why, you little…" She rounded on her niece again, but Bella stood firm.

"Go on, Aunt," she said. "I dare you. But what would it do to the Ponsford name if I turned up to dinner with a marked face? Would Dunton still want me?"

"*You* should be more concerned about that than me, girl."

"It seems as if the prospect of being the aunt of a duchess is of more value to you than the prospect of being a duchess will ever be for me," Bella sneered.

"Ungrateful child! To think, all I have sacrificed for you."

"What sacrifice, Aunt?" Bella asked. "It was my fortune that paid for everything—the house in London, even the gown you're wearing now."

"Your fortune will mean nothing if the world learns of your ruination."

"What ruination?"

"You may have fooled Dunton, but I'm not so out of my wits that I cannot recognize a whore when I see one."

"Will you be so bold as to call me a whore when I'm a duchess?" Bella said. "I could have you thrown out in a heartbeat. Best pack your things—*I'll* be mistress of this house in three weeks."

"Oh no you won't, girl. I've persuaded the duke to wait."

Bella suppressed the joy at the notion of delaying her condemnation to a life with Dunton. "What for?" she asked.

"Even *you* must understand the necessity of a delay."

"No, Aunt."

"Then you're a fool as well as a slut. We must wait until we know whether you're carrying some man's bastard."

Bella recoiled at the loathing in her aunt's voice.

"H-he didn't defile me," she said. "I—Oh!" She let out a cry as her aunt gripped her by the neck, pressing her bony fingers into the base of Bella's throat.

"Did you spread your filthy legs like a bitch in heat to satisfy your base urges, with little thought for the disgrace you bring upon *me*?"

With her free hand, she clawed at Bella's stomach. "If some rutting beast has planted his seed in your belly, then it must be dealt with before you can marry the duke."

"Dealt with?"

"I know a physician who'll undertake the task. He'll want payment for his discretion, but that's a small price to pay. Should you survive, you can reflect on the folly of your disobedience."

"Aunt, I—"

"Silence! I'll not hear another word. You will remain here until this sordid little affair is settled. Do not distress me any more than you already have by discussing it. And do not discuss it *at all* in the duke's presence."

Bella's aunt released her, then retreated to the door.

"You're to remain here until supper. I'll send Thomas to escort you to the dining room, and I expect you to behave in the manner expected of a woman of your rank."

She exited the bedchamber, closing the door. Shortly after, Bella heard the key turn in the lock.

She stood, her mind shifting in and out of focus. Then it sharpened into a single thought.

If some rutting beast has planted his seed in your belly…

Sweet Lord—was she…?

She placed a hand over her stomach, nursing the nugget of hope.

"Lawrence's child…"

Someone to love, without condition or requirement, to cherish and nurture—someone to hold in her arms, to kiss goodnight and read stories to. If it were a boy, she could teach him to love; a girl, she could teach to be strong, like Roberta…

Then her resolve faltered as she recalled Roberta's wail of desperation, her tear-streaked face. She might never see Roberta again—or William, or Jonathan—but it would be some consolation if she had a child to love.

Only she wouldn't.

A *problem to be dealt with*, Aunt had said.

Bella stumbled toward the bed and sank back, holding a protective hand over her belly while she surrendered to despair and grief.

Chapter Forty-Four

"Are you saying, Mr. Simms, that you'll *give* me money each quarter?"

The banker, a neat, balding man, eyed Lawrence over the top of his spectacles. "That's exactly right, Mr. Baxter. One half of one percent of the value of your deposit."

Lawrence glanced at Trelawney sitting beside him. "One half of... *what?*"

"I'm aware it's not much, Mr. Baxter," the banker said. "If you deposit regularly with us, we can increase the rate to one percent."

"Percent?"

"It means for every hundred, Baxter," Trelawney said. "So, for the fifty pounds you've just deposited, you'll earn five shillings each quarter—one half of one per cent."

Lawrence stared at his companion. "Five whole shillings?"

"It's called interest, Mr. Baxter," the banker said. "It would earn you ten shillings if you deposit regularly."

"Which he will do," Trelawney said. "Won't you, Baxter? Several of my acquaintances have inquired about your services—and they're willing to pay handsomely."

"Y-yes, of course," Lawrence said.

"In which case, that concludes our business," Simms said, "unless you wished to discuss anything, Mr. Trelawney?"

Trelawney shook his head, then rose. "No—my wife's meeting us at the Crown. I don't want her kept waiting."

"Of course." The banker offered his hand, and Lawrence took it. "Welcome to Simms Bank, Mr. Baxter. Mr. Trelawney, give my regards to your charming wife."

Simms opened the door, then Trelawney led Lawrence outside.

As they stepped out onto the street, Trelawney pulled a watch out of his waistcoat pocket. "Almost three o' clock," he said. "You'll join us for tea? The Crown does a good tea. Mrs. Folds always bakes a lemon cake especially for Alice—she has a soft spot for her."

"I'm not dressed appropriately to take tea with a lady."

"Nonsense!" Trelawney laughed. "Alice cares little about that sort of thing, and she particularly wished to see you."

"Me?"

Trelawney nodded. "She was most distressed—we both were—when we heard about"—he glanced around, then lowered his voice—"*Lady Arabella*."

Lawrence drew in a sharp breath to stem the ache in his heart. "I-I take it Lady Arabella's well?"

"I know nothing of her state of health, but she's to marry Dunton in a matter of days," Trelawney said. "We heard it from an acquaintance who saw Dunton at his London club. Apparently Dunton was boasting about his increased prospects now a fortune was forthcoming."

"Who told you this?"

"Whitcombe."

"Oh, *him*," Lawrence said. "He insulted Bella at your garden party. He may be a duke, but that didn't give him the right to distress her."

"Perhaps not Bella," Trelawney said, "but Whitcombe has only ever known *Lady Arabella*, who's been very cruel to his wife in the past."

"Bella's not cruel."

"*Bella* never existed. She was the product of an injury to the head, a lapse in senses."

"Perhaps Bella was the true woman," Lawrence said, "and Lady Arabella was the role she'd been taught to play by the folk around her."

"Are you bearing the loss?"

Lawrence let out a sigh. "With my first wife, I hardly had time to know her. We liked each other, and I grieved for her passing—but the pain lessened over time. But with Bella..." He shook his head. "It frightened me how quickly she found a place in my heart, as if we were meant to be together. Now she's gone, it's like there's something missing in my heart—a wound that can never heal."

"You'll heal in time, Baxter," Trelawney said. "You have your children, a flourishing business, and friends—good friends who'll stand by you no matter what."

"What of Bella?" Lawrence said. "She has no true friends. She might have fancy gowns, carriages, and big houses, but she's at the mercy of that vile man."

"Dunton?"

"Beggin' your pardon, Trelawney. I know it's not done to speak ill of them with titles, but a man like that won't make her happy."

"She chose him."

"Aye," Lawrence said. "In the end, she chose him. Not me, nor the children, but *him*."

"All right, my friend," Trelawney said brightly. "What you need is a good dose of Mrs. Folds's cake to cheer you up. She has the lemons brought over fresh. Or perhaps a drop of Mr. Folds's brandy? It's not too early to enjoy a glass, and it's the finest in Midchester." He gave Lawrence a wink. "I should know—I supplied it to him."

They crossed the road to the inn. The door opened to reveal a woman in a neat blue gown with a crisp apron, flame-red curls peeking out from beneath a lace cap.

"Mr. Trelawney! Such a pleasure to see you again." She cast her gaze over Lawrence, showing no sign that she'd noticed his lack of cravat, his frayed jacket, or the scuffs on his boots. "You've brought a friend?"

"This is Mr. Baxter," Trelawney said. "The finest garden designer in England."

"Praise indeed, for a man usually so prudent in distributing compliments," she said.

"Except when it comes to your lemon cake, Mrs. Folds."

"You're too charming for your own good, Mr. Trelawney," she said. "Now, shall I take you to the parlor? Mrs. Trelawney's already arrived—she's been here twenty minutes."

"Wonderful!" Trelawney said. "Less time at the shops is always good news for my pocket."

"Mr. Trelawney, if I didn't know you were jesting, I'd turn you over my knee!" Mrs. Folds replied. "How dear Mrs. Trelawney puts up with your teasin', I don't know. It'll serve you right if she's ordered from every shop in the street. She's brought a basket with her, filled with all sorts of things. Jewelry, bolts of silk—more ribbons than I've ever seen!"

Ribbons…

Bella loved ribbons—her beautiful eyes had smiled with love as he related the story about how he'd wooed her with an array of pink ribbons.

But that story had been a lie.

Fuck—what an utter bastard I am.

Mrs. Folds chattered on while she led them to a parlor overlooking a garden with a pond that sparkled in the sunlight.

Mrs. Trelawney sat beside the window, her face in profile, a serene smile on her lips.

"Beggin' your pardon, Mrs. Trelawney—your husband's here," Mrs. Folds said. "And his friend. Shall I have tea brought in now?"

Mrs. Trelawney turned her head slowly, and as she met Lawrence's gaze, her eyes narrowed for a moment before she smiled.

"Yes, of course, Mrs. Folds," she said. "My husband has spoken of nothing but your lemon cake this past week."

"Very good, ma'am. I'll be back directly."

Mrs. Folds curtseyed, then exited the parlor.

Lawrence approached Mrs. Trelawney, hands outstretched. "A pleasure to see you again," he said. "I—"

Before he could continue, she strode toward him and slapped him across the face. "You blackguard!"

Lawrence stepped back, rubbing his cheek. *Bloody hell*, that hurt!

"Alice!" Trelawney said. "What are you about?"

"You should be asking *him* that." She jabbed a finger at Lawrence's chest, and he flinched in anticipation of another blow.

"Alice, we spoke about this," Trelawney said. "Lady Arabella's back where she belongs. Why should you care? You never liked her."

"I never liked Lady Arabella," she replied, "but *Bella* was a completely different woman. I didn't even recognize her."

"She was the same woman," Trelawney said.

"I can see the likeness *now*, Ross," she huffed. "When a familiarity is pointed out, it becomes obvious, and you wonder why you missed it. But at the time, she was different enough not to be recognized."

"Why didn't you recognize her?" Lawrence asked.

She raised her eyebrows.

"I want to know, Mrs. Trelawney, if you'd oblige me."

"She was different from within," she said. "Someone like Whitcombe would recognize her. He's a man, and men are incapable of looking beyond the surface. When he sees a woman, he'll note her outward appearance—the color of her eyes, her hair, the shape of her mouth, the shape of her body. Because that's all a man cares about."

"What did *you* see when you saw Bella, Mrs. Trelawney?" Lawrence asked.

"A kind and clever soul," she said. "A woman determined to do her best for her loved ones, unafraid to express her opinion, and eager to make use of her talent and intellect. In short, I saw a rare creature—a woman whom I wished to have as a friend. And *you*, Mr. Baxter, took her away from me."

"Alice, had I known you were so angry with Mr. Baxter," Trelawney said, "I'd never have—"

"Never have what? Brought me to Midchester today?" She shook her head. "No, I suppose you wouldn't have. Instead, you'd have laughed at your wife's whims before reassuring Mr. Baxter here that he's better off without the harpy of the *ton* in his life. As for Bella, Dunton will destroy her."

"She willingly went with him," Lawrence said. "There was nothing I could do to stop her—she ignored even the children's pleas."

"You see, Alice?" Trelawney said. "It was her choice."

"Have you never known a woman to be mistaken?" she asked. "To be coerced into making the wrong choice because Society, or her upbringing, dictates it?"

Trelawney blanched, and his forehead creased in distress. "Alice, my love, you cannot liken that woman to the suffering you endured."

What the devil did he mean?

"Forgive me," Lawrence said. "I'm intruding. I should go."

"No, Mr. Baxter, stay," Mrs. Trelawney said. "I'm merely referring to my first husband."

"Y-your first…?"

"I was a duchess, once," she said. "Blinded by the expectations of my father, and of Society, I chose a duke over the man I loved. And it almost destroyed me."

"Alice, my love, don't distress yourself."

"No, Ross." She set her mouth into a firm line. "What better purpose can I put my past mistakes to than to teach others the folly of ignoring their hearts?"

She turned to Lawrence. "My first husband was a cruel man, Mr. Baxter. But the world revered him for his title. And even after surviving marriage to him, I found myself on the brink of marrying another just like him, just as cruel, to satisfy propriety. But I found salvation in another—in the man I loved, the man I had *always* loved."

Her voice wavered, and Trelawney drew her into an embrace.

"Alice, don't distress yourself."

"A moment's distress is a small price to pay when the liberty and happiness of another is at stake. Mr. Baxter, do you love her?"

"Lady Arabella?" Lawrence asked.

"No," she said. "*Bella*. Do you love Bella?"

"Yes."

"Did you lie with her?"

"Alice!" Trelawney said. "That's not a question a woman should ask."

"And yet I do ask. Mr. Baxter, answer the question. Did you lie with her?"

Fighting the urge to deny it, Lawrence nodded.

Trelawney shook his head. "Bloody hell."

"You unimaginable bastard..." she whispered, curling her hand into a fist.

Lawrence took a step back. His cheek still stung from her first blow, and he had no wish to discover the potency of her right hook.

"I tried not to," he said. "Many times, I drew back—restrained myself."

"That's *so* gentlemanly of you," she sneered. "Should we congratulate you for delaying her violation at your hands?"

"She wanted it," Lawrence said. "She wanted *me*."

"I say, Baxter, that's far enough," Trelawney said. "That sort of talk's not suitable when there's ladies present."

His wife snorted. "Spare my sensibilities, Ross! I'm well aware what happens between a man and a woman when they're in love. I'm merely trying to establish whether your friend ruined Lady Arabella out of gratification or lay with her out of love."

"Of course it was out of love!" Lawrence cried. "What kind of man do you think I am?"

"Most men are *that kind of man*," she replied. "Dunton most of all. You profess to love Bella, yet you ruined her. Try to view the world from her eyes. She's lost and alone, her body violated, and her reputation ruined. You deceived and betrayed her—made her believe that you were her husband, and your children were hers. And for what? A whim?"

"Not a whim," Lawrence said.

"What, then? An act of hatred? Are you a decent, hardworking man eager to make a better life for himself, or a revolutionary content to persecute those who have more than you?"

"You think I don't regret what I did?" he said. "I regret the misery I caused her, and the misery she'll endure. But I cannot regret the joy of knowing and loving her—the light she brought to my life, and the children's lives." He drew in a sharp breath and lifted his gaze. "And I'll *never* regret loving her, Mrs. Trelawney."

"There's little point in making such a grand declaration if you're not prepared to act upon it, Mr. Baxter."

"What can I do?"

"Fight for her," she said.

"I cannot fight a duke," Lawrence said. "Dunton won't let me near her—most likely I'll be shot on sight."

"Then seek the help of your friends, Mr. Baxter. Ross, can't you do something?"

"Dunton's hardly likely to be receptive to anything *I* say," Trelawney said. "Whitcombe's more likely to succeed. But I can't ask him—he loathes Lady Arabella."

She shook her head. "So, you'd forsake her as well."

"What if she doesn't want me to fight for her?" Lawrence asked.

"I didn't want Ross to fight for me," she said. "I too was lost and alone, blinded by fear, believing that everyone had forsaken me. But

I'm thankful every day that Ross removed the blindfold. He opened my eyes and taught me to hope again."

"Bella hates me," Lawrence said. "I saw it in her eyes."

"You're unwilling to risk a few sharp words from a woman you've wronged?" She shook her head. "Clearly you don't love her enough. Perhaps you never did."

"I did love her enough! I still do—more than life itself."

"Then prove yourself worthy of her."

"But what if she deems me unworthy?" Lawrence asked. "What if I do everything I can to bring her back only to find she's forsaken me?"

She let out a sigh and took Lawrence's hand. He flinched, anticipating another blow, but instead, she lifted it to her lips and kissed his knuckles.

"Poor Mr. Baxter," she said. "I can never condone what you did, but I believe you love her—and I saw the love she bore you every time she looked at you. So I urge you not to surrender to defeat. You must accept responsibility for what you did. You must accept the risk that she may never forgive you. But could you live with yourself if you gave up trying when there was still hope?"

Lawrence inhaled, shuddering as he fought to suppress his despair.

"You're right, Mrs. Trelawney," he said. "I cannot leave her at the mercy of that man while there's still hope."

"Then perhaps, Mr. Baxter, you may after all succeed in your endeavor to deserve her."

At that moment, the door opened, and Mrs. Folds entered, followed by two young girls each carrying a tray bearing a tea set and an array of cakes and sweets.

"Heavens!" Mrs. Trelawney said. "Is all that for us?"

"It is, ma'am. Seein' as you've brought a friend with you, I thought he might be deservin' of something a little special for his first visit to the Crown. We like to keep our patrons happy."

Mrs. Trelawney glanced at Lawrence and smiled, her gaze softening.

"Yes, Mrs. Folds," she said. "I had my doubts at first, but I believe Mr. Baxter deserves to be happy. And we'll do what we can to ensure that he is."

Chapter Forty-Five

BELLA LOOKED UP into a pair of clear gray eyes, filled with love.

"My Bella..."

She tilted her head back, offering her lips, while she moved her hands across her body. Her fingers lingered on her breasts—the silken skin with the little buds at the center that beaded as she flicked them with her thumb. Then she moved her hands lower, toward the downy curls that were already damp with need.

"Lawrence..."

Relishing her wantonness, she moved her fingers slickly against herself. Any moment and he'd kiss her and whisper wicked words while he slipped inside her.

But the moment never came.

She opened her eyes to find herself alone, in her chamber at Ilverton Manor.

A clock struck in the distance, seven notes in succession, and she pulled back the bed sheets and swung her legs over the edge of the bed, then froze.

A small patch of blood was visible between her legs.

The door was knocked upon, and, her cheeks warming with shame, Bella lowered her night rail then leaned forward, drawing in a deep breath to fight the swell of disappointment.

The knocking came again.

"Lady Arabella?"

"Come in, Connie."

Her maid opened the door. "Oh, Lady Arabella! You're not up yet. The master's expecting you to attend him at breakfast. Your aunt was most insistent you be on time, and the breakfast gong will sound any minute."

Bella cringed at the fear in the maid's voice. "Forgive me, Connie," she said. "Be assured I'll tell His Grace it was *my* fault for being late."

"That's right kind of you, Lady Arabella, but there's no need. I've set out your gown. I'll have you ready in no time."

Bella stood. The world shifted out of focus, and she stumbled against her maid.

"Steady, Lady Arabella! Are you unwell?"

"N-no," Bella said, fighting back tears.

"Oh, mercy!" the maid said. "I should have known, but you've been away. I didn't know when to expect it."

"Expect what?"

"Your..." The maid blushed. "Y-your *monthly bleed*. Shall I tell His Grace your health's delicate today? Perhaps your aunt can be persuaded to have a tray sent up for you."

"N-no—please don't trouble yourself, Connie."

"It's no trouble, Lady Arabella. I can get anything you need."

Bella placed a hand on her belly—her empty belly. "Nobody can give me what I need," she whispered.

"You'll feel all right again in a day or so," Connie said. "Some sweet tea will settle your stomach. I can bring you fresh cloths and change the bedsheet. Why don't I—"

"No!" Bella cried. "There's *nothing* you can do, Connie! Why can't you leave me be?" She sank onto the bed, the tears flowing more freely.

Connie placed a light hand on her arm. "Can't you tell me why you're so distressed? I want to help."

"There's nothing wrong," Bella said, forcing a hard edge to her voice. "Didn't you hear me the first time?"

"I know what you said, Lady Arabella, but there's more to knowing what someone's saying than hearing the words."

Bella looked into her maid's eyes. They were a pale brown—wide, expressive, and filled with compassion.

"Connie..." She hesitated. "I-I hoped... I mean, I believed that I w-was..."

The maid's blush deepened.

Bella rose to her feet. "It matters not," she said. "Perhaps it's for the best. After all, the duke..."

"I understand," Connie said. Then she spoke more brightly. "Now—how about I fetch your cloths, then get you dressed? You've been stuck inside these past few days. Some fresh air will revive your spirits."

Bella approached the window and looked out. Her heart ached as she spotted the hedge at the back of the garden, behind which was the site of the bonfire.

Perhaps what she endured now was retribution for the sins she had committed.

While Connie dressed her, Bella remained silent, staring out of the window, complying with her maid's instructions like a meek child. She lifted her arms, stepped into her petticoats, and turned her head from side to side as Connie twisted her hair into curls. Finally, she stood before the dressing mirror, looking every part the haughty heiress she'd always been.

Except for the expression in her eyes.

"There!" Connie said. "You look perfect, Lady Arabella. Nobody would know your health was delicate."

Bella sighed, and a tear ran down her cheek.

"Oh, miss," Connie said. "I know I'm behaving out of turn, but you look so sad. Is it because you wish you'd not returned here?"

Bella opened her mouth to admonish her, but the words caught in her throat, and she stifled a sob.

"Oh, miss! Were you happy there with"—the maid lowered her voice to a whisper—"the gardener?"

Bella fought to voice her denial, but she surrendered and nodded her head.

"Why didn't you stay with him?"

"It's not that simple, Connie."

"It is, if you follow your heart."

"*My* heart wasn't the problem," Bella said. "He didn't love me. He pretended, *tricked* me into becoming his wife, and mother to his children—as vengeance. He must have hated me so much for what I did."

"You burned all his tools, miss, and his drawings. They may have meant nothing to you, but to him, they were everything."

"Oh, Connie!" Bella said. "You make me quite ashamed. But, you see, that's why I can never face him. I grew to love him—I still do—but if he hates me so deeply to have taken such vengeance... I cannot bear it. I cannot bear to be hated by the man I love!"

"I think..." Connie began, then the breakfast gong echoed in the distance. "Heavens! Let's get you downstairs. Let me tidy you up."

The maid lifted her hand to Bella's face and brushed away the tears. Unable to withstand the simple act of kindness, Bella took her maid's hand and squeezed it.

"Thank you, Connie. I don't know what I'd do without you."

"You can trust me, Lady Arabella."

There was a knock, and before Bella could respond, Dunton's footman entered.

"The master doesn't like to be kept waiting."

Bella fixed him with a cold stare. "Thomas, how dare you enter my chamber! I'll have you whipped for that."

She exited the chamber, pushing him aside.

"Do not follow me," she said. "I know the way, and am not in need of a gaoler."

He merely grinned, then followed her to the breakfast room, where Dunton and Aunt Kathleen were already seated at the table. The duke rose to his feet.

"You're late, child," Aunt Kathleen said.

"I came as soon as I heard the gong, Aunt."

Dunton settled back into his seat as Bella took her place. "Thomas, my fiancée is hungry," he said.

Bella waved the footman away. "I'm not hungry. Fetch me some tea."

"You must eat, my dear," Dunton said. "Thomas, bring her some eggs."

"Yes, Your Grace."

The footman spooned eggs onto a plate and placed it in front of her.

Dunton nodded toward the plate. "Eat, my dear."

"I *said*, I'm not hungry," Bella snapped. "Must I always bow to your demands?"

"A wife must obey her husband," he replied. "It's better for her if she learns her place sooner, rather than later." He leaned forward. "Now. *Eat.*"

Bella shivered as invisible fingers brushed the back of her neck. She took up her fork and picked up a mouthful of eggs, which wobbled and glistened in the sunlight. Her stomach churned, but Dunton continued to stare, his gaze darkening. Ignoring the rising tide of nausea, she slipped the fork into her mouth, then swallowed.

"That's better," Dunton said.

Aunt Kathleen smiled coldly. "I told you my niece would learn her place eventually."

"Perhaps, but she'd benefit from a little more correction. She cannot be seen to deviate from the righteous path."

"Righteous?" Bella let out a mirthless laugh. "You dare lecture *me* on righteousness?"

Dunton's eyes narrowed. "Have a care, my dear. You forget to whom you are speaking."

"I know perfectly well to whom I'm speaking," Bella replied. "A man who's debauched countless young women, including my friend, Miss Howard."

"Friend!" Dunton scoffed. "Juliette Howard whored herself in an attempt to marry above her station. The devil knows who sired her bastard. But at least I'll not have that problem with you."

"What do you mean?" Bella asked.

"Hush, girl!" Aunt Kathleen said. "It's not seemly to speak of such things."

Her aunt and Dunton exchanged a glance, and Bella's cheeks warmed with shame.

"Has your maid been inspecting my bedsheets, Aunt?" she asked.

"I *said*, don't speak of it!" Aunt Kathleen said, rising to her feet. "I thought I'd raised you better than that, yet you talk like a whore. You should be grateful His Grace is still willing to take you on."

"Would he have been so willing were I carrying another man's child?"

Dunton's face reddened. "My dear, you're distressed," he said, rising. "You should return to your chamber to rest."

"I shall *not*."

"I expect you to honor me as a fiancée ought."

"Will you honor me in return," Bella asked, "or merely spend my fortune?"

He strode toward her. "It's my fortune now the marriage contract's been drawn up."

She stood, scraping her chair back. "Come no closer."

"Tut-tut, what a willful harpy you've become," he said, grasping her arms.

"Unhand me," she snarled. "Do you think I'd marry a man who

thinks nothing of abusing me to get his own way?"

He curled his fingertips into her flesh. "You've no idea what I'm capable of doing to get my own way," he said. "You think I can't control one silly, spoiled little heiress?"

He grasped her chin and forced it upward until their eyes met, his glittering with lust and fury.

"You will marry me, my dear, and you'll show me proper deference and gratitude."

"Your Grace!" Aunt Katheleen cried. "Please desist."

He released Bella's chin, and she could have wept with relief at her aunt finally coming to her rescue.

"I'll discipline the girl as I see fit," Dunton said.

"I did not mean to question your authority, Your Grace," Aunt Kathleen said, "but with the wedding approaching, it's better to leave her face unmarked."

Dunton smiled. "How sensible and practical! Arabella, you're fortunate to have such a caring aunt."

He forced his mouth over hers, and her stomach churned as he slipped his tongue along the seam of her lips, probing to gain entrance. She jerked her head back, and he let out a low laugh.

"I like a little spirit," he said. "It'll makes the victory so much sweeter when I break you in."

"You'll never have me, Dunton," Bella said.

"Where would you go?" he asked. "You're already ruined. Nobody in Society will receive you if you refuse to marry me. Whitcombe told me as much."

"Wh-Whitcombe?" Bella cringed as she recalled the contempt in the man's eyes the day he encountered her in the Trelawneys' garden. Whitcombe hated her, and with just cause, given how she'd ridiculed and tormented his wife. Why hadn't she befriended the gentle, purehearted Eleanor? Never did she need a friend more than now.

"I saw Whitcombe at White's when I was in London," Dunton

said. "He warned me that I'd suffer a lifetime of misery were I to indulge your whims." He grinned. "I do declare, my dear Lady Arabella, that he *loathes* you. Do you think you'd survive without the protection of my title?"

"You cannot force me to marry you," she said.

"I can, and I will." He turned to the footman. "Thomas, escort Lady Arabella to her chamber. I'm concerned for her state of mind."

"There's nothing wrong with my—"

"She's been having violent outbursts of late, and I fear for her safety and that of others. Take her to her chamber and let me know if she gives you trouble."

"Don't be foolish!" Bella cried. "There's nothing wrong with me."

"I beg to differ, my dear," Dunton said. "A woman in possession of her wits would not abandon her family and disappear for months, nor would she have violent fits of temper. What say you, Lady Smith-Green? Should we perhaps send for a doctor to determine her state of mind?"

Bella shivered at the undercurrent of threat in his voice. "Y-you wouldn't…"

"Not if you give me cause to believe that you're perfectly sane," he said. "But we must always consider whether you should be placed somewhere where you can be cared for properly."

An asylum… A cold, stark place, where sorry individuals were incarcerated by those who wished to be rid of them.

Bella cringed as she recalled the barbs she'd directed at Eleanor Howard, whom Juliette had once said was destined for an asylum due to her inappropriate behavior. To her shame, she'd joined Juliette in her taunts, reveling in the gratification to be had from ridding Society of undesirables.

And now she was an undesirable herself, a misfit to be controlled and punished—or incarcerated if she failed to obey.

"Thomas, take care of my fiancée," Dunton said. He leaned over

Bella and kissed her on the forehead, and she fought her revulsion as he flicked his tongue out, running it along her skin.

Then the footman took her wrist. Surrendering to defeat, she let him lead her back to her chamber. As soon as she entered, the door closed, and she heard the key turn in the lock.

Chapter Forty-Six

Lawrence leaned out of the kitchen window. "Children! Breakfast's ready."

Silence.

They were in that bloody den again—sulking about *her*.

He glanced at the kitchen table—at the day-old, half-eaten loaf of bread and the congealed mess in the bowl that might pass for scrambled eggs if he closed his eyes.

And held his nose. And ignored the taste.

It was better than nothing—and no different to what they'd been used to before. But he missed the aroma of freshly baked bread.

And he missed the woman who'd baked it with love.

It was true that, when enjoying a good meal, one could taste the love that went into the preparation. And, *by goodness*, she had loved. She'd loved cooking—she'd loved her home, and the children.

And she'd loved him.

Cursing, he strode out into the garden and approached the den.

The sign was different to before.

Keep out. On pain of death. That means you, Pa.

"You can't stay out here forever," he said.

He heard whispered voices, then silence.

"If you want to pretend you're not there, children, you must do better than that."

After a pause, Jonathan responded. "Who goes there?"

"It's your father."

"You can't come in," Roberta said.

"And we're not pretending," William added. "Unlike *you*."

The arrow hit home. Admitting defeat, Lawrence retreated.

As he returned to the kitchen, he heard whistling, and a young lad appeared at the window.

"Mornin', Mr. Baxter," the boy said. "I've got that cheese you ordered."

"Come in, Jimmy," Lawrence said. "I'll give you a penny for your trouble."

The boy's face creased into a smile as he entered the kitchen carrying a basket. Then he pulled out a small packet wrapped in brown paper.

"A right tasty bit o' cheddar, that is," he said. "My ma let me have a whole slice to meself."

Lawrence fished a penny from his pocket.

"Thank you, sir," the boy said.

"Would you like a spot of breakfast, Jimmy?"

The boy glanced at the scrambled eggs, then shook his head. "Best not—my grandma's needin' a hand at the farm. My ma wouldn't want me to be late."

"Be off with you, then," Lawrence said. "You mustn't get into trouble with your mother."

"That wouldn't happen," the boy said. "Ma loves me, she does. But she's not well today, and I don't want her worryin' when she needs to get better."

"You love your mother, don't you, Jimmy?"

"Aye," the boy said. "My real ma's dead, and when Pa married again, I didn't want anyone to replace her. But she's been so kind to Pa and me, and I love her more than anything. Grandma says she's a special gift, and we must treasure her."

Lawrence's chest tightened at the love in the boy's eyes.

"You're a fine lad, Jimmy," he said. "Go take care of your ma."

"I will, sir. And, beggin' your pardon, I'm sure Ma would like a visit from Mrs. Baxter if she can spare the time. Ever so fond of her, she is. She sat with Ma all day the last time she took a turn and said to send for her any time she needed a bit of company."

Lawrence glanced about the kitchen. "So, you don't know…"

The boy turned his wide, expressive eyes on him. "Is Mrs. Baxter not at home?"

Lawrence shook his head.

"Well, I hope she'll be home soon." Jimmy picked up the basket, then exited the kitchen whistling a merry tune.

Lawrence stared at the cheese, his mouth watering at the memory of the pie Bella had made with cheese in the pastry crust.

I hope she'll be home soon…

"So do I, Jimmy," he whispered. "So do I."

The desperation that had been festering inside his soul swelled into determination. Then it burst and he slapped his hands on the table.

"Fuck it."

It was time to end the prevarication. Dunton and his thuggish footmen might have the means to fend off a lone man, a gardener—a *filthy peasant*. But no man could withstand an army—or a band of brothers.

He marched across the garden until he reached the den.

"Ahoy there!" he roared.

"Who goes there?" Jonathan said.

"Admiral Horatio Nelson!" Lawrence bellowed. "I come seeking my brothers."

After a volley of whispers, Roberta spoke. "What for?"

"Bonaparte has kidnapped the fair Lady Hamilton. I'm recruiting an army to rescue her."

More whispers, then the bush shook, and three faces appeared.

"Are you pretending, Pa?" William asked.

"No." Lawrence shook his head. "I'll never pretend again."

Three bodies emerged to accompany the heads.

"You're wrong, Pa," Roberta said.

His heart sank—did his daughter have no faith in him? "I'm wrong?"

"We're not the army," she said. "We're the *navy*."

"Then, my fine bunch of sailors," he said, "let us recruit the rest of our band. We head for enemy lands within the week."

Chapter Forty-Seven

Bella sat up and blinked, her eyes adjusting to the darkness. What had woken her?

An owl hooted outside, followed by another, further away.

She heard footsteps and caught her breath as a shadow moved beneath the door.

Was it Thomas, who guarded her door at night—or worse, Dunton, come to anticipate the wedding night?

Trembling, she reached beneath her pillow and pulled out the candlestick she kept there, taking comfort from the solid metal as she curled her fingers around it.

The door opened with a creak, and Bella tightened her grip on her weapon.

"Lady Arabella?"

"Connie?"

The maid approached the bed. "We've not got long. The hallway's empty."

"Where's Thomas?"

"Outside, looking for poachers—with my brother. He's saddled a horse ready for you."

"*Thomas* has saddled a horse?"

"No, Luke has—he's ostler at the King's Head."

Bella tempered the flare of hope. "I can't ride off into the night."

"You can," Connie said. "I have your reticule here, with enough money to get you to London."

"London?"

"That's where your lawyer is, isn't it? He'll take care of you."

"I've never met Mr. Crawford," Bella said. "How can I trust him?"

"No, Mr. *Stockton*," the maid said. "Mr. Crawford was arrested. Have you never wondered why the duke found you when he did?"

Bella shook her head. "I don't understand."

"Not long after you disappeared, the duke stopped looking for you," Connie said. "He had all sorts delivered to the house: wine, furniture for that empty parlor in the east wing, a jeweler came from London for your aunt—he even ordered a new carriage. Then it was all sent back—your aunt and the duke argued about it for days. Begging your pardon, I know it's wrong to eavesdrop, but I heard your aunt call Crawford a fool, and the duke cursed Stockton for refusing to hand over your fortune."

Bella's gut twisted with nausea. *How dare they!* Dunton and her aunt had abandoned her so that they might take her fortune for themselves.

"The greedy, despicable…"

"Hush, miss!" Connie said. "Do you now see why you must go to London? Mr. Stockton might be your best hope for sanctuary."

Bella stared at her maid. How could Connie—the creature she'd dismissed as having no worth other than to dress her and fix her hair—possess such insight? And how could she, in her pride and arrogance, have overlooked it?

"Come with me, miss," Connie said. "Come and claim your freedom."

Bella stared at the open door, beyond which a world existed outside the realm ruled by a vindictive, vile pair who'd delight in bending her to their will.

"Yes, Connie," she said. "Quick, before my courage fails."

The maid helped her into a gown, followed by a thick woolen

cloak, then looped the reticule over Bella's neck. She led her into the hallway, pausing at the top of the stairs to check the house was clear before descending and shepherding her out into the night.

At the rear of the building, a horse stood tethered to a gatepost.

"There!" Connie said. "I knew Luke wouldn't let me down. Do you need help to mount?"

"No, I'll be fine."

"Good. Now, Thomas will be in the forest at the front of the house—that's where Luke's told him the poachers are. You must ride across the fields at the back. When you come to the London road, don't turn left—that's the way to Ilverton village. Turn right and head for Ancombe Mills. It's an hour's ride away, and you can hide there. The inn's called the Boar. The London coach stops there twice a week, and they'll have plenty of rooms free this time of year. The duke won't think to look for you there."

"Connie, why?"

"Because he's a dim-witted fool, and his men doubly so."

"No, I mean, why are you helping me?" Bella asked. "I've not been an easy mistress. I blush with shame at the thought of how I treated you."

"I always knew you had a kind soul," Connie replied, "even if you had to imprison it to survive the life you'd been born into. But you've had the privilege of living a different life now, and you deserve to have the freedom to choose the life you want. There's precious few of us able to follow our hearts, and I'll take comfort from knowing that you're following yours."

"Come with me," Bella said. "The horse can take both of us."

"I can't, miss."

"You cannot stay here. What will they do to you when they find I'm gone?"

The maid grinned. "They'll blame Thomas—he was supposed to be guarding your door. Besides, I'd only slow you down. You've a better chance of reaching London without me."

"Oh, Connie! Forgive my past rudeness—I never knew I had such a treasure in my life. I promise that as soon as I'm able, I'll send for you."

"Lady Arabella, there's no need for—"

"There's *every* need," Bella said. "The harpy of the *ton* is no more. In a world devoid of true friendship, you've been a true friend—and I'll not forsake a friend."

She embraced her maid, then mounted the horse and set off toward the fields.

The moon was almost full, which enabled Bella to see, but also made her prone to being spotted. The polished metal of the bit and bridle gleamed in the moonlight, and even her breath seemed to shimmer in the cold night air each time she exhaled. She steered the mare around the perimeter hedge to keep to the shadows.

An owl screeched close by, and her mount startled, letting out a soft whinny.

"Hush." She patted the mare's flank. "There's nothing to fear."

Was she trying to convince the horse—or herself?

She froze as she heard the crunch of footsteps on frost.

"Who goes there?"

Bella's gut twisted with fear as she recognized Thomas's voice, and she spurred the horse into a trot.

"Stop—poacher! Or I'll shoot!"

Footsteps crashed through the undergrowth.

Bella urged the animal into a canter, heading for the gate at the far end of the field, and she could almost have cried with relief when she spotted the road beyond.

Then a sharp crack filled the air.

The horse reared up with a loud whinny, then surged forward. Bella tugged at the reins, but her mount continued to gather speed. The animal sprang forward, and Bella felt a brief moment of weightlessness as they cleared the gate. Then the horse shuddered as its back legs clipped the top of the gate. The animal crashed forward, throwing her to the ground, then righted itself and galloped off, disappearing into the night.

Before Bella could move, another shot rang out.

"Come back, you thieving bugger!"

Footsteps approached, accompanied by wheezing.

"Bastard," Thomas panted. "Thought I'd got 'im."

Lighter footsteps joined the first. "You shouldn't have shot him, sir," a second, lighter voice said. "That was no poacher—poachers don't ride horses."

Bella heard the sound of a slap, followed by a sharp cry.

"Don't be insolent, boy. They could have stolen one of the master's horses."

"The poachers are in the forest, sir. I—Ouch!" The boy yelped at another slap.

"Witless boy!" Thomas replied. "They'll be long gone by now—I'll wager my arse on it. Be off with you!"

"B-but you said I could have something to eat if—"

"*If* we caught the poachers, boy. You should be thankin' me for not beating your hide for sending me on a fool's errand."

"And you should have gone to the forest."

Heavens, was the lad brave, or simply foolish? Thomas wasn't the sort to take kindly to challenge—the poor boy would find himself at the wrong end of a whip if he continued.

"We may still catch them, sir. The duke thinks ever so highly of you—he'd bound to reward you. I want no reward other than knowing I'm doing my duty."

"And a bite of somethin' to eat, no doubt," Thomas said, his voice mellowing.

"Only if we catch them, sir."

"Very well—but we'll check the stables first."

Thomas sniffed, then hawked and spat. Then the heavy clomp of his footsteps faded into the distance, followed by his companion's lighter tread.

Bella waited until she could no longer hear them, then she tried to stand. Pain shot through her ankle, and she stumbled against the gate, wincing as it creaked. For a moment, she clung to it, her heart hammering, but there was no sign she'd been heard.

But without the horse, she had no means of escape. If Thomas was headed for the stables, it was a matter of minutes before her flight was discovered. If the next village was an hour's ride away, she'd never make it on foot.

In the opposite direction, she spotted the spire of Ilverton Church silhouetted against the night sky. She might be able to lodge at the inn—provided she wasn't recognized—and wait for the next London coach. She reached for her reticule, uttering a prayer of thanks that Connie had had the foresight to secure it around her neck. Drawing her cloak around her, she limped toward the village.

※

BY THE TIME Bella reached Ilverton, her ankle felt as if it were on fire. As she approached the inn, raucous laughter erupted from within. A door burst open and a man stumbled out, reeking of ale. Grinning at her, he stretched out his arms.

"What's this? A wench to keep old Jakey warm? Come here, my lovely!"

"Don't touch me!" she cried, pushing him back. "Do you think I'm a harlot?"

He stumbled against the door, then laughed good-naturedly. "Oh, well, no matter, lovely! There's plenty lasses willing to warm my bed. It's right cold outside—get yourself inside and Tom will take care of you."

"Tom?" *Dear Lord*—was that brutish footman waiting for her?

"Tom Barnes—the innkeeper," the man said. "He'll see you right if you're needin' a room. Or perhaps you're waiting for your husband? A pretty thing like you shouldn't be on her own at night."

"Y-yes, that's right—I'm meeting my husband."

"Get yerself inside, then, ma'am." The man touched his cap. "Beggin' your pardon for thinkin' you were a…" He touched his cap again then stumbled off, singing.

Bella slipped inside, drawing her cloak around her, and found herself in a parlor crammed with people. They jostled each other, cheering and singing, and her stomach heaved at the stench of ale. A flame-haired woman crossed the parlor, dodging from side to side as an occasional hand flew out toward her skirts.

"Come here, my lovely!" a drunken man said.

"Be off with you, Matty," she replied, laughing, "or I'll cut yer balls off!"

Her voice seemed familiar.

Where have I heard it before?

"She'd have to find them first!" another man said.

The drunken man joined in the laughter. Then he leaned back, lost his balance, and toppled onto the floor.

"Serve ye right with yer wanderin' hands!" the woman said. "How are ye goin' to explain the bruises on your arse to your missus?"

"Tell her he got kicked in the arse by a lass!" another man cried. "He'll have no bollocks left by the time she's done with him."

Bella shuddered as she watched the woman weave her way around the parlor, swiping away offending hands, her bright-red curls gleaming in the candlelight.

Yet she felt a pang of envy at the woman's good-natured ease and merry countenance. Perhaps a place such as this—a den of iniquity— was safer than the drawing rooms of London Society. At least the predators here were overt in their nature. A very different kind of predator hunted in Society's drawing rooms: men—and women—who hid their evil beneath a veneer of gentility.

A cheer rose as another woman strode across the parlor, a tankard in each hand, her rough, homespun gown stretching over her voluptuous form. She placed the tankards before two men sitting at a table, her ample bosom in full view.

Bella shuddered at the lust in the men's eyes. She stepped back and collided with a body.

She whirled round. "Forgive me, I…"

Her voice died as she came face to face with the redhead.

Recognition slid into place. It was the doxy who'd been staying at the inn in Brackens Hill—the one Lawrence had lain with.

Perhaps he still patronized her. Though he had denied it, he'd lied to her about everything else.

"Amelia," Bella said.

"It's Millie." The woman's eyes widened with recognition. "I know you! You're Lady A—"

"I'm not."

"Yes, you *are*," the woman sneered. "The haughty creature who lives up at the big house—the one who destroyed my Lawrence's belongings."

My Lawrence…

A needle of pain stabbed at Bella's heart.

"Be off with you, *your ladyship*," Millie said. "There's nothin' for you here. Go back to your duke."

"I can't," Bella said. "I hate him! He's nothing like…"

"Nothing like who?"

"No matter," Bella said. "I'm on my way to London, b-but my horse threw me, and I hurt my foot. I…" She shook her head. "Forgive me. I made a mistake."

The woman cast her gaze over Bella's body. Then she took her hand. "Come with me."

Before Bella could respond, Millie pulled her through a door into a hallway.

"Now, tell me what you're about."

"I told you—I'm running away," Bella said. "Why don't you believe me?"

"Because you're a lady—and ladies never keep their word. Look what you did to my Lawrence."

Bella blinked, and a tear splashed onto her cheek.

Millie let out a huff. "Not the tears, please. You might be able to win your duke over by sniveling, but I see you for the spoiled madam that you are—lookin' down your nose at the likes of us."

"I'm sorry," Bella said. "I know now what it's like to feel trapped—to be in the power of those who believe they have the right to treat someone with cruelty merely because of their birth."

"And what about Lawrence?"

"Lawrence…" As Bella whispered his name, another tear fell. "H-he taught me so much."

"I'll wager he did," Millie said. "How to cook and clean—and how to fuck."

Bella flinched at the profanity. "It wasn't like that. I believed he was my husband."

"Husband, lover, customer—it's all the same," Millie said. "I'm not blamin' you, your ladyship. A darn fine fuck he is—I've never had such pleasure between my thighs. Is that why it took you so long to leave him, because your duke can never give you such pleasure?"

Bella shook her head.

"Perhaps you're thinkin' he'd rut you again once you've tired of that lecher…"

"No."

"Or you've come here to learn a thing or two about feigning pleasure for when the duke mounts you on yer wedding night?"

"Dear God, won't you desist?" Bella cried. "It wasn't like that, I tell you! It was an act of love."

Millie snorted. "Your sort don't know the meaning of the word. A good rutting—that's what you're after."

Bella surrendered to her fury and wrenched herself free. She grasped Millie's arms and slammed her back against the oak-paneled walls.

"Do *not* presume to know me! It may be just rutting to you, but I'll not have you cheapen what we had between us—what I had, with the man I loved."

"You didn't—" Millie began, moving forward, but Bella pushed her back against the wall.

"I did!" she said, thrusting her face close. "I did love him—and I still do. I'll love him until I draw my last breath, no matter how much he loathes me."

Millie's eyes widened, and for a moment the two women stared at each other. Then Millie let out a small moan of pain.

Bella released her and stepped back.

"I'm sorry," she said, awaiting a tirade of abuse. "I didn't mean to hurt you."

The tirade never came. Instead, Millie rubbed her arms and continued to stare. "Lawrence… You *love* him?"

Sweet Lord! Bella had revealed her heart to a woman who'd gladly betray her.

"Forgive me," she said. "I didn't mean it. Perhaps I should go."

Another drunken roar rose, and Bella stiffened and glanced at the door.

"I'm no fool, your ladyship," Millie said. "You spoke the truth."

"No, I—"

"There's never a truer word than that spoken in anger—or in the throes of passion. Stay, your ladyship. Perhaps I can help you."

"I don't want your help."

"I offer it anyway." The doxy's expression softened, and she placed a hand on Bella's arm. "I saw the fear in your eyes just now. If you wish to hide, you can stay here for the night. I'll help you get to London if that's where you're headed."

"I have money."

"Heavens, I don't need your money—I offer my help for your sake. And for Lawrence's. He'd want you safe."

Bella shook her head. "He hates me."

"But you lived as man and wife."

"Out of his desire for vengeance after I destroyed his belongings. H-he tricked me, Millie. He made me believe I was his wife, mother to his children—and it was out of a desire to punish me, nothing more."

Millie let out a sigh. "I know," she said. "It was wrong of him, and I told him so. That day I saw you in Brackens Hill, when I was staying at the Oak. I asked him to come and see me. Do you know what he did when he came?"

"No."

"He rejected me. Me—the doxy who's never wanted for a man's attention. I'm ashamed to say that I begged, told him I'd give him a night's pleasure and ask nothin' in return. And he said...he said that he loved another. He said that for the first time in his life he understood the meaning of love—the need within his soul to care for and remain faithful to another, until the day he drew his last breath." She took Bella's hand. "He was talking about you."

"Then he deceived you as well as I," Bella said.

"I told him he was a misguided fool, and that was the first time he ever raised his voice to me. Then I saw it in his eyes, heard it in the depth of his voice. There's few who can truly deceive a whore. Lawrence loves you, Bella. I'd stake my reputation as a whore on it— and my reputation is all I have."

Bella drew in a sharp breath. "You called me *Bella*."

Millie smiled. "That I did. And I'll help you get to London. But the coach won't be stopping here for days yet."

"Then I must go elsewhere," Bella said. "Dunton might come looking for me at any moment."

"Old Tom will send him away with a flea in his ear," Millie replied. "I can hide you in my room. Tongues might wag if a woman with your accent takes a room of her own. Then I'll see if Tom will let me take you over to Ancombe Mills in the cart tomorrow. I know the innkeeper at the Boar—he'll keep you safe."

"The Boar? Connie told me to go there."

"Connie?"

"My maid," Bella said. "I owe her my liberty." Bella shuddered at the thought of the discovery of her escape. "I wish she'd come with me. But I can better help her when I've reached London—I'll send someone to bring her to me once I'm safe."

A crash came from the parlor next door, followed by a stentorian voice. "Cease what you're doing this instant!"

It was Dunton.

"Sweet heaven!" Bella cried.

"Hush!" Millie whispered, pressing her ear to the door. "Consider yourself lucky you arrived this late—half the men in the parlor will be too drunk to recognize their own faces, let alone anyone else's. He'll not know you're here. But I'm leaving nothing to chance. Follow me."

Millie led her along the hallway to a narrow staircase.

"Take the stairs—mind the step at the turn, 'cause it creaks. Turn right at the top. My chamber's at the end, with a number eight painted on the door."

"But—"

"No time for questions—just do it!"

Bella approached the staircase as Millie returned to the parlor. She climbed the stairs, wincing as they creaked, and made her way to the chamber. The room reeked of cologne and stale cigars. A huge four-poster bed dominated the room with red drapes trimmed with gold, reeking of decadence. How many men had Millie entertained on that bed?

How many times had *Lawrence*...

Voices approached, and Bella froze as she recognized Dunton's thick, nasal tone, coaxing and whining like a petulant child.

"Why *not*? I'll show you a good time, girl."

"Aren't I the one supposed to show *you* a good time, sir?"

It was Millie's voice, though it seemed harsher than before. Had the doxy betrayed her?

"Just one little kiss, then, you delectable creature."

"I've told you before, I don't give my services for nothin'."

"I could make you rich beyond your wildest dreams, my dear."

Bella shuddered at the undercurrent of threat in Dunton's voice.

"That may be, sir, but I'll not let you touch me until you show me your coin."

"My man can see to that in the morning."

"Then come back in the morning."

"Miserable whore!"

Bella winced at the snarl in his voice.

"I'm a *sensible* whore, sir," Millie said. "If none of my customers paid me, I'd have to stop whoring, and then where would you all be with your needy cocks?"

"I'll soon have a fortune to give you," Dunton said.

"A man known in Ilverton for not settling his debts?" Millie laughed.

Bella found herself admiring the doxy. How could she defy Dunton with such courage? Then her gut twisted as she heard his next words.

"I'll soon have enough money to buy exclusivity from every whore in the county, when I've roped in that little bitch."

"Then I wish you luck in finding her, after which I'll service your every whim."

Bella grimaced at the wet sound of a kiss.

"There!" Millie said. "A treat to whet your appetite for when you return. And then I'll…"

"You'll what?" Dunton's voice sounded strained. "Will you let me fuck you on the floor?"

"Oh, sir, have you no imagination?"

"In the stables, then, on all fours while I rut you from behind? I'd give you an extra sixpence if you neighed like a mare."

Bella fought the urge to retch. Was this how men spoke to doxies? How could a woman bear such degradation?

"Ooh, *sir*, I'm quite overcome with the prospect. To think—all that straw sticking to our bodies, the scent of animals in the air…"

Dunton let out a strangled groan.

"Now, don't be spending out here in the hallway," Millie said. "The landlord won't be having any of that."

"Then let me inside your chamber."

"My *chamber* is not to be entered until we've come to an agreement. Go find your fiancée. If you're so desperate to find her, you shouldn't be spending the night with a whore."

Dunton let out a grunt, then Bella heard the sound of wet lips smacking once more.

"There," Millie said. "May my kiss give you all the luck that you deserve."

Dunton mumbled a reply, then his footsteps faded into the distance.

Shortly after, Millie opened the door. She glanced at Bella, then rushed toward a bureau containing a decanter and two glasses. She poured out a measure of dark red liquid and drained it in one gulp.

"Sweet holy tits, that man's repugnant!" she said, her tone returning to its former softness. "Every whore has her limits, and my limit is *him*. Why the devil would anyone want to spend the rest of their life with a man like that?"

Bella's cheeks warmed with shame.

Millie set the glass aside and took Bella's hands. "Forgive me," she said. "I understand you thought you have no choice before—I only rejoice now you've realized that you *do* have a choice, and you're exercising it now."

"D-do you think he'll come back?" Bella asked.

"Not likely. Tom told him he'd heard talk of your going to Midchester. And don't worry—Tom's agreed to let me take you to Ancombe Mills in the cart."

"Why would he help me?"

"Because I asked."

"And why would you ask him when you hardly know me?" Bella asked.

Millie smiled. "I'm doing it for Lawrence. Even if you never see him again, I know he'd rest easier if the woman he loves is safe."

Chapter Forty-Eight

THE FIRST STRAINS of birdsong heralded the dawn. By the time Bella followed Millie outside, creeping through the back door like a thief, the chorus was in full swing—male birds claiming their territory, calling to their females.

At Brackens Hill, she'd come to savor the dawn, surrounded by the songs of nature, when she could pause in her chores and take a moment to herself. At first, she'd loathed having to rise when it was dark and cold outside, to lay the fire or prepare breakfast. But the rituals of life as a laborer's wife had given her purpose and fulfilment.

"Bella! Come quick!" Millie's voice returned her to the present, and they crossed the courtyard, where a young man waited beside a cart fixed to a sturdy-looking brown pony. "Is everything ready, Luke?"

"Aye, Miss Millie," he replied, in a voice Bella recognized. "Bessie's not too quick, but she's a steady girl as long as you're firm on the reins. She'll see you safely to Ancombe."

"You're a treasure," Millie said. "Your sweetheart—Sara, isn't it?—is a lucky lass."

"Oh no, Miss Millie, I'm the lucky one. Will you be wantin' me to accompany you? It's a long way to Ancombe for a woman on her own in the dark."

"It'll be light soon," Millie said. "And I'm not alone—it's my friend wanting to get to Ancombe."

The young man frowned as he glanced at Bella, then his eyes widened.

"Bleedin' hell—it's Lady Arabella!"

"You're Connie's brother," Bella said.

"Aye," he replied. "Went to a lot of trouble for you, my sister did. You should be halfway across the county by now—I don't want you causing trouble for Connie."

"The horse bolted and threw me," Bella said. "And the last thing I want is to cause trouble for your sister. I intend to send for her as soon as I've reached London."

"Why, because you cannot survive without a maid?"

"No!" Bella replied. "I'm fond of Connie and cannot bear the thought of her suffering as a result of my flight."

"For pity's sake, Luke, don't be an arse," Millie said. "Help Bella up, then get your skinny hide back inside before you wake the whole village. Mind you say nothin', or I'll cut your bollocks off."

The lad let out a huff.

Bella held out her hand. "Your loyalty to your sister does you credit, Luke," she said. "You have my word that I'll do everything I can to ensure her safety. Tell her this when you next see her."

The lad stared at her hand, his eyes widening. Then he took it and nodded. "Perhaps what Connie said about you was true."

"Which was?"

Even in the low light of the dawn, Bella could see he was blushing.

"Did she perhaps say that the spoiled Lady Arabella has mellowed into a woman with the potential to be a little less disagreeable?" she suggested.

The lad hesitated, and Millie slapped him on the arm. "Stop your gawking, you fool. We need to get going."

"Right you are, Miss Millie."

The boy helped Bella onto the cart, and Millie followed. "Remember, Luke, not a word if you value your balls."

"You can trust me, Miss Millie. My Sara would chew my balls off herself if she knew I'd let you down." The boy touched his cap and nodded to Bella. "I wish you well, your ladyship."

Millie grasped the reins, then issued a soft command, and the horse set off. She steered the cart across the courtyard, and Bella winced at the clatter of hooves. But other than a boy scurrying along the street carrying a basket, the world had yet to wake.

※

BELLA RELAXED INTO her seat, lulled by the motion of the cart. This time tomorrow she'd be safely on the London coach—perhaps even under Mr. Stockton's protection.

The road led through a forest, but the sun, which had long since conquered the dawn mist, filtered through the trees. Bella tipped her face upward, relishing the birdsong in the air, together with the distant rush of water from the nearby river.

"Look!" Millie cried.

Bella opened her eyes. The cart rounded a bend in the road and the forest thinned out to open country. On the horizon was a line of trees, above which rose a square tower with battlements.

"That's the church at Ancombe Mills."

"It looks more like a castle," Bella said.

"It dates back to the Norman conquest."

"How do you know…" Bella began, but trailed away with shame.

"How can I know history, seein' as I'm a whore?"

"Forgive me, I didn't…"

Millie laughed good-naturedly. "I'm fond of history, and like nothing better of an evening than to tuck myself into a chair with a book. Don't believe everything you see at first glance, Bella. You have to look closer. The painted peacock who earns her keep giving pleasure to lonely men is nothing like the woman inside. Just like *Lady Arabella* is nothing like *Bella*. We women must disguise our true selves to survive in a world ruled by men."

"Then I thank you for honoring me with your true self, Millie," Bella said. "It's a mark of true friendship—and I can think of no one better as a friend."

"Lawrence is a fool for lettin' you go," Millie said.

She resumed her attention on the road, and Bella watched the tower loom higher as they drew near.

Safe at last.

The clip-clop of the horse's hooves was joined by another, heavier tread from behind.

Millie glanced over her shoulder. "That'll be the mail coach from Midchester."

The air vibrated with the beating of hooves, and Bella's stomach twitched with apprehension.

"Steady, Bessie girl!" Millie said as the pony tossed its head from side to side. She steered the cart to the edge of the road and stopped. "Someone's in a hurry. We'll let them pass."

Four horses emerged from the bend, pulling a carriage that swayed from side to side. Bella winced as she heard the crack of a whip.

"That's not the mail coach," Millie said.

Bella's gaze settled on the coachman. His livery was red, and though it was too far away to notice any detail, she caught a gleam of gold.

It can't be…

"Dunton…" Bella's throat constricted with fear. "Dear God, he's found me!"

"Run!" Millie cried.

Bella glanced at the coach bearing down on them, then she leaped off the cart and ran along the road.

"No!" Millie screamed. "Get off the road—head for the river!"

Bella slipped between the trees at the side of the road. The ground sloped away, plunging down a bank toward a roaring, raging torrent of water. She caught her breath as a surge of fear gripped her, paralyzing her with the memory of bitter cold that stabbed at her flesh like a thousand knives. A face swam into her vision—a ruddy, fleshy face, watching her through the bushes, eyes gleaming with satisfaction. She opened her mouth, fighting for breath, willing her body to scream, while icy fingers clawed at her legs, pulling her down in a spiral, sending her into hell…

"No!"

She raised her hands to cover her ears, but the roaring ripped through her senses. She retreated and collided with a solid form.

"At last!" a familiar voice cried. "I have you, my dear."

Her vision cleared and she caught sight of a familiar face.

Dunton.

The same face that had watched her fall into the river.

"It was you!" she cried. "You left me to die."

"What nonsense," he said, and she fought the ripple of nausea at his sour breath. "Come with me now."

"Let me go!" She struggled as he dragged her back to the road.

"Leave her be, you—Oh!" Millie cut off with a scream, and Bella caught sight of Dunton's footman holding her limp form in his arms.

"Millie!" Bella said. "What have you done, you brute?"

"Leave the whore, Thomas," Dunton said. "I have what I want."

"You'll never have what you want," Bella snarled. "You'll have to drag me down the aisle in chains."

"That can be arranged."

Dunton pulled her hard against his body and forced his mouth over hers. She twisted her head to one side, then he slipped his hand inside her gown, and she winced at the sound of the material tearing.

"You mean to take me in the dirt, like the rutting pig that you are?"

He began to drag her toward the carriage. "I'll take you in there," he said. "No need to wait until our wedding night to claim you as mine." Bella kicked out, but he merely chuckled. "I shall enjoy breaking you."

"Sir!" Thomas cried. "Someone's coming."

Bella glanced up to see a second carriage approach. Dunton squeezed her wrist until she could feel the bones crunching.

"Say nothing, Arabella, or you'll regret it."

The carriage slowed to a halt. Then the door opened, and a man climbed out.

Hope swelled within her—any reasonable creature would listen to her plight.

The man leaned into the carriage. "Remain inside until I say otherwise," he said. Then he approached, and Bella's hope died.

It was the Duke of Whitcombe—a man who loathed her.

He stared at her, the familiar sneer on his lips. "Dunton," he said. "What have we here?"

"My wayward fiancée, as you see."

Whitcombe lowered his gaze to Bella's torn neckline before resuming his attention on her, his expression cold and hard.

"Your Grace, please," Bella said. "I—"

"Be quiet," Dunton said, tightening his grip. "Whitcombe, I'm afraid my fiancée is suffering from a fit of nerves. But she's under my control now."

Whitcombe lowered his gaze to Dunton's hand still gripping Bella's wrist. "So I see."

"The little slut thought she could elude me," Dunton continued. "You know how women are like."

"Yes, Dunton," Whitcombe said icily. "I know *exactly* what women are like. And Lady Arabella deserves to be in her rightful place."

Bella's gut twisted with horror. "Please…"

"Hush, my dear," Dunton said. "Did you not hear what Whitcombe said?"

"Help Millie, at least, Your Grace, if you won't help me," Bella said.

Whitcombe glanced toward Millie, who'd begun to stir in Thomas's arms. Then the corner of his mouth twitched into a smile.

Bella's fear gave way to indignation. "You find her predicament amusing?" she said. "Millie is my friend. And even if she is a whore, better that than a duke with no morals who believes that his title gives him the right to destroy the lives of others!"

"Then you don't love this man?" Whitcombe asked.

Bella glanced at Dunton, then let out a laugh. "Of course not. I *loathe* him! You dare ask me about love when you don't understand the word?"

"And you do?" Whitcombe asked.

"I understand more about love than you ever will."

"Then tell me," Whitcombe said. "Tell me whom you love."

She tilted her chin up and fixed him with a glare. "You deserve no such consideration."

"Damn you, woman!" Whitcombe said. "Tell me or I'll leave you to rot as Dunton's duchess."

"Very well, if you require satisfaction then you shall have it," she replied. "I love a gardener—someone you'd call a *filthy peasant*. And though he may hate me, I love him, and I always will. And I'd rather be alone for the rest of my days, because I cannot begin to imagine loving another when my heart belongs to him. Now please, let me go."

Whitcombe glanced toward the carriage, then his mouth curved into a smile. "You can come out now!"

The carriage tilted sideways, and a man emerged. Tall and muscular, his hair caught the sunlight and sparkled with gold—hair she knew to be silken to the touch. He stood, regarding her with clear gray eyes that she knew and loved—eyes that she knew darkened to the color of coal at the point of pleasure.

"Lawrence..."

CHAPTER FORTY-NINE

Lawrence fisted his hands, fighting the instinct to spring forward and smash Dunton's face to pieces.

That vile bastard had his filthy hands all over Bella. Nausea clawed at his stomach as he caught sight of her torn neckline, below which he could discern the outline of her breasts.

Even with her in the clutches of her tormentor, Bella's eyes flashed with spirit. But as she caught sight of Lawrence, the fire died in her eyes.

"Lawrence…"

His heart ached at the sorrow in her voice. Did she really believe what she'd said to Whitcombe? That he hated her?

"H-how did you find me?"

"Your maid—Connie, is it?" Whitcombe said. "She told us where you'd gone."

"Is she all right?" Bella asked.

"She's safe, Lady Arabella. Her brother's with her."

"A-and you came to help me?"

Whitcombe smiled. "Trelawney can be a persuasive man when he wants to be."

Dunton stared at Whitcombe, dim-witted confusion in his expression.

Her captor having lowered his guard, Bella twisted herself free, then she rammed her knee into Dunton's groin. He toppled forward with a groan, landing on his knees.

"Miserable whore!"

"Better a whore than your wife," she sneered.

Dunton clutched his groin and groaned. "Thomas..."

Whitcombe barked, "Rutley! Smith!"

Two footmen climbed down from Whitcombe's carriage. The first drew a pistol.

"I came prepared," Whitcombe said. He gestured toward Millie. "Rutley, see to it that *Thomas* remains where he is. You're at liberty to shoot if he moves. Smith, take care of the woman."

Millie let out a sigh and opened her eyes, and Thomas tightened his grip on her.

"Let her go!" Bella cried.

She stepped forward, but Dunton pulled her back.

Lawrence sprang forward. "Get your filthy hands off my wife."

"Wife!" Dunton scoffed. "She was nothing more than a slut who spread her legs for you."

"She's my wife in everything that matters," Lawrence said. "I didn't need no piece of paper to know that I loved her—and love her still."

Bella's eyes widened, and Lawrence's heart ached at the disbelief in them. He held out his hands, holding his breath. She stared at them for a moment, then met his gaze, a sheen of moisture in her eyes.

"You love me?"

"Aye, my Bella," he said. "You're the air in my lungs, the blood in my veins, and the light in my soul. Without you I am nothing."

A flicker of hope flared in her eyes, and she reached out and took his hand, sliding her fingers between his.

"I can never atone for deceiving you," he said, "though I'll spend the rest of my life trying, if you'd permit me. But that deception brought you into my life. My beautiful, kind, clever Bella. You may not be my wife in name, but you are my equal—more than my equal.

You are my heart, and my home, and I am incomplete without you. We *all* are.

"All?"

Lawrence turned toward Whitcombe's carriage, where the children, bristling with need for their beloved mama, but tempered by Whitcombe's orders to remain in the carriage, were watching the exchange.

"The children..."

Hope swelled in Bella's eyes, and his heart ached at the love there.

"Spare me this nonsense!" Dunton said. He stumbled forward, reaching for Bella.

"Charge!" a high-pitched voice cried, and the children tumbled out of the carriage, brandishing sticks, then raced toward Dunton.

"Don't touch my mama!" Roberta said.

William raised his stick. "Begone, foul Napoleon!"

Dunton whimpered and raised his arms, and Lawrence's heart soared as Bella let out a giggle.

"Mama—we're here to rescue you from enemy hands," Jonathan said.

Bella reached for the little boy and drew him into her arms. "I thank you, kind sir," she said. "My, how you've grown during my incarceration!"

"Foolish brat!" Dunton said. He raised his hand, but before he could strike, Whitcombe caught his wrist.

"I'd advise you to think carefully, lest you wish to add the assault of a child to your list of crimes."

"Crimes?"

"The attempted murder of Lady Arabella Ponsford..."

"Don't be a fool!" Dunton replied.

"How else did she end up almost drowned in the river?" Whitcombe said. "Not to mention your abandonment of her."

"Abandonment?"

"You were seen at Drovers Heath, claiming not to know the woman who was your fiancée. Trelawney and I obtained written testimony from Dr. Carter."

"Preposterous," Dunton said, though his voice wavered.

"Not to mention your attempts to defraud Lady Arabella out of her fortune. A certain Mr. Crawford has been overly willing to talk while residing in Newgate."

Dunton narrowed his eyes, the glare of arrogance fading as he glanced toward Lawrence then back at Whitcombe. "You can't prove anything."

"There's enough doubt over your innocence to destroy your reputation," Whitcombe said. "And, with enough debt to land you in Newgate as Mr. Crawford's cellmate, your reputation is all that you have. Unless you agree to my demands."

"What demands?"

Whitcombe made a dismissive gesture. "We can discuss that later. But now, I'm sure these good people are anxious to enjoy their reunion. Is that not so, Baxter? I know Trelawney—and Mrs. Trelawney—is anxious to know that your wife is unharmed."

Bella's smile disappeared. "I'm not his—"

"Hush," Lawrence whispered, holding a finger to her lips. "Let me remedy that."

He lowered himself onto one knee.

"Lady Arabella Ponsford, would you do me the honor of becoming my wife? I have nothing to offer you, but I ask you to fill my heart and home, and to love my children as your own—as they love you."

She took his hand and lifted it to her lips. "You're wrong," she whispered.

He swallowed the stab of hurt and lowered his gaze. It was too much to expect her to forgive him after what he'd done.

"Won't you ask me *why* you're wrong, Lawrence?"

He glanced up to see her smiling at him, her eyes glistening.

"Never say that you have nothing to offer me," she said. "A hardworking, honest soul, a doting father, and a loving husband—what are titles and fortunes compared to that?"

"Then…" he said, hardly daring to hope.

"Yes," she whispered. "Yes, I'll marry you. I was never happier than when I believed I was your wife—and mother to your children. I treasured the memory of our life together as a beautiful dream. And now you offer me the dream—a life with the man I love, and children I adore, as if they were my own…" She shook her head, and a tear spilled onto her cheek. "I cannot imagine such happiness."

"Oh, Bella!" He rose and pulled her to him, crushing his mouth against hers. She molded her body against his, and his manhood twitched with eagerness as he felt her two little peaks pressing against his chest.

"Ahem."

She broke the kiss, her face flushing, but Lawrence pulled her close.

"Whitcombe, would you deny me this moment?" he asked.

"Of course not, my good man." Whitcombe chuckled. "I only wished to offer my carriage, which is at your disposal. I can see to Dunton's." He gestured toward the pathetic figure cowering before him.

Lawrence stared at Dunton. To think he'd once envied men such as him. But he was the richer of the two, because while Dunton had known desire, lust, and greed, he had never known love. And he never would.

He held out his hand, and Bella took it, smiling up at him with her soft blue gaze. Together, they climbed into the carriage with their children, a family reunited.

Epilogue

Bella lay on the bed, her gaze wandering across the ceiling—the paintings depicting rosy-cheeked cherubs with their serene smiles and soft, feathered wings. Her body still thrummed with the ripples of her climax, and she squeezed her thighs together, chasing the pleasure that had made her scream with ecstasy only moments before, savoring the delicious soreness from her husband's attentions.

Chatter and laugher filtered through the house. No doubt the wedding guests were gossiping about how the groom, as soon as the toasts concluded, had tossed the bride over his shoulder and carried her upstairs, like a barbarian eager to bed his mate.

And what a bedding it had been! Her discarded wedding gown lay torn on the floor, unable to withstand his fervor as he forsook gentility and thoroughly claimed her as his.

And she had relished every moment.

She yawned and stretched, and a warm hand caressed her face. Then light fingertips traced an invisible path toward her neck and down her throat, until, finally, the hand cupped a breast. A fingertip flicked her nipple, and she caught her breath at the pulse of pleasure in her center.

"Mmm… Is my wife ready for me again?"

"Lawrence, you're an insatiable beast."

"Beast, am I?"

He caught her wrists, and the bed shifted under his weight as he mounted her, then he thrust forward, and she let out a low cry of pleasure.

"Ah… What greater delight is there for a man than to bury himself inside his woman?" His low growl reverberated in her chest, and she arched her back, parting her legs further. "Beast I may be," he said, sliding out before plunging inside her once more, "but I'm *your* beast."

"Lawrence…" she panted, "the guests will—Oh!"

A small burst of ecstasy ignited in her center, and she looked up into her husband's eyes, which glazed over with satiation as the newlyweds came to pleasure.

At length, he captured her mouth in a kiss and then climbed off the bed. She rolled onto her side, feasting her eyes on his body—the toned, muscular form, the broad chest that tapered to his waist, and the firm, sculpted buttocks she'd clung to while he drove into her with such primal fervor.

How could she have ever believed that fulfilment could be had in the staid, genteel world of a lady?

He turned to face her, and she lowered her gaze to that part of him that had given such pleasure, nestled among a thatch of dark blond curls. When she lifted her gaze to his eyes, she saw a wicked glint in their depths.

He reached for his breeches and slipped them on, then he picked up her wedding gown and sighed.

"You must forgive me, love—perhaps Connie can mend it if it's not too badly torn."

"I love the rips," she replied. "They're the marks of your desire."

"They're evidence that Lady Arabella Ponsford has married beneath her."

"No, Lawrence," she said. "Rank, position—that's nothing. In everything that matters, we are equals. You think I'd have been happier married to a duke? They make the worst husbands."

"Not all dukes," he said. "Whitcombe dotes on his wife. They could hardly keep their eyes off each other today."

"Whitcombe's an exception because he chose the perfect wife," Bella said. "Eleanor's a delightful creature—quiet and unassuming, but when she does say something, it pays to listen. They're utterly in love."

"Unlike Dunton and your aunt," Lawrence said with a chuckle. "'Miserably ever after,' Trelawney said when they married. It was generous of you to invite them to *our* wedding."

Bella grinned. "I'll not have the world admonish the harpy of the *ton* for being ungenerous toward her only living relative. And I confess a wickedness in wanting them to witness our happiness. Aunt seems satisfied enough as Dunton's duchess, but I wonder if she knows he only married her at Whitcombe's insistence to preserve his liberty. An unusual punishment—but Whitcombe's an unusual man."

"That he is—and in forcing Dunton to marry your aunt, he's ensured that London's debutantes are safe from being debauched, and their fortunes are safe from being squandered. With little income and not a soul willing to give him any credit, Dunton must live a very quiet life from now on."

Bella glanced at the mantel clock. "We should return to our guests," she said. "They'll think us poor hosts."

"Our guests will delight in our love." He looked up and down her body and curved his mouth into a hungry smile.

She glanced at the bulge in his breeches. "Lawrence—we can't!"

"Perhaps not yet," he said. "But when the guests are gone, I intend to claim you as mine in every room in this house."

"It's not properly furnished yet," she said. "The drawing room's empty, and—"

"It has a serviceable rug, yes? And the dining room has a sturdy table. As for the stables, just think of those bales of hay we can bury ourselves in while I bury myself in you among the soft scent of grass, with the fresh air on our skin as we come to pleasure…"

She caught her breath at the image before her—her beast of a husband riding her like a stallion while she howled her pleasure like a mare in heat.

"Hmm," he said. "We must explore that idea further once we have the house to ourselves." He kissed the tip of her nose. "And I must cover up that delicious body of yours before I lose control and take you on the carpet, here and now. Shall I send for Connie to find you another gown?"

"Leave her be," Bella said. "Today she's our guest. Besides—Ned's with her, and he'll not forgive us."

"How come, Bella, love?"

"He's smitten with Connie—or so Millie said. I can dress myself, you know."

She crossed the floor into the dressing room, aware of her husband's gaze on her body. But she was no longer ashamed of the scars adorning her thighs—not when he'd worshipped every inch of her with his hands and mouth.

A pink day gown had been set out. Dear Connie must have slipped upstairs during the toasts. Bella put it on. As she brushed her hair, her husband appeared over her shoulder, resplendent in his newly tailored jacket, which he filled to perfection.

"My wife's attire is incomplete," he said, pulling something out of his pocket. "May I?"

She nodded, and he reached forward and placed a necklace around her throat—a simple gold chain with a single pearl pendant.

She caught her breath as her gaze settled on the familiar, beloved object she thought she'd never see again.

"Is that..."

"Yes, my love," he whispered, his breath caressing her neck as he secured the clasp. "Your mother's necklace. It broke my heart when I realized you'd sold it out of necessity to pay for my son's spectacles. I think that was the moment I understood the depth of my love, and I resolved to return it to you one day. What better day than this—the day we declared our love to the world?"

She blinked, her eyes blurring with moisture, as the pearl glistened in the sunlight.

"I have another gift for you," he said, reaching for a trinket box on the dressing table.

"I want no gifts," she said. "You are all I need. You and the children."

"Who are, most likely, stuffing themselves to the brim with wedding cake," he said with a grin. "Consider this a token of my love, nothing more." He opened the box and pulled out the contents.

Ribbons—dozens of them—in every conceivable shade of pink.

"I-I don't understand," she said. "That story about our courtship, though it touched my heart, was a lie."

"Aye," he said, "and it fair broke my heart to see the love in your eyes when I told you that story. It made you so happy, and I wished beyond anything that it could have been true. But my love for you *is* true. I love you enough to seek out every ribbon in Midchester as a gift for the finest woman in the world."

He dipped his head and brushed his lips against her neck.

"So, here I am, my love, with my token for the finest woman in the world. May I choose one for your hair?"

She nodded, and he plucked a pale pink ribbon, then secured it on a lock of her hair.

"I doubt it looks fitting for a lady."

"But it's perfect for your wife," she said. "Lady Arabella Baxter I may be by title, but in my heart, I'm your Bella. Your lover and helpmate—mother to your children and, I hope, many more in the future."

He placed his hand over her belly and smiled. "Perhaps, even now, another member of Nelson's band of brothers is on the way."

She grinned. "We'll have much work to do—there were fifteen

sailors in total, if you recall."

"I shall relish our efforts," he said, licking his lips. Then he offered his arm. "Come on love—it's time we returned to our guests."

She took it, and they exited the bedchamber and descended the stairs to rejoin the wedding party. As they passed a window, Bella glanced out and caught a glimpse of a shirtless gardener digging a border, lifting up spadefuls of earth.

To think—the first time she'd glimpsed a semi-naked gardener she'd been a bitter harpy, taking pleasure in asserting her superior rank over her subordinates. But now, with that same gardener on her arm, she had shed the mantle of the lady and found fulfilment in the love of a good, honest, hardworking man.

About the Author

Emily Royal grew up in Sussex, England, and has devoured romantic novels for as long as she can remember. A mathematician at heart, Emily has worked in financial services for over twenty years. She indulged in her love of writing after she moved to Scotland, where she lives with her husband, teenage daughters, and menagerie of rescue pets—including Twinkle, an attention-seeking boa constrictor.

She has a passion for both reading and writing romance with a weakness for Regency rakes, Highland heroes, and Medieval knights. *Persuasion* is one of her all-time favorite novels, which she reads several times each year, and she is fortunate enough to live within sight of a Medieval palace.

When not writing, Emily enjoys playing the piano, baking, and painting landscapes, particularly of the Highlands. One of her ambitions is to paint, as well as climb, every mountain in Scotland.

Follow Emily Royal
Newsletter Signup: subscribepage.io/RKBvRE
Facebook: facebook.com/eroyalauthor
Bookbub: bookbub.com/authors/emily-royal
Instagram: instagram.com/eroyalauthor
Amazon: amazon.com/stores/Emily-Royal/author/B07NCBKJZ4
Website: www.emroyal.com
Goodreads: goodreads.com/author/show/14834886.Emily_Royal
Twitter: @eroyalauthor

Printed in Great Britain
by Amazon